July 4/20

D0665011

LOWCOUNTRY

BOIL
Special Edition

Also by Carl T. Smith

Nothin' Left to Lose

LOWCOUNTRY

BOIL

—Special Edition—

Includes a chapter
from the forthcoming
Louisiana Burn

CARL T. SMITH

For Jim + Jean Anne,

Enjoy this taste of the lowcountry!

My Best,

Carl T.

RIVER CITY
PUBLISHING
Montgomery, Alabama

Published in the United States by River City Publishing,
1719 Mulberry St., Montgomery, AL 36106.

Printed in the United States.
Designed by Nancy Stevens.

Library of Congress Cataloging-in-Publication Data:
Smith, Carl T., 1937-
  Lowcountry boil : a novel / by Carl T. Smith.
     p. cm.
  ISBN 1-57966-065-7
 1. Ex-convicts--Fiction. 2. Government investigators--Fiction. 3.
South Carolina--Fiction. 4. Conspiracies--Fiction. 5. Drug
traffic--Fiction. I. Title.
  PS3569.M5127L69 2003
  813'.54--dc21

                                        2003006791

Special Paperback Edition 2005

For Daryl "Dede" Hayden, whose unwavering friendship, encouragement, and faith have helped me steer a true course and provided a key ingredient to this work.

Firs' you takes you shawt ea's a cawn, 'bout tree inches, an' you puts in some taytas, some sausages, some chicken parts, onions and you puts 'em all in watta or beah—I kindly likes de beah myself—an' den you adds you hot spices and den you flavor spices. When it done boiled fo' some time, you adds you shrimps, mix it all up and lets it cook fo' jest a little while, an' it be givin' you a lowcountry boil dat'll sting you insides an' slap you outsides so's you won't fo'get it. Kindly like when you mixes some peeples together.

Riles Moultrie
Lowcountry Resident
Age: 103 years

PROLOGUE

There was no moon to speak of, a slender cut that chiseled shafts of light through the limbs of the live oaks and created quiet shadows and sequined reflections on the surface of the water. Turner Lockett, worn, grizzled, and looking older than his forty years, sat in his boat and looked toward the mouth of the Palachocola River. He was wearing a black rain suit—for camouflage rather than protection—and hip waders. His face was blackened with charcoal from the fire hole in front of his trailer. The others laughed at his caution, but it didn't bother him in the least. Nothing much did, especially other people.

Although there was no human sound, there was little silence on the river. A light breeze tickled the dried palm fronds and oak leaves along the bank. Jumping mullet launched themselves and splashed loudly when they re-entered the water. And there were soft sounds, unseen creatures sliding through the water or making their way through the marsh. Somewhere out there, beyond the river's mouth, in the open water of Matthew's Island Sound, out of sight and hearing, was a boat headed in Lockett's direction.

He had to urinate. The feeling had been there for some time, ever since he pulled his boat away from the dock behind his trailer and moved toward his position. Excitement and fear were building within him and made the necessity to empty his bladder more imperative. It happened every time. He stood in the stern of his old twenty-foot Grady-White and relieved himself; however, the urge returned as soon as he zipped up.

A sixty-eight-foot shrimp trawler moved inland along the Southeastern parameter of the Sound. The captain had planned the voyage carefully, so the boat would be at sea until eleven P.M., at which time it would begin to make its run inland. It carried nine thousand pounds of sensimelian—high grade, resin-heavy marijuana. When the boat entered the river, the captain contacted the pilot boat on his radio.

"Comin' in."

11

"Got you covered," came the reply.

"Big Dog, the package is arriving," Lockett said into his walky-talky.

"Okay," the lead man answered, smiling at Turner Lockett's ridiculous code words.

The trawler crew, despite the inherent risk of such a venture, had been relaxed until they entered the mouth of the river. Then the adrenaline in their bodies began to accelerate, and nerve endings extended themselves to the surface of the skin. They were in control, doing something most people couldn't imagine, unrestricted, masters of their own fates as much as one could be in such a situation. Body and mind were sensitive beyond their normal physical capabilities. They were experiencing the beginnings of criminal euphoria, the best drug of all.

Turner Lockett heard the engines before he could make out the shadow of the large craft coming around the bend. He was sitting in the mouth of Drake's Branch, a small creek that ran inland off the southern side. He raised anchor and moved out into the channel. Aboard the shrimper, the captain spotted the soft, blue light flashing from the small boat in the middle of the river. Since the trawler would be pushing the size limit the creek could handle, it was important to stay in the center of the pilot boat's wake. Once out of the river and into the narrow estuary, a variation to either side would be disastrous.

When the big craft was in position behind him, Lockett began leading them on the final leg of a journey that had begun on the Florida coast, taken them to Jamaica, back to Florida and up the eastern coast to South Carolina. The river was quiet. Lockett passed the opening of Patch Creek, used on a previous operation, went another mile and a half and veered left into Falling Creek. Each movement of the pilot boat was matched by the trawler as if the two crafts were attached by a steel rod.

The channel led to an abandoned dock, left that way when the house on the property had burned down several years before. Two small boats were anchored next to the landing to assist with the off-load, and two eighteen-wheel vans were backed up to the end of the dock. There was also a black Mercedes parked on the access road. When the trawler was docked, the task of unloading the boat's cargo began.

The work went swiftly, with little conversation. Once the trucks were loaded, they would proceed to a safe house where the goods would be stored. The vans would then be swept clean, vacuumed and returned to the site where they did their day-work.

When they were safely on their way, the door of the Mercedes opened. A well-dressed man, carrying a briefcase, got out and walked to the landing where the captain of the trawler was waiting for him. They went aboard and, in a few minutes, the man returned to his car and drove away. He was the last of the onshore contingent to leave the area. It had all gone smoothly.

Turner Lockett had the final responsibility: to get the trawler back into the Sound. He talked himself into being patient, didn't rush, didn't want to cause any attention despite an urge to get out of there fast. Who knew where the DEA people might be?

His excitement was dissipating. After the tough years of shrimping and fishing and picking oysters, the knowledge that one night's work had netted him more than twenty thousand dollars was satisfying. Leaving the trawler headed out to sea, Lockett turned for home, telling himself he deserved every penny of it. Let the rich bastards laugh at the poor people. He shook his head in glory. "If they only knew," he said out loud to the darkness. Life was good.

Almost good. Jared Barnes worked with him in the small shrimping business he had begun when he quit working for the larger shrimpers. There wasn't much money in it, but, between that and fishing, crabbing, picking oysters, doing a little guide work, bootlegging wild game and all of the other practices common to natural outlaws, it allowed him to survive. That was then. Now that kind of survival was not in question; he could probably afford to live at The Ritz, wherever the hell that was.

But Barnes was asking questions, using sly smiles, pretending he knew something, though Lockett was sure he was just fishing, hoping to get in on whatever he suspected was going on. There was threat in the man's eyes when he asked questions. He had probably heard a few rumors, figured out a little and thought he knew more than he did, but even a little was too much. Life was going to be too sweet to take a chance.

The others in the company would not condone violence. Hell, it was a game to them; that was explained to him when he was hired, but Barnes wasn't going away. Fortunately, the man was a loner with no kin, as far as Lockett knew. If something had to be done, no one would miss him, but Turner Lockett had never killed a man and wasn't sure he could.

CHAPTER 1

The sun room was dark. Sam Larkin, lean and naked beneath the robe that hung loosely from his body, sat looking up through the skylight at the stars suspended above his house, defying, by their very position, any human logic. His long, sandy-gray hair, newly washed, was splayed on his shoulders. It was only in the privacy of his home that it wasn't neatly combed straight back into a ponytail and clasped with a hand-tooled, silver holder. He was handsome by the standards of people who didn't judge worth and bearing by the length of one's hair or what one wore. Sam Larkin abided by the old Hemingway quote that "wearing underwear was as formal as he ever hoped to get." Sharp, hazel eyes cast an aura of a man at peace with himself.

His bare feet rested on the polished Mexican tiles that still bore some remembrance of the day's heat, their remaining warmth just a few degrees south of the night air that was now cooling. It was April. Hot in the daytime—though not as hot as it would be in full summer when the devil seemed to fan the flames—and dropping to a full chill during the night. The preface to summer and a reminder of winter, such as it is in the lowcountry of South Carolina.

Larkin's house was situated to look out over three hundred yards of marsh to Jones Run Creek, a brackish tributary like hundreds of others that flowed through the marshes and against dry land before emptying into the sea a mile or so from where he sat. There were other houses on the four-mile-long spit of land called Fiddler's End, but the closest was out of sight and sound. It was the quiet and solitude, energies he had been deprived of for four years until he moved to Matthew's Island, that had drawn him to the place. At first look, he decided it was where he would live. Maybe forever.

Occasionally he saw diffused light flash from distant heat lightning. No sound except Nature's own and the subdued ticking of a wall clock. His body was relaxed, approaching sleep until the sound of a boat-motor easing through one of the marsh capillaries offended the quiet and turned his attention from the stars to the water. He listened for a moment. It was an Evinrude. Light and tinny, shallow, not sounding the power of a Merc.

The sound, the night and his imagination transported him backward in time to a place he didn't want to be and couldn't avoid remembering. He could feel the damp moisture forming on the skin of his forearms. He felt a shiver as rational thought worked to relocate him from the past to the present.

He got up from the chair where he had been reading, until he caught the stars through the skylight, opened the screen slider and walked onto the deck, which extended to within twenty feet of the water's edge. A ghost light moved slowly, in concert with the sound of the motor, along a water path, its glow interrupted by dwarfed stands of wax myrtle that grew wild on the dry-land holidays that peppered the marsh. It appeared not unlike a summer firefly. Someone running a trotline. Maybe not.

Nothing was ever what anyone supposed it would be, but maybe there was no way anything was supposed to be. It wasn't a new idea, but it was bothering him more lately. During the short time Sam Larkin had lived on the island, he had seen and heard a lot of things that left questions and suspicions in his mind. Questions he didn't want to know the answers to. Boats running the creek in the middle of the night, shrimp trawlers moving around when there was no season to work, and conversations at Harry Tom Cooper's Boat Dock that were hushed when he came within hearing range.

He was in this place, had chosen it, because he didn't know anyone, and no one knew Sam Larkin. No ties, no relationships, no past, no personal responsibilities save his own. It was the way he wanted it. Now he was seeing and learning too much and felt himself being drawn in to things he didn't want to know, much the same as he had been in Louisiana. He wouldn't let history repeat itself, no matter what.

He stood in the dark watching and listening, knowing the man on the water was unaware of the eyes and ears that followed his light and the sound of his boat. Larkin didn't want to watch, but, out of an instinct for self-preservation, felt compelled. After a few minutes, he concluded that whoever it was had finished whatever he had been doing and was on his way home.

When he came to the lowcountry, he hadn't planned to work, just to leave everything behind, to paint and think and put his shattered life back together. But, plans aside, he had invested too much in the house, and, even though he did a lot of the work himself, his finances dwindled and work was the only option. Though he didn't fit the mold, he was qualified and managed to get a job teaching biology in the local school district. The job wasn't intrusive and allowed him time to read and develop his skills as an artist.

The painting came to some degree of proficiency rather quickly. He had drawn since he was a child and later took a few classes at The University of New Orleans. Here subject matter abounded. Matthew's Island teemed with wildlife living out its struggle for survival against a magnificent background. From the smallest fiddler crab to the largest antlered buck, that challenge was present in almost any direction one looked. It was the subject of most of his pictures: the war between serenity and violence, the Garden of Eden and Hell. A contrast of light and dark, much as his life had been.

The fading rumble of the Evinrude brought him out of his thoughts. It was one-thirty and another workday was looming. He went back into the sun room, secured the screen and glass sliders, picked up the book he was reading, took one last look at the beautiful emptiness surrounding him, felt grateful for where he was, and went into the house to go to bed.

Isabel Reichert was stylish and smart. Anyone looking at her and observing the way she operated recognized that. She wasn't classically beautiful, but the well-coifed, short, auburn hair, her height and figure drew attention. She appeared more a lawyer or doctor than a public school administrator. Other administrators— male and female—viewed her with cautious admiration and a small sense of fear. They knew little of the holes in her life and the emptiness that threatened to bury her.

She was irritated when she got out of her car and walked toward the entrance of Covington County High School. As principal of Walklet Middle School, she was required to attend all district in-service days. They were a waste of her time and everyone else's.

The other administrators knew it also, but forcing staff attendance was an exertion of their minor power. The appeal and pres-
tige of her position had faded for Isabel Reichert long ago. When
she embarked on her career, she, like so many others, believed
she could make a difference. It was naïve, but her idealism
guided her. She smiled ruefully when her marriage came to mind
as a parallel. She had thought hers would be unlike that of her
parents, the constant bitching and ultimate divorce. In both cases,
it had taken only a short time for reality to set in.

Coffee and pastries for the attendees were available in the
cafeteria, where the crowd was already assembled. The teachers were gathered en masse to load up on the freebies. Isabel
couldn't deny them that; coffee and pastries were the only perks
they could ever hope to get. She wished she could avoid the
cafeteria, find a seat in the back of the auditorium and be as
insignificant as possible. However, not only was being present
a requirement, but being seen was a necessity.

Administrators, board members and district officials
clustered in a corner of the room and watched—with obvious
superiority—as their charges complained about the educational
whimsies of the moment. They were children teaching children,
she thought. No touch of the real world or real-life experience
among any of them. Well, except one, she thought, as Sam
Larkin walked through the cafeteria doors.

He went to the coffee urn, filled a cup and walked out to the
plaza where students were allowed to eat lunch in good weather.
He put his coffee down, lit a cigarette and sat on one of the table
tops, his feet on the bench. He wore jeans, a blue denim work
shirt and moccasins with no socks. Socks were required by the
administrative dress code, and smoking was restricted to one
small area that was difficult to get to and surrounded by odorif-
erous cafeteria dumpsters. It went without saying, however, that
Sam Larkin would never adhere to those or any other rules he felt
were unreasonable if he so chose.

Looking at him, she felt a mild sense of skepticism and
uneasiness. It was exciting. Few men stimulated that kind of
reaction in her. Larkin was an enigma, building that house and
living out on Fiddler's End all by himself. She wondered what he
did out there all alone. In the district four years and no one knew

anything about him. He certainly didn't look like a high school biology teacher. There were no rumors or gossip about him that she knew of, and that in itself, in a public school district, was unusual. She had never come into contact with someone so insulated. The man was intriguing.

"Isabel. How are you?" Harold Taylor asked with a smile that caught her by surprise and made her skin crawl. What she resented most about his interruption was losing the fantasy she was creating.

In Isabel Reichert's opinion, no one in the administrative cluster was more obsequious than the principal of Covington County High School. She was glad their paths didn't cross often. He was fat. Not obese. Pear-shaped. And he was a classic bully; she recognized that the first time she met him. Gracious and subservient to anyone with any strength or power, and demanding, unreasonable and threatening to anyone he perceived to be weak.

"I'm fine, Harold. I'd rather be in bed, but all things considered . . . " She left it hanging.

"Sounds good to me," he said with a suggestive grin. Isabel cut him to the ground with a look. "I'm trying to find Dr. Hamilton. Have you seen him around? He said he would be here this morning. I want him to introduce the chairperson of the evaluation committee." The purpose of the in-service was to welcome the committee from the Association of Southern Schools—commonly referred to as "ASS" by the teaching staff—who were to begin their five-year evaluation of the Covington County Schools.

"No, I haven't seen him. Cedrick doesn't usually come to these things." She knew Taylor would resent the intimacy with which she referred to the Superintendent of Schools.

"I guess I'd better check around then. He said he would be here. If he doesn't show I guess I'll have to do it myself," he said, already scanning the room.

"You can handle it, Harold." She couldn't help smiling. On the scale of assholes, Harold Taylor was a ten. She turned back to where Sam Larkin was sitting.

"Bitch," Harold Taylor muttered under his breath as he walked away. Shame, he thought, bustling from group to group, playing his role as principal of the host school, her figure was exceptionally good for a woman her age. Of course there were no children, he knew that. In fact, there were rumors that she preferred women, but she was married, so he didn't take those seriously. He visualized her naked. She looked more like a thirty-something than a forty-three-year-old.

His musings were interrupted by the PA system. "Mr. Taylor? You are needed in the auditorium. The committee has arrived." Taylor looked around to see who had heard the announcement, stood up straighter and strode across the room.

"I'm coming," he said to no one, but loud enough for several people near him to hear. As he passed the windows that looked out on the plaza, he shook his head in disgust. Sam Larkin was incorrigible and flaunted it. He had tried to get rid of him, but could make no progress. The man stood in the face of authority, unshakable. Teachers were known for their lack of courage, but that didn't apply to Larkin. He was quietly intimidating and that was threatening in Taylor's eyes. There was little he could do, however. The man had a continuing contract, tenure by any other name. He would have to catch him committing a felony, which he didn't believe he was likely to do.

Sangaree Island, the outermost of the barrier islands and nineteen miles east of Covington, could not be considered a playground for the rich, but no one poor lived there. Rumored to have been frequented by pirates during the golden age of privateers, the island had remained sparsely settled and mosquito-infested until the fifties when a visionary real estate entrepreneur saw it as a paradise in the rough. It had developed slowly into a gated, private island with only a limited tourist business. It had, indeed, evolved into the island the visionary had seen.

Morgan Hannah, widowed and comfortable at thirty-six, owned a beachfront home toward the southern end of the island. She had come to Sangaree from Atlanta. Her husband, Ben Hannah, a manufacturer of highly critical optical lenses used in bombsights and other military applications, had been brought down by a massive coronary one Christmas Eve as he drove home from his office. Morgan, with neither the desire nor the expertise to carry on the business, liquidated everything they owned there, invested the proceeds and moved to Sangaree.

It was a good life. She didn't expect it to be permanent, but it was a good interim place. She didn't allow herself to become deeply involved in island activities or the social scenes either on Sangaree or in Covington, but she was seen often enough that most people knew who she was. She was admired by men and envied by women who saw her life as an impossible dream.

Morgan was sleeping peacefully when the telephone awakened her. It was only seven-thirty. Bright sunlight was cascading through the open windows that faced the beach, and the sound of a quiet surf provided a reassuring heartbeat that the world had begun another day.

"So what are you doing at this early hour?" She heard Bill Reichert say. His smile carried through the line.

"Me? What about you? Are you at work already?"

"I asked first."

"I was sleeping. What any sane person would be doing at this hour of the morning."

"I didn't know that sleeping at seven-thirty in the morning was a guaranteed certification of sanity."

"Depends on why you're awake."

"I wish I were there," he said.

"That would be a good reason." Morgan enjoyed playing these little games, though they weren't games in the negative sense. She didn't love him, but she could apply it for the moment, and the moment was all she was really concerned with. For the moment.

"What about this afternoon?" he asked.

"Where?"

"I'll come out there."

"That's fine with me if you're willing, but you said you were worried about coming out here so much."

"If anyone asks, I'm doing a drive-by of a house we're considering financing. The perks of being a banker," he said. "I've got a loan approval meeting at ten-thirty, which will be over by noon, and a meeting with Charlie Clay at twelve-thirty, but he never dallies. It won't take long. Do a quick swing through the bank, greet the girls on the teller line, and I'm out of there by two."

"Brave and brazen, aren't you?" she said.

"As long as I can hide the car in the garage."

"Of course." He sounded like a little boy sneaking out for a smoke. She had to stifle a laugh.

"I'll be there at two-thirty, quarter to three."

"Good. That'll give me a little beach time. My garage will be open."

He laughed. "See ya."

When she hung up the phone, Morgan sat in bed and gazed out at the vast expanse of ocean stretching out before her. She was happy. There were no worries about self-worth or accomplishments, though it wasn't because of a lack of intelligence. There was no reason or compulsion to move on, pressure herself, get entangled or achieve or any of the other things people drove themselves crazy over. She didn't need to "get a life," as some of her friends suggested. She already had one.

She cared for Bill Reichert; they were good for each other. If her husband hadn't died at forty-two, if she needed money and were forced to work, if she were desperate enough to seek occasional lays that held no promise save a small hope for future security, she wouldn't have gotten involved with Bill Reichert. A married banker, of all things, but he was exciting and good-looking and they had fun. No responsibility. She didn't believe, under the circumstances, that was a bad thing.

His money intrigued her. She didn't want it, didn't need it. The mystery was that it was there. He spent a lot more than banker's wages, regardless of position, and she didn't believe he had the courage to embezzle. There was no talk of an inheritance, and his wife was principal of a middle school. It didn't add up. She found that fascinating.

Morgan pulled herself from bed, went into the bathroom and began to fill the Roman tub. A stimulating whirlpool to wake up, an hour or so at the beach, and she would be ready for whatever the day offered. Catching a glimpse of her body in the mirror, she paused and approved, picked up a couple of mail-order catalogues and stepped into the tub to steam while it was filling.

Sam Larkin sat in the meeting, but he wasn't there. He was outside himself. When Harold Taylor announced a mid-afternoon break at one-thirty, he left the building. He had heard enough. Most of the teachers he came into contact with were quite different than those he remembered from his own youth, people who took pride in what they were doing, had dignity and were involved. He remembered them as strong people, role models. This new breed seemed to have no interests outside of their own families and complaining about their positions. By the time they were thirty, they were counting the years to retirement. He often wondered if they had ever done any kind of work they truly loved and enjoyed.

He castigated himself for his criticism. The teachers were, for the most part, good, well-intentioned, honest—if naïve and insecure—people. They were only dishonest with themselves. That thought made him ask some pretty probing questions about himself and his own honesty.

He never considered himself incompetent because he had done too many things far removed from the classroom. Teaching wasn't his life, but for now the job worked for him, gave him time to put himself back in order. It was something he did well because of the other things he had done in his life. He taught what he knew, what he considered important, and even in the field of biology, those things didn't come off the pages of a textbook. He never allowed the job to intrude on the part of his life that he considered vital. If that made him a bad teacher, so be it. Someone had once told him that anytime a job becomes your life, you don't do well at either.

As Larkin walked across the parking lot to the green '81 Land Rover that had been in service for more than two hundred and fifty thousand miles, Isabel Reichert was heading toward her car as well. She spotted him and stopped.

"It looks like we caught each other," she said as he approached.

"I guess it does," he answered. He had the most beautiful eyes she had ever seen on a man—large, amber-brown and liquid. He wasn't physically imposing, but the eyes, the graying hair pulled back in a pony tail that hung well below his shoulders, the lean, tanned body and the lack of compromise in his demeanor gave him stature that height and weight never could.

"I hate these things," she said. "Guess I shouldn't say that in my position."

"I won't tell anyone."

"Hey, it's Friday; what can I say? How's life out on the island?" She saw the puzzled look on his face. Was she trying to keep a conversation going where there was none?

"Best place in the world to live as far as I'm concerned. Of course I didn't know it was so much work to maintain a house, which is the main reason I left the meeting."

"What's waiting for you to do?"

"General stuff," he said.

She took his point. "Guess I'd better let you get about your business then. I won't tell on you if you won't tell on me. Good to see you."

"You, too," he said and continued toward the Rover.

She had heard that he was highly intelligent, well read and artistic but couldn't imagine it to look at him. He looked rough, yet in the few times their paths had crossed she heard a gentleness in the way he spoke, and he spoke well when he did speak, which wasn't often. She had the impression that he preferred to listen and draw conclusions. "Rough" was probably closer to the truth. When he looked at her, his eyes never leaving hers, she got the impression that he knew everything about her without knowing anything at all. That was unsettling and appealing.

"You're being paranoid," she said to herself and smiled.

The drive from Covington to Matthew's Island was quiet time for Sam Larkin. Occasionally he would put in a tape, some Jimmy Reed or Dale Hawkins. Most of the time he just listened to his own internal music and took in the beauty of what he saw passing by. He was looking forward to the physical work awaiting him.

He had undertaken to extend the small deck off the master bedroom in both length and depth. A mason had put up the cinder block columns; the rest of it he was determined to do himself. He found it interesting and calming to build. Each new tool he used for the first time and each new construction problem he faced was a learning experience. He had never done any building before and was surprised to find that he possessed some minor talent for it. Being forced to finish what he couldn't pay the builders to do had given him a college degree in the manual arts.

From a distance his house was hardly visible. The entrance, a long dirt road canopied by huge live oaks hung heavy with Spanish moss, seemed to close in behind any traveler who ventured there. The house was an abbreviated lowcountry-style structure that blended into the growth and earth colors that surrounded it. It was situated so there was a long-distance view in three directions, yet from the marsh, it was virtually invisible unless it was night and the lights were on. It was a purposeful placement.

Stopping the Rover, he noticed a boat moored to the dock he had built on the channel that passed within twenty yards of the dry land on which his house sat. Once in awhile, someone would get confused in the maze of the marsh and tie up to ask "how the hell to get out of here," but this was not that kind of boat. It was a Cobia with two 200-horse Mercs on the back. Built for speed. He got out and started toward the house.

"Sam Larkin," a voice called out. "Ray Breslin, South Carolina Environmental Resources Officer."

He was focusing on the boat when he parked and hadn't seen the uniformed man standing next to one of the cinder block pilings that held up the sun room and the deck. There was a woman with him, also in uniform. She was as attractive as her uniform and no make-up would allow her to be, he thought. Female law enforcement officers had their place, he guessed, but maybe not out in the wild. There was a different kind of outlaw in the natural environment.

"What can I do for you?" he asked as he approached the pair. He was apprehensive, a hangover from Louisiana.

"Nothin' in particular," Breslin said. Sam had seen the man in Covington once or twice at waterfront festivities and several times at Harry Tom Cooper's Boat Dock out near the inlet. He looked to be the consummate good old boy. Sam could imagine a sticker on his tinted-window pickup truck that said, "American Born, Southern By The Grace Of God." He was overweight, but he looked strong. Probably an ex-Marine. Sam smiled at the oxymoron.

"What kind of nothin' in particular are you lookin' for?" he asked.

"Just that. Nothin' in particular. This is Karen Chaney, new officer in the district. She'll be replacin' Jimmy Lee. I was out showin' her around and thought you ought to know who she was. You might be seein' her patrollin' the marsh on occasion, and I wouldn't want you to shoot her for trespassin' or anything. This is Sam Larkin."

Karen Chaney stuck out her hand. Five feet seven, he guessed, medium-length blond hair streaked by the sun, a good figure that wasn't hidden by the uniform. Blue eyes. Her face and arms were burnished brown. She would be a pleasant addition to the area. Her eyes locked on his as they shook hands. Sam sensed a professionalism he rarely saw in the local wildlife officers.

"Pleased to meet you, Officer Chaney," Larkin said. "And I don't shoot people. Besides you can't trespass on the marsh; it's everybody's." Her handshake was firm, practiced to fit in a working environment with men. However, unlike some of the occupational ball-breakers he had come into contact with, it didn't appear designed for intimidation or equalization. The Ruger .357 magnum she wore precluded any necessity for that.

"I'm pleased to meet you, too, Mr. Larkin. Nice to know there's someone out here if I get in trouble." He waited for "I've heard a lot about you," but it didn't come. He guessed she didn't lie. There was an awkward silence. "Your place is beautiful. I would never have seen it if Officer Breslin hadn't pointed it out." She was smiling.

Sam Larkin decided that his first impression was valid; she was definitely attractive. And her eyes flashed. They broadcast energy while she stood perfectly still, took him in and saw him, or so he thought. Some people had that ability. He had come to the conclusion long ago that people seldom saw each other or themselves as more than just a part of whatever background they surrounded themselves with. Knowing that and avoiding it was an advantage. Seeing people and the world as most everyone else did was dangerous, a lesson he had learned the hard way. That would never happen again.

"I like it," he said. "I just regret it took me so long to get here."

"You're from Louisiana aren't you, Larkin?" Breslin pronounced the state's name with an emphasis on lose.

"Yes," Sam answered. He wouldn't give the man anything. It was obvious, for whatever reason, that the man didn't like him, which was fine.

"Where 'bouts?"

"All over. Shreveport, Baton Rouge, New Orleans and lots of little parishes here and there." He paused. "Officer Breslin, Officer Chaney, I don't mean to be inhospitable, but I've got some work to do on that new deck over there, and if I don't get busy, I won't get anything accomplished before dark. Y'all are welcome to hang around; I can visit while I work. You might even be of some help. I've got two hammers." He smiled.

"Naw. We've got to be gettin' along. Just wanted you to meet Karen here." The name change was pointed; it seemed to make the female officer uncomfortable. She would have to deal with Ray Breslin sooner or later. Sam had no doubt she could handle it.

"I'm glad you did. Been a pleasure," he said. "If I can ever help . . ."

"Thank you. I'll count on it. It was my pleasure also," Karen Chaney said. The two officers headed down to where their boat was tied up. Sam Larkin watched them leave.

The uniforms, the boat, all of it put him back in Louisiana. Back among men who drank Everclear grain alcohol when they didn't make their own, men who could slide a pirogue through a cypress swamp in darkness as deep as an underground cavern. Among women who served up boudin and crawfish and etouffée and gumbos that would scorch the whole internal body of the toughest man. Those were good memories, and in some moments, he wished he could go back to that time, make more memories like those. Others were not as pleasant.

He had no idea what Ray Breslin wanted, but surmised it was more than his meeting Karen Chaney.

CHAPTER 2

Bill Reichert was sleeping soundly. Morgan Hannah leaned up on one elbow and looked at him. He had a good body, although there was a little softening, a bit of extra thickness around the middle, which had developed over the three months since their first encounter. His breathing was steady, but his eyes moved frantically beneath their lids. What they were seeing? They began to flutter and gradually opened. Her own eyes had, in that unexplained subconscious way that everyone experiences, awakened him. The nipple of her breast brushed against his chest. He reached up and filled his hand with the other.

"You have beautiful breasts," he said with a smile and closed his eyes.

"I'm glad you approve." She leaned forward and made the nipple available to his mouth. He pulled it in gently. "That feels good," she said. He kept at it, circling his tongue around the areola as he suckled her, then pulling harder, biting gently. She closed her eyes. He knew where this was leading, and there wasn't time to get involved again even though his body was telling him differently. He let his mouth relax and his head fall back on the pillow.

"What's the matter?" she asked. "Want me on top?" She was playing with him, knew he had to get back to town.

"I don't think I could get it up if you tried," he said, grinning at his own humor.

"Wanna bet?"

"You destroy me, lady."

"I'm glad," she said. "I just wish you didn't have to go." It was her game. She knew she couldn't expect more. Afternoons such as they had just shared and an occasional trip when he could come up with an iron-clad reason for going out of town were all she wanted or needed.

"Well, I do and you know I do, so quit trying to make me feel terrible," he said as he sat up and pulled her to him. He kissed her deeply, feeling the puffiness in her lips and the heat in her mouth.

"I felt something move," she said when he released her.

"Involuntary muscle spasm," he said and got out of bed laughing.

Morgan watched him as he got dressed. "Not gonna shower?" she asked.

"When I get home. I don't have time right now."

"I think I'd know."

"Know what?" he asked.

"If my man came in the door freshly fucked," she teased, knowing he found it attractive. Morgan Hannah had mastered the art of being bawdy and a lady at the same time. She exuded femininity and class and used it. She could also let it go.

"Such language."

"You bring it out in me, and thank you."

"For what?"

"This afternoon. It was lovely," she said, then laid back on the bed.

"You're more than welcome. Just another service of Covington County National Bank. Many banks have branches; we have roots."

"I like yours." Bill Reichert felt himself blushing.

"Call you later?"

"Make it tomorrow, but not quite so early?"

Bill Reichert had become a different man over the last two years. He no longer discussed banking as though it were his sacred mission. He was more confident and self-assured. It was a quality Isabel Reichert could have admired ten years earlier; now it was suspicious. For years they had been reluctant partners. No, not partners, she was just an appendage, but, one way or another, he was in for a surprise. She would see to it.

The charade had gone on long enough. The few women friends she considered close had asked time and time again why she put up with Bill, why she didn't leave him and take him for everything he owned. She certainly had motive. She never had a real answer. Pride maybe? Covington was a small town. People had gossiped about her marrying below her class. Revenge? Possibly. She did enjoy the times she made him sweat, though they were rare. She had accused herself of weakness, which she hoped wasn't true. But, she had to admit, she had done nothing but look the other way.

She had a difficult time accepting that for all those years there was, perhaps, hope for the marriage. That a part of her, despite everything, still felt love for Bill Reichert, the most illogical and indefensible of motives. The last few months had changed that. Not because of the screwing around, but because he appeared truly happy, something she had never seen before. She could not allow that. It negated any rational excuses she could find.

Isabel spent the afternoon searching the house for any clue to her husband's change in behavior. She knew about his lover out on Sangaree Island. The woman was of no consequence, just the latest in a long chain of affairs. With Bill, it was any time, any place, anybody. There was something else though, something bigger. She trusted her intuition. There would be no rest until every possibility was checked and eliminated.

At four o'clock she went to the bank. Bill was out as she expected, but, ever covering his backside, he had told his secretary that he would be back within the hour. After some pleasant, meaningless chit-chat, she went into his office, ostensibly to make some calls. Isabel knew it irritated the secretary when she acted proprietary about her husband's office—hallowed ground.

After closing the door for privacy and taking a cursory glance around the room, she went to the telephone on his desk and hit the recall button. She recognized the number: Charlie Clay, their attorney. Nothing of consequence there; Bill spoke with him regularly on bank business. It was a good trade-off. All of their personal legal matters were handled without fee in return for the bank's business, as well as mutual referrals. Bill had received offers from larger banks, but always brought up Charlie Clay as one of the perks of being president of a locally owned bank, regardless of its size.

There was nothing on the desk. It was clean, not one piece of paper, and the drawers were locked, as was the five-foot-tall mahogany filling cabinet. It had been custom-made when he was elevated to president, the youngest in the bank's history. Even the waste basket was empty. "You've surely changed, you son of a bitch," she muttered as she looked around the room once again. Bill had left little evidence that the space was even used. Isabel had never seen his office so pristine.

There was nothing to be accomplished and it frustrated her. He wasn't that perfect. Nothing had changed financially as far as she could tell, no unusual withdrawals, no liquidating of assets. In fact, she had noticed on the last statement that there weren't as many checks being written on their joint account as usual.

Isabel Reichert felt like the only kid in class from whom everyone else was keeping a secret and laughing behind her back. It was humiliating. She left the office in a fury though she tried not to show it. At a loss for ideas, she got in her car and started toward home, a large antebellum structure two blocks off Main Street in Covington's historic district. It was more realistically their house; it hadn't been home in a long time. There was no alternative for her, nothing else to do.

At times Covington itself felt as claustrophobic as the house in which she lived. The town closed up after nine o'clock in the evening, even on Fridays. There were a couple of small bars down along the river, but the clientele was so consistent, they were like private clubs. No one bothered someone unusual coming in; they just didn't acknowledge them. The town existed within its own cocoon, untouched. Its size was not indicative of its power. It was the landlord, and the residents were the tenants, regardless of their station in the community. Yet, it did embrace its tenants, held them close, gave them a comfort zone of familiarity that allowed them to become an integral part of the whole.

The houses along Main Street, grandiose, historic mansions, columned and white, looked out over the Chester River. Huge and ancient live oaks, gnarled and heavily draped with shrouds of Spanish moss, lined the river's edge. Coming across the Marion Bridge from Matthew's Island, seeing the picturesque town, the adjacent yacht basin crowded with cruising class sailboats and the sentinel manses, one could easily imagine driving into a calendar photograph.

As she pulled into the driveway, small droplets of water began to collect on the windshield of her car. It would be another night like the night before and the night before that. Her husband was out fucking and she was left to her own devices.

She went in the house, left her bag and briefcase in the foyer and went to the liquor cabinet. It was becoming a ritual. Tonight, she decided, would be different. She would consider possibilities.

By the time Sam Larkin finished cleaning up his work site, putting his tools away and stowing the wood scraps in a barrel under the soon-to-be bedroom deck, only a razor-thin edge of the top of the sun was visible, sinking fast, as if it were being extinguished in the brackish waters of the marsh.

It had been a long day, but the euphoria of physical labor and visual accomplishment subjected any exhaustion the long hours created. He went to the kitchen, opened a beer and began putting together a dinner that could cook while he showered. A chicken breast covered in salsa, sliced bell peppers, onions and artichoke hearts were put in a cast iron skillet rubbed with oil, covered and put on low heat on the top of the stove. He cooked it slowly so the salsa would burn and caramelize on the chicken. He put long-grain rice on to steam. Sam covered spears of chainey briar, a local wild asparagus he had cut a few days before, with water. It would be ready to cook when he got out of the shower.

Larkin ate on the deck. It was the best time of his day. He looked out over the marsh and silently thanked Providence or whatever power had brought him to this place. The sky was beginning to darken; there would be rain before the night was over, but he predicted sun for the morning.

After dinner, he was sitting in the sun room sketching when the telephone rang. He looked at the wall clock. It was close to nine, an unusual time for anyone he knew to be calling.

"Hello?"

"Mr. Larkin?" It was female and the formal address precluded anyone he knew well.

"Yes?" his voice was quiet and resonant, not an affected telephone voice that many people use to hide their insecurity.

"This is Karen Chaney." Pause. "Environmental?" His warning systems went on alert. The earlier visit by the law enforcement officers had been hiding in a corner of his mind ever since they left. "Out at your place with Ray Breslin this afternoon?"

"Yes?"

"I hope I didn't disturb you. I realize it's late and you don't know me at all. I'm sure this is presumptuous." She was talking a mile a minute without striking a period. Nervous, which made him nervous.

"Not at all. How can I help you, Officer?" Give away nothing. Calm. Unemotional.

"Karen?" she said, offering him the familiarity of a first name.

"Okay, Karen. What can I do for you?" Yes, she was presumptuous.

"Nothing major and please don't misinterpret this, but I'm going to be out in the boat on my own tomorrow and wondered if you'd like to come along? Officer Breslin showed me places, but I'd really like to get familiarization from a different perspective. From someone who lives in the area I'm working." There was silence on the line. "I thought maybe since it's a Saturday you could help," she added.

Larkin weighed the possibilities. Spending the day on a boat with Karen Chaney was not the worst of all possible prospects. Perhaps it would put his paranoia about the earlier visit to rest.

"Sounds like it might be fun," he said. "It would be good to be in a real boat for a change. I guess you saw what I drive." Larkin's boat was an old, inboard-outboard that on the outside appeared to have seen much better days. Only he knew what was on the inside. "Tell you what, I'll ice down some beer in the cooler, and—"

"Whoa!" she interrupted. "We're gonna be in a state boat." He stifled a laugh. Then she laughed, too. "Guess you got me on that one, Sam. May I call you Sam?"

"You already did, and I'm calling you Karen."

" 'Bout nine?"

"I'll see you on the dock."

"If I can find it. Good night. And thanks." He liked the sound of her voice and didn't have a doubt she would find his dock.

"Good night, Karen."

The day would require some caution. Questions about Karen Chaney rolled around in his mind. It was curious that the primary officer in the area was being replaced by a woman. He also wondered why Ray Breslin had given the new kid on the block the familiarization tour; he didn't work the area. Most puzzling was that she had called. Her excuse didn't wash in his mind. There had been few women and fewer friends in his life since he arrived in Covington. A couple of casual encounters, nothing more. He wasn't looking for a relationship; life was quite good as it was. However, Karen Chaney, Law Enforcement Officer, might prove interesting.

When the rain began pelting the glass in the skylights above his head, he was just finishing a drawing of a shrimper hauling in his drag nets. He put the work down and walked out the sliding doors onto the deck. There was a four-foot overhang from the peaked roof that allowed him, without getting wet, to stand and watch the rain cover the marsh and the creek. The overhang was a requirement when he designed the house. There was no music more sweet to him than the sound of rain on water, a singular rent in the night silence.

He knew where each species of bird and animal would go in such weather and what they would do for cover and protection. It was a life study for him. He visualized them in the landscape he was seeing and knew they were safe. There would be no wars on this night. They were listening and watching even as he was doing.

The rain would stop before morning. Years in the outdoors provided immutable insights to nature and its ways. Insights into the ways of man were a different ball game. He stepped out from under the overhang and let the rain take its pleasure with him, the prickles of cold water like so many tiny electrical shocks on his face and arms brought to his skin a new freshness and washed his mind clean. Without stars and with the moon buried opaquely behind the low cloud cover, the darkness beyond Sam Larkin's deck was dense and impenetrable. An absence of light.

He took off his clothes and let the rain bathe his entire body. It was a cleansing he required on occasion. He didn't know how long he stood there—oblivious to everything except the feeling of the rain on his skin—before the chill of the night air prompted him to pick up his clothes and go back into the house. He took them to the laundry room, dropped them in the washer, dried himself briskly with a coarse towel and went to bed. There would be no hot shower to wash off the softness of the rain.

Turner Lockett had just finished eating a fried baloney sandwich and was opening his fourth Budweiser when he heard footsteps outside his trailer. He was sitting in the threadbare easy
chair facing the small television set, which was on but at very
low volume. It was the way he watched it. Too much volume and
you could miss something.

Something like he just heard. Footsteps. Even though it was
raining. He prided himself on having an animal's hearing, vision
and instincts. He considered himself closely linked to the animals. It was the way he survived.

Footsteps were not a sound that he welcomed. Living where
he did, there was no reason for anyone to be at his trailer at midnight, unless it was Jared Barnes or someone come to do him
harm. His shotgun was in a corner on the far side of the room
next to the table where he reloaded shotgun shells and concocted
fishing lures. A skinner's knife lay on the counter next to the TV
and a piece of lead pipe two-and-a-half feet long with black elec-
trician's tape around one end and a cap on the other lay next to
the chair in which he was sitting. Once he had started accumulat-
ing money, he made up his mind never to be more than arm's
length from a weapon. If someone did come to do him harm, they
would pay for it.

The rap on the door was firm, accompanied by Jared Barnes
drunken voice.

"Turner? You in there?" Barnes pulled on the door handle.
"It's me, Jared."

"I know who the hell it is," Lockett responded as he moved
to unlatch the door. When he opened it, Barnes, disheveled and
wet, was sitting on the steps. "Jared, what the fuck are you doing
wandering around out here in the rain?"

"Come out to see you. Come by last night, but you wudn't
home. Waited till near 'bout twelve o'clock. Where was you? I
thought maybe you'd gone to see one of them girls on Wallace
Street, but your truck was here. Cain't go see 'em by boat." He
giggled. "You got anything to drink?"

Lockett reached down, grabbed him under the armpits and
lifted him into a standing position.

"Come on, Jared. Yeah, I got something to drink."

"Not beer. Cain't drink no beer. Makes me burp and fart. Why 'on't we go on in to Wallace Street. I could use me a little pussy." He laughed. "Course, don't know what I'd do with it. Not tonight leastways."

"I hope you ain't plannin' on spendin' the night here, you sorry son of a bitch. I was just gettin' ready to turn in."

"Ain't gone stay long. Jus' wanted to check an' make sure you was all right. I come by last night."

"You already said that."

"Oh yeah. Where wuz you?" Barnes asked with a sneaky smile. "You wuz out doin' somethin."

"Settin' a trotline. You want that drink? I picked up some good last week."

"All of it's good."

Lockett went into the kitchen area and came back with a clear glass jar filled with colorless liquid. He handed it to Barnes, who held it up to the light.

"I bet this come from Georgia. Clear as a bell. They got the secret over there." He removed the two-piece canning lid, raised it to his lips, took two big swallows, leaned back and yelled. "Hoowhee! That is good stuff! Smooth as a new mama's milk."

"Like it?"

"Man, whatchu talkin' about. Gone have me another." He lifted the jar.

"You had your drink now . . ."

"Yeah, but you ain't answered my question."

"Ain't goin' to, Jared. And you best keep your mind in your own bidness." Lockett was staring at the floor. It was time. Everything was in jeopardy. It had worried him for weeks and he was tired of worrying. If Barnes started shooting off his mouth, it would all be over. The sweet life would be gone. The others would let Turner Lockett hang. Lawyers and doctors and such as they were, they were smart enough to cover themselves; ol' Turner wasn't.

"We friends ain't we, Turner? Cain't you share what you got goin'? I know it's somethin' and I'm pretty sure I know what. Hell, you can trust me, man."

"Time for you to go, Jared." Lockett moved toward him. "Come on. Get up." He reached out to help the man.

"You throwin' me out?"

"Sure as hell I am. Now come on. You come back when you ain't been drinkin' and maybe I'll tell you all about it. Might make you rich." Barnes smiled.

"I knew you had somethin' goin'. Knew it. Smugglin', ain't it? Bet it is. I'll be beholdin', Turner, swear I will. Get me outta this place. Go somewhere nice. Hell, we could go together." The man's breath was sour. Lockett could feel his stomach turning. He felt like he was going to puke, but it wasn't because of the bad breath. He got Barnes down the two steps and into the yard.

"We gone live on high ground, Turn." He was laughing. "Yessir, high ground. Me and you." He turned toward Lockett just as the lead pipe was winging toward his head. He never felt the blow. At the last second, Lockett closed his eyes, but he heard the dull thud and felt flesh and bone give way as the pipe made contact with Barnes's head. He also felt a warm, liquid spray hit his face.

Barnes was down. He had done it. It was over. Then he heard the moan and knew it wasn't finished. The baloney sandwich was coming up and he couldn't stop it. He bent over and let go, gagging. When the heaving stopped, he looked down at Jared Barnes and raised the pipe above his head. It was too late to stop. The road to hell was already paved.

Lockett took off the man's bloody clothes and dragged the body down to the boat. Between the alligators, gar and other predators there would be nothing left of Jared Barnes for anyone to find. He went back to the clothes, put them in the fire hole and covered them with wet ashes. They would be burned in the morning. He got some baling wire and a couple of cinder blocks from under the trailer and took them to the boat.

Lockett was beginning to feel sick again and he wanted to cry, wanted someone to hold him, forgive him and tell him it was all right. Wanted to feel safe. He was shaking uncontrollably, like a seizure. He felt his bladder go, looked down at the spreading wet spot on the front of his pants and sobbed. Barnes had brought it on himself. His pain turned to anger. Barnes had forced him. Thoughts were cascading through his brain with the speed of a spinning kaleidoscope. He couldn't focus, couldn't remember untying the boat or moving out into the creek, but that's where he was with a naked body in the bow. He headed inland into the backwaters.

Morning broke bright and sunny, as Sam had predicted it would. By seven o'clock, the sun was already beginning to remove the night chill, and, according to the last weather report, it would reach the mid-eighties before day's end. Pulling on his shorts and putting on his shoes for his morning run, he was looking forward to the day ahead.

After stretching out his leg muscles against the steps that led down from the entrance to his house, he began his morning routine. The run was painful until heavy sweat began to run into his eyes and soak the tee shirt he was wearing. From that point on, his rhythm became smooth and fluid. He seemed to glide just above the surface of the pavement, barely making contact. A feeding deer, grazing by the side of the road, raised its head as Larkin passed but didn't move, just looked. After two and a half miles, he slowed to a cool-down pace as he approached his house. Fifty crunches, twenty minutes of light lifting, and he would be ready for a hot shower and coffee.

He was finishing a bowl of fresh fruit when he heard the twin Mercs in the distance. It was almost nine. Karen Chaney was punctual. He took a last sip of coffee, lit a cigarette, which always seemed hypocritical after a workout, took several drags, extinguished it and went into the kitchen to fill two traveling mugs with hot coffee before she docked. He returned to the deck and saw the Cobia moving up the creek. She cut the engines to slow forty yards out and eased the sleek craft against the floating platform. He was impressed.

"Good morning," Karen Chaney called out as she jumped on the dock and tied the boat off. She was shining. The sun caught the blonde of her hair and blended it, like so many gold strands, with pins of light on the water. Instead of her uniform, she was wearing denim shorts and a navy blue sweat shirt, with the collar of a lighter shirt exposed around her neck. Sam waved from the deck and started down the stairs.

"Good morning," he said as he approached her. He handed her one of the traveling mugs. "Didn't know if you used cream and sugar, so I put in a little bit of each."

"Thanks," Her voice held a note of surprise.

"Got a good morning," Sam said as he looked over the boat. "You people sure know how to travel." The Cobia wasn't like any other state boat he had ever seen in this area.

"This is a loaner. I'm sure I'll get a standard issue in the next few days." Karen stepped back into the boat. "You drive. You know where you're going."

"You'll have to tell me what you want to see. I don't know where Breslin took you."

"He didn't show me much of anything except fishing docks, waterside bars and Sam Larkin's place. Other than that, we just rode around. In circles, I think. I don't believe he was much impressed with me. As an officer, I mean."

"How much time do you have?" he asked as he untied the bowline and stepped aboard.

"All day," she answered then felt chagrined. "I don't mean you have to spend all day showing me around. I just meant there's no rush." Larkin gave her a smile. Serene, confident, reassuring with just a touch of pleasant condescension at what she had said. "I don't want to ruin your day." He enjoyed her nervousness.

"I won't let you ruin even part of it," he said. "Been a long time since I've driven a boat like this, and there's nothing better than spending a sunny day on the water."

"Just let me know when you've had enough. I don't want to intrude."

"You won't," Larkin said and hit the starter. The deep-throated sound of the engines energized the whole craft. He eased away from the dock and out into the channel. After what he said about the boat, Chaney sat down and held on to the rail, expecting him to go full throttle when they got to deep water. Instead, he accelerated only enough to slowly move to the main creek from which his tributary originated.

There was little talk in the beginning. Larkin took her through connecting branches and small water courses, pointing out landmarks he thought would be helpful to her, told her who lived in the ramshackle houses and trailers, including Turner Lockett's, lying half-hidden in the waterside growth. He also showed her Cobb Palace, a plantation house built at the turn of the seventeenth century, the house a shock of white amid the natural colors that surrounded it. It was huge, with smooth columns, a large gallery and a massive lawn leading to the water.

"Did Breslin bring you here?" Sam asked.

"He pointed in this direction and said it was over here, but we didn't come in close enough to see it. He doesn't seem to have much use for blue bloods, as he called them."

"Not many locals do, except the other blue bloods, but they do like the money they spend. It's not much different than anywhere else. Even people who have lived here for twenty years are still considered outsiders by the insiders." Karen Chaney laughed. "I'm going to take you by the Sangaree Island Marina in a few minutes. I assume he didn't take you there either. Out in this area, it's the place to go if you have trouble."

"That gives me two places," she said with a cautious grin. "He did point out how to get there, but he said I probably wouldn't have much cause to patrol there. I think he was anxious to get rid of me."

"Uh-huh." Ray Breslin's intelligence dropped a few points in Larkin's estimation.

The marina was different from anything else she had seen out in her territory. It breathed wealth and pretensions of wealth. Gingerbread, three-story houses barely one room wide, painted in pastel greens, yellows and blues with white scrollwork trim, a marine store, restaurant and bar, gas pumps, a large parking area and dry dock buildings formed a commercial compound lying against the water. It was a piece of upper-class Florida retirement dropped, out of place, in the natural lowcountry environment that surrounded it.

"This is the poor side of the island," Sam said. "Houses on the beach are much larger, a million or more. You hungry?"

"Not yet. I brought some lunch in case we were out that long."

"Sounds good to me."

"Least I could do with you giving up your Saturday morning," she said. "This is quite a place."

"Nice to visit, but I wouldn't want to live here."

"From the looks of it, I might." Sam turned to look at her and headed back out the creek into the main channel.

"Where to now?" he asked.

"You're the guide." Chaney leaned back and felt the full sun on her face. It was actually hot when they were moving slowly.

"So what did Breslin tell you about the lowcountry?"

"Not much of anything. He talked about himself mostly, what a tough job it was to patrol these waters, how to catch illegal shrimpers, and the proper procedure for arresting drunks during Water Weeks. Oh, and I forgot, some people I'm not supposed to arrest."

They spent another hour traversing the creeks and waterways that crossed and recrossed and intertwined like a new hatch of snakes in a nest. Names such as Wineau, Palachocola, Utchee and Coftacheque rolled off Larkin's tongue and then around in Karen Chaney's head. They were as confusing and unidentifiable in their locations as they were to pronounce.

As he maneuvered the craft through marshlands with no apparent landmarks, years of experience showed in the casual, off-hand manner with which he chose his paths. By one o'clock, without warning, and miraculously in her eyes, he brought them back to his dock.

"Now how about that lunch?" he asked when the boat was secured.

"I'm starving," she answered and retrieved a cooler from the stern.

After a quick tour of the house, Sam opened a couple of Coronas and pushed a wedge of fresh lime down the neck of each, as Karen Chaney watched. He escorted her to the deck to sit while he got place mats for the table. When that was done, he went back into the kitchen, put the sandwiches, potato salad, chips and a small jar of olives she had brought on a tray and carried them out to the deck.

"You go fancy, don't you?" she asked when he joined her.

"No, just civilized," he said. "I once made a pact with myself that I would never eat another meal without at least the minor graces."

"You're a tough one to figure, Sam."

"I hope," he said, unloading the tray and putting the plates and food on the table.

"It is truly beautiful here," she said.

"That's why I came."

"Not to teach school? Breslin said you taught at the high school."

"Didn't plan on that, but things don't always go the way you plan. I put too much money in the house and had to do something to put grits on the table. Teaching's okay. Gives me my summers."

"You don't complain much, do you?"

"You just said it: it's beautiful here. How could I complain?"

"Most people have something to complain about or they come up with something."

"I'm not most people."

Karen shook her head. "That's for sure," she said. "Seems funny, I've been with you all morning, and I don't know anything about you."

"It's kind of hard to talk with two Mercs blasting away. And there's really not a lot to know."

"I find that hard to believe," she said with a skeptical grin. Sam shrugged his shoulders. "As you said, you seem to have a good life."

"I do. If I didn't, I'd change it." He took a bite of his sandwich. "I appreciate the lunch," he said. "What about you? Where did you come from, and how did you wind up here?"

"I'm from Alabama, but I've worked in Florida. I wasn't coastal in either place, and that's what I wanted. This seemed like a good place."

"Pretty tough duty to get, I'd imagine. How'd you manage?"

"Friends," she said. The vague answer bothered him.

They finished eating and the conversation lagged. Although any day out on the water was a day of contentment for him, this one had been better than he expected. As far as he was concerned, they could have stayed on his deck the rest of the afternoon without talking; it wouldn't have bothered him in the least.

She rose from her chair and looked at him. "I guess I'd better get back to my little rented hovel and see what I can remember to write down. Let me help you clean this up."

"No need. I'll take care of it. I enjoyed this morning."

"I'm glad you did."

Sam followed her down the steps to the dock.

"We'll have to do it again sometime. I'm sure there's a lot more to learn."

"More than you or I will ever know," he said. "It'd be my pleasure."

He stood on the dock and watched her head the boat back out to the creek.

CHAPTER 3

On Saturday morning Bill Reichert left the house on Legree Street before Isabel got up. Saturday morning was her day to sleep late—late being nine o'clock—before beginning a day at the beauty parlor, grocery shopping and running errands that would take up the better part of the day. Bill would disappear for the day and the evening and return without explanation. It was standard operational behavior unless there was a social event at which their mutual attendance was required.

As she lay in bed, Isabel wondered in amazement how she could have let the marriage go on so long. Despite her thinking and rationalization over the last few weeks, she found it unconscionable that she had tolerated his behavior. There was no hope, never had been, though she had refused to admit that. Now it was over, and she was determined to exact some measure of retribution for what he had done to her life. What she had allowed him to do to her life. At this moment she held as much bitterness toward herself as toward her husband. Regardless of regrets on her part, tonight Bill Reichert was in for a surprise.

She went about her usual tasks during the day, fixed herself dinner, watched a movie on video and waited for him to come in. It was just after midnight when she heard the key in the lock. She had ingested enough single-malt Scotch to throw her glass at him when he came through the door. It smashed against the wooden molding around the arched doorway in which he stood, shocked, watching the amber liquid running down the wall and puddling on the antique heart-pine floor. She had seen him flinch, a break in the composure he prided himself on. There had never been any violence between them; it caught him by surprise. When he recovered, she saw explosive anger in his eyes, another drop in the calm façade. Score two.

"What the fuck was that for?" he screamed. Score three. She smiled, feeling she was embarking on a very pleasant and exciting time in her life. The question of why she had waited so long was no longer an issue.

"It's just a new ritual I've designed for welcoming home my wayward, thoughtless, philandering husband. Worked pretty well, huh? Got your attention. It worked so well, I think I'll use it on a regular basis." She laughed.

"What the hell is wrong with you? Are you drunk?"

"Maybe, but I'm honest. I never lie when I'm drunk." Bill Reichert stood silent. "How's your girlfriend? That's where you've been all day isn't it? Out on Sangaree? You must be worn out."

"What the hell difference does it make where I've been? We've been over this a hundred times. You want a divorce, I'll give you one." It was a shallow threat she had heard so many times before, it rolled right past her. She was his protection against involvement with the carousel of females that circled though his life.

"You'll *give* me one? Bill you're pathetic." He stared at her, the anger in his eyes subsiding, being replaced by something else. Hatred? Fear? "No, I don't want a divorce. Not right now anyway. I won't make it that easy on you. And when I do, it won't be easy. You were my mistake, Bill, and I have to rectify that."

"And how do you propose to do that?" He had moved into the room and gone to the liquor cabinet.

"This is a good start, don't you think? Tell me, Bill, what have you got going? Not your love life. What else? I know there's something. You're too happy. Of course I guess screwing your life away can addle the brain. Come on. Something has made you very happy. Relaxed. What is it?" He turned back to face her and she saw it. Fear. It was a first.

"I don't know what you're talking about."

"Sure you do. You won't tell me, but I promise you I will find out. As I said, you're too happy, Bill, and it isn't because of me. I can't allow that."

"Why don't you just kick me out if you think you can."

"There is no doubt I can, but that wouldn't be punishment, would it? You'd consider that a victory. No guilt. I did it. It's the cheating man's saving grace. Force her to throw him out, and all guilt is absolved."

"I've heard enough unless you have something reasonable to say." He turned and started from the room. Her voice stopped him.

"I could say more, but I don't want you to see it coming. It will come though. Remember that every time you walk through that door. What was it Dante said? 'Abandon hope all ye who enter here?' " There was a question on his face. She was in control for the moment. It wouldn't last, but it was a beginning. It had gone better than she expected. "Fix me another drink, would you? I seem to have dropped mine." Now his questions would begin, but he would get no answers.

The telephone rang at eight-thirty on Sunday morning. Bill Reichert answered it. Isabel didn't move. The argument had lasted until early morning when her words became slurred, and her eyes drooped from the Scotch she had ingested. He could still smell it.

"Hello?" There was only the sound of someone hanging up the phone on the other end of the line. "Son-of-a-bitch," Reichert said putting the receiver back in its cradle and falling back on the pillow.

"Who was it?" Isabel moaned. He was surprised she was conscious.

"Your boyfriend," he said sarcastically.

"Good. Tell him I'm ready," she said without opening her eyes. Her humor didn't raise a response in her husband. "Did you hear me?"

"Uh-huh." He said already drifting off.

"Oh, okay then. Are you ready?" She knew that would irritate him.

"No, I'm not ready, Isabel. I haven't been ready for a long time. I don't even know why I'm sleeping in here except to appease you. It was the only way I could get you to go to bed."

"Who was that?"

"I don't know who it was. Probably some salesperson who could hear the irritation in my voice and was too weak to say anything."

"Probably just somebody who got my name off a men's room wall, checking to see if the coast is clear."

"Probably," he said. "Are we going to talk or sleep? I thought we did all the talking last night." She could hear his breath become more measured as he slept.

"Not by half, my friend," she said to herself.

She must have dozed off because when the telephone rang for the second time, it startled her. It was ten-thirty and she felt worse. Her head was encrusted with white pain that hit with the searing electrical force of lightning.

"Hello?" she heard. Whoever was on the other end of the line caused Bill Reichert to come to attention. He pulled himself into a sitting position on the edge of the bed.

"Little early, isn't it, Charlie?" Isabel couldn't imagine why their attorney would be calling at ten-thirty on a Sunday morning and could discern nothing from the one-sided conversation. "Okay. I'll be there by noon. Goodbye, Charlie."

She was having trouble focusing. The room wasn't spinning; it was undulating. There was no sense of touch or control. Everything ached. Her mouth was dry and her tongue diagnosed her lips as being grotesquely swollen. She tried to watch her husband, but had difficulty putting any order to what she was seeing. She was still in a dream, or so it seemed, yet she knew she was awake. She tried to concentrate. There was a question she wanted to ask him, but she lost it. Just there moments before, it had left her completely. She ran her hands up and down her body to see if she could experience any feeling. The nerves beneath her skin seemed dead.

There hadn't been a hangover like this since she was in her twenties. Isabel wasn't sure whether she had experienced a celebration or a wake. She knew what would come next; it was already beginning. The contractions in her stomach, her throat closing up, trying to keep the inevitable from happening. Struggling, she got to her feet, held on to the bedpost for a moment, then let leaning momentum take her to the doorway to the bathroom. When she reached the toilet, she fell to her knees and let her stomach purge itself. She was still in the bathroom, helpless, when she heard her husband leave.

Crossing the Marion Bridge, Reichert could see that the Spartina grass in the marsh was already showing green halfway up, though it remained a light pecan color at the top. Despite the rising temperature, a sea breeze was forming small white caps on the water all the way across the river. It was a glorious day. The drive out to the Oyster Creek Inn took about thirty minutes the way Reichert drove. He loved the power and the feel of the white 740i BMW. It was only five months old, and each time he got behind the wheel, it was like the first time.

The restaurant, named for the small creek that ran behind it, was located on the northern side of Matthew's Island on the Palachocola River, just west of its convergence with the Chester, Skudahee and Dunn Rivers into Matthew's Island Sound. It was not open on Sunday, so he was surprised to see two other cars in addition to Charlie Clay's black Mercedes in the parking lot. The attorney had bought the eatery a year before and was spending more and more time there. His wife had been dead for several years, and he had no hobbies or interests. He had said nothing about anyone else meeting with them but left no quarter as to whether Bill Reichert should come to the restaurant. That gave Reichert a little concern, but he dismissed it.

Set in an old oyster-processing factory, the place was originally nothing more than a galvanized metal, warehouse-type building where oysters were graded, shucked and packed for shipping to retail stores, restaurants, and wholesalers throughout the state. The building itself had been converted to an eating place years before Charlie Clay became its owner. It was anything but ostentatious. The exterior metal siding was covered with weathered barn wood, and a large porch with cane-backed rocking chairs was added to the landward side of the building where patrons entered. The rear of the structure extended on pilings over the water to the dock. Another deck and more rocking chairs were put there to allow the occasional overflow crowds to sit while waiting for a table to come available. After dinner, diners could exit through the rear and walk along the dock looking at the shrimp boats, watching a sunset or a moonrise.

Inside was a large cypress bar, stained dark and aged by elbows, cigarette burns and years of spilled Jack Daniels, beer and other emollients that were drinkable. Dusty, nicotine-yellowed pictures of locals, smiling and holding up a day's catch for the camera, politicians, few of whom the present patrons could identify, as well as a few visiting movie stars who had filmed in the area, took up all the wall space not covered by old tin beer and liquor signs and the newer neon displays.

The dining area was set apart and hidden from the bar, its walls paneled with wind-cured, salt-sea wood and decorated with antique implements of commercial fishery. The tables were covered with linen table cloths and napkins and set with silver and crystal. Depending on the time of day or night, the clientele varied from hard-nosed lowcountry locals and men who made their living from the sea to the town's upper-class. The dinner hours—especially on weekends—could be pretty high-toned.

Charlie Clay, a man in his mid-fifties with a natural aura of southern dignity and power, was sitting on a high stool behind the bar drinking a cup of heavy chicory coffee when Bill Reichert, dressed in tan slacks, a navy golf shirt and tasseled loafers with no socks, walked in. The overhead lights, which were never turned on when the doors were open for business, exposed the dirt, dust and wear of the place that the public never saw in its subdued lighting effects. It was like a mediocre plastic surgery that had begun to fall after post-op years of smiling.

Turner Lockett was sitting at the bar with a bottle of Budweiser in front of him and a sullen look on his face. Reichert also knew the man sitting beside Lockett, but couldn't put together why he was at this meeting. Jerry Salyer owned a large highway construction company based on Palmetto Island, an upscale resort island fifty miles south of Covington that catered to well-heeled retirees and tourists from the Northeast and Midwest. Salyer was a forty-year-old inherited millionaire who had doubled or tripled his original nut.

"Jerry." Reichert nodded to the young construction mogul. "So what's up, Charlie?" he asked as he took a stool a space away from the other two.

"First things first. What can I get you? Can't sell it to you on Sunday, but I can give it to you," Clay said. "Silliest damn law I ever heard of. Makes me mad once a week."

"Heineken."

"I can do that." The lawyer pulled an icy green bottle from the cooler, opened it and set it in front of Reichert. Pieces of crushed ice that stuck to the bottle began sliding to the bar's surface, creating a puddle. Reichert reached for a bar napkin and wiped it dry.

"I'm sure you didn't call me out here to give me a beer and have social interaction with Turner and Jerry, Charlie. What are we doing here?" he asked, impatience apparent in his voice.

"Now don't get arrogant, Bill. We got bidness to tend to and some decisions to make."

The banker resented the patronizing attitude Charlie exhibited when he assumed his older, more experienced and wiser mode.

"I'm not being arrogant, Charlie. Just a little curious, that's all. What's so important that we need to meet on a Sunday morning?"

"No need to be anxious. In fact, there could be reason to celebrate. I might as well tell you right off that I've enlisted Jerry here to join our company."

It wasn't a surprise. As soon as he saw Jerry Salyer sitting at the bar, Reichert assumed things were going to change. In his mind, Charlie was playing a dangerous game. "The more the merrier" philosophy was not smart in his opinion.

"Why?" he asked. He turned to Salyer, "Nothing against you, Jerry. I'm just skeptical of any change when things are running smoothly."

"No reason for change that I can see," Clay said. "In fact, I think with Jerry involved, things will run even more smoothly. We can increase our income, and it will be safer."

"Would you explain that to me?" Bill Reichert's mind was racing. Despite the amounts of money that were passing through him, the idea of more was exhilarating. The problem would be how to handle it. The operation had grown in the last two years, far beyond original expectations. It began as a lark and had grown into a business. He was surprised that neither Jerry Salyer nor Turner Lockett had said a word. It was obvious they were briefed to be quiet until Charlie presented the plan. Charlie was pretty transparent at times, which worried the banker.

Reichert got a hard stare. "I'll try, Bill, but you've got to have an open mind. First off, nothin's going to change.

Everyone will take care of the same responsibilities they've been handling. I'll still arrange the buys, the backup money and delivery. Breslin and his crew will carry out the off loads. Turner here will be the water man, and you will continue to wash and dry our ill-gotten gains. You do a good job with the money, Bill, but you're naïve about the problems out in the field. We need more transporting vehicles, more off-load sites and, more than anything, we need storage space. Now neither you nor I nor any of the others have any logical or legal reasons for purchasing and providing any of those items. Jerry does. That's why I asked him to join us. Does that make any sense?"

"It would seem to, but . . ."

"We're bringin' in eighteen tons next time," Clay said.

Surprise or elation were not the first reactions to pass through Bill Reichert's face. Anxiety was first. The amount was double what they had ever dealt with before. Clearing the money would require some strategies he didn't know enough about to implement.

"That's a lot of grass," he said. "You're talking eight or ten million dollars. I'm not sure I know how to handle . . ."

"I'll help you. Don't worry."

"Do we have buyers?"

"Bill," Charlie said with a patronizing smile, "we always have buyers. You know that. They'll show up as soon as we get the word out. Just like always. I don't want it hanging around any more than you do."

"What's the arrival date?"

"Not definite yet. There are still some things to be put in place, but I thought you'd need some time for your end."

"I'll get to work on it. Anything else?"

"Not that I can think of just yet."

"Then I've got people to see and places to go. I'm sorry I can't stay longer, but you caught me by surprise, Charlie. Isabel had already scheduled my day for me," he said, adding the last to appease the attorney, who worried about his friend's marital status. Charlie's marriage had been good, and he wanted everyone else's to be. He'd seen too much of divorce and misery in his practice. Reichert stood up, nodded to Jerry Salyer and Turner Lockett, and left.

Charlie Clay knew Bill Reichert was disturbed, but that couldn't be helped.

"Man didn't seem too happy," Salyer said.

"Dudn't like change," Charlie said. "Bill likes to think he's the most important cog in the wheel. And I guess maybe in some ways he is, but . . ."

"Dudn't know shit about what we do," Lockett said. "I ain't seen him at no off-loads."

"No, Turner, but you wouldn't have the money you've got without Bill Reichert. Don't ever forget that. But don't worry about him. He'll get whatever's stuck in his craw out when he sees the money."

"You the boss," Lockett said. He wondered if he looked any different, if anyone could tell what he had done. He hadn't slept in two days. Though his body was under water, Jared Barnes was still with him.

"Not really," Charlie Clay replied with a stern look.

"Jerry, I want you to start looking around for an additional couple of eighteen-wheelers and a larger storage area."

"How soon do we need them?"

"Prob'ly a month or so. I'm not sure how fast I can put all of this together."

"It won't be difficult."

"Good. Then that's it as far as I'm concerned. I'll give you a call in a couple of days for lunch or something. There's a lot more we need to talk about."

"I'll wait to hear from you." The meeting was over.

When Salyer and Lockett had gone, Clay locked the doors and went outside to sit on the deck. There was nothing pressing to do except sit and look out over the marsh. He thought of the marsh as a microcosm of the society around him. It changed with the seasons. When the tide was out and the mud creek bottom exposed, it was as bleak as some people and some days. However, when the sea came back in, it was dressed in its Sunday best. It was coming alive again, resurrected from the dead of winter. Resurrection was the one difference in the marsh and the human race, and that, he felt, was unfair. It made his grief for his wife, Margaret, a reality because it removed any hope.

He never realized, until she was taken by a weak blood vessel in her brain, how much of his life was her. The money he had made was inconsequential. There was no desire for material possessions; he had all of those he had ever wanted or needed. His practice, the largest in Covington, no longer held any interest for him. Beyond that, he wasn't needed. A handful of associates did the work unless there was a sticky question to be answered. He had community standing and respect. Consequently, there was little to strive for and even less reason to live.

He was still a relatively young man, yet he felt old and had lost interest in his life except for what excitement the smuggling operation provided. Without a care for risk or security, that break in the monotony was stimulating. Greed was not his motivation for getting involved, as it probably wasn't for the three friends who brought it to him. Like himself they were professionals, not in need of money. It was the adventure of it all. Risk. Those things gave him a reason to stay alive.

The wind appeared to be picking up; he could feel a chill in the air. It was time to go home. On a whim he decided to go to his beach house on Sangaree instead. He sensed a storm might be coming and wanted to watch it. He hadn't been out there in months, though it was cleaned every week and was kept stocked with non-perishable and frozen foods. The house was not a pleasant place for him to be alone. He had bought it for his wife and she loved it. They had spent every weekend there even though the house in Covington was only thirty-two miles away. It had been a place of happiness.

Sam Larkin spent most of the day working on the bedroom deck and made quite a bit of progress. More than half of the deck planking was done. When that was complete, only the surrounding benches would remain to be built. He looked forward to being able to get out of bed and step outside at any time of day or night.

The wind was picking up and the temperature dropping. There was lightning somewhere out at sea. He couldn't see the fiery streaks, but the flashes they gave off were visible over the marsh and getting closer. It was a fast mover. By four-thirty the sky looked like it had been brushed in an ink wash. The sun was completely hidden, and only filtered light kept it from being fully dark. Marsh grasses lay flat in the wind and vines in the trees swung loosely like restless snakes. Small dead limbs and twigs fell from the trees and dried palm fronds and winter-brown oak leaves played a thin and tremulous music in the wind. Jones Run Creek was capped with white froth.

When Sam felt the first drops of rain, he brought the deck chairs and the table in under the overhang, turned them upside down and went into the house. He stood inside the door looking out. In the glare of some refracted light source, the creek might have been ice. For a short while it was white, then it gradually grayed until disappearing in the deepening darkness. Violent crashes echoed over the marshes as unbridled electricity strobed from point to point. Rain came in sheets hitting the ground with the sound of ripping canvas. It was a concert. The sound of the telephone removed him from the glory and power of the storm, and for a moment he resented it.

"Hello?"

"You gettin' wet yet?" Skeeter Crewes asked. He lived a mile and a half up Osprey Landing Road. They had met at Harry Tom Cooper's Boat Dock when Sam first came to the island. Skeeter was day-working, sanding the bottom of a twenty-eight-foot sailboat and minding the store, when Sam came in for gas. In conversation they realized they were neighbors. Sam subsequently hired the black man to help in the final stages of the house when he was available and there was two-man work to be done. Skeeter Crewes was Sam Larkin's first and best friend in his new home territory.

"No, I've got sense enough to be inside the house," Larkin said. "What about you?"

"I'm dry, but we ain't got no lights," Skeeter answered. "Course, what's new about that?"

"Power's still on here, so it's not the transformer."

"Naw, it's just us poor colored folks that loses power. Lightnin' knows where the white folks live." He laughed a deep bass laugh. It was an ongoing, good-humored repartee they had established soon after they began working together. "Who the hell knows what it is. Lights go out on this road ever time a cloud passes over."

"What's going on? I know you didn't call to talk about lightning discrimination."

"Wondered if I could borrow a couple of your crab traps this week if the weather settles down. Mine's done rotted through and cain't be fixed. Course they so old, I cain't complain. It's early, but I thought I might pick up some shedders. "

"You don't have to call about that. You know where they are. Just come over and get anything you want. I've told you that. Anything except the boat, and that's only because I can't afford another one and don't want you feeling black man's guilt if something should happen to it."

"I feel better askin'," Skeeter Crewes said.

"They're there for you, my friend."

"Thanks, Sam. Everthin' goin' all right? Ain't seen you in a few days."

"Good as can be expected."

"I seen you out in that boat with the blond Saturday. You gettin' ready to put you'sef into some big time trouble?" Larkin heard the man chuckle.

"No, that's one thing I don't need."

"Everbody be needin' a woman, man. One of 'em gonna get you sooner or later. We be seein'. I'll talk to you later."

"See you, Skeeter."

When he got off the phone, he went into the kitchen to put something on for dinner. He looked through the freezer and came up with a couple of quail a student had brought him during the winter. That and a salad would do it. After he cleaned up.

He got in the shower without worry about the lightning, figuring that if it took the trouble to come inside to get him, it was his time to go. There was no need to do anything constructive; he had been doing constructive things all day. He wondered what Karen Chaney was doing in this weather.

CHAPTER 4

At ten o'clock on Monday morning Bill Reichert picked up the telephone on his desk and dialed Morgan Hannah's number. She answered on the third ring.

"Hello?"

"Hi," he said brightly, trying to hide the irritation he felt at her not being available the day before.

"And how are you this morning?" He wondered if she ever said anything that didn't have the sound of promise behind it.

"I guess I'm fine. A little disappointed maybe."

"Disappointed?" Her tone didn't change.

"I tried to call yesterday afternoon from about one-thirty on until about ten. I left a message," he said.

"I was at the beach in the afternoon, and didn't get in last night until late." He knew she wouldn't tell him where she had been and he couldn't ask. It was an unspoken part of their arrangement.

"I wanted to see you," he said.

"If you had called in the morning . . ."

"You said not early." There was displeasure in his voice.

"I was up by nine-thirty. That's not early, and I didn't go to the beach until noon. Why didn't you call earlier?" she asked.

"I had a meeting at twelve and wasn't free until one-something."

"I'm sorry. I would have liked to see you, too." She didn't sound convincing. He wondered if someone else were there with her.

"What about lunch? Busy?"

"I've got a hair appointment in town. Then I think I'll do a little shopping. May even go over to Palmetto. I haven't been off the island in days."

"Should I call this evening?" Bill Reichert was angry at her coyness. He wouldn't beg. Never had; never would. She was just a piece of fluff. But a good piece of fluff, came the afterthought.

"Why don't we wait until tomorrow. Call in the morning. Maybe we can do something in the afternoon if you're free."

"I don't know what's on my calendar," he said coldly, knowing there was nothing he couldn't avoid or wouldn't cancel. "I'll call."

"Hey, lighten up," she said. "We'll try for tomorrow, okay?"

"Okay. Tomorrow," he said and hung up the phone.

He sat at his desk being bored. The whole business of banking had become monotonous to him. There was little to do. He had been promoted up and out of useful work. Loan meetings, if there was an important loan, handling a rare employee problem and attending the weekly Rotary Club meeting. That was pretty much it, other than at audit time. The bank was well-organized, which he considered his major talent. Vice-presidents and branch managers did all of the day-to-day work. He selected them carefully for that very reason.

He decided to call Charlie Clay and see if he was available for lunch. He wasn't comfortable with the idea of expanding the business and adding new people. The additional money was appealing, but how many BMWs could he drive at one time?

"Charles Clay, Attorneys-at-Law," the secretary answered.

"It's Bill Reichert. Charlie available?"

"Not yet, Mr. Reichert. He called in from the beach house and said he wasn't sure exactly what time he would be in. Any message or anything I can do for you?"

"No, just tell him I called. I would like to talk to him when he gets a minute."

"I'll tell him."

"Thank you." When he hung up the telephone, he had no idea what to do next. However, with additional currency coming in, there was research to be done. The thought of reorganizing The Company's system was aggravating.

It was cold when Karen Chaney woke up on Monday morning. The room felt wet. The blinds were closed, making it impossible to determine whether it was day or night. She pulled herself out of bed and opened the blinds. It was day, gray and raining. If she were staying in a better place, she would have gone back to bed. It was that kind of day—a depression-booster. The only positive thing that had happened to her since coming to Covington was meeting and spending the good part of a Saturday with Sam Larkin. Didn't know why that was positive, but it seemed that way.

She had participated in a number of difficult and dangerous operations since being assigned to the Special Operations Unit of the DEA, but she had never felt so isolated. She was on her own; there was no team. All decisions regarding her activities were hers alone. Kind of like a one-person Special Forces unit dropped behind enemy lines. The objective was simple: infiltrate the Covington District Environmental Service and determine if information received by the administration regarding the importation of marijuana and hashish into the area had any validity.

Neil Dougherty, the supervisor who assigned the project to her, believed the information was sound. However, the procedures appeared haphazard, which made her nervous. She was simply put in place, told to observe and report anything she thought important. A fishing expedition. If it was justified, a full unit would be sent in. She was to report to Dougherty every third day. Today was the day, but not now. Neil could wait.

When she finished dressing, she left the motel for the Environmental offices. Three Hispanic men were sitting on milk crates in front of the room next to hers drinking Colt 45 Malt Liquor. The thought of drinking at this hour made her gag. She glanced at them and their heads went down. As soon as her back was turned, she heard a laugh.

"Hey, *Puta*, come back in the room with us and make the day worthwhile. You can have all three of us," one of them said.

Chaney turned and walked back to them. She put her hands in her pockets, opening her jacket just enough to show the Ruger .357 clipped to her belt. The heads went back down.

"Come on. Don't you want to see what you're going to get?" she said. They looked up and took in the gun wide-eyed. "I don't think all three of you together could make one good bone." She turned and headed toward her car. The three men were silent.

The office of the Covington County Environmental Service was located in the Wylie Building, an old, dirty, red-brick, two-story structure built by the W.P.A. in the thirties. The entrance consisted of two framed glass doors at street level. On each floor a long, narrow, dark hallway ran the length of the building. Office doors with opaque glass windows bearing identifying titles such as Tax Assessor, County Records, Zoning Board, Licenses and Permits, District Attorney and South Carolina Division of Motor Vehicles were lined up symmetrically on both sides of the corridor.

The Environmental Services office was at the end of the hall, housed in a large room, crowded with furniture: six desks, which were seldom used, numerous filing cabinets, a water cooler, and a large conference table in the center. The government-green walls were stained by water leaks, years of coal-furnace dust and cigarette smoke accumulated before the facility was declared a "smoke-free" environment. They were hung with citations, regulations, framed newspaper articles and agents' pictures. Outside the supervising officer's private office stood an American flag and a South Carolina state flag. Only a fire would remove all of the accrued grime that Karen Chaney was looking at as she sat at her desk, located at the furthest end of the room from the entrance.

Sunday had been devoted to looking for an apartment. It was surprising to her how little was available and the prices that were being asked. Seven hundred a month was all she was allowed. She finally gave up on the owner-ads late in the day and stopped into a realtor's office, where she found a two-story townhouse listed that she fell in love with. It was in a pleasant location and looked out over the river. Two bedrooms—the master upstairs, guest down—living room, kitchen, bath, powder room and a small dining area. A wrought-iron spiral staircase led to the second floor. The river side of the unit was all glass, which gave an exquisite view from both the living room and the master bedroom. It was well-furnished, including a king-sized bed from which she could see a wide expanse of the river. More than perfect. It was also nine hundred and fifty dollars a month, but too beautiful to pass up.

If she had to hit her savings to supplement the allowance, she would. Covington wouldn't be long term, which created another problem. She was looking for a month-to-month or a sixty-day lease with two months' rent up front. The salesman told her the owner wanted a full year lease. He was doubtful, but said he would see what could be worked out. The thought of starting her search all over again was depressing.

In her short time in Covington Karen Chaney had learned nothing about the people she would be working with. The office was loosely run, each officer pretty much on his own.

The word was, keep up with your arrest quota, which was very small, do your paperwork, and check in at the office occasionally. Other than that, you were kind of an independent contractor. It was foreign to the work environs she was used to: duty rosters, red-tag cases, surveillance reports, and all of the other common and basic elements of law enforcement.

She needed boat time, but it was no day to be out on the water. Consequently, she found herself in the office with little to do other than hope for a call from the real estate agent. There were two other officers present, each working on their own paperwork projects. They didn't seem predisposed to conversation. She finally faced the inevitable and put in a call to Neil Dougherty.

While the phone was ringing, she assumed her professional demeanor and rehearsed what she was going to say.

"Neil Dougherty. Karen Chaney calling," she said when the switchboard operator answered the phone.

"Belle Starr," came the smiling voice on the other end of the line. He had given her the name when he was a trainer and she was a trainee. Said it was because of her tenacity and willingness to bend the law when solving classroom problems. In retaliation she started calling him Blue Duck after Belle's emasculated paramour. "What's up?"

"Just checking in as instructed. What about you?"

"Tryin' to find some bad guys to put away. What's going on in Carolina?"

"Haven't been here long enough yet. They don't hand out brochures on drug smuggling in Covington County to newcomers," Karen said, keeping her voice low.

"Covington may be the hub, Karen, or maybe not, but if it is and it's a growing operation, it may have already spread to Charleston and beyond. Don't get near-sighted."

"I'm not a beginner, Neil. I don't close my eyes to any possibilities, but give me a chance." There was a pause in the conversation.

"Have you met anyone yet?" Dougherty asked.

"Professionally, a couple of environmental officers and the head man. Socially? None of your business."

"Sounds promising. I was asking about the investigation." I'll bet you were, she thought.

"That's about it at the moment. Think you could get me an extra two hundred a month for rent?" she asked.

"You renting a penthouse?"

"Almost. Need a place to entertain. See what you can do." Nothing pleased her more than needling Dougherty.

"Not a chance."

"Just asking. As the good book says, 'Ask and you shall receive.' It doesn't say 'Bitch and you shall receive.' Guess I'll have to keep looking. Call you in a few days."

"Karen, I . . ." He heard the phone click.

Once again she faced the loneliness of nothing to do. In some ways Dougherty was her best friend. In others, he was a pain in the ass. Big Brother. She found it amusing when he asked if she had met anyone; Sam Larkin came to mind. Interesting. She knew nothing about the man. Could be a Bluebeard, hiding women's bodies around that isolated house of his. Or the chief smuggler. It was time to check out Mr. Larkin. It would keep her busy.

He said Louisiana, which was next to home territory for Chaney. She had also worked a couple of operations there, which left her with a number of nonfederal contacts. First, she called Buck Link, a divisional commander of the Louisiana State Police and asked for a run on anyone named Sam or Samuel Larkin, gave him a time period, a brief description and asked for anything he could find. He offered to check the records he had access to and the Bureau of Vital Statistics if she would stand him for dinner the next time she was in Baton Rouge. Second, she called her older brother, a banker, to use his network to check on credit cards, loans and credit records. When she was finished, she was pleased. Within a few days, the picture of Sam Larkin might be fully developed.

Before she could decide what to do next, the telephone rang.

"Hello?"

"Miss Chaney?" She recognized the deep southern accent of the real estate agent and felt a sinking feeling in her stomach.

"Yes?"

"This is Chris Blackwell. Dowdy Real Estate?"

"Yes?"

"Let me tell you what I was able to work out with the owner of the townhouse, and then you can make your decision. He wants at least a three-month lease. Said it's just not economically feasible to clean the place thoroughly and advertise with the possibility of only a one- or two-month rental. Now I know—"

"That's fine," she said, catching him off guard. "How soon can I move in?"

"Well, stop by the office, sign the lease, and I'll give you the keys. You can be sleeping in your own bed tonight if that's what you want. The utilities are all on, but you'll have to get them transferred to your name within the next couple of days."

"I'll be by in an hour. That long enough for you to get the lease ready?" she asked with anticipation. It would only take her that long to pack and get over there.

"Of course."

"I'll see you shortly, Mr. Blackwell," she said and hung up. "Yes!" she exclaimed and watched the two other officers turn and look at her. "Found a place to live." She picked up what she needed to take with her and left the office.

School district superintendent Cedrick Hamilton was as striking in appearance to men as to women. Although he had just turned fifty, his trim physique, cafe-au-lait skin and uncharacteristic Romanesque features created a presence that turned heads and commanded attention. To say assessments and opinions of him were conflicted in the black community would be an understatement. To some, he was a shining symbol of the rising power and position of their race, an example that served as an inspiration. To others, he was just another Oreo pandering to the white power structure of Covington County. To the white community he was either their contribution to affirmative action or another uppity nigger. Cedrick Hamilton was brilliant at walking a very thin line.

He was sitting at his desk when his secretary buzzed to advise him of Isabel Reichert's arrival. She was a frequent visitor in the superintendent's office. Hamilton knew when he hired her that her ambition would make her a valuable ally. Whenever there was a problem or he anticipated a problem within the administrative infrastructure, he liked to run it by Isabel. She was not only intelligent, but exemplified class and represented the school district's image well. She also had a handle on things that were going on in the district. And she was white, which gave him a conduit into white attitudes and the inner workings of the political elements in the community. They had become friends. He rose from behind his desk to greet her at the door.

"Isabel. Come in," he said with a broad smile.

"How are you, Cedrick?" she asked as he ushered her to a chair.

"I'm fine." He seated himself. "How about you?" His voice was gentle, which tended to relax people, give him time to work.

"I'm okay. Was in the building. Thought I'd drop by and say hello."

"Okay doesn't sound very good." Cedrick Hamilton knew the status of Isabel Reichert's marriage. She had confided it to him one afternoon at the end of a principal's meeting. "Bill?" he asked.

"Of course. He's the bane of my existence."

"Well," he said with a smile, "I can't really comment on that, but I think I understand how you feel."

"That's not your problem, Cedrick; it's mine. I'll handle it."

"Anything I can do, all you have to do is ask. You said *that* wasn't my problem. Do I have any problems?" He sat back in his chair and twisted a pencil in his hand. He was wearing an expensive-looking, sand-colored linen suit that was exquisitely tailored, a pale blue shirt and a brown and green figured tie. *GQ*. He bought the whole package down to his sand-colored socks and highly-polished tan Cole-Hahn loafers. Cedrick Hamilton was never not "put together."

"Not that I've heard."

"Anything new?"

"No. What about you? What's happening in the charmed life of Cedrick Hamilton?"

"Charmed life? If only. I'd like to get rid of Harold Taylor. He's a pain in the ass, but with the bond issue coming up, the board won't admit they made a mistake, and neither will I. I don't think he can do too much damage in that length of time. You want the job?" He was smiling. It seemed he was always smiling.

"A high school? Not in a million years. I'm tired, Cedrick. I'm not sure I might not hang it up altogether." Her words caught him by surprise.

"You're not serious."

"Probably not."

"Don't scare me like that. I can't afford to lose you; you're too valuable."

Isabel Reichert chuckled. "Cedrick, you know and I know why I'm valuable to you. I don't think either one of us has ever been in the dark about that," she said. "And don't deny it."

"Got me."

"Right. Now I've got to figure out a way to get rid of a husband while seeking the appropriate retribution." She smiled as if it were a joke. It wasn't.

"I trust your ingenuity," he said and came around his desk to give her a hug. It was their usual ritual. "You know the door is open anytime you need to talk."

She looked at him. "How well do you know Sam Larkin?"

"Not at all. Teaches at the high school. Science, I think. He the reason for your dropping by?"

"Not really, but you should know your employees better, Cedrick."

"A character fault," he said. "Why Sam Larkin?"

"He's interesting," she said.

"First time I've heard you express interest in anyone. I think that's good."

"Time for everything, Cedrick. But it's just a momentary fantasy, and we all have those, don't we?" She was grinning as she left the office.

Hamilton's telephone buzzed before he got back to his desk.

"Mr. Clay on line one," his secretary said.

Bad nights didn't come often for Sam Larkin, but when they did, there was little rest. It had been one of those nights when a single thought or memory presents itself, opens a door, and, from that point on, the mind will not turn itself off. It was frustrating and exhausting.

The week had gone quickly, but only because he forced himself to work. The deck was finished except for treating the wood, a weekend project. He spent every evening doing sketches for a series of paintings he was planning. He was master of his own time, except for his job, something he was beginning to rethink. The job—done right—was more demanding than he wanted, yet there was no other way he could do it.

He had done a lot of thinking during the week and made up his mind to crunch some numbers and see if he could walk away from it. The house was finished. He had a small savings, and he could always get a part-time job. Nothing was out of the question. It was just sad that the system made him feel this way. If it were just the teaching, there would be no problem. It was all of the other meaningless tasks that boggled his mind.

He lit a cigarette, put on a quiet Sinatra tape and zoned out. The world was dancing on the ceiling overhead. It was Friday. The next two days were his.

Turner Lockett had not gone into town for his usual Friday night visit with the girls on Wallace Street. Used to be four or five times a year. Lately it had been a weekly occurrence. It was the only thing he spent his money on. Charlie Clay warned him about spending too much money, which was no problem for him; there wasn't anything he wanted. Now, the girls on Wallace Street seemed a thing of the past, something he would never enjoy again.

The trailer was hot. He was sweating beneath the covers, but the chills came when he threw them off. It had been the same every night since Jared Barnes disappeared. Someone was watching him he was sure. Someone knew what he had done. He could feel a presence and it was evil. But how could anyone know? He had made sure to cover his tracks. Even used the slow trolling motor instead of the outboard to take Jared's body up into the headwaters.

At the time he laughed at himself for being so cautious. Now it wasn't funny.

He shook as thoughts he couldn't stop paraded through his brain. Vivid thoughts: the feel of the lead pipe meeting bone with no more resistance than a pillow and making the sound of crushing peanut shells, Jared's moan after the first blow, the deadly silence when he stopped after the second, the dead look on the man's face when he dumped him overboard, the man's eyes looking into his own as if they could actually see.

His own screaming brought him back to where he was. Sobbing, he got out of bed, turned on every light in the trailer and the flood light outside on the power pole. He was exhausted. The same sequence of events had recurred every night since the killing. The next step was to get dressed, get his shotgun and go outside to sit in the broken lawn chair in the shadows. He had never seen nor heard anyone during his vigils, knew it was a creation of his own guilt, but couldn't convince himself to let it go.

He was still sitting in the chair when pale light came through the fog that lay heavy on the marsh. He couldn't remember sleep and wondered if he weren't as dead as Barnes.

Since there was no requirement that she physically make an appearance at the office on any regular schedule, Karen Chaney made the townhouse her base of operations. She could call the office to pick up urgent messages, and she had a beeper for emergencies, though she couldn't imagine many of those in Covington. There was an answering machine that signaled what kind of call she had received and the urgency to return it. A facsimile machine and a computer. A telephone extension cord ran under the carpet from the answering machine on the kitchen counter into a walk-in closet in the guest bedroom where there was a filing cabinet and a small table for the computer and fax machine. When the louvered closet doors were closed, the decor was undisturbed.

On Friday she awakened early, put on a pot of coffee and decided there was no hurry to do anything. After a wake-up shower—hot as she could stand it, then a switch to stone-cold water for three minutes—she wrapped a white terry cloth robe around her, got a cup of coffee, sat on the overstuffed, white couch and looked out over the river. A marine fog covered the water when she woke up, but it receded quickly. The sun—a scarlet orb signaling the beginning of the new day or, perhaps, the end of the world—played on the water, throwing red diamonds at anyone who took the time to look.

Karen Chaney was not one to believe in synergy, but as she was questioning why she had received no responses from her inquiries about Sam Larkin, the telephone rang.

"Hello?"

"Karen? Buck Link."

"I was just thinking about you. How are you?" It was difficult to be conversationally gracious when your curiosity was killing you and hard not to smile at his name, which always reminded her of a hard-nosed private-eye out of a detective novel.

"I'm fine. I got some of that information you asked me for. Don't know if it's enough to get you to spring for dinner or not though." He laughed.

"Let me hear what you've got and I'll pick the place for dinner."

"It's pretty slim and may give you more questions than answers. Samuel T. Larkin, if it's the same guy, worked for the State of Louisiana Environmental Service for four years, ten years ago and left without reason. No record of anything in this state since then, as far as I can tell. No arrests, tickets, anything like that. Not even a car registration. A clean record as far as the law is concerned. Haven't gotten over to Vital Statistics yet, but I thought you might be gettin' curious."

"I am, Buck, and thanks. I do owe you that dinner. Let me know if you come up with anything else."

"I will, Karen. You take care now."

She remembered Larkin saying this was his fourth year at the high school, which meant that if he stayed in Louisiana all that time, he had neither registered a car nor had a traffic violation for five or six years. That was strange enough, but the fact that he was an environmental officer and never mentioned it was even more astounding. She felt the hairs prickle on her arms and warning bells go off in her chest.

She picked up the phone and dialed her brother's number. What he had found was incredible, the reason he hadn't called. Nothing. There was no financial trail from Louisiana or anywhere else except in Covington where he had a modest savings account and a checking account at the Wachovia Bank. He could only go back eight years without a lot of digging, which he was working on, but for that period there were no loans, credit cards, accounts, anything.

The questions she was left with were shocking. Where did he get the money for the house? It was a place she could only dream about, and there wasn't even a mortgage. More important, what happened to the six years between the environmental service and Covington County High School? She wondered if Sam Larkin was under a deeper cover than she was.

Throughout the week she had resisted the temptation to make contact with him. She thought maybe he would call the office, but no such luck. He wasn't scratching at the shell of her curiosity; he had broken through it. The best way to handle curiosity is to satisfy it, she thought. Frustration? Face it full on. Both techniques had gotten her into trouble more than once, but she had to know whether Sam Larkin was a good guy or a bad guy. It looked like he was the only one who could tell her.

She made up her mind. She would take the boat out and drop by Larkin's place unannounced. See what she'd find. Nothing ventured, nothing gained. "Ready, Sam?"

CHAPTER 5

Bill Reichert was pouting. Morgan Hannah knew that, but she was making no move to solve his problem. He had called three days in succession, and each time logistics made it impossible for them to connect. Now she hadn't heard from him since Wednesday. It was his problem. They had decided at the outset of their relationship that there would be no demands; demands were not a part of what they wanted from each other. It was becoming apparent, however, that she could more easily accept that arrangement than he.

At three o'clock she walked across the dunes path to the beach. The wind had died, which made it even warmer than it had been earlier in the day. She ran her tongue along her upper lip and tasted the salt of her perspiration. It was too early in the season for the pink and purple gerardia to color the dunes, but the sea oats, pennywort, and other plants she could not name were greening up and creating a quilt of earth colors.

Walking along the water's edge, she reminisced about her first meeting with Bill Reichert. She had been alone for more than a year when he came into her life. They met at the bar at a charity auction. Neither of them wanted to purchase anything they saw displayed, and the bar seemed like a good refuge. The physical attraction was immediate. Reichert knew who she was, but since she didn't do business with his bank, he was a complete stranger to her. He had to introduce himself, which, she later decided, must have been a huge blow to his ego.

He didn't lie to her. Told her he was in an unhappy marriage that hadn't been a real marriage for a number of years. After asking around among the few lady friends she knew in the area, she substantiated his story. He called several times in the following weeks and, eventually, she invited him to dinner. They chatted over drinks and hors d'oeuvres and went to bed. The rack of lamb she prepared went uneaten. It had been a long time for her. They were insatiable and met at every opportunity for weeks. Now the mind-fucking was beginning, and, for the first time, she considered the possibility that it might be ending. That wasn't her game. It would be her call.

The beach wasn't crowded; it was too early for most tourists. Even in the height of summer, it was barren compared to other beaches. She saw two men walking toward her—one, average height, medium build, a little thick around the middle, but not bad. The other was six-two or -three, lean, extremely tan with brown, sun-bleached hair. As they got closer, Morgan recognized Charles Clay, the attorney, but the other man was a stranger. She didn't really know Clay, just who he was. When they approached, she had difficulty averting her eyes from Clay's companion.

"You're Morgan Hannah," the lawyer said when they came face to face.

"Yes, and you're Charles Clay." She put on her most promising smile.

"I'm flattered that you know who I am."

"Most everyone does," she said, looking at the man standing next to Clay.

"Hardly," he said with a laugh. "We've been neighbors for some time, but I haven't been out here much in the last couple of years."

"I'm sure it must be difficult for you to come out here," Morgan said. "I was sorry to hear about your wife. I didn't really know her, but we did speak on the beach a couple of times."

"Thank you. Oh, you must forgive me. This is my friend, Brad Coleman. Brad, Morgan Hannah." Brad Coleman's smile was iridescent. The white teeth against the deep tan along with the lightest golden brown eyes she had ever seen—yellow ochre she would have said—created a striking picture that demanded attention.

"I'm pleased to meet you," she said and extended her hand.

"And I'm pleased to meet you." His voice was smooth, southern and gentle. He gave her hand a squeeze that was neither intimidating nor condescending.

"Are you from Covington? I don't think I've seen you around," she asked, never moving her eyes from his.

"No. Just visiting."

"Are you here for long?"

"I'm afraid only for another couple of hours. Just a quick business trip to see Charles. I will be back though, I'm sure. You have a beautiful island. Must be like living on a cruise ship."

"That's a good description," she said.

"Well, much as I hate to say it, we have to get along," Charlie Clay said. "I've got to get him to Charleston to catch a plane. I hope I'll see you again, Morgan."

"I do, too, Charles." She nodded. "Mr. Coleman."

"Pleased to have met you," he said as he turned and continued down the beach with his friend.

"Wow," Morgan whispered to herself as she picked up her walk.

The Oyster Creek Inn was not a frequent lunch stop for Bill Reichert. He much preferred going to The Covington House, an upscale, decidedly Southern bed and breakfast, one block off Main Street on Jackson. It was only a few blocks from the bank. The food was better and served more graciously than any other place in the city. It was a meeting place for the community's movers and shakers, of which Bill Reichert considered himself a member in good standing. This was not a day for The Covington House, however. It was time to lock Charlie Clay into a conversation. He had been unable to reach the attorney for a week, and his concerns about the upcoming operation were becoming serious, if not paranoid.

Reichert's research into international banking left his head spinning with cross-purposed laws and restrictions. Off-shore, blind corporations were obviously the easiest places to deal with large amounts of cash, and, to the unaware, they appeared to be the safest, but—always the inevitable "but"—there were also some very scary traps to fall into.

He knew Charlie would gently scoff at his fears, simplify his concerns and leave him wondering who the naïve one really was. Not this time. Reichert had made up his mind that if he were going to turn over more millions of dollars than he had ever imagined, in cash, to a foreign entity, he wanted to go to the place and meet the people he would be dealing with. Find a friend of his own that he could trust. Someone to protect his own interests if the shit hit the fan. That was the way it would have to be.

Charlie Clay was tending bar himself, as he often did during the lunch hours. It was relaxing and allowed him to bask in the pride of ownership, talk to old friends and new, and have a drink or so himself. It was a great place to pick up information about what was going on in town. He was surprised when Bill Reichert walked through the door.

"Bill, what are you doin' all the way out here on a Monday?" he said as Reichert took a seat.

"Slummin'," the banker said.

"What can I get for you? You havin' lunch?"

"That's what I came for. I'll have a beer first though. Give me a Corona for a change."

"Comin' up," Clay said as he bent into the stainless steel cooler and withdrew an icy, clear-glass bottle. "Maybe I'll join you for lunch, if you don't mind the company. Roger's supposed to relieve me at one."

"I'd like that," Reichert said.

Thirty minutes later, sitting at a dockside table, Reichert's demeanor changed from the casual appearance he had displayed at the bar.

"Charlie, how well have you thought through this next venture?" Reichert asked. "I mean ever since I was out here Sunday a week ago, I keep asking myself the same question: why change things when everything is going smoothly? It just doesn't make sense to me. How much money can we want?"

Charlie looked at him carefully, trying to perceive any hidden agenda in his face. "Let me ask you a question, Bill; how much longer do you want to keep doin' this?"

Reichert sat back. "I don't know."

"Well, see, that's the point. I don't really know either. I mean it's fun and all. I like the risk, and I don't think we're hurtin' anybody, except maybe the other people who would be doin' it if we weren't, but I really think the time for me to be bailin' out might be gettin' close. Despite all the positives, I think I'd like to get back to a normal life sometime soon. Have it all behind me, be out safe and secure. Maybe retire. I been thinkin' about that. One venture like this, and we can all decide when we want to quit."

"Damn, Charlie, how much money are you going to need?" Reichert asked.

"It's not the money, Bill. I've got enough of that, but I want to make sure everyone else does. It'll only be safe if all of us get out at the same time. I don't want any of our group to try to carry on. Leaves us like sittin' ducks if they get caught."

"Okay, say we do it. How am I going to move that kind of cash? What are we talking about? Six, eight million?" A satisfied grin crossed Charlie Clay's face.

"Top dollar? Ten to fourteen. Somewhere in there." Bill Reichert looked stunned.

"How am I going to handle that? Think about it, Charlie."

"Sounds pretty, don't it? I thought money was your area of expertise. I'm just a poor ol' country lawyer." He smiled.

"Oh, yeah, Charlie. You are that." Reichert sighed. "Okay. I've been doing some research, and I came up with a couple of options, but working with these kinds of figures is new to me. I'm not sure which is the best way to go. It's going to take some thought. And, I'd want to meet the people I'm working with, no matter what we decide."

"That's no problem. You can go anywhere you want, see anybody you choose. We can afford it," he said, amused. "I do have a guy comin' in a week or so that I want you to meet, and I have a foreign banker I've been in contact with who I think may be of help."

"Who's that?"

"Let's wait and see if this whole thing has a chance of working out. I'll let you know."

"I think we're getting too many people involved. I worry about that."

"Who are you worried about?"

"Nobody specific. Well, yes. Jerry Salyer. I just don't see—" Charlie cut him off.

"I explained that. Or at least I thought I did," Clay said calmly. "Look, I've known the guy for twenty years. I've handled a lot of legal work for him. He studied law, too. Did you know that?"

"No, I didn't, but—" Charlie held up his hands.

"Trust me, Bill. Hell, I don't want to go to jail."

"I couldn't," Reichert said. "No way." Just the thought created a chilling sweat on his skin.

"We need his position. His company is a perfect conduit for most of the big stuff we have to have. Hell, a company as big as his—building fifty miles of highway over the next five years? Pretty hard to keep up with all that equipment and storage. And, come to think of it, money. You might give that some thought."

"That's my point exactly. Why would he want to get involved? He's not a sixty-thousand-dollar-a-year banker. He's already got more money than he can spend."

"Two reasons: greed and fun." Clay looked at Bill Reichert steadily. "Ever ask yourself why I'm involved? I'm not a sixty-thousand-dollar-a-year banker either." Reichert was silent. "Neither are you, as I see it. Not now anyway. How many millions have you got that nobody knows anything about? Even I don't know how much you have, but I don't see you gettin' out, sayin', 'I've got enough.' *Enough* is a hell of a big word, Bill, and I've never heard anyone who could define it accurately.

"And do you know what I've come to realize? The addiction to money is probably the greatest addiction of all. I don't mean greed. Hell, I don't even mean spendin' it. I mean the money itself. The makin' of it, seein' it, feelin' the power it gives you. Lemme ask you somethin'. You ever ride around for a day with a quarter of a million dollars in the trunk of your car and only you know it's there? Hell of a feelin'. Somethin' I never figured on. You ought to try it sometime.

"Jerry Salyer? Don't give him a thought. Bill, you know construction people; they're rich one day and broker than a field hand the next. Let me worry about the employees. You just keep doin' your research and find us a nice, safe place to hide our booty." Clay laughed. "You hear that? 'Booty.' I'm even starting to talk like a pirate."

"I'll do my best to find a place." Reichert said and looked at his watch, "Looks like I'm going to have to be heading back. Monday's a busy day at the bank, and I've got some function to attend tonight. I'm not even sure what it is. I just saw a notation on my calendar."

Charlie Clay gave him a knowing smile. "Isabel goin' with you?"

"I don't know," he lied.

"Just wondered how you all were gettin' along."

"We get along necessarily, Charlie," he said, as he got up and pushed the chair back under the table.

"What's that?"

"When it's necessary, we get along." Charlie Clay laughed and gave him a wave as he turned to leave.

Reichert was still upset. Charlie Clay, with all his wise platitudes, did not resolve his concerns. Fears? Like the man said, it was the thrill of risk that got him involved in the beginning. That and the money. He had never dreamed of the sums of money they were making, the cash that had passed through his hands. It was like collecting rent on Park Place and Boardwalk, and so far no one had gotten a "Go to Jail" card. Monopoly money. It was euphoric, but the euphoria had turned to worry. Maybe because he felt his position changing.

With each new person's involvement, his role appeared to become less critical. Now with this "mystery man or men" Charlie mentioned, he was beginning to wonder where he stood in The Company. It was time for Bill Reichert to start looking out for Bill Reichert.

Morgan Hannah was also on his mind. He didn't know what was going on there. That was another blow that interrupted his focus. It had been more than a week since he had seen her. Every time he called and said he was coming out, there was some reason she wasn't going to be there. She knew he wasn't able to arrange his schedule to fit hers, knew that from the beginning, and the idea that she might expect it burned him. At the time they met, their agreement to make no demands on each other, no commitments, seemed appropriate to the situation, but he found himself rethinking that arrangement. Even the thought of getting a divorce had crossed his mind. There was certainly nothing scandalous about divorce in Covington, and he could afford it. However, now it appeared that Isabel would make that more difficult. He couldn't understand why their fractured marriage suddenly wasn't acceptable to her; she had put up with it for years. He wondered if it was the onset of menopause.

CHAPTER 6

She heard the voice before she saw the man. "You headed out this mornin'?" Ray Breslin asked as he walked toward her slip at the Covington Municipal Marina. The one thing she didn't need was Ray Breslin interfering with her plan for the day. That he was in uniform at the dock on a Saturday made her wonder if he was watching her. Paranoid, Chaney, she thought. What she had learned and not learned about Sam Larkin was making her very insecure, but Ray Breslin would not be her salvation. "Be glad to go along if you want some company or guidance." He was smiling. The smile exposed him: *I know everything. You don't know anything, and, by the way, I'd like to fuck you.*

"Not today, Ray. I've got to get out and learn it on my own. I've been getting in a couple of hours a day. I'm getting there, but it might be awhile before I'm very effective. Lot of water to cover."

"Yeh, it is," he said. "What time you gettin' back? Thought maybe we could have a drink or somethin'."

"I don't think that's very smart, Ray, but I appreciate the offer," she said, lifting a twenty-gallon cooler into the boat. Breslin didn't offer to help.

"Why not?" he asked.

"Well, I think you mentioned a wife, didn't you? And, besides, 'work and pleasure' you know."

"Well, honey, the first part dudn't mean anything, and as far as the second part goes, sometimes the pleasure outweighs the risk." He was leering at her. Chaney gave him a look that would crack granite. The DiNero 'You talkin' to me?' look. It was practiced. Breslin put his hands up in surrender. "Okay, I know when a 'no' is a 'no.' Don't take offense. Change your mind, just say the word." The smile on his face changed to one of condescension. "I'll see you later. Have a good day." He started to leave.

"Oh, and, Ray, don't call me 'honey' again. It'll never get you that roll in the hay you were just asking for." Breslin shrugged his shoulders and walked back up the dock.

The sun was a quarter high and bright. It was a glorious day. She decided to take the long route to Jones Run Creek and Sam Larkin's place. North on the Chester River, past the waterfront park and the bleached-white manses on Main Street until the street made its big turn inland as the river widened. Then across open water to the northern perimeter of Matthew's Island and to Oyster Creek, all of which she knew would give her navigational skills a test. The course was narrow and winding, but she had her chart. She was good at reading water, learned from her father when he started taking her along on his patrols through the backwaters of the Georgia coast. She always knew she would return to the low-country. However, there was no way to predict it would be in the capacity that it was or under the present circumstances. That had come about quite by accident or a quirk of fate, though Karen Chaney did not put much stock in such things.

Traversing the inland creeks and estuaries, she marveled at what she saw. One could spend days just categorizing the vegetation that was observed from the island's waterways. Live oaks, water oaks, wax myrtle, and swamp gum trees, and bald cypress along with tupelos and mixed hardwoods stood tall in the backwater swamps. There were also dwarf palmettos and cabbage palms. She passed blooming glasswort-rimmed ponds that showed blood-scarlet in the sun. Blue water iris, hooded pitcher plants and spider lilies grew in profusion along the shore. In a tall live oak, she spotted a bald eagle watching her progress. Its power and austerity took her breath away. A flock of wood storks passed over as she approached the entrance to Jones Run Creek. There was no full-day scenic tour that would ever show a tourist what she had seen in the past hour.

Isabel Reichert was stunned by her husband's sudden change in behavior. In the past week, he had come home for dinner five nights in a row, explaining that he had been working too hard, the bank didn't own him, his salary wasn't big enough to justify such long hours, and, last, that it was time to sit back and enjoy the fruits of his labors. Isabel did not accept his reasoning or his behavior, but she decided to go along and let him play himself into a corner, which she was certain he would do.

Having her second cup of coffee, on the second floor gallery, she couldn't help smiling when she thought about the night before. For the first time in months, Bill Reichert had awkwardly made it known that he wanted to make love to her. She allowed him, but it was perfunctory, much as it had been the last time, though she couldn't put a date on when that was. She wondered why he made the effort. That had been her thought as he moved inside her. When? Why? Afterwards, she could tell he was angry—humiliated—that he wasn't able to arouse her. He was easy to read.

"Well, we're up bright and early this morning," Reichert said as he came onto the gallery and sat down to join her.

"Coffee?" she asked, reaching for the carafe that was on the glass-topped, white, wrought-iron table.

"That would be good."

"Sleep well?"

"As a matter of fact, I did," he said.

"It's been very unusual," Isabel said, watching his expression. He was looking toward the river, but she felt his mind working, traveling far from where he sat.

"What has?" he asked.

"Your being home in the evenings, not to mention Saturday morning, of all things. How come?"

"I told you, I think it's time to ease off a bit at the bank." He didn't look at her.

"Don't try to kid a kidder, Bill. What's going on?"

"Nothing. I told you."

"Whatever you say." Isabel sipped her coffee. "So what's the plan for today? You going to be around?"

"Should I leave?" He turned his face toward hers.

"I wasn't suggesting that. I was just asking."

"What's on your schedule?" he asked.

"I have a hair appointment at eleven, and I'm supposed to make an appearance at the district art show in the park this afternoon. Other than that, I have no schedule."

"Well, I do have to go to Palmetto sometime today. I was going to ask if you—"

"I could cancel the hair appointment, and the art show's not a must." She enjoyed watching him squirm; she had no intention of canceling her hair appointment. Lisa, her hair-dresser, had been on vacation for two weeks, and every time Isabel looked in the mirror, she saw a disaster.

"No. No need to do that. It was just for the ride. I have to see a contractor about a new project, and I have no idea how long it will take. You know how these financial things go." He tried to throw it off, but it didn't work.

"You're not making sense. Easing off and working on Saturday? Go along for the ride, but you don't know how long you'll be?"

"Look, Isabel, if you would like to go, you're more than welcome. It's just that . . ."

"No, Bill, I don't want to go, and you don't want me to go wherever it is you're going. I just wanted to see your reaction. Don't lie to me. That's not much to ask. I don't know why you're suddenly at home in the evening, but I do have my suspicions. Suddenly horny last night?" She smiled. "It all seems to fit." She wanted to say more, but didn't. It wasn't a fight she wanted this morning, just the upper hand.

"Damn it, Isabel, I'm trying to recoup some ground here, make amends . . ." He ran out of words.

"Get serious, Bill. I don't know what this week has been all about, but it has nothing to do with making amends."

"Have it your way," he said.

Isabel finished her coffee, got up, and started back into the house. When she reached the screen door, she turned to him.

"I will," she said.

"What?" he asked without looking at her. Bored.

"Have it my way."

Bill Reichert felt uneasy. For all his bravado, he had a healthy respect for his wife's steel will. Between Charlie Clay, Morgan and now Isabel, fear was becoming his constant companion. Whenever it had threatened to get the best of him before, he always had home, the house on Legree. It was a safe haven, a fortress against all things bad. He had always felt protected by the familiar streets, the houses that surrounded him. However, at this point he was beginning to feel like a stranger, unwelcome, with all the doors shut against him.

The deal with Clay—the dollars involved—was too big for him to handle. It was all crashing down. He couldn't go to prison, but he was certain that would be the ultimate result if he did what Charlie asked. Why couldn't the others understand that? It was all cowboys and Indians to them; if they got shot down, they believed they would get up to play again the next day. But they were wrong. He knew that, but he couldn't just get out, take his broomstick pony and go home. He never perceived any of the men in The Company as violent, but who knew what they might do if they were threatened.

And now Isabel. She could take away the safety of his home if she wanted to. They both knew that. What then? Bill Reichert had never spent one day of his life alone, completely dependent upon himself with no one to shore him up. He didn't know how to do it. When he got up from the table, his hands began to shake and he dropped the cup and saucer he was holding. On his knees, picking up the broken pieces of china, he felt helpless. He didn't know whether it was a beginning or an ending, but it was maddening. He wanted to disintegrate.

Sam Larkin didn't recognize the boat easing its way up the creek. It was a twenty-foot Bass Master with a walk-through windshield. Dark green. As it got closer, the sun picked up the long, blond hair—down again. Karen Chaney. He was wearing a pair of cut-off jeans, no shirt and was down on his knees treating the new deck with a mixture of tung oil and turpentine. The mix of weather in the lowcountry was tough on wood, and he didn't want the yearly chore of painting it some unnatural color. He had gotten the formula from a retired builder who hung around Harry Tom Cooper's Boat Dock. The man said it would last for three years; Larkin hoped he was right.

He went in the house and put on a shirt before Karen was close enough to communicate. Walking down the steps toward the dock, he saw her wave and yell something that the sound of the engines drowned out. She maneuvered the boat up to the dock, and Larkin grabbed a line and tied it off.

"Good morning," she said after she cut the engines. Her smile was as brilliant as the sun.

"You're about three minutes late," he said looking at his watch. Karen Chaney looked confused. "It's afternoon," he said with a laugh.

"I was beginning to wonder if I was missing something here. I didn't think I had an appointment." She was wearing a tan safari shirt and matching shorts.

"What brings you out here on your day off?"

"Seems like every day is a day off around here. I don't see much work being done in my office."

"Nature of the area," Sam said. "You want a cup of coffee or iced tea or something? I assume that's a state boat or I'd offer you a beer."

"It is. My standard issue. I knew the Cobia was too good to be true. I'd love a glass of tea if I can sit on your deck and drink it, but I don't want to interrupt what you were doing. I can watch while you work. The new deck looks great."

"You're not interrupting me. That's something I can stop and pick up anytime. Don't have to worry about getting it on even or stop-start marks."

"Then, yes," she said.

"How was your first week at the new job?" he asked when they were seated with tall glasses of tea in front of them.

"Busy. Spent a good deal of time finding a place to live and getting moved in."

"What did you find?"

"Actually, I was very lucky," she said, sipping her tea. "It's a two-story townhouse overlooking the river. Great view and not far from the marina. Beau Rivage. Are you familiar with it?" Sam Larkin took a long look at her.

"I've seen them from the outside. I'd guessed they were pretty expensive."

"More than I can afford, but I cater to myself when it comes to where I spend most of my off-work hours." There were a few moments of awkward silence.

"You never did say what brought you out here," he said, staring into her blue eyes.

"Reconnaissance mission to further acquaint myself with the territory." She laughed. "My reason for coming out here." She said it as a declarative question. "What I said, to a degree. Just getting better acquainted, and it's too beautiful a day to stay ashore. This is what I love." Sam could see her eyes taking in the whole of what was in their field of vision.

"I believe you," he said. "I do, too. If I could afford it, I don't think I would ever leave this place except to get on the water or go into town for supplies. Maybe walk the beach once in awhile."

"So what do you do for entertainment, Sam Larkin? I mean other than losing yourself in the outdoors and painting."

"Oh, I get out," he said. He took another sip of his tea. "A movie once in awhile if there's something I want to see and can't rent. And once every couple of weeks when I get bored with my own cooking, I treat myself to dinner out."

"No girlfriends, or is that too personal?" Karen Chaney was smiling.

"Pretty personal." He smiled back. "Nothing serious. I go out on occasion. When someone asks me," he threw in.

"I'd think that would be rather often. Single, wonderful home in a beautiful spot."

"You flatter me, but I'll take all the flattery I can get. Not many people have seen this place."

"It's beautiful. I keep saying that." She laughed. "How long have you been in the lowcountry?"

"Came here in eighty. We in the Great Inquisition here, Karen?" She looked embarrassed.

"I'm sorry," she said.

"No need to be. Hell, all the world wants to know about everybody else. What about you?"

"What?"

"What's your story?"

"We in an inquisition here, Larkin?" she asked with a mischievous grin. It was appealing.

"Probably."

"Well, I was born in the sea islands of Georgia and lived there till I was sixteen, at which point, we moved to Alabama. My father was a wildlife officer at the time and got a better job offer in Alabama as a regional supervisor. I don't think he was ever

happy there though. He missed the lowcountry. It's not all in South
Carolina, you know."

"That depends on who you ask." Sam said.

"It's not. Anyway, went to college, studied criminal justice and
biology, and followed in my father's footsteps. End of story." She
sat back in her chair, closed her eyes and let the heat of the sun warm
her face.

"Guys?"

"Too personal, Larkin. I don't keep count, but none at the
moment." She didn't move her head or open her eyes.

"In that case then, I guess I ought to ask you if you'd like to stay
for dinner." She opened her eyes.

"Now? I mean today? Tonight?"

"Three questions. Let me see if I can answer them. I am asking
you now. Today? Well, I'm asking you today, but dinner's usually at
night, so I don't know how to answer that one. And, third. Tonight?
Yes. Dinner tonight."

"Why?"

"Well, you don't look like you have plans to go home anytime
soon. Look pretty comfortable and if I don't invite you, I won't be
able to eat. So I thought I might as well ask." Karen couldn't help
laughing.

"Here?"

"Doesn't have to be here, although that's what I had in mind.
Don't want to frighten you though. If you'd rather eat somewhere
else, I'd . . ."

"No. No, here is fine, but I'd like to take the boat back and clean
up."

"That's up to you," he said, pleased that he'd caught her totally
off guard. "Do you want me to pick you up?"

"No, I can drive." Doesn't want to be stranded, he thought. "But
you'll have to tell me how to get out here by land. I don't think my
compass would find you."

At three o'clock, Sam gave her directions and watched the boat
out of sight. It appeared to move with more purpose than it had coming in. Or so he imagined. She would be back at six.

Morgan Hannah stood in front of the full-length mirror in her
bathroom. She was naked, performing a self-examination ritual that

she went though every three or four days, usually after a four-mile walk to the stone jetties at the end of the island and a long bath in the swirling waters of her Roman tub to ease the muscles. The body was better than good for her age. She was always irritated by good-looking women—many younger than she—who constantly berated themselves, looking for a compliment, she guessed. Or maybe they believed it. Sad.

She was not a small woman, five feet eight inches tall, one hundred and twenty-eight pounds, constant as long as she exercised, and well-proportioned. Her breasts were full with medium-sized nipples that darkened to burnt umber when they hardened. She cupped them in her hands to feel their weight. A plastic surgeon friend of her husband's had told her that when they began to feel heavier, they were falling, losing their firmness. Firmness was difficult for her determine, since she had never felt another woman's breasts, though she had imagined it on one or two occasions. In fantasies. Her stomach was flat, and the natural shape of the hair on her pubis was well-defined, no razor stubble to hide. Her looks pleased her.

She was ready to turn away from the mirror when she heard the sound of a car in her driveway. She slipped on a terry cloth robe and walked into the living room to see who it was. Bill Reichert was just getting out of his car when she looked through the window. She locked the front door and went back into the bathroom. She ran her fingers though her hair to fluff it and heard the front door knob being tried. It would surprise him to find it locked. She waited a moment until the doorbell rang, dropped her robe to the floor and went to answer it.

When the door opened, Bill Reichert could not speak. He didn't know if he had caught her in a compromising position, if she were drunk or stoned, if she had gone over the edge, if she were expecting someone else, if there were something about her daily life he didn't know—it was the first time he had ever arrived unannounced—or if she somehow knew he was coming and planned a grand welcome after their extended time apart. All of that went through his mind in the blink of an eye.

"Bill, come in," she said, as comfortable as if she were wearing jeans and a sweatshirt or an Oleg Cassini dress. He couldn't move as his eyes traced the geography of her body. After what seemed like endless minutes of silent petrifaction, he stepped into the living room.

"I'm speechless," he said, attempting to smile but still in awe of what was happening.

"I noticed," she said.

"How did you know it was me?" he asked.

"I didn't," she said, enjoying the discomfort she was putting him through.

"Morgan?" She noticed him trying to look toward the bedroom without being obvious.

"Did you like it?"

"Well, of course I liked it, but . . ."

"Then don't question it. Why don't I make drinks while you take a shower, and we'll talk about it in bed." She turned away and headed toward the kitchen, still naked, and totally uninhibited.

She made brilliantly cold, extra-dry martinis on the rocks from a bottle of Chopin Vodka she kept in the freezer, calamata olives instead of green, as he preferred, and waited until she heard the water go off in the shower. Two minutes to dry, and she went back to the bedroom, where she knew she would find him stretched out naked on top of the sheets with his eyes closed. They opened as soon as he heard the tinkle of the ice cubes in the glasses.

"Thank you," he said as she handed him his drink. "I need this after that opening." He took a sip, held it in his mouth and swallowed. "Wonderful."

"What did you think?" she asked, getting in next to him, sitting with her back propped against the wrought-iron headboard.

"I didn't know what to think. I still don't."

"Expect to find someone else here?"

"It crossed my mind," he said. "Among other things."

"Tell me," she said. As he began to talk, explaining all of the thoughts that had gone through his mind, she put her drink on the bedside table, leaned over and without warning took his flaccid penis in her mouth. No teasing, no foreplay, all at once, while he was still soft. His breath caught, and he fumbled to get his drink to the night stand on his side of the bed. It dropped to the floor. He fought to get his breath back amid involuntary moans that were emanating from within him. He hardened immediately as her tongue worked sensually on the underside of the shaft. She slowly rode her lips up and down, pulling on him. When he came, he had no control of the sound that broke from his lips. A scream that couldn't be defined as one of pleasure or pain. The sudden attack on him created an intensity he had never experienced before. It was as if the usual foreplay prepared his body and nervous system for what was to come. This time her actions caught them by surprise, vulnerable.

Reichert was confused. He lay with his eyes closed unaware that Morgan had gotten out of bed, picked up the ice cubes, his glass, which did not break on the thick carpet, and gone to the kitchen to mix him another drink, until he reached for her.

She came back into the bedroom, handed him his drink, then sat facing him with her legs crossed Indian style.

"Do you have any idea what the most sexual thing about you is?" he asked.

"Tell me." Her smile only added to the exquisiteness of her body.

"You are completely uninhibited. Entirely happy with yourself. I've never known anyone like you before. Male or female."

"Now maybe, but there was a time."

"Your turn to tell," he said.

"I've told you before, living a facade of a life, being upwardly mobile, constricted by social standing and all of the standards that requires. Trying to maintain myself in others' eyes without ever thinking of me. Being basically dishonest with myself and everyone around me. It's what life in the real world seems to be all about."

"What changed you?"

"It didn't work, and I wound up going through life chemically dehanced, if there is such a word. Valium, Xanax and various other downers. When Ben died, I finally said 'Time for me,' threw all the chemicals away and decided to do whatever I wanted. Being selfish is what most people would call it."

"I can't imagine you ever being what you just described."

"Well, I was," she said. "Now. Do you want to tell me why you just popped out here this afternoon?" It wasn't said with malice or any form of chastisement.

"First, because I missed you. It seems like forever since we've been together. And, second, I haven't been able to get any-where with you on the phone. Don't get angry, but I thought you might be playing games with me. I can't take that."

"I told you, Bill, I don't mind-fuck. It's simply been impos-sible to put our schedules together the last couple of weeks."

"I can accept that, but . . ."

"We made a pact that we both enjoy. Why change? You're married; I'm not. I accept the limitations that imposes, but I have a life I have to live and these times will occur now and then. They've happened before."

"Suppose there were no limitations?"

"What do you mean 'no limitations'? You do have a wife." Morgan didn't know how to react. She enjoyed Bill Reichert but couldn't imagine a life with him. He was silent.

"Surprised?" he finally asked.

"I'm not sure what you're saying."

"If there were no limitations. No Isabel. If I weren't married any longer."

"Bill, I've never even given that a thought. That's not what I'm looking for right now."

Reichert looked stunned. It obviously wasn't the reaction he expected. "Isn't that what all of this was about?" he asked.

"What all of what was about?" She took a sip of her martini, now warm, and grimaced at the taste. He lay back, rested his head on the pillow and stared at the ceiling.

"I thought, if you weren't playing games, that maybe you were tired of the arrangement, wanted something more perma-nent and didn't think I would deliver."

"That never entered my mind. I told you I don't do that. If marriage was what I was looking for, we would never have got-ten involved. If I was tired of the life we share, I'd have told you. We're happy, or at least I am and thought you were. We both have sole possession of our lives. I was happy with Ben, but I didn't have my life; it wouldn't have been as easy for me to do what you do. I thought this was what you wanted."

"I do. . . . I don't. . . . I don't know. I'm feeling very shaky right now. Not just about this, about a lot of things. I don't want to lose you." He shook his head. "I can't believe I said that."

Morgan lay down and put her head on his chest and crossed one leg over his.

"Do you want to tell me? About the other stuff, I mean?"

"I can't. Not now anyway. Maybe someday. I love you, Morgan."

"I love you, too." They had both said those words many times, but only in the context of their situation. She kissed his chest and ran her tongue around one of his nipples. "Why don't we quit talking and you make long, slow love to me." And he did that.

Shortly after six o'clock, Sam heard a car come to a stop at the side of his house. He had surprised himself by inviting Karen Chaney for dinner. A pork roast was almost done, and the rest of the meal would only take minutes. The table on the deck was covered with a linen table cloth and set with china, silver and crystal he had purchased at a roadside auction on his way through Georgia to South Carolina. It wasn't expensive, and he laughed at the idea of having it. However, as he settled into his house, he took pleasure in using it. He didn't open the door until she rang the bell.

Karen Chaney wore a white, cotton dress with a wide, navy blue belt around her small waist and sandals on her feet. She and Sam looked at each other and laughed. He was wearing white shorts, a long-sleeve white guyabera, one cuff turned up, and huaraches.

"We look like two lab technicians," he said.

"Or sanitation workers."

Karen's appearance on this evening gave no evidence of what she did for a living. It was the first time he had seen her with make-up.

"State car?" he asked.

"No," she answered. "All mine."

"What do you drive?" he asked.

"A Mustang."

"Convertible?"

"Hardtop."

"A girl-car with attitude," he said with a smile. "Not as much as a Jeep, but it has more class. Seems to fit."

"You flatter me, Sam Larkin," she said.

"All that being considered, what would you like to drink?"

"Do I have to be a lady and say 'white wine'?"

"I don't have any." He shrugged his shoulders, looked helpless.

"Then I'll have a Jack Daniels on the rocks."

"That I've got," he said.

He went into the kitchen to pour the drinks and she followed him.

"You know, I can't get over this house. It's absolutely beautiful."

"Thank you again." He handed her a drink.

"And not only that, I've never seen a bachelor as immaculate as you are. Most guys' places have toothpaste globs in the bathroom sink."

"You haven't been in my bathroom yet. Cheers." Sam touched glasses with her. He put the vegetables in the oven to roast and turned on the heat under the rice. "Thirty minutes okay?"

"Are we on a schedule?" she asked.

"No. No schedule." He smiled.

"Then thirty minutes is fine."

"Feisty," he said to himself, shaking his head. "Let's go into the living room."

It wasn't an easy evening, wandering in unfamiliar territory with no parameters. At sea without a compass or chart. The usual polite conversation between two people in such circumstances passed too quickly, and they found themselves fighting awkward silences: Sam, at times, wondering why he had suggested the evening; Karen wondering why she had accepted the invitation. In this situation there was no flora or fauna or other passing scenes of interest to distract their discomfort. They were both relieved when they finally sat down to dinner.

"You are something, Sam Larkin," Karen Chaney said as she sat at the immaculately set table. She pointed at the china and crystal. "This cannot go without explanation."

"All in good time," he said. "And now I will get the white wine I said I didn't have."

Karen shook her head and laughed.

The food was excellent and eating it allowed enough holidays in the conversation to alleviate some of the discomfort.

When they were finished, Karen helped clear the table and clean up the kitchen, which took little effort given Sam's penchant for neatness. He put a carafe of coffee, cups, saucers and the condiments on a tray, and they went back to the deck to watch the moon bathe the marsh and creek in an icy white light that contradicted the season.

"Kind of like being in a movie here, Sam. Who's your landscaper?"

"I wish I knew for sure," he said.

"I have to apologize."

"For what?" he interrupted.

"My self-consciousness earlier. I really didn't know what to say or talk about."

"I remember the same feeling in ninth grade." He was smiling.

"Who was she?"

"Helen Baker. We called her H.B. I was deeply and sincerely in love."

"It's been awhile since I've been out socially, and you're a difficult man to know how to proceed with. Everything I know about you is contradictory."

"Keeps 'em guessin'."

"Tell me some things," she said.

"Like what?"

"Like what you have a passion for. Why you made the choice to teach. Anything, really. I'd like to know you better." She sipped her coffee in defense. "I'm sorry. I'm sure you didn't invite me out here to pry." Sam was silent.

"My passions. That's hard to say. Right now I think it's painting. A little while ago, it was pork roast." She laughed. "How the hell do you know whether something is a passion or not?" He heard the irritation, born of doubt, in his voice. Karen Chaney did as well.

"I don't know, and I promise I won't ask any more personal questions. Okay?"

"Deal."

The rest of the evening went smoothly. They talked about books and movies they liked—everything according to the first date handbook—and Karen told him a little about her family:

father, mother and three brothers. She also asked about several pieces of art that were hanging in the living room. None of them was his. Walking her down to her car, he looked at his watch.

"Ten o'clock," he said. "Not much of a Saturday night."

"It's been a long day," she answered, "and it's been a lovely evening, especially after I stopped tripping over my own conversation."

"I think we both did a bit of that."

"There will be other times. . . . I hope."

"There will be," he said. He made no move to hold her or kiss her. He opened her car door and held it while she got in.

"Thanks, Sam."

"You have the long drive; I should be thanking you." He closed the door and watched her turn the car around and disappear up the road. He was weary when he climbed the stairs. Karen Chaney was right; it had been a long day. He made up his mind to take an early run and work out in the morning and then settle into a day's painting and reading.

On the drive back, her anxiety returned. She had learned nothing. When she did try to probe, he cut her off. The feeling that he was hiding something was growing. He was too sharp to be easily trapped. She could come out and ask him, but even if he answered her, she would be exposed and her investigation compromised. She didn't know what to do. It was her own mistake. She allowed herself to like the guy, and he was getting under her skin.

That line of thinking brought forth another puzzling thing—in addition to all of the other mysteries about Sam Larkin—he didn't make any kind of move on her, not even a friendly, good night peck on the cheek. She had never met anyone quite like him. She pulled the sun visor down and looked at her face in the vanity mirror.

CHAPTER 7

I do know what it feels like to be ass-deep in alligators, Cedrick Hamilton thought, as he toyed with the round, walnut and brass paperweight that he kept on the desk in his den. Some organization somewhere had given it to him for something, but he couldn't remember who or what, and, though it was inscribed, he couldn't come up with the energy or curiosity to pick it up and look. He just rolled it across his desk from hand to hand. On a normal Sunday he would have been getting ready for church, a political requirement of the job, but his depression was becoming oppressive. There was too much he couldn't control.

Four years before, when he was made superintendent, his life became dream-like. He was young for such a position, handsome, an upwardly mobile black man—though not too black in his color or his thinking—who was generally acceptable to both races. He learned early that public school administration was ninety-five percent politics and five percent educational expertise. The controlling force in the industry, the Boards of Education, were lay people, some without a high school education; it was they who determined what he could or could not do. It was an irrational situation. He could imagine IBM being run by outsiders with no knowledge of technology. It wouldn't be a Blue Chip.

After undergraduate school at Clemson, where he ran track, he earned an M.B.A. at Georgetown University and stayed on for a Ph.D. Being black was not as much of an asset in business as in education, so he had chosen education, and it had served him well until now. With his background, it hadn't taken him long to realize that if the public schools were a business, they would be bankrupt in a month. The money was there and he was its victim.

Now, four years later—as in the old cliché—the dream had become a nightmare. There were guarded accusations of racism in hiring from the whites and a feeling among his own race that

93

there were not enough blacks in administrative positions. In addition, there was Harold Taylor who needed firing before he created serious problems, and a board that wouldn't hear of it until after the bond issue passed, about which he had grave doubts. Those were the small issues. The most serious problem was a district-wide audit that had been called for by a senior citizens political group and would take place within the next three months. Audits never bothered him, but this one was different; the district would have no input in choosing the firm who would conduct it. If whomever was chosen was even mildly efficient and looked in the right places or asked the correct questions, he knew they would expose gross improprieties.

It was easy to corrupt the system. Kick-backs from vendors in education were as commonplace as payola was in the music business in the fifties. Student trips could be scheduled and "paid for" from numerous funds that were virtually unaccountable and then quietly canceled—the cancellation fee being split between the travel agent, the comptroller and the superintendent. No one ever bothered to follow the funds even if they could have. School moneys passed through inept hands, and those hands were so caught up in their own self-importance and greed, that the granting of a few small perks, inclusions in travel to conferences and meetings—some legitimate, some not—and pats on the back here and there, awarded Cedrick Hamilton immunity from question. Incompetent people put in positions that monitor a maze of ill-defined financial cubbyholes seemed a perfect way to operate, and that's what he had done. Now he sensed it all coming apart, and there was nothing he could do.

Power corrupts, and absolute power corrupts absolutely. The quote had stuck with him since he first heard it in a History of Economics course at Clemson University. Professor Robert Childs, although he was white, had been like a father to Cedrick Hamilton, taken him under his wing and guided him through the social inequities faced by a young, black man in an essentially white college.

The professor had also uttered the most astounding words young Cedrick had ever heard to that point in his life. They were sitting in a university coffee shop when Childs said, "You know, Cedrick, I've thought about it a lot, and if I ever get the chance to come back to this planet after I have 'shuffled off this mortal coil,' so to speak, I would like to come back as someone like you: intelligent, black and not angry. And that last part may be the most important. You have the world at your feet. Fuck worrying about being a token, and don't expect sympathy from either race because you'll get none. And don't expect your ethnic leaders, as sincere as they might be, and I'm sure they are sincere for the most part, to make advancements and carry you along with them. They won't, and you're too smart to expect them to. If you wait for that, you'll be waiting forever.

"You're educated and intelligent, and those two do not necessarily go hand in hand, as I'm sure you're aware. You have also, by the grace of God, been fortunate enough to master the social graces, something few of either race have done. You have it all, and because of that you will be resented by whites who think you're an 'uppity nigger'—excuse the word—and to others, those 'brothers' who want to wallow in reparations, who are envious of you and too angry or unmotivated to do anything for themselves, you will be nothing more than another 'Oreo.' Last word: don't ever begin to hate because when you begin to hate, you forget to think. Jimmy Hoffa said that. Who the hell knows where wisdom might come from? Another good lesson.

"Lecture complete. I am very proud of you, Cedrick, and we will never mention this again; however, if you ever hear a young, black man say, 'I want to be like you and do what you've done,' you'll know who it really is. Hell, I might even wink." Robert Childs smiled. Hamilton would never forget the man.

When he was appointed superintendent, he had, for all intents and purposes, been granted absolute power, and, true to the theorem, he had been corrupted absolutely. Or so he sometimes felt. Try as he might, he could not reconstruct the naïve reasoning that projected him in that direction except, perhaps, that he had never tasted power before and saw it as an opportunity, and, of course, the money, which now seemed redundant. He presently possessed more than he ever imagined possible. The system had given him everything any person—white or black—could hope for. He could not find any reasonable answers, except his own lack of wisdom. He wished he could talk to Robert Childs right now, at this moment, but he had died shortly after their coffee shop conversation. Cedrick Hamilton had been looking for him ever since.

He unlocked the bottom drawer of his desk and took out the thirty-two-caliber pistol he kept there. With it in his hand, he thought, "If I just do it without thinking about it, without giving it any consideration, just a reflex action, pull the trigger . . . ," but then he considered it.

When the telephone rang, he slipped the gun back in the drawer, looking around as if someone were watching. He allowed three rings, to compose himself before he picked up the receiver.

"Cedrick Hamilton," he said.

"Well, how are we doin' this mornin', Cedrick? Thought you might have already left for church," Charles Clay said in his quiet, good-natured way.

"I'm fine, Charles. How about you?" Hamilton said flatly.

"Fit as a fiddle. Listen, I need to talk to you about a project that's comin' up. Wondered when you might have some time."

"Let me look at my calendar," he said, covered the mouthpiece and stared into space for a minute or so. He didn't need another project. How much deeper was he going to bury himself?

When Charles Clay recruited him to grease the racial wheels and use some of his northeastern acquaintances in their "business" endeavor, he had no choice but to go along. He was in trouble. An affair with a white attorney had gone sour, and she had committed suicide when he wanted out. Though only a few people knew of the relationship, the young lady's death raised some questions and created rumors. Made public, Cedrick Hamilton would have been finished in Covington and maybe the whole state, maybe even education period. Charles Clay was one of those who knew, and he protected Cedrick Hamilton. Indentured him.

"When did you have in mind, Charles?"

"What about Thursday evening? We could have dinner."

"Charleston?" Hamilton asked.

"If it makes you more comfortable, Cedrick, I suppose Charleston is all right, but you know I hate that drive."

"It's not what I prefer either, but you know I can't go any-where near this town without being accosted by parents, teach-ers or politicians."

"I know. Charleston. Thursday night. Five-thirty too early for you? I don't want to get back to Covington too late."

"That's fine. Where?"

"Millon's. Haven't been there in awhile," Clay said.

"Millon's it is," Hamilton said.

"I shall look forward to it, and so should you, Cedrick."

"I'll let you explain that when I see you."

"Have a good day."

"You too, Charles." In all the times they had been together, he had never confided anything to Clay about what he was doing in the school district. They discussed the political aspects of his position, and they talked about bond issues, school taxes and those kinds of things, but never any of the finances of the district. Maybe it was time. Perhaps Charles could come up with some ideas that would help solve his problems. He didn't know how, but the man was a master of manipulation. He had proved that.

A Cooper's hawk sailed across the marsh as if it were being propelled by Zephyr's own private winds. Sam watched its movements and gloried in its freedom. The bird made a large circle, took a sharp dive into the grasses and came out with a small rodent in its beak. The price of carelessness, Sam thought. He respected freedom, knew it was taken for granted by most people. The luxury of day-to-day decision-making was unappreciated for most of his own life; fortunately, experience had taught him the value of that luxury. The one discomfort in his life at the moment was that he couldn't support himself with some self-employable skill, be beholding to no one.

Sam sat on his deck eating his breakfast. He wore only a pair of denim cut-offs and well-worn boat shoes, which at some point in their history had been white, but were now the gray of dried plough-mud. He had done his run early before the heat became oppressive, followed it with a twenty-minute workout, and after a shower came out to the deck feeling as good as he thought it was possible to feel. It was still a wonder to him that he had come to enjoy exercise. For years it had held no place in his daily regimen.

It was only eight o'clock. There were no plans for the day other than to pick up a fiberglass repair kit at Harry Tom Cooper's Boat Dock and do a small resurfacing job on some spider-cracks in the surface of his boat. It was at the top of his to-do list. However, when he got the repair kit if he decided he didn't feel like working on the boat or if something more appealing came up, it would remain at the top of his list for tomorrow or the next day. It was the way he had come to live.

Breakfast done, he lit a cigarette, leaned back in his chair and rested his coffee cup on his bare stomach. He couldn't imagine a better life than he was living at the moment. If teaching was a requirement to make all this possible, so be it.

Harry Tom Cooper's place could never be mistaken for a yacht club, though there were a few large sailboats and cabin cruisers moored there. It consisted of a working dock that served as home base for half a dozen shrimp boats, a retail fish store, and a general store that sold everything from fishing gear to picture books about the lowcountry to beach toys and souvenirs for the tourists.

Sam parked the Rover and walked across the parking lot that was covered in oyster shells crushed to pumice by cars, trucks and boat trailers. The early morning warmth was accelerating. A couple of fishermen were already at the cleaning tables working on fish they had caught during the night. The fish weren't large, so from a distance, Sam could only suppose they were sea bass or trout. Skeeter Crewes was on the dock filling the tanks of a twenty-eight-foot Grady-White, and another customer was backing a boat trailer carrying a mid-sized Whaler toward the launching ramp in front of the store's entrance. It looked like Harry Tom was going to have a busy day.

"Mornin', Sam," Cooper said when Sam came through the door. "What gets you out so early this mornin'?" Harry Tom was the consummate "good-ol' boy"—overweight, big smile that no one could read, bourbon-rosy cheeks, an unpressed and questionably-colored Exxon shirt that hid his belly, which extended well-over the Harley-Davidson belt buckle that held up his jeans. Hc had no visible ass.

"Not early, Harry Tom; it's after nine."

"Just don't see you down here much in the mornin'." The display case Cooper was standing behind, looking at the newspaper and sipping coffee, served as the counter, bar and checkout station.

"I have to work. Don't have mornings except on weekends. And don't you rub that fact in, you ol' sumbitch." Larkin was smiling.

"Well, school be out soon; maybe you'll come around more often. Spend some of that fuckin' money you makin'. You here to buy somethin' or see Skeeter? He's workin' today, you know." Harry Tom never passed up an opportunity to get in a shot on Larkin.

"Come to buy something, but I'll probably say hello to my neighbor before I leave."

"Sure wish I could put him on regular, year-round. I know he needs the money, and he's a good worker, but I just cain't. Too much dead-time outta season."

Three black men came in, pulled four six-packs of malt liquor from the beer case, paid Harry Tom and left.

"I don't know how they can drink that damn stuff," he said. "Tastes like horse piss to me, but they come in ever mornin' 'bout this time." He laughed. "Hell, I don't even know where they get the money, but it's two or three times ever day."

"Always a way," Sam said.

"I guess so. Now what you come to buy? I gotta get that money outta your hand 'fore you change your mind."

"I need a fiberglass repair kit."

"Shit, that boat's been in the sun too long, Sam. You do it this year, there's just gonna be more surface cracks next, and you'll have to do it all over again." He leaned forward on the counter, as if sharing a secret. "Now I've got a real nice—mint condition, actually— twenty-six-foot Mako I can give you a good price on. Want to take a look at it?"

"What kind of motors?"

"Twin hunderd and fifty Mercs. Sumbitch will flat fly."

"Not fast enough, Harry Tom." Sam tried not to grin.

"Don't fuck with my brain now, boy. I know I ain't the sharpest knife in the drawer, but I seen your boat, remember? All I can do is offer. Cain't save people from themselves or their mistakes."

Skeeter Crewes came in through the back of the store just as Harry Tom was going to get the repair kit.

"Happenin', Sam?" Skeeter said, holding out his fist to touch knuckles with his friend.

"Just doin' chores. You workin' all day?"

"Looks like. I hope. Been a short month, but I got three mouths that don't stop eatin' even if I do." Skeeter went to the beer case and pulled out two Coca-Colas. "Have a drink on me," he said. "Gone be hot today looks like."

"Yeah, I may just have to turn on the air-conditioning," Sam said with a superior smile.

"Fuck you, white man. I may just have to invite all my friends and family over to sit in your house. How 'bout that?" Skeeter said with an even broader smile.

"Oh, Lord. Well, you know you'd be welcome, Skeeter."

"I know I would, but you ain't met all my family and friends." He took a swallow of his Coke. "How you and that Miss Blondie Blonde doin'? I seen her in a boat headin' toward your house. You in trouble yet?" Skeeter Crewes grinned.

"Maybe I better ask if you've been keepin' tabs on me?"

"Just watchin'. She was out here the other day. I don't think she knew we were neighbors."

"Why do you say that?" Sam asked.

"Well, she was askin' 'bout people who live 'round here, familiarizin' herself she said. Seemed nice enough, but a little . . . uh . . . what the hell's the word, Sam?"

"Pushy? Smart? Ignorant? Naïve?"

"Naïve. That's a good word for it. Anyway, she was askin' 'bout people, but when I mentioned your name, I got the feelin' you were the only one she really wanted to know much about. Didn't hide it very well. See what I'm sayin'?" He laughed. "You are in trouble, boy."

"You love that, don't you?" Sam asked.

"What?"

"Callin' me 'boy.' "

"Absodamnlutely."

"Well, I think what's on your mind is your imagination."

"What is it then?"

"I don't know, but don't tell all my secrets, okay, son?"

"Hell, I don't know any of your secrets, but don't worry 'bout me tellin' 'em anyway."

Harry Tom came back with the repair kit and put it on the counter in front of Larkin. "Twenty-nine ninety-five," he said with a grin. "Sure you don't want to look at that Mako?"

"If I was before, I'm not now. How much mark-up have you got on this damn stuff?" Sam asked, as he put a ten and a twenty on the counter.

"You pay for that Co-Cola?"

"Skeeter said it was on him. Told me he gets 'em free," Sam said as he turned and headed for the door.

"On your ass, he gets 'em free. I'll put both of 'em on your tab, Larkin." Cooper said. Sam was already out the door.

During the drive back to his house, Sam saw that the three black men who had come into Harry Tom's for beer had gathered a couple of friends and settled in around a large, wire spool that made a shaded garden table in front of a mobile home he assumed belonged to one of them. Sam knew he could come back at five o'clock and find them in the same place, maybe with a few more friends. He wondered what they talked about all day and what they would talk about tomorrow when they would be in the same place.

What Skeeter Crewes said about Chaney's apparent interest in him was bothersome. Why was she asking about him? How could she afford to live in Beau Rivage if her salary were commensurate with that of the other officers in the area? And, regardless of what Skeeter said, why did he feel every time he was in her company, that she was picking his brain, probing into his personal life? Maybe Skeeter was right; maybe she was looking at him for carnal purposes, but he didn't think so.

During the week Karen Chaney tried to put Larkin out of her mind and concentrate on her mission. It wasn't easy; the man challenged her abilities as an investigator. She spent time in town, visiting shops, going to the library, taking a carriage tour, asking questions about the town and its people of anyone she could engage in conversation, but never wearing her uniform unless she was in the office.

On Wednesday she ate dinner at the Oyster Creek Inn. She was the only woman sitting by herself in the dining room, but that didn't bother her; she was used to eating alone. It came with the territory. She was nicely dressed in off-white, linen slacks and a pale blue, long-sleeved, silk pull-over. One man in the place stood out, he was in his mid-fifties, she guessed, not bad-looking, probably handsome when he was younger. He circulated the room, glad-handing customers and operating in a proprietary manner. She was not surprised when he came to her table and introduced himself as the owner, Charles Clay. In Ray Breslin's orientation tour, he had mentioned Clay as Covington's most prominent attorney, not one to arrest during Water Weeks. He would be worth checking out.

The ambiance in the dining room surprised her. It wasn't stuffily formal, but gracious beyond any other place she had been in the area. Observing the clientele was interesting—the regulars easily identifiable from the tourists. And the food was good. It was a pleasant experience.

The red light on the answering machine was blinking when she entered her townhouse. She closed the door, locked it and went to retrieve whatever message awaited her. She immediately recognized Neil Dougherty's voice.

"You out shootin' up the town or somethin', Belle? I'll be in the office catching up on paperwork until about ten-thirty if you want to call tonight. Or you can catch me at home in the morning. Talk to you."

It was ten o'clock when she sat down and dialed her friend's number. She was sitting on the oversized, sectional couch in the living room. Quite a few of her nighttime hours were spent there, watching the light-adorned boats trading up the river toward the marina where they would bunker in for the night. It was a spectacular view.

"Dougherty," the voice on the other end of the line said.

"Hey, Blue. I got your message."

"Why hello, darlin'. How are things up in the lowcountry? Is that a paradoxical construction or what? 'Up in the lowcountry'?"

"I have no idea what it is; something that would stump a Mississippi-born Irishman, I suspect. How are you? You're working awful late."

"I'm fine. Workin' late because I went fishing this afternoon."

"Get anything?"

"A few king mackerel and a new informant. What about you? Catch anything?"

"No bad guys."

"What about good guys?" he asked probing her personal life. It was tiresome.

"Couple that may need checking out. Lawyer here in town. Pretty powerful. Probably nothing, but he does own a restaurant, knows everybody and everybody knows him. There is no present reason for suspicion, but it's all I've got for the moment."

"You said a couple . . ." Decision time. Dougherty could find out anything there was to know about Sam Larkin, but she didn't want to expose Sam Larkin to Neil Dougherty. She wondered if she was afraid to find out anything bad about the man. Sam could wait. Clay would satisfy Neil for awhile.

"Let me get a better line on the other one. As far as I know, there's really nothing there, and I wouldn't want to waste your time. Too many real bad guys out there." There was silence on the line. "What?" she asked.

"You're talking fast. I know you, Karen. What's going on?" *Karen*. The professional approach. He was serious.

"Actually, me and this other guy, we been sleepin' together since an hour after I arrived in town. He's fantastic and if it keeps up, I'm gonna be too tired to work." It was mean, meant to hurt. Neil Dougherty was, in spite of everything, her best friend. She felt guilty. More silence. "I'm sorry, Blue. I'm okay. Leading a nun's life up here, not that it's any of your business. I'll let you know when I want something. Just check out Clay for me. I can handle this. I'm beginning to think we're on a wild goose chase anyway."

"Be careful," he said and hung up the phone. Angry, she knew.

Her mind was spinning in a thousand different directions. She was in limbo, getting nowhere, but maybe there was nowhere to get. She liked Sam Larkin. In an investigation you weren't supposed to like anyone. At least not to the extent that it affects your judgment. His past had to be pursued.

She looked out the window, saw what looked like a thirty-eight-foot sailboat heading toward the marina, leaned back on the couch and closed her eyes. What a life, she thought.

CHAPTER 8

Turner Lockett had heard tales his whole life long about people "going mental" and laughed about them. He never considered it for himself, but now he was beginning to wonder. He searched the area around his trailer every morning and every night, but had found no footprints, man or animal, yet he still heard the sounds. Heard them plain as day. Marsh grass breaking, the sound of rubber boots walking on dry land, footsteps and a humming sound like a man preoccupied with the performance of a task, making idle music.

He could feel eyes watching him. Shadows brought panic. When he did manage to doze off, there were dreams, serpents coiling around his body, dragging him through familiar places where everyone knew what he had done. Through it all, he saw Jared Barnes. When the blood got to boiling temperature in his veins, he woke up, wet from sweating beneath the covers he was under to ward off the phantom cold. And he cried.

Only on the water did he feel safe. Once he was away from land, security seemed to surround him. He was drinking more, as well. Running the creeks, finding an isolated spot, anchoring and drinking to clean his mind. He could accept all of the bad things that were happening as his own creation. Imagination. But whenever he came back to the trailer, it all returned and he couldn't think. He was glad when Charlie Clay contacted him, told him The Company was in need of a secure off-load site and asked him to put an around-the-clock watch over the weekend on Skeeter Crewes's place as well as Sam Larkin's. They fit the profile for what The Company needed.

Heading west from Covington toward Charleston, Cedrick Hamilton saw the color of the sky deepening from pale blue to bruised purple and heard the distant rumble of thunder, low and growling like a dog who makes raw, guttural sounds just to tell you he's mean. *It was a dark and stormy night*, he thought as he drove. It brought a guarded smile to his face, the first smile of any kind in weeks.

The wind began to blow, and the glow of lightning flashes signaled that the oncoming storm was getting closer. A stand of wild, white oleander next to the road sent flower petals across his windshield where, like misguided snow flakes, they adhered themselves until he flipped the wipers on to knock them off. He hoped the weather was not portentous of his meeting with Charles Clay.

His depression had not dissipated. He was no more confounded by the natural complexity of the storm he saw forming than he was by the intricacies of his own situation. Despite his ability to skate and manipulate, he could not come up with any foolproof way to avoid the consequences he knew lay ahead.

There was the slim possibility of sacrificing the district financial officer and the superintendent of buildings and construction, and he had thought about it. The financial records of building projects and the bidding processes were so full of holes and dark corners that they were always subject to question. In school districts across the country, the controllers of those two areas were often made the sacrificial lambs. With a little skewing here and there and a few unanswerable questions, he could lay it right in their laps. They were both hired for their ignorance and arrogance, which made them vulnerable. Get the fingers pointing in the opposite direction, and he was home free. He couldn't understand what misguided sense of morality discouraged him from doing that, but, for whatever reason, he placed it in a position of last resort.

Ten miles out of Charleston, huge drops of rain began pelting the windshield of his car. Even with the wipers going full speed, the landscape melted before him. Huge puddles formed in low spots on the highway, and the car hit walls of water causing it to hydroplane to the edge of control. Hamilton's mind was not only on the troubles he was facing, but also on surviving the drive into town.

He found a parking lot on Meeting Street, a short distance from Millon's. Even though he carried an umbrella, by the time he entered the foyer of the restaurant, the blowing rain had dampened his light tan suit.

"Mr. Hamilton," the maitre d' said as if he knew him. "Mr. Clay is already seated. If you will follow me, please."

Millon's was, by far, the most elegant and formal dining place in the city. Tables were covered with white Damask cloths and set with a full set of silverware—some pieces with very obscure uses that were never seen elsewhere—three crystal wine-glasses to accommodate the various wines served with each course, and the finest china. Waiters wore tuxedos and carried white serviettes over their forearm. The menu was prix fixe and expensive. On most occasions Hamilton found dinner at Millon's a grand experience. This evening, however, was tempered by what was going on inside him.

"Cedrick," Charlie Clay said as he rose from his chair while his dining partner was seated.

"Charles," Hamilton nodded.

"You don't look very happy for a man who's about to partake of Charleston's finest. And free at that," the lawyer said with slight admonishment. "What would you like to drink?"

"A Rob Roy on the rocks." The waiter, who, after seating his guest, had been standing a private distance away, nodded and turned to place his order.

"Thank you, George," Clay said to the man's back. He noticed Hamilton examining his suit jacket. "It'll dry, Cedrick; don't worry about it. You look miserable. Now what weight of the world are you carryin' on your shoulders tonight?"

"Just a lot of district business on my mind."

"Well, why don't you tell me about it, an' maybe I can help. Don't guess there's any secrets between us now, are there?" There was a question in his grin.

"No, I guess not." Hamilton paused, trying to put together what, if anything, he wanted to tell his friend. The waiter brought his drink and he took a sip, which gave him a little time to consider.

"Must be pretty heavy, if it's takin' you all that time to make up your mind whether or not to tell me about it."

"I'm in trouble, Charles, and I don't know how to handle it."

"Now that is a first." Clay gave a quiet chuckle. "I've never seen you stumped for a solution to any problem, and even if you didn't have one, you've always convinced everyone you did. What could be so bad this time? Tell me about it. Maybe we can solve this little dilemma of yours." Clay's eyes were piercing as he looked straight-on at Cedrick Hamilton.

"The audit," Hamilton said.

"Oh, yes. I heard about that. Stirrin' up quite a fuss, idn't it?"

Hamilton sighed. "More than you know, Charles. More than you know."

"Tell me."

"It's going to put me out in the cold, probably in jail." He took another sip of his drink. "There's a lot of money unaccounted for, kickbacks that will become apparent, false vouchers; you name it. It sounds terrible, but, in reality, it's not that unusual. Done in almost every school district in the country if the truth were known. It's just that most of them never have to face an audit they can't control.

"School boards are the closest thing to the old Russian *Politburo* we have in this country, and I was naïve enough to think mine would never knuckle under to pressure. But they're anxious and impatient about this bond issue. It's as if it doesn't pass the first time around, they won't get another shot at it. Hell, we passed the last one for a hundred and forty million without even trying. But we didn't have the senior citizen population then that we have now."

"And they're worried about taxes. Stands to reason."

"They've been assured that taxes won't go up, but they want the audit to prove it, and they want an accounting of all the moneys from the last bond issue to make sure it wasn't misspent." He took another sip of his drink.

"Which, of course, taxes will and the money was." Hamilton, stared into his drink. "How much we talkin' about, Cedrick? In question, I mean."

"Six hundred thousand, maybe a million. Who knows? "

"I hope you're not sayin' what I think you're sayin'," Clay said.

"I'm guilty as hell, Charles. There will be questions about employees' salaries, skimming, falsifying records. I'm scared. I don't even know how it got started. It was easy and seemed victimless. If I didn't take it, it would be wasted somewhere else."

"Seems like you got yourself in a tough situation, Cedrick, though I can't, for the life of me, understand why. You sure as hell don't need the money. Whatever. I'm sure it's solvable. Who's doin' the audit?"

"The board hasn't made a choice yet."

"The board gets to choose? That's the damnedest thing I ever heard of." Clay sounded flabbergasted. "That's a new one. A demand audit and the auditee gets to choose the auditor. What's the problem?"

"Well, choose from the three firms they were given by the citizen's committee."

"Oh, don't you just love bureaucracy. Makes it possible for us lawyers to do all the stuff we do."

"You all were the ones who created it."

"That's right. Smart of us, wudn't it?" Clay said with a Cheshire grin. "Do you know who the firms are?"

"Taylor and Bradshaw from Greenville; Shelton, Kline and Davis from Charleston; and Roger Herrington and Associates from Columbia. Why?"

"How soon are we talkin' before the board makes a choice?"

"A couple of weeks or longer."

"Well, I think that gives us enough time."

"For what?" Hamilton asked, suddenly picking up.

"To do a little finagling." He thought for a moment. "We want Herrington."

"Can you reveal your reasoning to me about that?" Hamilton asked with the merest edge of sarcasm.

"Trust me. They're political. Roger Herrington wants to be in the Governor's cabinet and eventually governor himself. Tell you anything? Give me till Saturday, and I'll have a better handle on it. Now if that's your only problem, I think we can take care of it."

"But it's the board that has to choose Herrington . . ."

"That's the easy part."

"How?"

"Cash and influence, Cedrick. Cash and influence. It's the magic formula." He smiled.

"Here comes our dinner. Let's forget all this stuff and enjoy."

There was little conversation during dinner; Clay didn't like anything to disturb the event. It was only when coffee was served that the two men turned back to the business of the evening.

"That was good, wudn't it?" Clay asked.

"The best, as always," Hamilton said.

"Okay, Cedrick, I've listened to your problem, and I think— actually, I'm sure—I can help, but I also need some help from you on the next company venture." Clay made it an offer he couldn't refuse.

"I've still got my northeast connections in place."

"On this one, the requirements are a little bit different, and you're the only man I can think of who can handle it. We've not done anything as big as what we have planned; consequently, the site's gonna have to be extremely secure, accessible by road for a coupla eighteen-wheelers, relatively deep water and more space than usual."

"What are we talking about, Charles?" He found himself getting nervous as he looked at Clay's face.

"Eighteen tons of product and enough money for you to tell the whole State of South Carolina to go hang, not to mention auditors and school boards. Hell, you can go live in Paris if you want to." Cedrick Hamilton's mouth went dry. His accountant's mind was already doing the calculations and the figures were staggering. "I need you to secure the off-load site; you're the perfect person for the job."

"But I have no idea where—"

"I do. I've got Turner Lockett doin' some research on two sites. Some reconnaissance missions, you might call 'em." He laughed. "One I don't think much of, in fact, I'm a little scared of it; the other I believe you could help us with."

"I'm listening."

"The one I don't think we should pursue, even though it does fit the criteria, is Sam Larkin's place out on Fiddler's End. Now I don't know the man, though I suppose I might have seen him around town at some point, but all I know of him is that he teaches school and has a pretty fancy house that nobody knows how he paid for. Hey, maybe he's in the same business we are. That'd be a hoot, wouldn't it? But you pro'bly know more about him than I do." Clay paused, waiting for a reaction.

"Not that much more. Does a decent job, I guess. Haven't had any complaints. Kind of a loner from what I've heard. I've hardly seen the man; I would stay away from him. Who's the other?"

"Lives in the same area, coupla miles up the creek. Skeeter Crewes. You know Skeeter, don't you?"

"Yes, I know Skeeter. We go back a ways. He's a good man, but I'm not sure he'd be approachable either. Got a wife and one or two kids. I haven't seen him in quite awhile."

"Two kids. Works for Harry Tom Cooper when there's work," Clay said, "but I think he's havin' a pretty rough time. Bill checked on his bank account, and it varies between empty and nothin'."

"Well, that's motivation. What kind of a deal are we talking about?"

"I just want him and his family to be gone for the night. They must have a relative somewhere they could go visit. I don't want 'em to go to a motel in town or anything; that would be a little obvious. Hell, we could even send 'em to Myrtle Beach for a coupla days if they want. Take a little vacation."

"And what does Skeeter get for his trouble?"

"Well, dudn't sound like much trouble to me, just take a trip and keep his mouth shut. Not even any risk to amount to anything. I was thinkin' maybe twenty-five thousand."

"Just to not be at home for a night?"

"That's all. What do you think?"

"I don't know. If he's as hard up as you say he is, I would guess he'd consider it."

"You feel okay about prospecting him?"

"Skeeter and I have been pretty close over the years. I think I can trust him. He's a pretty quiet guy; I don't think he'd turn on me even if he didn't want to do it."

"We need him, Cedrick. We're talkin' millions here. Maybe the last hurrah, who knows?"

"Yes, who really does know." It was a statement. "About any damned thing."

Hamilton's mind had wandered back to his own troubles. He wondered if this would just add pressure and compound them.

"Cedrick, you take care of Skeeter Crewes for me—for us—and I'll take care of your audit for you. Deal?" Clay smiled.

"I don't know where your confidence comes from, Charles, but I really don't have much choice, do I?"

"None that I see. I'm gonna have Turner out there this week keepin' an eye on both of them. Even if we don't approach Larkin, I need to know what his schedule is and what he's doing."

"I'll see Skeeter this week." Hamilton rose from his chair. His back was stiff from sitting. "Thanks for dinner. And let's keep our fingers crossed for each other on this one. Okay?" Clay held up both hands with the first two fingers on each hand crossed.

"My pleasure, Cedrick. Drive carefully."

It had been a long day, but now all the work days felt that way; the job and its people were getting oppressive. He felt independence slipping away. When Sam entered his house with only a cold beer and the deck lounger on his mind, he was stopped by the blinking answering machine. He went to the phone and pushed the REWIND/PLAY button.

"Hi, Sam. It's Karen. Remember? Haven't heard from you, and since you fixed such a great meal for me last week, I thought I would offer to return the favor and invite you to dinner, if you're not busy. I know I should have called earlier, but it's a spur-of-the-moment decision. I'll be home today, so give me a call." The machine clicked off.

With what Skeeter said and what had gone through his own mind, the invitation was unnerving. The idea of her making moves on him didn't ring true. He didn't know Karen Chaney very well, but she appeared to be the type of person who would let her intentions be known, if that was her purpose. He took off his shirt, got a beer from the fridge, opened it, took the phone with him out on the deck to decide what to do.

Under most circumstances, he would trust his gut instinct: call or don't call, go or don't go, but this one required more consideration. Depending on her motives, if he didn't go, it would likely end a purely social relationship that he wasn't sure he wanted to end. If he did go and she had other objectives—though he couldn't imagine her purpose—he might expose himself to more questions and a deeper probe into his personal life, which he definitely didn't want. From another angle, he didn't want to appear paranoid or ungrateful, regardless of her reasons for inviting him. And, most important, if he refused the invitation, he might never discover her purpose. He dialed her number.

She picked up the telephone on the second ring.

"Hello?"

"That anxious, huh?" he said.

"Just happened to be sitting at my table doing some paper-work. Hi, Sam." Her voice was soft and glad.

"Hi to you."

"My invitation forward enough?" she asked.

"That thought never entered my mind."

"Can you come?"

"When?" he asked.

"Tomorrow night?"

"What are you having?"

"Liver and eggplant," she answered.

"Damn! My favorites. How did you know that?"

"If they're your favorites, you're uninvited." He didn't say anything. "I was only kidding. About what I was having. You said you'd lived in New Orleans, and I have a restaurant cook book from New Orleans, so I thought I would make barbecued shrimp from a restaurant named Pascal's Manale. Ever heard of it?"

"One of my favorite places and barbecued shrimp is what made them famous."

"Maybe I'd better not try it. Not if you already know how it's supposed to taste."

"It couldn't be bad if you follow the directions," he said.

"I never follow directions. Want to give it a try?"

"I'd love to. What time and how do I find your place?"

"Six-thirty and it's number seven, on the end, toward the marina."

"Got it. I'll be there. Anything I can bring?" he asked.

" No. I never invite people to dinner and then ask them to bring what I'm going to serve them." She paused. "Sam? Do you really eat liver?" she asked with distaste.

"Not if I can help it. See you at six-thirty."

"I'll look forward to it."

"Me, too. Thank you, Karen."

CHAPTER 9

On Saturday morning Brad Coleman chartered a plane in Miami and flew to Montego Bay, Jamaica, where a car would be waiting to take him to Runaway Bay, halfway between Montego Bay and Kingston. He had flown into Kingston on his last trip, and it was his compulsion never to fly into the same place on consecutive trips, no matter how much time intervened. It was common sense, as far as he was concerned. The car, as Peter Walker promised, was waiting when he arrived, and within ten minutes he was on his way to Peter's estate.

The exotic green of the island created a sense of rebirth in him, fresh and new, much the same as the experience of putting a new venture together. It had been four years since he'd worked a deal with Walker. The last one netted him two million dollars, which was only a small fraction of what he had earned since that time. For him, the business had ceased to be about money some time ago, something he knew would be difficult for most people to conceive. One had to be born to risk to understand that. Not much different than mountain climbing. He sat back and watched the landscape pass by.

The island was unspoiled once one got out of the city. He often thought that if there truly were a Garden of Eden, it must have been in Jamaica. He was taken with the vibrant and lush bougainvillea that grew without care, the banana trees and other trees hanging heavy with mangos and aqui. It was only when he saw the abject poverty of small towns like Saint Anne's or when he visited Trench Town, the slums of Kingston, that he could imagine what it must have been like to be expelled from the Garden.

Peter Walker's house was at the top of a hill that overlooked the Runaway Bay Hotel and the aquamarine sea beyond. It was a low, sprawling structure, L-shaped, with a foyer and living room at the apex. Lying in opposite directions from the apex were two bedrooms on each side, which opened onto the pool. There was an open-air, covered dining area that adjoined the living room and also fronted the pool. It was here that all meals were taken. A tennis court lay adjacent to the house and looked out over the ocean. The dwelling itself was shaded by a gargantuan guango tree that dwarfed men and automobiles. It was paradise, Coleman thought, as he got out of the car and headed to the front door.

A six-foot-tall, black woman opened the door before he could ring the bell. She wore a broad smile on her face.

"Mista Brad, how nice to be seein' you. Been a long time now—tree? Four year?"

"At least. I know it's silly to say, Doris, but you haven't changed a bit. I think that's the same head kerchief you were wearing the last time I saw you." He gave her a mischievous grin.

"Oh, pshaw! You know it ain't." She dismissed his foolishness with a hand gesture. "I had to wash dat one jes' yestade'." She laughed at her own joke.

"Well, you look wonderful."

"Den dey's no reason to change, is dey? Come in; get out de heat. We got de fans goin' and shade in de house. No sense you be out here gettin' you clothes all wet an' sweaty."

Coleman followed her into the foyer, dropped his hanging bag and briefcase and surveyed the place. Like the housekeeper, it had not changed either.

"Mista Peter, he just called in. He be comin' in jus' a minute. Been out fishin', but he at de dock now. Ten, fifteen minute at de mos'. Now, you bein' thirsty?"

"Do you have any tea?"

"You go sit down; I bring it right to you."

It was as Doris promised, only ten minutes before Peter Walker came striding through the front door. He was an average-sized man, but the musculature of his upper body, combined with the strong jaw line, wide smile and confidence created an overpowering presence. He wore a pair of white shorts that were in dramatic contrast to his dark-chocolate skin. There was no shirt. His eyes were ice-blue and his teeth as white as the shorts he was wearing.

"Bradley, my mon. How you be doin'? You de sight fo' some sore eyes. Ain't dat de way you say it?" he asked with the melodic rhythm of his native speech. It was happy, so unlike flat American speech patterns. Coleman wondered if the man ever experienced a worried day in his life.

"I'm fine, Peter; how about you?"

"What it look like? Hey, it be a long way from Trench Town. I got inside plumbin'." He laughed. It was hearty. "How long you be stayin'?"

"Like to stay forever, but I've still got some things to do in the north islands and Miami and then get back to South Carolina if everything looks good."

"Doris," Walker shouted into the kitchen. "Bring me a Stripe, please. So, how's de people in South Carolina? Tell me." Before he finished his question, the housekeeper had put a coaster, a glass and a bottle of Red Stripe beer on the coffee table in front of him. "She always givin' me a glass, like I got class or somethin'." He took a long swig from the bottle.

"Oh they're okay, I guess. They've been at it quite awhile. Descarté in Miami put me on to them or them on to me; I'm not sure which came first. He's worked with them before and seems to think they're okay."

"You meet any of 'em?"

"Only one. A lawyer and, I assume, head of the operation. I only need to meet one."

"Not like you to be assumin'." A concerned look crossed Walker's face.

"I won't be if we go into business. You know me better than that, Peter."

"Been a long time. I jus' wanna make sure you ain't gettin' careless on yo'self. How 'bout I get you some more tea? Dat glass 'bout empty. Doris? Get Mista Brad some mo' tea, please. So how dis lawyer be?"

"Seems all right. What can I say? He's a lawyer. I'll know more after the next trip."

Walker appeared to be reading the label on the beer bottle while Doris filled Brad's glass with tea.

"You don' seem too, whatchoo say, settled 'bout all dis."

"No, I'm okay. It's just that they've never done anything this big before—five, six tons at a time, maybe less—eighteen tons is a lot of product. It requires a division, not a squad, and the more people you get involved, the greater the risk. You know that."

"Mebbe de risk too great. Mebbe we pass on dis; I got some udder t'ings brewin' you be interested in." Coleman could see the skepticism on the other man's face.

"Peter, I'm not going to take on anything I'm not sure of. Lot of big upstanding citizens involved in this company. The thing that bothers me is that I'm not sure just how serious they all take it. It's kind of like a game to them from what I saw up there. They're innocents. I don't think they've ever thought through the possible consequences if they get caught. Maybe I'm wrong. Whatever, I'll know everything before we load the boat."

"I doubt you wrong, mon. Till you been caught, you don't t'ink you eva will be. 'Cept maybe you. You betta make dem see dat befo' we be doin' business. Smugglin' used to be a profession, now it be mo' like amateur night down de hotel."

"You sound like you're getting ready to retire," Coleman said with a smile. "I know you can afford it."

"Oh, no, mon. It not de money. It be de fun. I got mo' money den some banana republics. Hell, dey be comin' to me to borrow money fo' dey nex' war. Like I say, long way from Trench Town." He paused and grinned. "And I want it to stay dat way. What kind boat dey got?"

"Gettin' a sixty-eight-footer. I'm supposed to go to Eleuthera Island to look at it. They found it through an acquaintance on Great Abaco. I'll be going there when I leave here."

"You frontin' de buy?" Walker asked.

"No, the lawyer is. I'm just in for a percentage."

"Twelve, eighteen, twenty ton don' make no difference; I got de product, and we get de trucks from the bauxite people to bring it out de hills and load it. Dey goin' big time; all right, den." Peter Walker smiled. "I trus' you, mon. You say we go, we go. You take care de details. You de masta planna. Dat mind a yours. Don' know how it work, but it do." Walker stood up. "Le's go for a walk on de beach an talk 'bout you an' me, an' all dem years done passed since you be down here."

Like so many things about Karen Chaney, her condo did not fit the image of a law enforcement officer. It was as soft as a generically furnished living space could be, enhanced, he was sure, by Karen Chaney's touch. He liked that it was white. Carpet, furniture, drapes and sheers. There were several fresh flower arrangements in the living and dining area, to give it color. Again, he wondered how she could afford such a place.

"What would you like to drink?" she asked from the kitchen.

"Vodka on the rocks with lime, if you have it," Sam said. He was standing at the sliding glass doors looking out at the river. "Your place is beautiful, and the view is spectacular."

"As I said, it's a stretch to pay for, but it's where I live, so I won't let myself scrimp on that. I'm not into squalor," she said as she handed him his drink. She was wearing white slacks, an emerald green blouse and gold sandals that matched the wide belt around her waist. She looked more like a Charleston socialite than a quasi-police officer. "How hungry are you?" she asked.

"I'm not in a rush unless you are."

"Not really. Why don't we go out on the deck and watch the world float by for a few minutes?" She opened the door and they went outside. "In another few weeks even the nights will be too hot to sit out here."

"You'll always have a breeze; it won't be bad."

"So what did you do today if that's not too personal a question to ask on the second date." Sam turned and looked at her.

"Is that what this is?" he asked. "The second date?"

"The way I count," she said.

"Okay then. In that case, no, it's not too personal seeing as how this is the second." He smiled. "I never tell about my day on a first date, a rule I adhere to religiously. There's really not much to tell. Sketched. Read. Not much accomplished. What about you?"

"The same. Not much accomplished. Got my hair cut, listened to the ladies gossip. Met a woman you probably know; she's involved with the school district. Isabel Reichert? Husband's a banker."

"I know Isabel," Sam said, "but we don't work together; she's at the middle school."

"She and I were waiting together. Appears to be one charged-up lady."

"What do you mean?"

"Intense. After we were called, I was in the chair next to her. All she could talk about was her husband. I don't think there's much love lost there. Said she'd like to kill the son-of-a-bitch."

"You got all that in a beauty parlor?" Sam couldn't help laughing.

"Women have no secrets from their hairdresser. It's like a guy and his regular bartender. Nothing's sacred."

"She's a pretty hard woman from what I've heard," he said, "but I don't really know her other than seeing her at a few school district meetings."

"Well, it seems her husband has been home for dinner every night this week, and she can't understand why. Assumes it's because his other lady has cut him off."

"And she talked about all that? That's interesting," he said.

"Sounds like a soap opera," Karen said. "Wish I could have heard more, but they went into another room for a color job. You need freshening?"

"No, I'm fine." He had barely touched his drink.

They sat for a few minutes watching the river. There was a pall of discomfort between them. Karen looked at her watch.

"I've still got quite a bit to do in the kitchen. Why don't you come in and talk to me while I work."

"Can I help?" he said, getting up to follow her.

"The salad stuff is on the cutting board. You can toss it with the greens in that wooden bowl. I didn't ask what kind of dressing you liked. I've got . . ."

"I'm not particular," he said as he moved toward the cutting board.

"I'm feeling strange again," Karen said as she freshened her own drink.

"What do you mean? How?"

"I'm having a hard time with our conversation. It's the second time and that's never happened to me before."

"Hard in what way?"

"I don't know exactly. I mean I don't want to talk about work, and I know you don't either, and I don't feel comfortable questioning you because I know that you're a very private man or at least that's my impression. I feel like I'm forcing things, and I don't want you to be uncomfortable." She stopped. "Listen to me talk. I'm essentially a quiet person, and I'm prattling on."

"I'm not uncomfortable," Sam said. "Well, maybe a little. I guess I'm not sure what's going on here." Karen tensed at his words.

"I'm not either. You weren't in my plans, Larkin," she said with her back to him.

"Do you want to explain that?"

"I mean I came here to do a job, and now I find myself getting caught off guard and heading in another direction."

"What kind of a job did you come to do?" She had said something she didn't intend to say, a slip. He was sure of it.

"To work with the environmental service. My job." It was a quick response, but the comment still bothered him.

"And what different direction are you headed in?" Karen Chaney turned and looked at him, her back against the stove.

"You, Larkin. Okay? I like you."

"I like you, too."

"Dammit, Sam, that's not what I mean. I mean 'I like you.' "

"I just said, I like you, too, Karen." He was having fun.

"Oh hell." She came to him, put her arms around his neck and kissed him full on the lips. It was a hard kiss that softened as their lips opened. When the kiss ended, she said, "I've never done that before."

"What?"

"Kissed a man before he kissed me. Am I too forward?"

"No. It is the second date after all. I'd have gotten around to it. Actually thought about it on the way out here."

"You were planning?"

"Absolutely."

"So what were you thinking?" she asked in a husky voice.

"Whether you would kiss me back or put me in handcuffs."

"We could do both." She grinned.

"Now you're being too forward; I'm not into handcuffs," he said, "but I am into dinner because if we don't get back to that we'll never get back to this."

"Is that a promise?"

"I don't see any way out of it now," he said with a smile.

It wasn't exactly Pascal's Manale barbecued shrimp, but it was close enough. There wasn't a lot of conversation; they were both trying to determine what their position was now that their relationship had obviously changed. She asked him about his travels with the merchant marine, which he had told her about, and he asked about her family. He never mentioned his and she didn't ask.

After they cleaned up the kitchen, Karen poured coffee, turned off all the lights, and they went to sit on the sofa and watch the river. There was always boat traffic on the weekend— travelers, day sailors and fishermen—a river of lights trading back and forth. Karen curled her legs under her and leaned into him, putting her head on his chest.

"What are you thinking, Sam?" He didn't know what to say because he didn't know what he was thinking. He was just enjoying the comfort of her presence. "Would you really have made the first move if I hadn't?" she asked. If he said he didn't know, she would be insulted, but he truthfully didn't know.

"I think so." His answer didn't seem to bother her.

"I choose to think so; I just didn't want to wait for you to get around to it."

"Probably a good idea. I'm not very fast," he said putting his hand under her chin and lifting her face to kiss her. This was a different kiss. He could feel the texture of her lips, her tongue moving inside his mouth. He felt the smoothness of her teeth and was aware of the sweet smell of her.

"Can I be forward again?" she asked.

"I like forward," he answered.

Karen got up from the couch, took his hand and led him up the spiral staircase to her bedroom. There were no words. She took a book of matches from an end table beside the king-sized bed and lit several candles. The candle-glow, picking up the highlights of her hair and creating soft shadows from her high cheek bones, complimented her.

There were ten or twelve large, white, decorator pillows carefully arranged on the white duvet that covered the white wrought-iron bed. It looked like a cloud. She removed half of them and left the rest, pulled back the duvet and, without hesitation, began removing her clothes. Larkin felt his heart surge as she revealed herself to him. There was no shy coyness in her actions, yet there was a shared privacy in what she was doing. Her breasts were not large, nor was her waist, her hips or her thighs, and her stomach was flat; she was perfectly proportioned. He could only look with admiration.

When she was completely naked, she came to him and gently kissed his lips, as she began unbuttoning his shirt. She moved her head down and kissed his chest. He was lean and smooth, the build of a dancer.

Lying on the bed, facing each other, they kissed as he rubbed the small of her back. The perfume in her hair and the heat in her body enveloped him. He kissed her breasts. He moved his tongue between them and slowly eased down her stomach. He could hear her breath getting labored. Her hair was soft. He took her in his mouth gently until he felt her responses quickening. He moved up to kiss her lips, and she lifted a leg over him. When he entered her, there was no awkward searching; they joined without effort and made love slowly. He heard her try to say something as she reached her climax, but the spasms constricted her throat and no intelligible sound came out. He felt the tension lift from her though the muscles in her stomach and thighs were still contracting. She put her head on his shoulder.

There was no need for talk. There were no questions because there were no answers. They both understood that. They wanted each other on this night. There were no presumptions about tomorrow or the day after that; those days would take care of themselves. Neither of them knew if it would ever happen again, though they supposed that it would. This night had been an exploration.

It was close to three o'clock when Sam pulled himself from the bed and began putting on his clothes. He could not take his eyes off Karen Chaney, lying on her side, facing him, still sleeping, the curves of her hip and her breasts as perfect as any artist might make them. It was hard to believe that only a few hours before he had been inside her, sharing an intimacy so private, so guarded and protected.

He didn't slip into his boat shoes until he was downstairs. Turning toward the front door, he saw a red light flashing on the answering machine sitting on the counter that served as a pass-through from the kitchen. There were no telephone calls while he was there, and he couldn't imagine Karen ignoring a call-received signal before he arrived. It was puzzling. For a moment he considered that they might have been so taken with passion they didn't hear the phone ring, but he remembered seeing one on the table beside the bed. He paused and listened for any sound from the second floor, but there was only silence. He couldn't let it lie. He turned on the counter light and looked at the machine. It was different than any he had ever seen before.

There was a ringer switch, which was turned to the OFF position, a switch that was labeled "message center," which was turned to the ON position, and a MUTE switch that was turned on. The digital message display button was set on a four hour delay, which meant that the call did come while they were in bed. There were three lights: blue, red and green, which he didn't understand. It was obviously not equipment that could be purchased at your local Radio Shack. His curiosity about what words were behind the flashing light gnawed at him, but there was nothing he could do.

He looked around the room. Nothing else caught his attention. He went into the guest room. There was a double louvered-door closet, but it was locked. The lock itself appeared to have been recently installed; the paint around the key receptacle was scratched. It was curious. Who locked louvered closet doors? As he let himself out the front door, his mind was in turmoil. Of one thing he was certain, Karen Chaney was not just a wildlife conservation officer. What unnerved him was why she was here, what she was doing and how he might be involved. He tried to convince himself that what Skeeter Crewes said was accurate, and after what had just happened, it seemed plausible, but his self-protective instincts couldn't accept it. He wondered if their lovemaking were job-related then put that thought aside.

When Sam walked into his house, his own answering machine was signaling a message. He pressed the PLAY button. It was a musky, feminine voice.

"I heard you leave, Sam. It wasn't very kind; you didn't even say goodbye, but I'll forgive you. I loved everything you did to me, and I miss your being here to hold me. As I said, I didn't plan on you. I didn't intend to ever miss anyone again. When can I get another appointment? Good night and thank you."

He was smiling when the message began to rewind.

CHAPTER 10

The sun was hot, and she had been lying in it for two hours, chastising herself for all the damage she was doing to her skin. She used a thirty sun block, heavily, but didn't kid herself. Her problem was that the heat on her skin, the quiet hush of the ocean, and the salt air was an addiction, and since it lay just outside the door to her house, Morgan Hannah found it difficult to resist. Her relationship with the sun and the heat was cleansing on a spiritual level, but it was also sexual. She loved the feeling of the little rivulets of perspiration that coursed down her arms, between her breasts and down her thighs. It was a purification, quite sensual.

It was surprising to her that at her age her body had developed a new level of eroticism. During the courting years and her marriage, sex was always enjoyable; Ben Hannah was not unskilled and it had never been a problem. Now, however, she seemed to be operating with a new-found freedom. She was more adventurous, open to new things and saw her body as a source of pleasure. Without reason, the restrictive boundaries in all areas of her life had disappeared and that made life sweet.

She was considering an offer Bill Reichert made to her on Wednesday to go to Las Brisas in Acapulco for a few days. He had business in Mexico and could use the resort as his base. It would be a vacation, no heavy thoughts or decisions, and, other than the work he had to take care of, they could do whatever she wanted. The idea was exciting. It was strange that with all the traveling she and her husband had done, they had never been to Mexico. Ben was afraid of running into Mexican bandits, being kidnapped or, on a less serious level, getting sick from bad water. What she knew really held him back was that he couldn't abide seeing the poverty of the country. He had heard devastating horror stories from friends, and Ben Hannah possessed a well-maintained guilt about being successful and wealthy. Lying on the beach, she made up her mind that when Bill called, she would agree to go. Maybe, for once, he could relax into several days of pleasure.

Morgan was just opening her eyes to get up and gather her beach gear when a shadow fell across her.

"I hardly ever see you and now twice in a couple of weeks," Charlie Clay said. "It's quite a pleasure. How are you?" he asked as she sat up.

"Hello, Charles." He was wearing white shorts and a blue denim shirt, unbuttoned all the way down the front.

"Do you do this every day?" he asked.

"Most. I know it's not good for me, but what can I say?"

"I can't see that it's done any great physical damage."

"Not yet; wait a few years. You must be spending more time out here. I don't think I saw you at all last year, just heard rumors of your existence."

"I hope the rumors were good ones," he said.

"Well, now, if they were good, would you want them to be rumors?"

"Point taken. You think logically, too. I believe I'd better consider you dangerous, Ms. Hannah."

"I hope so." She smiled. "Everything I've heard has been good, Charles. You didn't answer my question: Aren't you spending more time out here? Seems I've not only seen you, but I've seen your car in the driveway more than usual."

"Guess I'd better start using the garage; looks like I'm too easy to account for." He laughed at their parrying. "And, yes, I have become a little more at ease about being out here. It's a lovely place. I had almost forgotten." His mind wandered elsewhere for a moment.

"Yes, it is. Would you like to come in for a drink?" she asked.

"I would love to. Unfortunately, I have to get back to town. You know, Morgan, may I call you Morgan?"

"Of course."

"I have to be honest with you; I didn't come out on the beach by accident." She could see the discomfort growing in his face.

"That sounds ominous," she said.

"Not really. I just thought you might help me with something."

"And what is that?"

"Bill Reichert." It wasn't a surprise that he knew about their relationship; many people did, but it was the first time someone she didn't know ever faced her with it. And why Charles Clay? "I don't want to pry, though I guess that's what I'm doing. Bill and I do a lot of business together, and I've noticed he's been kind of on edge lately, a little short-tempered, hyper. You know. He's also a good friend, and I just thought you might give me some insight into what's bothering him. You don't have to say anything if you don't want to."

His statement threw her. She sat silently, not knowing what to say. There was no way to know whether Charles Clay was aware that Bill had invited her to Mexico, and she didn't want to get Bill in trouble with a business partner. Answers were difficult to come up with. Oblique attack.

"What kind of business do you all do?" she asked.

"Oh, just banking stuff. You know how it works: he does the banking for me; I do legal work for him. Normal stuff, but he's a friend and I'm concerned."

"I don't know of anything, Charles. I haven't seen as much of him lately as I used to. He gets that way, you know. The bank. Isabel." Bring it out in the open.

"I guess it is something like that. Just thought I'd ask."

"Can't help you, I'm afraid," she said with a smile that put an end to his questioning.

"By the way, how's that friend of yours I met?"

"Friend? Oh, Brad Coleman. Haven't talked to him since that day."

"He was intriguing," she said smiling.

"I'm sure he would say the same about you. Well, I must be going. Good to see you again, Morgan."

"You too, Charles," she said as he turned and started back up the beach toward his house.

"That was interesting," she said to herself as she gathered her things to go back into the house.

She had only been inside for a few minutes when the telephone rang.

"Hello?"

"Hi," Bill Reichert said. "I tried earlier, but you must have been on the beach."

"I just came in," she said.

"Have you thought it over? The trip?"

"Yes, I think it would be fun. Three days?"

"Actually four nights and three days. We'll get in Tuesday night and leave on Saturday morning. I'll come over tonight and give you all the details."

"Not tonight, Bill; I already have plans."

"Do you want to explain that?" he asked, obviously angry.

"No. I have plans for this evening, that's all. I thought we agreed—"

"Fuck. I invite you to a world-class resort for a few days of living the high life, and you've got 'plans' you can't tell me about? I don't believe this, Morgan."

"I think I went a week without hearing from you."

"You know what that was." His anger was growing, which fomented her own.

"No, as a matter of fact, I don't because I didn't ask. Look, let's forget it. It was a bad idea anyway. You go and do your business and call me when you get back."

"No, godammit! I don't want to go without you, but I have to go." There was silence on the line. "I'm sorry, Morgan. I'm sorry. I want you to go with me. I won't ask about your plans; just say you'll go."

"I want to, Bill, but I won't be curtailed by any relationship. It's for fun, remember? That's what you said when it started, and that's what I told you a couple of weeks ago. I'll go and we'll have fun, and maybe neither of us will be able to walk when we get back—I hope so—but please, please don't get possessive. That will end it all faster than you can dial my telephone number."

"I'm sorry. Look, can I call you tomorrow? I'll have times and flight numbers and all of the information."

"Why don't you just come out tomorrow and tell me. Bring some brochures if you can. I'd like to see where I'm going. Four o'clock?"

"Four," he said. "I love you, Morgan."

"See you tomorrow."

Morgan Hannah put down the receiver. She didn't hear Bill Reichert throw his telephone across his office, putting a hole in the wall.

Isabel Reichert was smiling. It was a beautiful day and she was working in her yard. She enjoyed the feel of the earth on her fingers as she weeded and mulched the flower bed that lined the walkway to her house. It was good therapy. Old jeans, a sweatshirt and a bandanna covering her hair, planting flowers, no district hassles; it was all good, but it wasn't the reason she was smiling. Bill Reichert had made a mistake.

Earlier in the week, he had informed her of an upcoming trip to Salt Lake City for a banking conference. She could accompany him, but he didn't ask, and she had been to enough banking conferences in her life. Strait-laced accountant types and old men flaunting their dishonesty and net worth. The idea of going did not appeal to her at all. San Francisco, New York, L.A. maybe, but not Salt Lake City, Utah.

Then she picked up a call on the answering machine from a clerk at the Las Brisas Resort in Acapulco. It seems they had lost his office number, and an aggressive clerk had sought out the home phone of the only William Reichert in Covington, South Carolina, to determine if he had received the confirmation and information regarding his upcoming trip. Las Brisas was a long way from Salt Lake City.

She didn't know what she would do with the information, but the possibilities were exciting. She had time to think about it. Regardless, it would provide her with another kick in the balls for the arrogant bastard. Putting that aside, she began to think about herself, her freedom and the possibilities of a future.

After their one evening together in her townhouse, Karen Chaney's job forced a postponement of any further trysts with Sam Larkin. It wasn't the way she wanted it; she had replayed their time together a number of times to the point that some of their most intimate moments invaded her dreams and caused her to awaken warm and moist. They spoke on the telephone without shyness or hesitation—on her part anyway. The Monday after, she was assigned an undercover operation in cooperation with the U.S.

Fish and Wildlife Service in Myrtle Beach to expose an illegal clamming operation. Posing as an outlaw clammer's wife, she sold clams taken from illegal beds to seafood suppliers. The takedown was successful, and she returned to Covington on Thursday.

Sam had not called. She had been at odds with herself all afternoon, and it was now past eight o'clock. She would wait another hour.

The ring of the fax machine brought her out of her thoughts. She went to the closet, unlocked the door and watched the paper feeding out of the top of the machine. When it stopped, she tore it off.

FROM: Commander Buck Link, Louisiana State Police
TO: K. Chaney

> *Karen:*
> *I received a follow-up call from my friend at Vital Statistics. It appears the subject of your inquiry was married to a Celine Aguillard in Lake Charles, LA, on February 3, 1975. They divorced in November of 1976. No other details. Hope it is helpful. I'm counting on that dinner you promised.*
> *Buck*

Karen felt her knees go weak and sat down on the floor. Married. Why hadn't he said anything? Why hadn't it come out in their conversations. More rationally, had she told him about her personal life? It was different; she was working. No, it wasn't different. He appeared as closed in his everyday life as she was undercover. She read the name again. *Celine Aguillard.* Maybe a check on her would reveal something. Link could do it, but she didn't want to be a bother. Not yet anyway. Dougherty could do it, but she was nervous about where that might lead. It was almost nine and Sam had not called.

"Shit!" she said, went to the phone and dialed.

"Dougherty," came the voice on the other end.

"Hello, Blue."

"Belle. Been wondering about you. What's going on?"

"How many times a day do you ask that question?" she asked.

"I have no idea. What's happening? I haven't heard from you."

"I've been buying clams undercover up in Myrtle Beach. Takedown went smoothly and I'm back."

"I guess clams is a start. One small step for clams; one giant leap toward a drug bust." She could imagine his grin.

"Don't be sarcastic. I made an arrest this week, have you?" she asked.

"If you're trying to hurt me, you did. Anything else to report? Any progress?"

"Nothing specific. Listen, I need some information. A name came up. I don't think it means a thing, but I'd like you to check it out. No alerts to anyone because I don't think there's a chance she's involved in anything. I just want to make sure."

"Boyfriend's girlfriend?"

"Fuck you, Neil. No. The name came from an undisclosed source, and I'd like it quietly checked out without ruining her life. Write it off to curiosity or good investigation. Take your choice." She was angry, but that happened every time she talked to Dougherty lately.

"Name?"

"Celine Aguillard." She spelled the name. "The only location I have is Louisiana. Maybe around Lake Charles."

"Louisiana?"

"People move around." She said it flatly.

"See what I can do and call you."

"Thanks." She hung up the phone, went to the sofa and laid down. She was tired, wondered if it were depression and closed her eyes.

The nap on the couch lasted less than an hour. When she awoke, it was only ten-thirty, and her mind was a collage of thoughts, all centering on Sam Larkin and Celine Aguillard. Thinking about what she had accomplished in her investigation, she could come up with nothing. So much for being a government agent. Unless Sam Larkin turned out to be a bad guy, she had pretty much neglected her duty.

Questions and recriminations kept her awake most of the night. Reading didn't work, soft music and sinking into the comfort of the sofa didn't bring rest, and the bed brought Sam back into the picture. It was miserable. When she went for a run at five-thirty, it was still dark. She ran to the marina, sat briefly on a swing at Riverfront Park and then jogged back. She took a shower, fixed some fruit for breakfast, read the paper and waited for someone to call and tell her what to do with her day. Then she went back to bed.

At three-thirty she was awakened by the telephone.

"Hello?" she said, trying to wake up.

"Did I wake you?" Neil Dougherty asked.

"I guess you did; I didn't sleep much last night."

"How come?"

"I don't know. Just one of those nights."

"Is the information you asked me to get enough to keep you awake?" he asked.

"Just an inquiry, I said. Nothing critical." Oh, how the lies roll off the tongue, she thought. "I can't imagine that you've found anything this quickly."

"Never underestimate a Blue Duck. Hold on a second." She could hear him shuffling papers and Wilson Pickett singing in the background. "Okay, here we are. You owe me for this one, Belle. I'm working in the dark here. I like to know what I'm looking for, makes it easier to find. But I did find something interesting. Confusing really."

"So kill the foreplay and tell me what you found." Her hand began to shake.

"Celine Aguillard. Spelled it right by the way. Celine Aguillard married a Samuel T. Larkin in Lake Charles, Louisiana, on February 3, 1975, and divorced him in November of the following year."

"What grounds?"

"Desertion. He pleaded *nolo contendere*."

"So he didn't admit or deny it, and she agreed to no further action." Desertion didn't sound like the Sam Larkin she knew. "No settlement?"

"That's the interesting thing. Nothing then. Not a dime, but four years later, according to her 1040, she listed sixty-eight thousand dollars of income designated as alimony."

"Where in the world did that come from?"

"Be patient and I will tell you, my love. It wasn't real difficult to run the banks in Shreveport, where she now lives, and locate her accounts. It was, however, difficult to get the bank to run a record of her 1977 accounts without getting a warrant, which I could not have done in any case, since I am not involved," he said with a note of sarcasm.

"Put a lid on it, Neil. So, tell me, how did you do it?"

"You don't want to know, but it took less than an hour. I'm good."

"Give," she said.

"In February of 1977, she made a single deposit to her savings account of sixty-eight thousand dollars. Of course, a deposit of that amount had to be reported, as well as the check—if it was a check—being copied. Guess what?"

"What?"

"It was a check, and it was drawn on the account of . . . ready?"

"Damn it, Blue." It was his game; a carryover from childhood, she often told him.

"The United States Treasury Department." There was a stunned silence.

"Wait a minute; I thought you said it was alimony," Karen said, her voice reflecting her confusion.

"That's what I said." She knew he was rejoicing in her bewilderment.

"So you're saying the government paid her alimony."

"That's what I said."

"I've never heard of anyone being divorced from the government, although I do know a few people who are married to it." They both laughed. "What does it mean?"

"I have no clue, but I do have a couple of ideas."

"Would you like to share them?" she asked.

"Not yet. Give me a couple of days."

"Don't panic, Blue."

"Maybe someday you'll be confident enough to confide in me. Watch your back, Babe."

"I will," she said and put the receiver down. She looked out the window and saw what looked like a thirty-eight-foot sailboat heading toward the marina. For some reason, the slow movement of the sailboat and the useless lethargy she had been experiencing coincided and forced her to make a decision.

She put on a pair of white shorts, an open-collar shirt, and sandals, then headed for the city dock. All the way there she wondered if she were making a big mistake. He might not be home. That would not be a big mistake, just a waste of time. He might not want to see her, not invite her in. Humiliating. A mistake. He might have someone else there with him. Very big mistake. None of those cautionary thoughts made her turn around, however. When she started the boat and began easing it out of the slip, her adrenaline was surging. Nothing ventured, nothing gained.

She was nervous as she pulled into Sam Larkin's dock. There was no movement that she could see, or any indication that he was at home. For a moment, she thought about turning around and heading back to Covington, but she had come this far. Her legs felt weak as she climbed the stairs to his deck. Facing the sliding glass doors, she became totally confused as to what her next step should be. She leaned away from the sliders to eliminate the glare, so she could see into the sun room. There was no one there.

She waited a moment, giving anyone who might have heard her coming up the stairs time to make their presence known, but there was nothing—no sound, no movement. The doorbell button stared at her, but she was reluctant to push it. Who knew what might be going on in the rooms she couldn't see into? The more she thought, the more paranoid she felt. She pushed it, and there was no response. It was a relief. As she turned to leave, Sam came down the driveway in his running clothes. He carried a towel in his hand and had slowed to a cool-down pace before he saw her.

"Looks good from here," she said, leaning over the railing. She felt the blood come back into her legs and her heart rate begin to slow.

"Hey. I didn't know you were back; I thought you'd call," he said.

"I thought you'd call to check. I'm tired of chasing you, Larkin."

"Well, if that's what it takes," he said with a grin and a shrug of his shoulders. His clothes were soaked with perspiration. "You don't want to touch me, but if you'll make yourself a drink and let me get cleaned up, we can talk about dinner."

"I'm in a state boat, Sam."

"Not planning on going home, are you?" She looked at him and smiled.

"I guess not. Get in the shower."

CHAPTER 11

Even in the shade it was hot. Turner Lockett was sitting in his boat, pulled up against the bank of Jones Run Creek under the spreading limbs of a huge live oak. Despite the heat, he wore a dark green, long-sleeved shirt and worn jeans to protect his skin from the sun and hungry insects.

It was late Sunday afternoon, and he was dividing his time between watching Skeeter Crewes's place and Sam Larkin's house. Clay was adamant about knowing the schedules of the people at each place and who came and went. The time spent watching Larkin's place moved faster. Nothing at all to see at Crewes's, other than his going to work in the morning and a couple of pickaninies playing out in the dirt yard that Mrs. Skeeter swept with a grass broom every afternoon. Larkin's was more entertaining, especially for the past two days when the female water cop came to spend the weekend. More than once he wished he could see what was going on inside the house. "Bet she fucks like a mink just to prove she ain't a lesbian," he told himself the first night she spent there.

On Saturday morning he watched her come to the sliding glass doors. He thought she was naked, but by the time he got his binoculars up, she was gone. The woman had a good body; even when she was in uniform, he could tell that. Both mornings she and Larkin had come out to the deck to have coffee, and, from what he could see, she was only wearing an over-sized tee shirt. Probably one of Larkin's. Through the glasses he could tell her tits weren't huge, but they were more than a handful.

He opened his cooler and saw one, lone beer remaining. He popped it and made up his mind to go to Harry Tom's for more. He wasn't about to sit out in the heat all afternoon and another night with nothing to drink; the eyes would come back. A couple of times since he had been on watch, he had felt the eyes. At one point he'd even imagined he saw something in the grass and scrub along the edge of the bank, but it only looked real for a few

136

seconds, then it was gone. A shadow. He had a couple of high-powered joints in the cooler that would help if old Jared's ghost tried to spook him again. He resented being given all the shit work to do, but it was better than sitting at the trailer surrounded by spirits.

It was only a twenty-minute run to the dock. The last beer was empty by the time he got there, and he was beginning to feel it and the eleven that went before it. After docking, he picked up the cooler and went inside. Harry Tom put in two six-packs and topped it off with ice while Turner made a phone call. Charlie Clay answered on the first ring.

"Charles Clay."

"Charlie? It's me, Turner. I been watchin' them two houses for two days an ain't nothin' happenin' in either one of 'em."

"Nothin'? Nobody come or go?"

"Skeeter goes to work and comes home; missus don't go nowhere. She's got the kids to look after."

"What about Larkin? Nobody comin' or goin' there either?"

"Oh, I imagine there's lotsa comin' goin' on there." He laughed. "That female water cop—name's Chaney, Ray Breslin told me—she's been out here since Friday night. They've been eatin' regular out on the deck, but that's about all I've seen."

"Been there since Friday night you say?"

"Yep. Hardly come up for air near as I can tell. Probably won't be able to get her knees together, she don't leave soon." He found himself laughing; it had been awhile.

"You drunk, Turner?"

"Hell, no," he said. "You give me a job to do, I do it. Now do you want me to stay out there?"

"Give it till the woman leaves. I doubt she'll stay tonight; tomorrow's a work day. If she leaves, wait a half hour and see if Larkin goes anywhere. If he dudn't, call it a night."

"I still don't know what all this is for; I thought you already decided on Crewes's place?"

"Dammit! Shut up, Turner. You don't know who's listening to you prattle on, on the phone. I am sure there are other people in the store."

"But why, if—" Lockett tried again.

"Because we have to know everything that goes on in that area all the time. I don't want any surprises. You never know what might happen and what contingency plans we might need, and why in hell am I explainin' myself to you? You're gettin' paid."

"Okay, Charlie, I'll go back out there."

"Call me tomorrow, Turner."

"Yeah." Lockett hung up the phone and went to pay Harry Tom for the beer.

After pulling out of sight of the dock, Lockett let the boat idle in open water while he opened a beer for the trip back to Larkin's. He would pass by Skeeter's on the way and give it a glance, but it was Larkin's he was interested in.

He let the boat idle back into the shade of the oak tree, two hundred yards across the creek from Larkin's house. The water cop's boat was still there. Maybe she was planning to spend the night again, get up early and make it into work. "Man, would I like a woman like that. Might even marry her," he said to nobody. He opened another beer, sat back in the boat and focused on the house. He knew he should eat one of the fried baloney sandwiches he'd brought with him, but he wasn't hungry.

He wondered what it would be like to be married. It wasn't something he'd ever thought about. Never thought there was much chance of it. Especially to someone like the Chaney woman. One who could hunt and fish and shrimp with him. One who could see in the outdoors what he saw and appreciate it. One who could recognize in him smarts that indoor people never saw and who would realize he wasn't dumb. That and her body to hold all night, every night. "Whew! That would be more than a man could stand," he said. Of course, he didn't know whether she felt that way about all those things or not, but it would seem so, given her job.

As the day waned, Turner found it more difficult not only to focus on Larkin's house, but also to stay awake. He had been up for over fifty hours straight. He thought he might have dozed briefly because he remembered something about being married, which had to be some kind of dream. The third six-pack of beer was gone. There was another, but he left the beer and moved on to one of the joints he brought with him.

The grass took its toll. Charlie said to wait until the woman left, stay another half hour and then go home. The only problem was that it didn't look like she was going to leave, and he couldn't last much longer. He lit the joint, took a couple of deep hits then put it out and back into his shirt pocket. Two hits at a blow with this stuff was enough.

It got to dark without his noticing. He must have fallen asleep again because the woman's boat was no longer at Larkin's dock. There was no recollection of seeing her leave, and no way of knowing if Larkin had gone with her. "No way of knowin' nothin'. Shit!" he said to the boat. It was the one familiar thing he had to talk to; they had shared three days together. "Fuck!" he yelled. There was no way to know when the Chaney woman had left, so he didn't know if he had stayed a half-hour afterwards or not. Fifteen more minutes and he would head home. He fumbled in his pocket, brought out the joint, lit it and took three big hits before he put it out.

He waited what he thought was fifteen minutes, though he couldn't be sure because the high from the grass was accelerating. Regardless, he was going. He pulled anchor, started the engine and began moving the boat away from the bank. He waved goodbye to an imaginary Larkin standing on his deck. Maybe he was standing there; he couldn't see clearly enough to tell. His eyelids felt like they weighed a thousand pounds each.

"That's some shit," he said to himself. When he turned back to look at where he had been anchored to judge the distance to the channel, Jared Barnes was standing at the edge of the woods, staring at him. His head was as misshapen as it had been when he'd dumped him overboard. One eye was closed and the other was staring straight at him. Lockett rubbed his eyes and looked back. He was still there. He could almost discern a smile on the man's face. He stood perfectly still, but the eye had life and it was burning into him.

"You're not Jared, you son-of-a-bitch," he yelled, unconcerned that anyone might hear. "You leave me alone. I know you're not there. Fuck you, Ghost," he screamed and then sobbed. "Oh Lord, oh Lord, oh Lord." He hit the throttle hard and headed toward the channel. He wanted to get away, get home. Suddenly he was flying. Not going fast, literally flying.

The boat had gone up in the air for some reason. Everything was moving slowly. Half-speed. Like in a movie. Graceful. And then smacked into the water. He tried to hold on to the steering wheel mounted in the small console, but the weight of his body and its forward momentum forced his grip apart and launched him into the darkness.

He struck the water on the back of his head, causing him to skip across it like a flat stone thrown at a low angle. On his last skip, his back arched and forced him down into the blackness, wrenching his arms backward and upward, tearing the muscles and tendons in his shoulders. He couldn't see anything; it enveloped him. He realized he was underwater and had to get to the surface. The air in his lungs was expended when he hit the water and went under. There was no reserve. A fire burned in his chest. He thought about the boat circling and coming back over him, cutting him to pieces. He feared being cut up. Blood mixing with water was one of the most frightening sights he could think of. He had to swim out a few yards from where he was and then move to the surface. He began swimming as hard as he could, the pain in his shoulders and arms excruciating, trying to hold on to the last vestige of oxygen in his body.

When he realized he could go no further, he pulled toward the surface, but something was wrong. Terribly wrong. He felt plant growth all around him. Suddenly his hands, reaching out to pull the water behind him and propel him toward the surface, struck mud and shell. He tried to recover, turn himself upside down and go in the opposite direction, but it was too late; he was out of air. He fought the deep breath that he took, tried to halt it, but he couldn't hold it back. He felt the water filling his lungs, inching its way up like the red line in a thermometer is the way he saw it. Maybe there was a bubble of air at the top that would save him, but there wasn't. His last thought was of Jared Barnes watching him from the edge of the woods.

Karen Chaney's spending the weekend was a total surprise, albeit, as it turned out, a pleasant one. But Larkin was not accustomed to allowing anyone else to make his plans for him, and she had taken it upon herself to show up unannounced. It amazed him that he allowed it to happen. Once she was there, it all became too comfortable. It continued to be difficult to relax around her, which was ridiculous considering all of the things they had done together; however, her unbridled curiosity caused him to guard everything he said. If she was after something, she hadn't gotten it. Still, it bothered him.

The call came into the sheriff's office at one o'clock Monday afternoon. They, in turn, notified the Matthew's Island Fire Department and the Covington office of the South Carolina Environmental Service. By one-thirty, two sheriff's department cars and a fire department rescue vehicle with a boat trailer were parked in the area surrounding Sam Larkin's house. Karen Chaney and Ray Breslin, notified of an overturned boat on Jones Run Creek, made high-speed runs from their respective positions in the Marion River backwaters near Covington and were anchored next to a twenty-foot Grady-White, the propeller of its Evinrude motor standing above the water's surface like a buoy marker. Upon his arrival, Ray Breslin identified the craft as belonging to Turner Lockett, which two of the deputies already knew.

After an hour of searching, no body had been recovered. Tramping through the mud edges of the creek bank, sheriff's deputies, who had been ferried across by the fire department rescue boat, began to weary of fighting the intense afternoon heat and seemingly repellent-resistant mosquitoes. The fact that the boat belonged to a man known for making his living off the waters of the area stimulated a more intense search than normal for clues as to what might have happened or, best case scenario, any sign of the survival of Turner Lockett.

"The only thing I can figure is that it was dark, and, for some reason or other, he didn't see that spit of land yonder and that dead pine stickin' out in the water." Breslin said to Karen and the deputy he had picked up on Larkin's dock when he arrived. "But even that dudn't make sense. That tree fell nine months ago durin' what we thought was gonna be Hurricane Chloe; he knew about that. Must've thought he was further away from the bank when he hit the throttle. Had to have been a ways back up the creek for that motor to get up enough speed to throw the boat upside down." It was obvious Breslin was enjoying his position of expertise.

"I can't imagine someone who knew these waters making a mistake like that," Chaney said. Breslin's explanation sounded logical, but it didn't sound realistic. She had known a lot of watermen in her days in the service, and the ones she knew could take a boat through a cypress swamp in the dead of night without a second thought.

"That's what dudn't make sense. Turner knew these waters like the back of his hand. Hell, I been out night fishin' with him, and he could maneuver through these creeks like he had night vision. There's somethin' in the grits that ain't gravy."

"Maybe somethin' went wrong with the boat," the deputy said.

"What could go wrong? It's a damned outboard. If the throttle had stuck, he'd of just killed the motor. He wudn't stupid."

"And we have no way of knowin' when all this happened." The deputy stated a fact that was a question.

"No way to tell until we find a body or Turner walkin' around somewhere. Body more'n likely," Breslin said.

"Well, he could be under the boat," the deputy said. "We'll have a diver in the water in a coupla minutes."

"He wouldn't be under there if he hit something," Chaney said. "He would have been thrown clear." The deputy gave her a disgusted look.

Shortly after the diver entered the water, a cooler popped to the surface next to the overturned craft. One of the deputies on the bank used a boat hook to pull it within reach. He put on a pair of gloves and pulled it up on land and opened it.

"Well, we might have a reason here. We got about sixteen, no, eighteen empties in here and a six-pack that idn't opened. Nothin' else."

"Still dudn't seem right," Breslin said. "Turner's been drinkin' on the water all his life."

"Got a body!" a voice from back up the creek hollered. Everyone turned toward a deputy on the bank about a hundred yards to the left of where they were anchored, directly across from Sam Larkin's dock.

Turner Lockett was wedged in the branches of a fallen water oak. The color of his wet shirt was a perfect match to the color of

the water, and the filigree of the leafless branches on the tree provided a camouflage that might have left him undiscovered for
days were it not for the face turned toward the sky at just the right
angle to catch the sun. It glowed like a warning beacon. One of
the deputies waded out to the body and, after fighting the entan-
glements of growth and dead tree limbs, managed to pull it to
land. Chaney and Breslin edged their boats to the bank, got out
and watched as the EMT began to examine the body.

"Can you tell anything?" Breslin asked.

"Well, he wasn't hit in the head with a hatchet or shot that I
can see, but, beyond that, who knows? I'd say he drowned, but
I'm not the coroner. I guess we'd better see about getting him in
a boat and across the creek. Want to give us a hand here?"

Sam Larkin was cutting a faculty meeting that would explain,
in detail, how final exams, final grades, locker clean-out and the
closing of school for the summer would be handled. It was
exactly the same way that it had been done for the past three
years. He decided when the meeting was announced that he
would not spend two hours hearing a repeat of things he already
knew. When his last class ended, he left.

He was shocked when he attempted to enter his driveway to
find two sheriff's department cars and a fire department emergency vehicle blocking his way. He parked on the shoulder of
Osprey Landing Road and hurried up the dirt drive. There was no
one in the vicinity of the vehicles. When he walked around the
house, he spotted the gathering across the creek. There was an
overturned boat and two Environmental Service boats, but, at the
distance he was standing, it was impossible to recognize any of
the people. He ran up to the deck, took the binoculars from the
hook where he kept them for wildlife observation, and stood
watching the operation that was going on across the water.

Lockett's boat was easily recognizable, even upside down.
He could see Karen Chaney and Ray Breslin observing as the
EMT technicians worked over a body he assumed to be Turner. It
was obvious there was little to be accomplished, and it was only
minutes before they began the task of putting the body into the
boat for transport to his side of the creek. When the boat moved

out, Larkin walked down the steps to meet them. Karen Chaney was the first across and pulled her boat into the dock, tied it off and walked toward Sam.

The fire department craft was much slower and was directed toward a part of the bank where it would have closer access to the emergency vehicle.

"Quite a reception, huh?" Karen said as she approached.

"What the hell happened?" Larkin asked.

"We really have no way of knowing, Sam. Somehow the boat turned upside down and threw Turner Lockett out. He drowned, as near as we can tell, but the coroner will have to make it official."

"That doesn't seem reasonable," Sam said. "Turner was born on this creek."

"Well, there are eighteen empty beer cans in his cooler, and, as they say, everybody has his day." As Sam looked at her, he had difficulty placing her only as an officer on duty and not the companion he had shared the weekend with. Somehow her job was lost during those two days. They hadn't spoken since she left the night before, so merging the two images was difficult.

"That doesn't make a lot of sense either. What would he be doing out here in the creek long enough to drink eighteen beers, and, even if he did, I don't think that would have stupefied him enough to make a fatal mistake. Was anyone with him?"

"Not that we can tell. They've walked the entire bank. If there was anything to find there, they wiped it out. It took quite awhile just to find him; he was hooked up half underwater in some tree limbs. What were you saying about why Turner was out here? That it didn't make sense," she said.

"Nothing maybe, but I know he doesn't have to fish long enough to drink eighteen beers to get all the fish he wants. He's a pro. And I don't think he would load the boat with that much beer if he didn't intend to drink it."

"Maybe some of the cans accumulated over several trips."

"Not likely."

"So what's your opinion?"

"I don't have one," he said. Conjecture wasn't a part of Sam Larkin. "Where'd Breslin go? I thought he'd stick to you like glue given a good excuse."

"He went ahead to get the report started."

His mind was still on why Turner Lockett was on the creek with eighteen empty beer cans in his cooler. It wasn't right, but he didn't want to get into that discussion.

"This beer can thing is bothering you, isn't it?"

"Not really."

"You lie," she said with a smile. "Never can predict people, Sam." She turned to see the gurney being lifted into the emergency vehicle. "I need to go talk to them," she said gesturing toward the EMTs. "And then I need to get back into town. Don't want to expose our friendship, do we?"

"I think we exposed it all weekend," he said with a smile.

"Hush. You gonna call me sometime?"

"When I get lonely."

"That could take years. Don't worry about the deputies, I'll answer whatever questions they might have for you. By the way, you didn't notice anything out of the ordinary or see anything suspicious over the last couple of days did you? Any unusual activities?" she asked with a grin.

"Nothing to speak of," he said, threw a hand in the air and started back up the stairs.

In ten minutes all of the vehicles, deputies and Karen Chaney were gone. Sam opened a beer, walked out on the deck and stared at the bank across the creek. Turner Lockett's boat, still upside down, was tied off to a tree at the water's edge. He wondered how long it would be there as a reminder. Flipping it would be a major salvage operation, but the boat wasn't his primary concern; Turner Lockett's presence in the creek was.

"Charlie, we might have a problem," Ray Breslin said into the phone at Harry Tom's boat dock.

"What's the matter, Ray?"

"Turner's dead." There was silence on the other end of the line.

"What happened?"

"Drowned, far as we could tell. He'd been drinkin' pretty heavy. We found eighteen empty beer cans in the cooler. Looks like he hit a submerged tree. Have no idea when it happened, so

I don't know if it was dark or not. The boat turned upside down and threw him out."

"He must've been doin' somethin' besides drinkin' beer. That dudn't sound like Turner. Where'd it happen?"

"Right across from Larkin's; that's why I called," Breslin said.

"Anybody have any questions as to why he might have been out there?"

"Not really. Karen Chaney couldn't believe that someone like him could have that kind of an accident."

"I been hearin' that name a lot lately. Does seem peculiar though, and I'm sure there will be questions and theories. I don't think there's anything to be done right now except for you to go over to his place and take a look around before the sheriff's deputies get out there. Make sure nothin's there that's not supposed to be there, nothin' obvious. But don't change anything unless it's somethin' that needs to be changed. He dudn't have any family, does he?"

"Not that I know of. I'll head over there right now. I don't think the deputies have thought that far ahead yet, but even if they have, I can get there faster on the water."

"You do that, Ray, and thank you. I'll be talkin' to you."

When Breslin got back in his boat, he headed directly to Turner Lockett's trailer. He didn't know what he was to look for, but he was certain that if there was anything that would give The Company away, he would recognize it.

It was a shame, he thought. He liked Turner. What he knew of him.

CHAPTER 12

Turner Lockett's trailer, ravished by years of wind and weather, was a collage of putty-colored metal and rust. Pieces of siding hung loose off the main body. That it was standing appeared a heroic feat. Turner's ten-year-old pick-up truck was parked in back, its road-worn and weather-beaten condition a perfect complement to the trailer.

A wire-spool and three cane-bottom chairs. whose seats were half-rotted and stretched to the falling-through stage, sat in the yard. To the left of the front stoop was a top-loading, collectible, red Coca-Cola box that still worked, evidenced by the orange electrical cord that ran to a junction box mounted on a two-by-eight stanchioned at the side of the trailer. When Ray Breslin lifted the top of the drink box, it was obvious Turner used it as his refrigerator. It was filled with a variety of early local vegetables that were in season, some from the small garden patch he kept in the side yard, milk, bread, mayonnaise and mustard and lunch meat, mostly bologna, he noticed.

There was nothing outside to indicate to Breslin that anyone had been there before him. The door was locked, but having apprehended poachers, out-of-season hunters, illegal clammers, shrimpers and various other kinds of outlaws for more than fifteen years, a mobile home door, locked or unlocked, was an open invitation for entry. He popped the lock, stepped inside and was hit with several days accumulated heat and the smell of something rotten.

To say the interior was a shambles would be an understatement. It wasn't that the place had been tossed; it was just the way Turner Lockett lived. Dishes filled the small sink; one corner was piled high with stacks of outdoor magazines; fishing rods were leaned in the others. One small table held a manually-operated shotgun shell loader, and a small television set sat on the kitchen counter next to the stove. One wall was mutilated with gutter nails that served as a hanging place for all of Turner Lockett's clothes.

There was no way to tell if anything had been disturbed because it looked as though what he saw was its normal state. He checked the kitchen table and the telephone stand to make sure Turner hadn't left anything written down that would jeopardize The Company. Satisfied that no one could find anything of an incriminating nature, he reset the lock on the door and stepped back outside. His shirt was wet and clinging to him. Droplets of sweat coursed down his back and continued downward between his buttocks. As he walked down the path to his boat, he shook his head in disbelief and disgust at the way the man lived.

He was tired. The heat in Lockett's trailer had sapped what little energy he had left after the morning's patrolling and working the accident scene all afternoon. It wasn't a long run back into Covington; there would be plenty of time to call Charlie Clay. Everything was all right; he was confident of that. Moving the boat into the creek, he turned for a final look at Turner Lockett's "home" and wondered what in hell the man spent his money on. Charlie told all of them to live conservatively, but what he had just seen was ridiculous. Turner had made a bundle. The money question was interesting; he'd have to remember to ask Charlie about that.

Karen Chaney had a premonition that it was a mistake, but her work ethic dictated that she should stop by the office and see if she could add anything to the report that Ray Breslin was filing. When she walked through the door, she knew she should have heeded her inner warnings. There was only one other officer present, and he assured her he had been there all afternoon and Ray Breslin had not come in. Her initial reaction was to turn around and leave—let the bag fall on Ray—but she didn't. She was angry that he so graciously offered to relieve her of the paperwork and then left it hanging. By tomorrow details would be fuzzy, and, perhaps, something of importance forgotten or overlooked. It was with great reluctance that she sat at her desk and began the process of detailing everything they knew or suspected concerning the death of Turner Lockett. She made the right decision in doing the work, she decided. Protect Ray. It wouldn't be wise to create enemies at this point; there was no way to know whom she might need on any given day.

She guarded herself in writing the report. It couldn't be perfect; they weren't used to that in the Covington office, and she didn't want to send up any red flags. Let them regard her lightly; it was safer that way. When it was adequate, she placed it in the supervisor's mail slot and left the building. She was weary, which was tougher than being tired.

After a quick stop at the grocery store to pick up a frozen dinner, she arrived at her townhouse at eight-fifteen. It was an ungodly hour to have to cook dinner when one was alone, but she was hungry; there had been no food since breakfast. She checked for messages and saw that there were none, which she accepted with mild disappointment. She put the Salisbury steak dinner in the oven and got in the shower.

When the hot water hit her body, its relaxing effect tempted her to forgo dinner and just go to bed, but, although she was tired, her mind had not ceased working. All of the questions Sam Larkin posed to her were still active. He was proving impossible to crack, and that was keeping her off balance. She toweled off, put on a terry cloth robe, and went back down to the kitchen. She took the foil container out of the oven and poured a glass of iced tea, then she went into the living room to eat.

With Sam came Turner, imposing himself into her thoughts. It wasn't only Sam's questions about the improbability of a man like Lockett's having such an accident, but Ray Breslin had found it implausible himself. She was confident Sam was correct: there was more to it than an extended period of fishing and drinking beer, but she hadn't pushed him on it. The one thing she didn't need was Sam Larkin getting in the way.

She was halfway through dinner when the telephone rang.

"Well, Belle, you are behaving." Dougherty said. "Home this early. Of course there could be ten people in the other room." He laughed.

"If there were, I wouldn't have answered the phone, Blue. To what do I owe the honor of this call?"

"Anger," he said firmly. She was startled.

"Anger?"

"Yes. I'm damned angry, Karen." There was no humor in his voice; he was serious. "I'm your supervisor and your friend, I thought. That was what we decided, wasn't it?"

"Well, we did. What are you talking about?"

"Why in God's name aren't you honest with me?"

"Honest? Neil, I . . ."

"Samuel T. Larkin." She felt her knees go weak. "He just happens to live in Covington, South Carolina. Did you know that?"

"Yes," she said quietly. There was nothing else to do.

"You don't know him of course."

"I know him."

"In the biblical sense or just casually?"

"Fuck off, Blue. Okay? I screwed up taking the approach I did. And it's none of your business if I know him in the biblical sense or not. We're not married anymore and this is the reason why. You don't have to be my protector; I'm a big girl. I was when you met me, and you could never accept that. You treated our marriage like it was a stakeout." There was silence. After a moment she said, "I'm sorry. I shouldn't have said that; it was nobody's fault. It just didn't work. But it's over. I'm sorry I wasn't up front with you about Larkin."

"I'm sorry, too." It wasn't an apology; it was an admonishment.

"Obviously you pursued Sam Larkin. Why? I haven't even classified him yet," she said.

"Why did you want to know about Celine Aguillard?" She didn't have an answer. "I'm not sure you'll be able to classify Mr. Larkin very easily; it might have to come from the horse's mouth. The reason I pursued him was that the payment to Celine Aguillard wasn't right. Isn't right."

"Will you share what you found with me?" she asked without emotion.

"That's the reason I called. I think you should be very wary of him. I don't know everything yet, but I will."

"I'll take what you have."

"It's getting more interesting by the minute. It seems that the same year Celine Aguillard made her sixty-eight thousand dollar deposit from alimony, compliments of the U.S. Treasury, Samuel

T. Larkin came into money as well. It wasn't easy to trace, but I managed. He used S.T. Larkin and several other variations on his accounts."

"Accounts? How much was there?"

"There were separate payments over an eight-month period, direct deposited in nine different banks."

"How much total?" she asked.

"Best I can figure, two hundred eighty thousand dollars."

"You're kidding me."

"No, I'm not. I haven't been able to find out where his money originated; however, I think it would be a no-brainer, given the time frame, to assume the source was the same as Aguillard's. Problem is, his transactions were much more sophisticated and insulated."

"I guess that accounts for the house," she said, half to herself.

"House?"

"His house is too nice for a school teacher. Built a lot of it himself."

"You must know him pretty well," he said.

"Not as well as you do, obviously. It would be interesting to know what he did between Louisiana and South Carolina. From my calculations, there's six years missing; I don't know how long he spent on the house."

"I'll see what I can find." He paused. "It's because I care, Karen."

"Thanks, Blue, but let's not get into the past again, okay?"

"It's in the past," he said and hung up.

It was too late to finish eating dinner and she had lost her appetite. She packed the leftovers in a container and put it in the refrigerator with all of the other meals she had not finished lately. She turned out the lights and went up the stairs to bed. It felt solitary. She thought about Sam Larkin—damn him—and hoped sleep would come quickly.

Isabel Reichert thought about booking a flight to Mexico herself. Bill might have business there; she was willing to concede that, but she was certain he wouldn't be traveling alone. Morgan Hannah was just the latest in a long line of women he had cajoled into bed since their third or fourth year of marriage, maybe before that for all she knew. All of the reasoning she had come up with for hanging in the marriage for so long—even if it was hope or pride—transformed itself into self-admonishment and weakness. It was time to change all that.

For that very reason, she knew the fantasy of flying to Mexico might not be just a fantasy. It was something to consider.

Standing at her bedroom window, running through these thoughts, she couldn't help marveling at the view before her: the water, tar-black at night, shimmering like smoky silk in the moonlight, the bridge over to Matthew's Island, lit like a Christmas tree with the cars crossing it, producing the effect of blinking lights. She loved it, and she loved this house, this room, everything about it. If Bill Reichert ever tried to take it away from her, there was no doubt in her mind that she would kill him or have him killed. That thought, so real and so honest and so frequent of late, made her shudder.

She closed the curtains and began to undress for her bath, always the loveliest part of her day. The tub was old-fashioned, not an antique, but a replica. At the time she and Bill had renovated the house, they couldn't afford real antiques, but they did the best they could to move the decor back toward the age in which it was built. There was a lot of consternation over the bathroom fixtures, and when they ripped out the '50s-modern, lavender tub and replaced it with a deep, white porcelain one that was raised above the hardwood floor on four cast-iron feet, she wasn't at all sure she would be happy with it. She quickly recognized, however, that the depth had its advantages. They installed a hand-spray to make it easier to rinse, but that and the shower were the only twentieth-century concessions.

Isabel liked to feel the steaming water engulf her as she eased into the tub. It was enveloping, comforting, and gave her safety. She allowed her mind to float to a time when she still felt desirable—her youth, young adulthood—when she was a target for the young men who considered her prime.

Her hands moved up the inner sides of her thighs, teasing, then leaving them behind. Her body was a wonderment that she discovered even before puberty. When her fingers reached her breasts, she allowed her nails to circle the areola. She lifted one of her breasts high enough that she could touch the nipple with her tongue.

She cupped her left breast in the palm of her hand, while the fingers pinched the nipple to a point just short of pain. It caused her breathing to become deeper, more stressed and forced. She ran the fingers of her other hand along the folds between her legs. She let the water caress her as her hand moved downward. She felt her stomach begin its small contractions as her hips involuntarily arched. She held off until, helpless, she gave into the wave of relaxation that engulfed her.

CHAPTER 13

Bill Reichert chose Las Brisas because it was close to the airport. He had seen the Acapulco resort eight years earlier when he was attending an international bankers' meeting. His familiarity with the site lent some confidence. He wasn't a member of the international organization, but, at that point in his career, he wanted to learn everything he could about banking. It was before his involvement with The Company, when he thought that banking would be his only source of income, and president of the Covington Bank was not his idea of being at the top.

There was another reason for choosing the five-star resort. He needed Morgan to come. Las Brisas was romantic and beautiful, a paradise with private casitas, set like pink and white jewels on a hillside, facing a bay with clear, azure blue water. To swim in it was like bathing in the center of an aquamarine mounted in a fine setting. Each casita had its own pool, in which fresh, brightly colored hibiscus and other native flowers were floated each morning before the guests arose. Bougainvillea abounded. There were no radios or televisions, which assured freedom from anything negative or worrisome for the guests, except those things within them, brought along only because the owner was unable to leave them behind.

When he showed Morgan the travel brochures, there was no hesitation, no more questions or conditions. She didn't even take exception to the fact that, though they were traveling on the same flights, they would be strangers for all intents and purposes. Nor did she react when he asked her to follow directly behind him as he went through customs. It was for her protection, he suggested, in case there were any questions about her jewelry or valuables. Should anything of that nature occur, he assured her, he would step in and straighten it out. She laughed at the idea but agreed, though she didn't accept his reasoning.

Reichert had also been told by Bernardo Heironymous Ortega, the man he would meet the day after his arrival, that since Acapulco was primarily a tourist area where the visitor's comfort and safety were primary objectives, customs inspections were far less stringent than in most areas. Reichert was more than a little nervous about the four hundred thousand American dollars he carried in his luggage; however, Señor Ortega told him not to worry. If the money was discovered, declare it, the man said. Do exactly as he was told, and everything would be taken care of. Carry five thousand in cash that he would declare and keep it easily accessible should he need it, though there was no reason to think it would be.

Whether it was by arrangement—which he suspected—or because the inspectors were lax in their duties, none of the instructions were necessary. There were a few questions, a cursory glance at the luggage by an inspector, who was far more interested in Morgan Hannah, standing directly behind him, than anything the American might be trying to smuggle in. He congratulated himself for positioning her there for that very purpose.

After arriving at their casita, it took only minutes for Morgan to coax Bill Reichert into a bathing suit and down the natural steps in the hillside, onto the beach and into the water. As beautiful as the water was, he thought, Morgan floating on her back complemented it. It appeared he had made her happy for the first time in weeks.

After the beach, they returned to their casita where they swam in the pool, lay in the sun and let the anxiety and tension of travel leave their bodies. South Carolina and all that went with it was left far behind. They made love before dressing for dinner. Bill Reichert began to feel they were a couple, that he was connected to her. He wondered if he were beginning to gain some understanding of what the term "love" meant. What he was feeling was different than anything he had ever experienced with Isabel, but he felt no guilt about that.

When dinner was over, he took Morgan to the cliffs of La Quebrada to watch the cliff divers. It was a tradition begun in the thirties, young men rock-climbing the steep cliffs to an area a hundred and thirty or forty feet above a narrow cut of water that rose and fell in depth with the incoming breakers. The diver had to time it perfectly, or he would find the water too shallow when he entered it and be severely injured or killed. It had happened a number of times. Night was the best time to watch, Reichert remembered.

As they stood and watched the divers climb to their natural platform, the tension of the climb itself became almost unbearable. It taxed Reichert's imagination that anyone would take such a risk. He watched Morgan and saw the excitement and fire that the prospect of what they were going to see brought to her eyes.

Once in position, the divers would hold their torches high, say a prayer, and wait for the precise moment to launch themselves out into space beyond the outcroppings of rock that stood between them and the water. The torches flickered, as shooting stars falling from the night sky, until they hit the water and were extinguished. It was spectacular and breathtaking. Morgan's eyes became more brilliant and wet as she watched, mesmerized, he was sure, as much by the danger as the spectacle. They remained for more than an hour before Reichert was able to pull her away.

They went to the Esplanade and listened to a mariachi band playing at a sidewalk cafe for tourists who sipped on their Tecates or Coronas. It was like a movie; everyone was in love or so it seemed. Maybe it was just the Mexican night.

Upon their return to the casita, they sat by the pool and looked out over the water. Low, flat, shadow-clouds, dark, though not ominous, crossed the moon, and the lights along the hillside formed a necklace around the curve of the beach. Exhaustion finally overtook them and they went to bed. Reichert was glad they had made love earlier because he knew he was not capable when he lay down to sleep.

At nine-thirty the following morning, he left Morgan sleeping soundly and went to the resort entrance where a black Mercedes was waiting to take him to his meeting. He was unaware that his every move was being observed and had been since he boarded the plane in Savannah.

Bernardo Hieronymous Ortega was the primary representative of a private bank that dealt with large sums of money needing to be taken beyond the scrutiny of the United States Government and protected from the laws that governed its currency. Money brokers such as Ortega might use a bidding system to convert U.S. dollars for a fee or buy the dollars at a discount of up to ten percent. Either way, the seller was protected. With Ortega's bank, unlike some others, the bank managed the funds exclusively, which made Reichert skeptical.

In his research, he was surprised to find that there were hundreds of such private banks in existence throughout the world, their activities funneled through financial centers with little legislation or restrictions. One of the primary techniques was "layering." A transaction initiated in Mexico would continue a path, via wire transfers and other financial instruments, through a number of countries and islands, such as Aruba, Columbia, the Netherlands, the Antilles, Venezuela, the Canaries and other areas with similar lax restrictions, to blind corporations that would make the proceeds legally available in the states. Of all the underground banks that practiced this technique, Ortega's group was reputed to be the most sound and trustworthy.

Charlie Clay had received a letter of introduction to Ortega from John Descarté in Miami. Clay had done business with him before, and there were never any problems in any of their joint ventures, which, in Charlie Clay's mind, generated trust. On the other hand, trust was a commodity that Bill Reichert did not dispense easily.

Ortega was staying at the Pierre Marques Hotel. Located south of Acapulco on Revolcadero Beach, it was one of the original fine resorts in the area. By the time the Mercedes passed by Guitarron Point, Reichert was nervous. Despite Descarté's referral, the idea of handing over millions of dollars to a Mexican "banker" and his compadres, none of whom he knew, was frightening. He was even more suspicious of falling into a government sting operation, which was becoming commonplace.

When the car stopped in front of the Pierre Marques, the driver, who had said nothing—Reichert assumed he spoke no English, so he didn't try to begin a conversation himself—escorted the American to Ortega's suite and left him at the door.

"Buenos dias, Mr. Reichert. Come in. It is a pleasure to meet you," the man said as he held the door for Reichert to enter the luxurious suite. "An enjoyable drive down from Las Brisas, I presume?"

Bernardo Ortega was not what Bill Reichert imagined. He wasn't old, wasn't wearing a white suit, wasn't overweight, nor was his hair pulled back close to his head into a pony tail. And he didn't speak broken English. There was an accent, but his English was excellent. The man's features were refined, more Spanish than Mexican. Although he was no taller than Reichert himself, he appeared so because of a lean physique resembling that of a matador. Surprisingly, his eyes were blue. Mixed breed, Reichert thought, the meanest and toughest to trust. Bill Reichert dealt in clichés, and he was working overtime on Ortega. Appearing calm was difficult.

"It's a beautiful part of the country," Reichert said, trying to affect a purely businesslike tone. He didn't come to be friends with the man.

"I took the liberty of having breakfast set up on the balcony. The heat is not so intense this early in the morning. I thought it would be nice to talk and eat in the fresh air. It is so beautiful a view. You will enjoy it."

"That's fine," Reichert said, as Ortega ushered him through the doors onto the balcony. A round table, covered with a white linen tablecloth, held two place settings, several silver chafing dishes, a coffee server, a bucket of ice and two carafes of juice.

When they were seated, Ortega uncovered the dishes and they served themselves. One chafing dish held tortillas covered with minced onion and chopped ham, each with two fried eggs on top, drizzled with a chili sauce and sprinkled with green peas and cheese. Another contained huevos rancheros, a Mexican staple dish of eggs on tortillas, topped with salsa. Bill Reichert picked at his food. His stomach was too shaky to bombard it with any-thing—despite the quality of the resort—he held questionable.

"I understand," Ortega said, flashing a smile that was diffi-cult to mistrust, "that we are to discuss a significant number of U.S. dollars that you wish to protect." Significant? Reichert almost laughed. Eight to ten million dollars is what this man calls "significant"?

"Yes," he said. "Excuse me, Señor Ortega, if I seem imperti-nent. I don't mean to, but before we begin discussing details, I would feel more at ease, perhaps, if you could tell me exactly what your background is concerning international banking.

Slipping four hundred thousand dollars across the border is one thing, but what we are considering is a much broader project with far more serious implications." Reichert knew that delving into a man like Ortega's background was not only improper but could be dangerous. In his mind, however, he was only exercising caution. He was out of his element.

"Your impertinence is excused, Mr. Reichert. I understand the trust between you and me is not here yet. I received my bachelor's degree in international relations, with a minor in business administration from Brown University in Rhode Island and a graduate degree with an emphasis on international finance from The Wharton School in Philadelphia. You see, I understood from a very early age exactly what I wanted to do for a career and decided to prepare for it in the best way possible. If your business is going to be pulling the wool, as you say, over someone's eyes—in this case a country—the best method is to study their ways. Fortunately, my father was able to afford it."

"Very impressive," Reichert said chagrined. "I hope you will forgive my asking."

"No problem. But, and I know it is difficult, you have to trust me. I understand that Señor Descarté referred you to me, but he also referred me to you. My bank does not do business lightly. Should you ever run into any trouble in your dealings, it will not be through us. We currently manage on average five point three billion U.S. dollars a year, and not one dollar has been lost through our inefficiency." It was said without hostility or braggadocio, just in a manner that let the American know that if they were ever going to be doing business, he must never question him again.

"I didn't mean to offend you," he said. Ortega smiled.

"You didn't. I just felt it necessary to let you know we are not—what you call—a fly-by-night organization. We make money together, or we don't make money at all. Now, let's put all this aside, shall we? How many dollars are we talking about?"

"Eight to ten million is a ballpark estimate."

"Very nice amount."

"May I ask how you would suggest we handle it? Exactly. The process?"

"Of course. Diversify, I think, and then bring it to three or four primary corporate accounts. This would, of course, be after eight or ten transfers, maybe even more. I would begin by using one of our New York importers. The way it works—and I won't go into detail—one of our manufacturers will obtain a permit to export, let's say, ten million dollars worth of household hardware to New York. What he will actually ship is two million dollars worth of hardware to one of the island Free Zones, where it will be re-labeled, repackaged and sent back to Mexico to be sold at a discount.

"At the same time, the manufacturer's agent picks up your eight to ten million in New York, which is covered by an export license, and brings it back here. Now we are ready to begin the transfers, taking the money in various amounts through eight or ten countries and islands, via wire, courier and, in some cases, bank certificates until it finally rests in three or four blind corporations, probably in the Canary Islands, Venezuela and the Antilles. Those locations would not be decided upon until the time comes, in order to find you the best rates. No need to let money sit and do nothing for you." He smiled.

"From there your corporations can use the money for real estate purchases in the states or virtually any other type of acquisitions the corporation might think is a good investment. To follow a paper trail, which seems to be your government's primary method of exposure, will be virtually impossible. After this is established, smaller amounts can be wired, even through your own bank, if you wish, directly to your corporations' accounts. Does this seem reasonable?"

Reichert nodded, thinking it over.

"Bertolt Brecht once said, 'If you want to steal, buy a bank.' Some wisdom in that statement I'm sure even he wasn't aware of," Ortega said.

Reichert had to bite his tongue to keep from asking what he knew were dumb questions. He could understand the simplified version of the technique that Ortega had just explained. That was no problem. It was the implementation of the procedures that was impossible for him to grasp. How could they keep track of the money with it going in so many different directions through so many currency exchanges? How many people were employed to manage all of what Ortega described? And how many individuals would be in control of The Company's funds while the transactions were going on? Even if he could trust Ortega, what about the others? And if it all got fucked, it would fall on his shoulders.

The questions raced through his mind, not one reasonable enough to ask. But then again, maybe he was just a patsy in Ortega's mind, an amateur, a hick from Covington, South Carolina, a chicken ripe for the plucking. Bill Reichert felt all of those assessments were valid at the moment. He was out of his league. The Company was out of its league. What were they thinking? Charlie Clay and the others. That they were invincible? His stomach began to roll. He felt like he was going to vomit. He didn't eat much, by design, but he thought he might lose what little he had ingested. There was a cool sweat on his body and arms that brought a chill with it that he tried to disguise.

"Is something wrong, Mr. Reichert?" There was a look of concern on Ortega's face.

"No, nothing. Just a bit of indigestion."

"I'm sorry. The spices in our food probably. Or maybe too much tequila last night? The water at Las Brisas is safe, so unless you drank some elsewhere, it couldn't be the infamous 'revenge.' Can I get you something for your stomach? There is a pharmacy not far from here."

"No, really, it's passing already. Just momentary. It's not unusual."

"So, does our financial planning meet with your approval?"

"We haven't discussed your charges." Get aggressive, he told himself.

"To do all that I outlined, with your only part being to get the currency to our agent in New York, would cost you fifteen percent of the total amount we handle."

"That's one point five million to handle ten."

"Your mathematics is good. Of course, you're a banker. It is a lot of work, Señor, and once it is in our hands, the risk is all ours. You could lose only your money. That can always be replaced. We could lose our lives or, worse, spend them in prison. We do not have 'country club' prisons in Mexico. For me, I would rather lose my life." Ortega took a sip of his coffee. "And, before you ask, the fee is not negotiable."

"It's acceptable," Reichert said. "What's the first step?"

"You will notify us twenty days in advance of the money being in your possession. It is essential for your safety that it remain in your possession as brief a time as possible. When you have it, you will be given instructions on how to deliver it to New York. In the meantime, during that twenty-day period, papers will be sent to you to be signed—in any way you choose—for corporate setups and access signatures. We get nothing except a handshake until our agent in New York receives the money. At that time our percentage will be deducted and the process will begin. Can I answer anything else?" Reichert's head was spinning.

"About that, nothing that I can think of; however, I will have to get approval from our principals."

"Of course."

"There is one other matter that we need to discuss and take immediate action on: the four hundred thousand dollars I brought in with me." Reichert said.

"That is all arranged. These are your personal funds, I recall."

"Yes."

"My driver will take you to Banco Privado de Ciudadanos, a small bank in Acapulco in which we have an interest. Ask for Señor Gallaggria. He is the vice-president and will assist you in setting up an account here and one in Guadeloupe—you did say this was a personal account in your name only, not part of your organization," Ortega said.

"Yes."

"Once the money is deposited here, it will be wired directly to your account in the islands. Señor Gallaggria will supply you with all of the necessary documents and will give you a secure access code while you are in his office. You may witness the whole process."

"How will I contact you when we are ready to proceed?"

"The same way you did this time. Mr. Clay will be in touch with Descarté, and he, in turn, will contact me." Reichert rose from his chair, balancing himself with three extended fingers on the table in case his knees were too weak to lift him upright without faltering. At that moment, for the first time, he thought of himself as a criminal.

"We will contact you," he managed to get out.

Bernardo Hieronymous Ortega extended his hand and smiled. "It will be good doing business with you, Mr. Reichert. I would tell you not to worry, but I can see that you will. That is you. But I will say it anyway. We have been in business for more than twenty years, and it is not all money such as yours, believe me. We have a number of legitimate, major American manufacturers and corporations among our clients. You would be surprised."

"I'm sure I would," Reichert said, his legs firming a bit.

"Juano has the car waiting for you. Buenos dias, Señor."

"Buenos dias."

Walking to the car, the heat of the day enveloped him, but the feeling was not as uncomfortable as the cold sweat he had experienced in Ortega's suite. He tried to focus on Morgan Hannah and the two days and nights that lay ahead. His overwhelming desire, however, was to get back to South Carolina. He wasn't sure he ever wanted to leave it again. Of one thing he was certain, this would be his last venture with The Company.

Neither Bill Reichert nor Juano was aware of the small car that followed them as they headed back to Las Brisas.

CHAPTER 14

It was five-thirty in the morning. Sam Larkin had slept little. At four o'clock he had dozed for the last fitful time and awakened ten minutes later. After that, he lay in bed staring through the sliding glass doors, waiting for the first vestiges of morning to appear. They were slow in coming. It was a black night, no stars, no moon, as if the heaven's electric service had been terminated. His mind would not close down and let his body go.

Uncertainties bounced around in his head like small flashes of white light. There was the death of Turner Lockett, which surely wasn't over yet, and Karen Chaney. He had allowed her into his life without thinking, a risk he couldn't afford and live as he had lived.

Now he wanted her out. Or so he felt at the moment. There were too many shady corners and puzzles to rationalize: her job, probing him with questions and checking him out at the boat dock, the hi-tech answering machine in her townhouse, the locked closet door. The woman brought out the paranoia in him.

The more he thought, the more his anger grew like the thrum of hornets at the first rattle of their nest. He sensed Karen Chaney as a threat to all he had done over the last six years. He could leave, but he wouldn't. His life and his house were all he had, his only identity, and he'd be damned if he'd ever let anyone take that away from him again.

There was no false dawn; the sky greyed into first light. Larkin got out of bed, put on his cotton running shorts, a tee shirt and went out on the deck to put on his shoes. Exercise and exhaustion were his bromides for anxiety. Let other people use Xanax, Valium and booze; sweat did it for him. Grey clouds, the color of warships, moved lazily out to sea. He could feel rain in the air. The hot-dry bugs were silent. The smell of something dead penetrated through the odors of plough-mud and greening Spartina grass. The air was heavy and moist.

Before he completed the first half-mile of his three-mile jaunt, the humidity and sweat drenched his light grey shirt to charcoal. In the second half-mile, the tightness in his legs, hips and shoulders began to loosen. His stride was no longer awkward and painful. He began to press harder. Cool perspiration formed on his arms and legs.

When he moved into the final sprint for home, blood was coursing through his arteries and his heart at a tremendous rate. He wondered at times like this if he might not fall forward and die as his heart exploded. When it didn't happen, it was a step gained on immortality. He slowed and ran a couple of cool-down laps around his property, then settled in to free-weights, sit-ups and push-ups. The tightness in his head began to ease.

It was a close day—not the closeness created by humid air— but one where all parts of everything in this one place, including himself, his thoughts, his body and voice melded into one entity, the water and grass understanding him and the mysteries of him as well as he understood them. It was an exhilarating aura that surrounded him and this place, and the aura was silent.

He poured a cup of coffee and was moving toward the deck when the telephone rang. He considered not answering, but at the last moment picked up.

"Hello?"

"Sam?"

"Hi, Karen." Before it began, he knew this was a conversation he didn't want to have. Maybe her call was synergistic. He could end it, solve the problem.

"That doesn't sound too chipper. I'm not calling to ream you out for not calling for the last few days." She paused. "Am I disturbing you?" He had the urge to say "yes" but didn't.

"No, I—"

"Good." She cut him off. He heard determination in her voice. "How busy are you today?" she asked.

"I have a couple of things to do. Why?"

"Because we need to talk, to have a good down-to-earth conversation. You've been in my bed, and I know nothing about you. Now, on the face of it, that's not very smart on my part or yours, and I don't know how I let it happen. On the other hand, I have been in your bed, and you know nothing about me. Somehow I don't think that's standard operating procedure for you either. Come to think of it, I'm not sure whether you know anything about me or not. See? That's how little I know about you; you might know everything about me, and I wouldn't even know it." She stopped. There was a silence.

"How long did you rehearse that?" he asked, a lightness creeping into his voice he didn't intend. *Karen Damn Chaney*, he thought.

"Obviously not long enough."

"Well, then, there, now," he said.

"James Dean. *Giant*."

"What?"

"James Dean said that line in *Giant*. 'Well, then, there, now.' " she said.

"I really have no idea how to respond to that. Have you been drinking this morning?"

"No. There's no need to say anything. Just wanted to impress you with my vast storehouse of useless knowledge."

"You like James Dean, I take it."

"Yes. *Rebel Without a Cause*, *Giant*, *East of Eden*, all of them. Loner, misunderstood, tries to do the right things, which always turn out wrong. Good guy who's perceived as bad. Sound familiar?"

"Not in the least," he said, having no idea where this part of the conversation was going, but wondering if Karen Chaney knew a lot more about him than he was aware of. "Karen, what is all this about?"

"You're a puzzlement, Sam, and I can't deal with that. Can we talk and decide if we have anything further to talk about?"

"Sounds kind of ominous, but, yes, I've got some time." Maybe this was the best way to deal with it and get back to life as abnormal, he thought.

"My place or yours?"

"Why don't you come for dinner?"

"What are you having?"

"Alligator."

"My favorite," she said and laughed. He liked her laugh.

"Six okay?"

"See ya, Larkin."

He waited for her to hang up and then put his receiver back in its cradle more than firmly. "Damn!" he said out loud to the room. Why hadn't he told her he wasn't interested in talking, that he was happy with things the way they were, that if she needed to know things that were none of her business, she should find somebody else to pal around with, that he didn't want to like her any more than he did because at nights sometimes, he still awoke thinking of Celine Aguillard, telling her to divorce him, to find a life for herself, knowing, even as he said it, that it wasn't a noble act, as he tried to convince himself, but a selfish one to protect himself, and feeling guilty about it. Her tears and his wanting to cry at his own hopelessness. There was no place for any more hurt in his life. Dealing with anger was job enough, and, though it was a daily struggle, like an alcoholic getting through a day without a drink, he had managed to do that so far. Without people.

The rain had begun pelting the creek and marsh, creating a landscape etched in silver. There was no lightning, but for more than two hours the near-black sky had borne the sound of conflicting air, not unlike two armies cannonading each other with a vengeance. Marvon Jefferies and Bitta Smalls, two black youths, were hunkered down next to a live oak that gave them some umbrella protection from the rain. It made little difference; they had been there for two hours, and their cheap cotton shirts and wash-worn jeans clung to them like a second skin. Marvon Jefferies was thirteen years old, and Bitta Smalls was eleven.

"I say we go on in," Bitta said, looking up at the older boy.

"I ain' ready yet," Marvon said.

"You ain' never ready. You won' ready yestaday, and you ain' ready today. De man done been dead mos' a week, and ain' nobody been out here. I think you scared."

"I ain' scared."

"Man, they's gots to be lotsa good stuff in there we can sell. Ain' nobody never gone live there no more."

"How you know dat?"

"I don't, but dey sure ain' gonna after we take the copper pipes out from under de sink and tear de wirin' outta da walls. Dat's what Bingo says he and his boys do when dey finds a empty

trailer. Dat stuff worf money, an' ain' no tellin' what else in there."
Bitta said.

"Shit. You b'lieve everything Bingo say. Where you gon' sell
it, Bitta?" They had had this same conversation, almost word for
word, at least four times a day, in each of the four days they had
been watching Turner Lockett's trailer.

"Down to de Exxon station. I done tol' you. Dey's a junk man
come by there ever mornin' jes to buy any stuff like dat you got,"
the younger boy said.

"You got de snips and pliers?"

"You know damn well I got 'em, an' I know you got de ham-
mer and de hatchet. You jus' scared."

"Well, pro'bly a good time. Ain' nobody dumb enough to come
out in dis mess anyway, 'cept us." Marvon said. Neither of them
moved.

"You right about dat."

"You ready?" Marvon asked, hoping the younger boy would
say "no" or "not yet."

Bitta Smalls took a deep breath and stood up.

"Le's do it," he said, like he had heard on TV.

They bent down and moved stealthily from tree to tree then
made a run for Turner Lockett's truck. When they got there, they
waited and listened.

"Ain' nobody out here," Bitta said, stood up and brazenly
headed around to the front of the trailer. He tried the latch, but it
wouldn't give. "Hit it with de hatchet, man," he said, and the older
boy followed his orders. The latch popped open on the third blow.

They eased the door open as if expecting to see a ghost, looked
behind them and went inside, closing the door. Neither of them
said anything, just looked at the dirt and disorder the dead man had
lived with.

"Man, dis is awful," Marvon said.

"Dat man white trash, sho' nuff," Bitta said. He looked at
Marvon who wasn't laughing. "Well, le's do what we come fo'.
You start pullin' wire; I'll work on de sink."

"I don' think Bingo knows shit. Why somebody gon' buy wire
done been pulled out of a wall. How'm I s'pose to pull it anyway?"

"Knock a hole in the wall, grab it an pull. Trevin say it easy."

"S'pose I get 'lectrocuted?" Marvon asked. Bitta stopped what he was doing, thought a minute and went back outside. In less than two minutes he returned.

"Now you ain' gon' get 'lectrocuted. I turned off de switch outside. It jus' like de one we got at my house."

"You sho?"

"Turn on de lights. See if dey come on." Marvon did as he was told. Nothing happened. "See? I done tol' you I turned off de switch."

"It dark in here. Cain't hardly see to do anything."

"Light enuff. Get busy. We ain' got all day," Bitta said, taking charge.

Bitta got down on his knees and opened the cabinet doors under the sink. What he saw made him sit back on his haunches.

"Shit! Ain' no damn copper under here. Ain' nothin' but silver pipe. Probly lead. Ain' worth shit," he said. "Wonder if this sink be worth anything."

"I ain' carryin' no sink to de Exxon station. Look like a damn fool an' get put in jail fo' stealin' it to boot." The wire Marvon was pulling on was making the overhead light fixture send down a shower of dust.

"I think dis wire go up to dat light yonder, Bitta. Get up there and see if you can cut it with dem snips. Ain' no copper pipes. Leas' we can sell de wire maybe."

Bitta Smalls pulled a chair under the fixture, climbed up and tried to pull it from its anchorage, but it wouldn't move.

"Hand me dat hatchet," he said.

"You don' need no hatchet. Jus' turn it on 'em screws, an it'll come off, an you can cut de wires, an I'll pull 'em through."

The younger boy grasped the fixture, twisted and it came loose, bringing a rain of dust and dead bugs with it. He pulled it down as far as he could and cut the wires, which freed them for Marvon to pull through the wall. He dropped the fixture on the floor, shattering the globe, stood on tiptoe and looked through the hole it left, checking to see if there might be any copper pipes in the ceiling.

"They's somethin' up here, Marvon."

"A ghos' in the ceilin' maybe?" Marvon said and laughed.

"Naw. Somethin' shiny. Maybe somethin' we can sell, but I cain' reach it," he said, trying to extend his arm through the hole.

"Lemme see," Marvon said. Bitta got down off the chair and Marvon climbed up. "Where?" the older boy asked.

"To you lef'. You see it? Shiny?"

"Yeah, I see it." He leaned away from the hole, extended his arm through it and turned his head aside to get maximum reach. "I feel somethin'." He went up on his toes. "Got it."

"What is it?" Bitta asked.

"How'm I s'pose to know? Somethin' wrapped in tinfoil," Marvon said, inspecting the small package. He got down off the chair, went to the kitchen counter and began unwrapping it. As the foil came off, the boys' eyes bulged, their mouths dropped open and they lost their breath.

"Holy shit! Holy shit! Holy shit!," Marvon said. "Look, Bitta. Mus' be a million dollars. Oh, Lawd, we gone die. I knew we shouldna come here. Holy shit!" The two boys stared at the neat stack of one hundred dollar bills. Neither of them could talk for several minutes. Marvon Jefferies kept turning away from the money as if he didn't want to look at it and then kept coming back and touching it and turning away again. He was moving like the floor was hot under his feet.

"Wha' we gon' do wif it, Marvon?"

"I don' know. It scares me."

"Me, too. S'pose 'ere's mo' up there?"

"I don' know. How would I know?" Marvon said impatiently. "Why would you axe me dat?"

"We oughta see," Bitta said, his eyes still wide. "Might be mo'."

Marvon climbed back up on the chair and tried to look through the hole again, but he couldn't spot anything.

"It be too dark in that hole to see anything. Hand me dat hatchet yonder," he said. He took the hatchet and hooked it in the thin veneer.

"Wha' you gone do, Marvon?"

"I'm gone jump and see if it pull de ceilin' down wif me. You ready? Get out de way."

Bitta Smalls moved back in the trailer, and Marvon Jefferies jumped off the chair. A large panel of the ceiling, dust, and dirt came with him. Also falling amidst the rubble were more tightly wrapped foil packages. They both stared at the pile of thin silver bricks scattered on the floor.

"Holy shit!" Marvon finally said. "Bitta, we in trouble. We better get outta here. Jus' leave dis stuff where it lay. I ain' got no truck wid dis. I ain' gone touch it. Dis be somethin' bad, Bitta." The younger boy looked at him astounded.

"Leave it here? You crazy?"

"Wha' we gon' do wid it? Cain' spend it. You gon' go in de sto' wif a hunert dollar bill? Shit! You be in jail so fas'." Marvon shook his head hopelessly.

"Well, I ain' leavin' it here. I might get a whuppin' when I gets home, but worse off happens, I gone tell daddy 'bout it, an' axe him what to do."

"You axe yo' daddy what to do wif it, you be in jail fo' sho'. I knows yo' daddy. He ain' gone put up wid dis shit."

"Well, I ain' leavin' it. Get me a bag. Mus' be one round here somewhere." He looked around the room. "There's one fulla papers. Dump 'em and bring it over here."

When all of the foil-wrapped packages were in the shopping bag, they picked up their tools, took a quick glance around, opened the door, looked in all directions and made a run for the woods. It was still pouring rain, and they had no idea what they would do with the cache of money. What they did know was that they were in trouble.

CHAPTER 15

Charley Clay was sitting in the screened-in Carolina room at his beach house when Brad Coleman's call came. It was a call he had been waiting for with anticipation. If Coleman gave him the right answers, money would rain down on Charley Clay and friends.

"I was wondering when I'd hear from you," Clay said. "How's the world traveler?"

"I'm fine."

"Everything all right?"

"Everything's fine." It was a go. The product was available; the price was right, the logistics and the boat were acceptable. Brad Coleman had answered all of those questions with two little words.

"Good. When are you coming back to South Carolina to finalize things?"

"About a week. Are the papers ready?"

"I got a million of them. How long do you plan to stay?"

"Maybe a day or two. I won't book a return until I see how things go."

"Plan to stay at my beach house. I know you like the beach and privacy. You'll have it all to yourself," Clay offered.

"I appreciate that. By the way, what was the name of that woman you introduced me to out there?"

"Morgan Hannah. Run into her, you might stay longer than you plan."

"That remains to be seen," Coleman said. Morgan Hannah had passed through his thoughts more than once.

"Fax me your schedule, and I'll have you picked up."

"Not necessary. I'll get a car and call you when I get in."

"There will be a pass for you at the gate in case you want to head on out to Sangaree. The house is never locked."

"Amazing."

"I'll look forward to seeing you."

When he hung up the phone, Charley Clay was smiling. "I love it when a plan comes together," he thought, stealing a line from Hannibal Smith. Everything was looking good. The only missing pieces were finalizing the off-load site, setting up a crew and making sure Reichert had accomplished what he set out to do in Mexico.

It was just after noon, but he felt like celebrating. He went to the bar, poured a generous two inches of Edradour Single Malt Scotch over a couple of ice cubes and went back to the sun room to take care of business. There were two problems that needed to be resolved. Turner Lockett's money and the lady officer who, according to Turner, seemed to be spending an inordinate amount of time at Sam Larkin's place. With an off-load a couple of miles down the creek, she could present considerable risk. Newcomers were always ambitious, and he didn't want to go through the process of buying her.

He picked up the phone and dialed Ray Breslin's home number. Although it was a weekend, Breslin seldom worked Saturdays and Sundays in the off-season.

"Hello?" A worn woman's voice answered the phone.

"Miz Breslin? Ray there?"

"Sure. Just a minute." Clay heard the phone being put down and the woman calling her husband. "Ray? Telephone."

"Who is it?" he heard.

"I don't know who it is."

"Damn it! I've told you to ask before you let them know I'm here. How many times do I have to tell you?" The phone was picked up. "Hello? Who is this?" The anger was obvious.

"Charley Clay, Ray." There was silence on the other end of the line.

"Oh, Charley. Hey."

"You doing all right, Ray? Sound a little stressed."

"No, I'm fine, Charley. Just bein' home with the old lady. You know."

"Then you won't mind my asking you to do a little work." Clay's voice was cold. He envied Ray Breslin's being home with "the old lady." Breslin was an ass, but he was useful.

"Any excuse, right?" Clay could imagine him smiling, as if they shared his good ol' boy philosophy.

"Dudn't have to be today, but a couple of things need checkin' out."

"You name it."

"Turner's money. You heard anything about anyone else goin' out there?"

"Not a soul I've heard. The guys from the sheriff's office ain't said a word, and they'd ask me. I did tell 'em I'd checked it out and didn't find nothin' of interest. That'll probably be the end of it far as they're concerned. Turner wudn't exactly important."

"Well, he was important to us, and we can't be too careful. Who knows what he did with it. I just want you to make sure nobody else finds it. It would create a lot of questions."

"Right."

"Ray, we'll split whatever you find. That fair?"

"More than. I owe you, Charley."

"And we won't say anything about this conversation or the money to anyone."

"Sure, Charley."

"I figure maybe sometime in the next couple of days would be soon enough. Now the other thing. Turner mentioned that new female officer in your department was spending the weekend at Sam Larkin's. What do you know about her?"

"Not much. Came up from Florida. Dudn't seem to know much. I thought she was a lesbo. Guess I was wrong. Been wrong before." He laughed.

"She worries me with Larkin being so close to Crewes's place. I'd like for you to check her out. I get the feeling there's something funny about her replacing Jimmy Lee out of the blue, and her being friends with Larkin makes me uneasy."

"I'll take care of it. It'll be a pleasure."

Clay hung up the phone feeling like he had just had an in-depth conversation with Dumbly Do-right. There was one more call to make, and it wouldn't be as simple.

"It's going to be a tough situation, Charles," Cedrick Hamilton said after hearing that it was time to move on Skeeter Crewes with their proposition. "I know the man pretty well, but it's been a lot of years since we were close. It's exposure, and you know how I feel about that. A lot of people take this stuff more seriously than you do; they've got a lot to lose or think they do." He sounded cynical.

"I know. I don't have anything to lose," Clay replied tersely.

"I didn't mean that, Charles. I meant—"

"You're right. I've been thinking about that lately, and I really don't have a lot to lose." There was impatience in Clay's voice. Sometimes Hamilton's "wiser than thou" attitude got to him. "I've been comin' to the beach house for the last couple of weeks, and it's brought back a lot of things. I think about what I'm doing and can't believe it. Other times, 'Why the hell not?' What other kind of a life do I have? You know, we go along thinking about the future and all its possibilities, and then one day, without warning, there it is. The future. And it's not a damned thing like what we expected. What do you think about then? The future doesn't last forever. Pretty fragile really."

"Charles, I didn't mean—"

"I know what you meant. But you, Cedrick? I don't think you have a choice. Remember back a little. Back to when you were fresh out of school with all those degrees, not knowing a damned thing about anything, wanting to come home, broke as a church mouse and in debt. Think about that insignificant arrest record for possession in D.C. that magically disappeared when I suggested you apply for the assistant superintendent's position down here. Remember that lady lawyer who threatened to kill herself and then did because you dumped her when you didn't think a black and white situation would work in Covington politics. And how long did it take you to become head man? One year. Oh, and all the money we've made together. You're a damned millionaire. I don't have anything to lose, but you do. Having nothing to lose makes me dangerous, Cedrick, but not dumb. I don't like to have to talk you into anything, but I do what's necessary."

"You're right; I can never repay you, and I'm grateful for all of it. I'll see Skeeter this week and get back to you."

"Thank you, Cedrick. I apologize. I don't know where all of that came from."

"From inside, I guess, but what you feel in there might not always be right."

"I know. I'll wait to hear from you." The man was getting skittish.

It would be like walking on the proverbial eggshells, Karen Chaney knew, as she crossed the Marion Bridge onto Matthew's Island in her dark blue Mustang. Her mind was in turmoil, yet it was important to bring some kind of fixity of purpose to whatever was going on with Sam Larkin. This dinner would either be a beginning or an end. Both prospects made her nervous. The thing to keep in mind, she told herself, was her reason for being in Covington, South Carolina. The job came first. What she had learned from Neil Dougherty only left bigger questions about Sam Larkin. Realistically, an ending would be better. Where could a beginning really go?

The major problem was how to get Sam to expose himself, discuss his past, clear up the vague suspicions surrounding him, without blowing her cover. He was smart and protective, but there was no way to open herself and trust him—even in the most favorable of circumstances against procedure—without knowing every detail of the life and times of Sam Larkin.

The drive out Route 37 to Osprey Landing Road was foreboding on nights such as the one she was experiencing. The rain stopped about four o'clock, but the sky had moved to full dark. The heat in the earth and on the macadam of the road combined with the moisture to create a fog that was almost impenetrable. Though no rain was falling, the storm surrounded her. Overlapping claps of thunder, like a roll of timpani, rocked the car with their impact, holding quiet for only seconds at a time and then shocking with staccato bursts that caught her by surprise. Lowcountry weather, she thought.

Several times she found herself flinching at the volume of the noise. Flashes of radiant, white lightning revealed glimpses of dilapidated mobile homes, nestled hidden among live oaks hanging heavy with wet moss that veiled them from view. Sights appeared ghost-like and menacing in the electric illuminations and just as quickly disappeared. She pushed the switch that locked all of the doors on the car, praying she would find a pair of tail lights to follow as the car behind her was doing. Whoever it was laid the responsibility on her. If she went off the road, they would surely follow.

Sam, wearing a pair of faded, green safari shorts and a light blue denim shirt, stood barefoot under the overhang on his deck watching the light show as the first drops of rain began to fall. Big drops, flattening on the surface of the water like soft-nosed bullets hitting an impenetrable obstruction. For a time in the late afternoon, he had wished Karen was not coming, actually dialed her number once to cancel then hung up before the phone began to ring. Now he was glad he made that decision. They would talk, as she asked; he was as anxious to reconcile their relationship as she, only he didn't think the final determination he had in mind was, in any way, similar to hers.

Dinner was already prepared. He looked at his watch. The rain was intensifying, and light, bleeding from the spotlights on the roof corners of his deck, exposed leaves being blown from the trees like dust motes in a ray of sunshine. Hanging moss performed ritualistic dances in the wind, and the rain began to impinge on the area in which he was standing.

Karen Chaney was having a difficult time seeing. The rain had begun to fall so fast and furiously that deep puddles covered the low spots in the road and eliminated any steering efficiency the car possessed. At times she felt the car was in control, and she was just along for the ride. It was foolish not to pull over and wait it out, but after virtually inviting herself to Larkin's for dinner, she didn't want to leave him waiting. There wasn't much farther to go. The visibility was so poor that only the sign on the Exxon station at the intersection of Route 37 and Osprey Landing Road allowed her to recognize her turn. The car behind her turned also. She hoped whoever it was knew where they were going; there were not a lot of houses on the road.

If Route 37 was dangerous, Osprey Landing Road was treacherous. Traversing the uneven macadam with its potholes and dips was little better than trying to blindly walk through a minefield. She had driven through lots of storms, but this was the worst. Hunched over the wheel, she tried to get her face closer to the windshield, but it didn't help. The wipers had little effect on the wall of water that was falling from the sky.

Suddenly the lights in the rearview mirror grew brighter, coming far too close in the conditions they were experiencing. Either her tail lights had failed or the driver was an idiot. The answer came quickly. She felt a firm nudge on the rear end of her car. A drunk maybe? She tried to accelerate to put more distance between them, but couldn't see well enough to go any faster. The driver behind her speeded up as well and hit her again. It was all she could do to stay on the road. The business of driving was losing ground to fear. The lights behind her dropped back. Maybe stop, get out and flash the Ruger. Not smart in this weather. Her thoughts stopped when she saw the lights coming on fast. She braced herself for the hit and it came. Hard and constant.

Her car hit a pocket in the road and, even though she was traveling at a low speed, launched itself in the air, coming down on a section of road that was completely submerged from side to side. The wheels could find no purchase. When they did, the car lurched to the right, ran up a dirt embankment, lifted on one side and hovered at a threatening angle that threatened to flip it. At the last moment, it circled down off the embankment, caught traction and shot across the road toward a drainage ditch. She saw the headlights flash by her. When her car hit the ditch, it leaped forward and stopped suddenly. Her head hit the windshield, and she saw spider cracks developing before her eyes, slowly moving out from the center of her forehead. Everything was reduced to slow motion and then she lost consciousness.

Walking from the shed in the side yard of his house, Skeeter Crewes saw lights dancing in the trees along the road. The movements were so erratic that it looked like a possum hunter's flashlight, scanning the limbs for quarry. The dancing stopped with unnatural suddenness and focused on one tree, white beams turned upward like the decorative lights rich people used to show off their oaks.

It was an accident; there was no doubt in his mind. The weather, the road, the huge pothole he had been after the county to repair for two years. It was bound to happen. He just hoped no one had to get killed to push the county into action. He left the shelter of the shed and ran in the direction of the lights. Even on foot it was tough going. Two times he stopped himself just short of running into one of the massive oaks on his property. It took several minutes to get to the accident. The car had not gone head-on into a tree, which was what he feared, but the back half of the automobile was submerged in the drainage ditch, which was the reason for the lights' angle.

It wasn't a local; Skeeter didn't recognize the car; however, he knew that if it sat where it was for very long and the rain continued, it would be flooded. There was no movement he could see, but the rain made that determination tenuous at best. Not enough time had elapsed for anyone to exit the vehicle and leave the scene. The rain-drenched, packed red clay had turned to a glass slickness, which made getting to the door difficult. He held on to a small wax myrtle that grew on the edge of the ditch and tried to ease himself down without slipping into what was becoming a swift-moving current. He leaned out toward the car and let go of his anchor to fall forward to reach it.

The doors were locked. A woman was behind the wheel, but he couldn't make out anyone else. Her head had hit the windshield. He pulled himself up on the hood, feet toward the driver's seat and began kicking the glass.

Kick by kick, the glass began to give until finally, when he was near exhaustion, one foot broke through, showering the person sitting there with small, geometric pieces of glass. He managed to remove enough of the windshield to reach through and flip the locks open, then worked his way back around to the door, holding on tightly to keep from being knocked down and swept away in the current. When he opened it, he recognized Karen Chaney. There was blood covering her face and she was perfectly still. For a moment he panicked. Having no idea how badly she was injured, he was afraid to move her. He removed his shirt, which was soaked with rainwater, and gently dabbed at the source of her bleeding. Head cuts bleed, he thought. It might not be as bad as it looks. She began to move.

"Quiet now," he said. "Can you hear me? Try not to move. I've got to get to the house and get some help out here."

"Sam?" she said, sounding as if she had awakened from a sound sleep.

"No. It's not Sam. This is Skeeter Crewes from down at Harry Tom's Boat Dock. You okay now. I gotta get some help. My house is jus' over yonder." He pointed in the direction of his house though he didn't know why. She didn't move her head. "I won't be gone a minute. You jus' try to stay still."

Karen Chaney's eyes opened. She was wet and it was cold. She tried to right herself, but couldn't. She looked down to see what was holding her and saw her blouse was covered with blood. She was confused. What happened? She was driving down Osprey Landing Road to Sam Larkin's house, and . . . Her memory went blank. There was a man leaning over her talking, but now he was gone. She put her head back and tried to remember, figure out exactly what had happened, what her situation was. Nothing came to mind. She felt the rain coming through the broken window and closed her eyes. She was very tired.

Sam Larkin was in the kitchen checking on dinner when the telephone rang. He was sure it was Karen saying the storm was too bad to drive all the way out to his house. He didn't want a cancellation; he was mentally prepared for whatever was to happen.
"Hello?"
"Sam?"
"Skeeter? Your electricity gone again?" He laughed.
"No, Sam, nothin' like that. That Miss Chaney, the wildlife officer, she ran into the drainage ditch in front of my house. The car ain' move, and she's bleedin' pretty bad. I'm afraid to move her; I don't know how bad she's hurt. I need some help out here."
"Hold on. Karen's hurt?" Skeeter was speaking too fast for Sam's mind to assimilate all the man was saying.
"Yeah. Her car's in the ditch in front of my house. I got to get back out there and stay with her. She's bleedin', an' the water in the ditch is gettin' deeper."
"Did you call emergency?"
"You know they ain't comin' out here tonight in this mess."
"Just stay with her; I'll be right there. She hit her head?"
"Yeah. That's where the blood's comin' from."
"Stay with her, Skeeter. Keep her awake. Don't let her go to sleep."

"I'll try, but hurry. And be careful, man. I ain' real good with this stuff."

"I'm on my way." Larkin hung up the phone, grabbed his keys off the counter, a high-beam search light from the utility closet and headed out into the night.

It took only minutes to get to Skeeter's house. Sam spotted the headlights pointed at a forty-five degree angle into the trees. He stopped the Rover in front of Karen's car and left the lights on. Skeeter was standing next to the driver's door leaning in. He straightened up as Sam came around the door.

"I couldn't keep her awake. She was already out when I got back out here. I been tryin' to keep a towel on the bleedin' and talkin' to her, but she ain' come around," Skeeter said, backing off to give Sam access to her.

"Looks like she's jammed under the steering wheel." He had to holler to be heard over the rush of the water, rain and thunder. "It doesn't look like she hit anything solid; we're going to have to take a chance nothing's broken and get her out of this mess."

"What you want me to do?"

"Go around to the other side and get in. I'll need you to put some leverage under her, so we can lift her out." The rain, if anything, had intensified. Water was cascading down Sam Larkin's face, making it difficult to see.

When Skeeter climbed into the passenger seat, Karen's weight shifted, and the angle of the car rolled her body slightly toward Larkin. The movement gave Skeeter just enough room to get his hands under her and pull her legs from beneath the steering column.

"I've got her," Sam said and lifted her free. "Open up the back of the Rover, and let's lay her out flat in there." Skeeter did as he was asked and climbed in to take her shoulders when Sam brought her around. He lifted and Skeeter pulled her inside. She lay with her head resting in his lap, his right hand applying direct pressure with a towel to the wound on her forehead. Sam got in the driver's seat and headed back to his house.

They carried Karen Chaney's limp body up the stairs and put her into bed. That done, Sam wanted to drive Skeeter home, but he refused, saying it was more important for Sam stay with her. Nor would he take the Rover. The bleeding from Karen's forehead subsided, but she remained unconscious. Sam checked her pulse and it was normal. He gently bathed her wound, which wasn't deep. There didn't appear to be any glass embedded in it, but it was located at her hairline, which made it difficult to clean.

His primary concern was her state of unconsciousness. He didn't know who to call, had never been to a doctor in Covington other than the school doctor who gave him his tuberculin shot when he began teaching. He tried that number and got an answering service. The young lady promised to have him call as soon as he checked in, but Larkin's natural skepticism made him doubt that he would hear from the doctor for hours, if at all. The service suggested the emergency room at the hospital in Covington, which was out of the question.

He removed her blouse and brassiere, both of which were soaked with blood, and her shorts. He cleaned her body with a warm, damp cloth, covered her with a light blanket, then sat down beside the bed to wait.

A soft moan brought him to awareness. She was moving beneath the blanket. He put his hand on her face to check for fever, but her temperature remained normal.

"Karen?" he said softly. There was little response. "Karen?" It looked as if she were trying to open her eyes, but they seemed glued shut. He squeezed out the cloth that was soaking in the basin next to the bed and began wiping her eyes. From the color that was showing on the cloth, he realized that her eyelids were sealed by dried blood. Gradually they loosened, and it wasn't long before they opened. "Hold still," he said and washed the rims of her lids.

"Sam?" She looked into his face.

"You're okay," he said. "Just a bump on the head."

"What happened?"

"I don't know; I wasn't there," he said and chastised himself for trying to add humor to a serious situation. "You had an accident on your way out here and wound up in a drainage ditch."

"The Exxon station. I turned at the Exxon station. I got that far. I remember lights and someone looking through the window of the car. I was lying on my back. There was a lot of blood. Was that you?"

"No. Skeeter Crewes. He found you and called me. He helped me get you here. Why don't you just try to be quiet and relax. We can talk later. Right now you need rest."

"My head feels like it's coming off my shoulders," Karen said.

"I'll get some aspirin." He left and came back with a glass of water and two tablets. She got them down in one swallow. "Rest."

"Sam?"

"Yes?"

"Hold my hand." Karen made a move to lift it and he took it into his own as she went back to sleep.

CHAPTER 16

Bill Reichert was livid. Sitting in a cocktail lounge in the Dallas-Fort Worth Airport on a Saturday night, with a woman who had all but scorned him, was not his definition of a good time. One day, twenty-four hours, was all it took for the whole trip to fall apart. When he returned from his meeting with Ortega, Morgan was already on the beach. That she wasn't waiting for him was infuriating.

By the time he changed and located her, he had calmed down, but her lack of enthusiasm or interest in returning to their casita brought everything back to the surface and the argument began. The following day and a half had passed emotionally strained, and the first leg of their flight home was spent in silence. His thoughts were interrupted by Morgan's voice.

"Is this the way we're going to leave it?" she asked.

"What do you mean?" He tried to sound as if nothing were wrong.

"Oh, Christ, Bill. What's wrong with you? Ever since you went to that meeting with whoever it was, you've been boiling. You haven't touched me; hell, you haven't even been mildly pleasant. I have no idea what's bothering you now. I thought we had worked that out back at the casita."

He turned on her, his face red with rage, the veins in his neck bulging. "What the fuck did we work out? I was ready to get laid, and you weren't. So what? My fault. I got angry. I bring you to Mexico, put you up in the finest resort I can find, feed you at the best restaurants, hell, I even offer to get a divorce and marry you, and you don't want me. I guess, by your standards, I should be happy as a lark; pussy without penalty only there's no pussy. I just offered to turn my whole life upside down, go through hell, and it doesn't mean shit to you. Hell, I can't imagine why I'm upset."

"We went through all that. It's not what I want. I thought you could accept that and enjoy what we do have, but I see that you can't."

"No, I can't." The words were out before he thought about what he was saying.

"Then we can't have anything, Bill, and I'm sorry about that. I thought we were having fun. That's really all I'm looking for, right now."

"You used me," he said.

"I used you?" He didn't know whether she was going to laugh or slap him. "You've got to be kidding. You wanted me and you got me. I will be honest, you were up front about it. No promises, just a little afternoon and evening delight. That's all I wanted, too, and still want. But when I feel like it, or, better yet, when 'we' feel like it. You can't handle that. You expected, I am sure, like your past flings, that I would be available at your whim, fall in love, start making demands—love me or leave me—and you could end things on your own terms. Hey, 'no strings' was what we agreed upon, so you would have a perfect out, but it didn't work that way and your ego can't take that. Me using you? Maybe I was, but you sure as hell thought you were using me and don't deny it." Morgan took a sip of her drink and looked at him squarely. Maybe that was what infuriated him most. All of the control and power he thought he had didn't exist. She was in control.

"Look," he said, trying to calm things down, "maybe it started out like that, but it hasn't been that way for quite awhile and you know it."

"No, I don't know it. For you maybe, but you can't change the rules just to suit you. There are—were—two of us in this thing, and you can't accept that a woman is self-sufficient enough, secure enough, to want to live her own life. That we can support ourselves, stand being alone, and enjoy a recreational fuck like you and your brotherhood can. I once warned you, I'm not one of P. T. Barnum's suckers. Your feelings may have changed some, but you're still using me and I don't mind. Just be honest about it."

"How am I using you? Tell me," he said.

"Well, first of all, I'm not sure you would actually go through with a divorce and marriage once you thought I was committed to you. That would take away the challenge; the thrill would be gone. And this trip. Other than companionship and sex, what other reason did you have for bringing me along?" He looked at her startled and felt the cold sweat that was becoming all too familiar of late.

"What do you mean? I love you, for God's sake. I wanted you with me."

"How dumb do you think I am, Bill?" He looked puzzled. "Why was it so important for me to stand directly behind you when we went through customs at the airport in Mexico. You were adamant. To protect me? I didn't have anything to hide. I could have answered any questions they might have asked. I've never been to Mexico before now, but Ben and I traveled most everywhere else in the world. Customs doesn't frighten me. You, on the other hand, were shaking. I was your distraction. It wasn't hard to figure out."

"You weren't."

Morgan lowered her voice to an angry whisper. "The hell I wasn't. And after your morning meeting, when you came back, your whole personality had changed. I don't know whom you met or what went on, and, at this point, I don't give a damn, but don't even suggest that you didn't use me."

"Morgan, listen, I—"

"There's nothing for me to hear, Bill, whatever we had is no longer. This is where it ends."

"Morgan!"

"Don't, Bill. Just be quiet. We came separately, and we'll go home separately." She stood up. "Goodbye, Bill." Morgan Hannah walked away, and all Bill Reichert could do was stare after her. Suddenly she turned around and came back to face him. "And don't ever think in your most egotistical moment that you could ever buy me with a trip and a fancy restaurant. That's insulting beyond anything you've ever done before." She turned again and left him with his head down, staring into his drink.

Neither of them was aware of Isabel Reichert sitting with her back to them, close enough to enjoy their exchange. A man sitting across from her caught her smile and returned it.

Bitta Smalls and Marvon Jefferies were in the old, dilapidated, wooden shed that stood in back of the double-wide mobile home that Bitta Smalls lived in with his mother and father. The neatly kept yard of their home was in great contrast to the shed, which was aged black and rotting and leaning heavily to one side, teetering on the brink of collapse. It was filled with ancient, rusted farm equipment that Bitta's grandfather had used when he worked the land, before the land and he wore out.

The inside of the shed smelled musty even on dry days, like a gunny sack that had lain wet and damp to the point of disintegration. There was little open space. Junk had collected for years, but Bitta and Marvon had cleared a small area in the back end where they could sneak cigarettes when they were available. None of the other family members ever came deep enough into the shed to discover them; it was their place. They sat on the dirt floor in the dark, the shopping bag of money between them.

"You ain' say what we gone do wid it," Marvon said. "I sho' ain' gone sit here in the dark all night while you make up yo' sorry-ass mind. I gots to be gettin' home."

"What you think?"

"It don' make no diffrunce what I think. You de one dat wonted to take it. I said leave it. You jus' a dumb-ass little boy, won' listen to nobody."

"I'm listenin'. What we gonna do wid it?" Bitta said.

"Hide it, I reckon."

"What den?"

"Wait. See what happens. We oughta keep watchin' dat trailer a coupla days. See if anybody else be comin' to look aroun'."

"An'?"

"An' what?" Marvon asked.

"An' iffen dey do, what we gone do? Go up to 'em and say 'Hey, we done foun' de money. Y'all might as well quit lookin'."

"Dat's the dumbest thing you eva said. Tell 'em dat, and dey kill us right off. You know we ain' s'pose to know 'bout dat money, but somebody do. Dat's fo' sho'."

"Den what we gone do?"

"Jus watchit. See if anybody come. If dey don' den we make a plan."

"What kinda plan?" Bitta asked.

"I don' know. Axe yo' frien's Bingo and Trevin. You say dey know everything." Bitta's eyes got wide.

"Dey don' know nothin' 'bout sumpin' like dis. We tell dem, hell, dey might kill us."

"Dey ain' gone kill you, Bitta."

"Cain' never tell. I hear Daddy say money do strange things. Turn peoples upside down ain' never been upside down befo'."

"Dat's yo daddy. Dat ain' Bingo and Trevin."

"Where we gone hide it?" Bitta asked. Marvon looked around.

"Seat on dat ol' tractor lif' up?" he asked.

"I don' know. Seem like I remember it do."

"Climb up and see." Bitta Smalls got to his feet and climbed up on the tractor. There was a home-made wooden box seat his grandfather had put on it when the steel one got too hard on his back. Bitta was right; it did lift up though the hinges were rusted, which made it difficult to raise. He guessed maybe his grandfather had kept his lunch in there or a bottle of whiskey.

"Any space up 'ere to hide it?"

"A little. I spec' if we stuff it, it'll go in."

Marvon picked up the shopping bag and climbed up on the tractor. By folding the top of the bag over, putting it under the seat and sitting on it, they managed to secure it out of view.

"I sho' hope nobody come out here and look under dere," Bitta said.

"Shit! When de las' time somebody come out here, lif' up de seat a dat tractor an' look under dere?"

"Never."

"Den why dey gon' do it now?"

"I don' know, Marvon. I'm jus' scared. Dat somebody's money, an' dey gone be lookin' fo' it, an' I don't wonna get killed."

"It's sho' is somebody's money, but dat somebody be dead. Now I been thinkin' on it. He hide it his own self, so nobody know 'bout it, so how anybody gone know?"

"Ain' you scared?"

"Course I'm scared. I wouldn't be sittin' out here on a dirt flo' in de dark wif you, I won' scared. But ain' much we can do 'bout it now 'cause you done brought it home."

"Won' jus' me."

"You de one brung it." He could see the younger boy was about to cry. "Don' worry, Bitta. Ain' nobody gone know we got it.

Somebody find dat money under dat tractor seat, we don' know nuffin' 'bout how it got dere."

"S'pose somebody saw us?"

"You see anybody see us?"

"No," Bitta said.

"Well den?"

"Okay." Bitta still wasn't convinced. Marvon took him by the shoulders.

"You know you tell anybody 'bout it, I ain' gone know nuffin', so don' go runnin' you mouf 'cause you 'fraid."

"I ain', Marvon, but I'm scared."

"Me, too, Bitta. You damn right I'm scared, but I gots to go home."

Bitta Smalls watched Marvon run up the road toward the lights of his own family's double-wide, and then he cried. It was several minutes before he calmed down enough to leave the shed and start into the house to face questions about being late and missing dinner. He might get a whipping, but he would never tell what he and Marvon had done.

"Ain' gon' tell nobody, no matta what," he said as he walked. His chin quivered, and tears began to form in his eyes again.

Sam Larkin dozed shortly after Karen fell asleep. When he opened his eyes and looked at the clock, it was just after eleven. The storm had subsided, but there was no shade of moonlight or stars. He was still holding Karen Chaney's hand.

When he moved to stretch out the settled vertebrae, her hand tightened.

"Don't try to get away," he heard her whisper. A subtle smile came to her lips.

"How long have you been awake?" he asked.

"Five minutes. Ten at most. You were sleeping soundly." She hadn't opened her eyes or looked at him yet. "Thank you, Sam."

"For what?"

"Staying here with me. Holding my hand."

"That's all?" She turned her head and looked at him.

"I could go on, but I don't think it's necessary. I think I could lie here all day." She lifted her eyes to look out the glass doors. "It's still night," she said.

"You slept about four hours."

"Seems like days."

"What can I get you? Are you hungry? Want something to eat?"

"What I want is not as important as my need, and my need is to get a shower and listen while you tell me what happened."

"You don't know?"

"Well, I wake up in someone's bed other than my own," she lifted the cover and looked down at herself, "naked, even though I don't remember undressing . . ."

"You didn't." He smiled, glad to see there were no obvious residual effects from the blow to her head. Her caustic humor was alive and well.

"See? I might have had a whole lot of fun that I don't even remember. I hate it when that happens."

"I can't imagine that ever happening to you under normal circumstances," Sam said.

"You might be surprised, Larkin. You don't know me that well."

"Of that there is no doubt," he said. "I'll go put some coffee on." He started toward the kitchen.

"My tee shirt still in the same drawer?"

"*Your* tee shirt?" He raised his eyebrows.

"Once I wear something, it's mine. That's the rule."

"How possessive of you."

"Sam?" He stopped and looked at her. "I'd probably kiss you in gratitude, but I don't think it would be too pleasant. I need to brush my teeth."

"I'm glad—considering the tee shirt—that it's just in gratitude. There's a new toothbrush in the bathroom. I keep them on hand for just such occasions." Karen threw a pillow at the retreating figure, put her hand to her head and lay back down.

"Ow, that hurt," she said. The movement caused more pain than she expected and caught her by surprise. For a brief moment, she felt dizzy.

It was not the first time she had experienced that kind of pain. The last time was when a suspect hit her from behind with a piece of two-by-four and gave her a severe concussion. The doctor told her that if it had been a longer piece of wood that created more force, it would have crushed her skull. As it was, she was put on leave for three months, and the case she was working on went to hell. She didn't want that to happen again, if, indeed, there was a case.

If she did have a concussion, she wouldn't be able to pull off her assignment by herself; however, she didn't want anyone else sent in from outside. The difficulty of her situation was intensifying. Sam Larkin would have to help her, if he would, and that meant telling him everything. Now she wasn't sure how to approach it; the playing field had changed, and she found herself dependent on him. Perhaps the accident was Providence. She would think about that as she showered. The thought of hot water beating down on her sore neck was absolutely the most appealing thing she could imagine. Almost. Anything else was out of the question.

CHAPTER 17

Karen couldn't guess how long she was in the bathroom, but it was obvious that Sam had taken a quickie in the outside shower and washed his hair. She was shocked when she saw him because she had never seen his hair any other way than pulled back tightly into a ponytail. He must have given it a quick blow dry because it fanned out over his shoulders. She liked the ponytail better. When he saw her, he pulled it back and flipped a rubber tie around it.

"Feeling better?" he asked.

"Much. A cup of that coffee I smell would make me almost perfect."

Her head was still hurting. All the thinking she had done while the water beat down on her, soothing the pain in her muscles, left her with no alternative other than risking trust with Sam Larkin and making every effort to reduce that to a calculated risk.

"Sam, could I make a phone call?" she asked. "My father always calls on Saturday or Sunday, and he panics if I'm not home and haven't called to let him know I survived another week." It was a lie she'd deal with later if she had to.

"Use the phone in the bedroom; it'll give you more privacy," he answered.

She had to let Dougherty know about the accident, how she was, and what she was going to do. If he said "no" firmly enough, she might respect his advice. Might. She used her credit card so Sam would not get a strange number on his phone bill, as well as to protect Neil.

"Blue?" she asked when he answered. "Did I wake you? I know it's the middle of the night, but I've got to talk to you. You don't sound sleepy."

"No you didn't, and I'm not. What's up?"

She told him about the drive out to Sam's house—as much as she could remember—her purpose in going, the accident, her fear

192

that she might be injured more severely than it appeared, the headache, possible concussion, and that she didn't want an outsider sent in. When she was finished, he sighed, which was not a good sign.

"I think I'm going to come in out of the cold with Sam Larkin."

"I can't approve that, Karen, and you're too professional to think I would. I'm considering bringing you in anyway." She was stunned.

"Why?"

"What do you have? Even a hint that our information is correct? That anything at all is going on down there? We can't afford wasting an officer sitting down there waiting to catch a high school kid selling a nickel bag on the corner, and I believe you've lost your objectivity."

"No, I haven't. Believe me, Blue, there's something here. I know it, and I think Sam Larkin can help me find out what it is. I need a local friend, a conduit to tell me where to look. Turner Lockett had to be watching Sam's house. There was no other reason for him to be out there. But why? And how could someone like that die in a boating accident? Give me some time."

"I'll see. In the meantime, 'no' to Larkin."

"You never reported anything on your check on Clay." There was a brief pause.

"Nothing yet. We're still working on it." Taking this much time was not Neil Dougherty's operational procedure, and the hesitant answer was unusual. She didn't want to think what she was thinking.

"Okay. I'll check in later, Blue, but if you undermine me on this . . ."

"Keep me apprised as to your condition. And 'no' to Larkin; I'm not playing games."

"I know you're not. Bad idea. See ya, Blue."

Her head still hurt, and the hurt must have shown because when she went back into the kitchen, Sam had a concerned look on his face.

"What?" she asked.

"You okay? I mean really okay?"

"I think so. Why?"

"You look like you're in pain."

"Thanks for the compliment. Actually, my head does hurt. I took some more aspirin, but it hasn't kicked in."

"Do we need to go to the hospital?" he asked.

"I don't think so. I looked at the cut when I showered; it doesn't need stitches. Let's give the aspirin time to work," she said, sitting at the counter.

"You took quite a blow. Still no idea what happened?" He put a cup in front of her and filled it. She caught him looking at the dark nipples that showed through the thin, cotton fabric of the tee shirt and smiled.

"Not really. It was raining; I couldn't see. Then I guess I hydroplaned or something. Next thing I knew I was lying on my back, looking up into the trees. By then the car wasn't moving; whatever happened was over. I remember blood, but that's all. No, that's not all. This is interesting now that I think about it: I wasn't afraid. I felt comfortable and then calmly passed out, but there wasn't any fear."

"I'm sure you were in shock. You were out cold when I got there."

"I have no recollection," she said, sipping her coffee.

"That might be good," he said.

"What?"

"No recollection."

"Why is that?"

"Memory of fearful things can cause fear to live with you, become a part of your life. That's not a good thing."

"I can't imagine you ever being afraid of anything, Sam."

"You have no idea," he said and got up from the bar stool. "I'm going out on the deck for a cigarette."

She took her coffee and followed him. The water lay still and the marsh grasses were quiet. They sat on the deck, not speaking, becoming absorbed in the comfort of the stillness. It was a time of silence.

"It's something, isn't it?" Karen said. He didn't need to ask what she was referring to; one could not be present in the moment and not know.

"Yes, it is."

"I think you're a good man," she said.

"I thank you for that, though I have no idea where that came from, and I'm not sure how you came to that conclusion. There's some that don't feel that way, as they say."

"I think you're a good man because I trust my instincts, and I'm going to have to put a great deal of faith in you. If that's not a good idea, I'd like for you to let me know now. I'd feel better than if you told me later."

She didn't look at him as the words came out.

"I'm not sure how to answer that, Karen. I can be trusted; that's not a question in my mind. What concerns me is why you need that. I'm happy here. I'm uninvolved. It's why I came, why I don't seek out friends. Running? Maybe, but I want peace. Other people don't respect that; they feel some kind of compulsion to impose themselves on you, save you from yourself. Most people can't accept that others don't need them. There's an old song that says, 'Everybody needs somebody.' I don't."

"Wow. That's the most personal thing I've ever heard you say." There was a hint of smile on her lips. "I don't want you to marry me, Sam; I just need to know I can trust you. That and honesty."

"Why don't we start with the first and see how it goes?"

"You're a tough negotiator. Do you always require a tilted field?"

"Absolutely." He smiled.

Sorry, Neil, I have to do this, she thought. "I have a confession to make," she began. "I am not what you think." She waited for a response and watched Sam as he thought about what she had said.

"You really don't know what I think, but I never, for a moment, supposed you were just an environmental enforcement officer. I don't know exactly what you are, but, pardon my grammar, that ain't it, and I'm pretty sure I don't want to know any more than that."

"Score one for you," she said. "The problem is that in my capacity as what I am—is that right?—I can't trust anyone I don't know everything about, and I need at least one person I can rely on."

"And you picked me." He shook his head.

"I didn't pick you; you evolved. When I met you, I didn't know what to think. I . . ."

"Could we cut to the chase?" he asked, lifting his eyes to hers.

"I don't know enough about you to trust you. It's as simple as that. There are a lot of dark corners in you, Sam."

"Is that why we went to bed? So you could get to know me better? See what's in the dark corners?" Her eyes shot up to meet his.

"That's not a reliable way to get to know someone, but if you think that, then fuck you. You disappoint me. Think about it." She got up and went into the house to refill her cup.

Sam stared out at the marsh. Embarrassed. What he. said wasn't him. He didn't know where it came from, since that idea had never crossed his mind before. It wasn't justified. He knew it was designed to hurt, to push her away. Good offense, Larkin, he said to himself as she came back through the door.

"I apologize," he said. "There was no excuse for that."

"You're damned right there wasn't." While she was in the house, she had put on one of his blue denim, work shirts over the tee shirt. "Sam, I'm offering you something that I guard very closely because it could cost me my life. That may sound dramatic to you, but it's a fact, and you're not helping me. You give off this confident, secure, sometimes even superior aura, but I'm beginning to wonder if there's anything inside to back it up. You won't let anyone in. I don't need anyone like that as a friend or anything else."

"How much do you know about me? I'm sure it's more than I've told you. I know you were asking questions at Harry Tom's."

"Not a lot; nobody knows much to tell. You're damned good at not blowing your cover. It's probably what made me think I could open up to you and ask for your help if I needed it."

"Tell me," he said.

"I can't tell you without exposing myself, Sam, something I've been ordered not to do. You might as well know, I'm stepping on thin ice here." He didn't speak, which didn't bolster her confidence. "I guess it's too late to stop now, in any case. I am part of the DEA Special Operations Unit, working undercover. At least I was undercover." She waited for a reaction, but Sam just smiled and shook his head.

"A hired gun of the highest degree. Impressive. I won't ask what you're working on because I know you can't tell me, and, truthfully, I don't want to know. So what has your investigation about me revealed?"

"I'll tell you, and then if you want to take me home, you'll not hear from me again. If that's the case, I can only ask that you keep this conversation as closely guarded as you do everything else."

"You can trust me."

"I hope so." She eyed him warily. "I know you're from Louisiana. I know you worked with the Louisiana Environmental Service, left without any reason we could find, and began teaching in Covington six years later. Based on local records, you were here a couple of years before you started working. And I know you've been married once. Beyond that, nothing else." She didn't like lying, but showing your whole hand at once wasn't ever smart.

"Pretty impressive," he said. "You know more than anyone, and I can't imagine anything else you'd want to know. Neat little invasion of privacy." She could see the discomfort in Sam's face and hear the anger in his voice.

"It was done with the best motives in mind," she said without apology.

"By whose standards"

"Mine, Sam. I had to know, but there are four years missing. Kind of unusual for a man in his prime." He looked at her.

"I'm not sure I want to share that, Karen. Like it or not, I'm going to have to think about that." He stood up. "I'm going to take a run. I'll be back in about forty minutes."

"In the dark? You'll kill yourself out here."

"I've done it many times," he said and went inside to change.

Sam Larkin left her with a decision to make. She thought about that as she watched him go down the steps, stretch out his legs against the Rover's bumper, and begin his slow warm-up pace up the drive toward Osprey Landing Road. Just beyond the arc of brightness cast by the deck lights, he disappeared into the darkness.

His mind was asunder, a mixture of anger, hostility, affection and admiration for Karen Chaney's honesty and trust, embarrassment at his paranoia, insecurity and, most of all, fear. Fear of the return of the dreams, the days and nights, all he had worked so hard to assuage from his memory. A living fear. The spotlights. That's what he remembered most vividly. Blinding. Lighting the entire slough where a boat was moored to a cypress stump. Lighting it so brightly that it seemed the moon had exploded. Sam Larkin was bent over, in the process of opening a hatch when the lights hit him. Two fast boats, hydroplaning sideways in a turn, broke the entrance of the slough, making it impossible for anyone—even someone with his knowledge, expertise and familiarity—to escape. There were shouts, warnings, a few moments of confusion, and one of the intruding boats sidled up to the one in which Sam was standing, his hand still holding the half-raised hatch on the untended craft.

He wasn't wearing his uniform and didn't have his badge, though, as things turned out, he was sure it would have made no difference. The federal agents were primed for a bust and nothing would deter them. From the moment he saw the lights, he knew that was the way it would be. He was arrested and charged with the importation and possession of an illegal substance for distribution, a half-ton of hashish. The fact that he was a law enforcement officer with the Fish and Game Department, that he was aware of the operation and had reported it to the county officials, who told him to "keep an eye out," held no weight with the arresting officers or the subsequent judge.

Judge Thornton Hunnycut looked down on the innocent he knew stood before him. There was no pity, no compassion and, above all, no suggestion of guilt or embarrassment on the judge's face. His voice held the emotion of a jackhammer pounding away at a mountain of solid granite when he spoke.

"Mr. Larkin, I won't dignify you with the title of officer because you broke the trust that allowed you to wear that title and that uniform, flaunted authority, and hurt your fellow officers. You, sir, are to be scorned. I cannot do that verbally any

more than I have already done in this court today, but I can,
and I do sentence you to fifteen years to be served at the state
penitentiary at Angola." Without moving his eyes from the laser
thread he had built between his own and Larkin's, he said,
"Bailiff, remand the prisoner into custody." Judge Hunnycut
punctuated his sentence with a firm stroke of his gavel.

Larkin returned the stare of the man sitting above him with
steel-cold eyes, knowing a crime far greater than that of which
he was convicted had just taken place. He had always looked
up to federal officers as being at the peak of their profession.
Now he knew better. His respect for them was gone with the
knowledge that they operated within their own club without
rules or regard for the truth or the law. His thoughts were spin-
ning out of control as he was led out of the courtroom. Fifteen
years of his life was something beyond comprehension, regard-
less of where it would be spent, and that those in charge had
chosen to prosecute on a state level rather than federal in order
to send him to a hard-time prison was unforgivable. It was an
easy way to hide their mistake. It was doubtful he would ever
get out.

Larkin served four years, during which he filed numerous
appeals and irrefutable evidence of his innocence was provided
by an unknown benefactor. A wrongful imprisonment suit then
moved through the courts unusually fast. Finally Larkin
received a substantial cash settlement from the government.
Only then was the matter resolved. No resolution, however,
could return what he had lost, and that thought never left him.

When he returned from his run, Sam showered outside,
wrapped a towel around his middle, and went upstairs. Karen
Chaney was curled up under the sheet on the bed, sleeping
soundly. He slipped in beside her and was soon asleep himself.

CHAPTER 18

Isabel Reichert sat on the gallery of her house, reading the Sunday paper. It was going to be a beautiful day. The possibilities that lay before her appeared endless. From the time she had made the decision to go to Mexico—the most bizarre thing she had ever done in her life—a new energy had overtaken her. And she had pulled it off. A wig, tanning makeup, some funky clothes, including a floppy hat, along with her husband's total interest in himself and his own problems, made it easy. When people are not looking for something, they seldom see it. She followed her husband's every step except to bed. Stood right behind him and his mistress, listening to what they said, as they watched the cliff divers. A party of three.

If she had been discovered, she had the confrontation planned. Now there were more scenarios than ever. Although she had bribed the desk clerk for his name, she still didn't know who the mysterious Mr. Ortega was. But she knew Bill hadn't gone to see him about a golf date. The beautiful part was that she could take her time in deciding exactly what to do. Beyond that, Isabel Reichert would only think about Isabel Reichert. For all intents and purposes, she was free.

Sam awoke early, despite having been up most of the night. Karen had backed into him, he held her in the spoon position while they slept. He managed to get out of bed without waking her, dressed, and called Skeeter Crewes to help him extricate her car from the drainage ditch. Skeeter said he could help if Sam came right over and afterwards gave him a ride to the dock. He wrote Karen a note and left it next to the coffee pot, which he loaded and turned on. He didn't take time for a cup for himself.

Good Morning!

I'm not still running. You were asleep when I got back. Have gone to get your car out of the ditch. If you regain consciousness, I'll see you when I get back.

The car was not difficult to remove. Sam took a tow-chain and pulled it out with the Land Rover. There was something disturbing, however; the rear end of the car was badly pushed in and the trunk was sprung open. Neither he nor Skeeter could come up with a path the car might have taken to cause such damage. They pulled it into Skeeter's yard, and then drove to Harry Tom's dock.

When he returned to the house, Karen was in the kitchen cutting up vegetables for an omelet.

"Well, Sleeping Beauty has arisen. A prince must have dropped by," he said.

"She may have arisen, but she doesn't feel like a princess. He couldn't cure the headache. Coffee?"

"That would be the best part of my day so far. If your head's still hurting, maybe we should see a doctor."

"It'll pass. Tell me about the car."

"You could drive it, but I wouldn't. The windshield's broken, maybe some undercarriage damage and something that's very strange. The rear end is pushed in and the trunk is sprung open. Anybody hit you recently?" Karen didn't respond, just sat on one of the kitchen stools and stared. "Karen?" She held up her hand for silence. There was a pained look on her face.

"Someone did hit me, Sam. From behind. I remember. It wasn't just once; it was three or four times. The last time was hard and pushed me off the road. My God, that's what happened. I got hit." He looked at her, shocked.

"Are you sure?"

"I was hit, damn it. On purpose. And because of the rain and the lights blinding me, I couldn't see what kind of vehicle it was. Had to be a truck; a car couldn't have done it without damaging itself."

"If that's true," he said, "somebody must know who you are, Karen. That or they want you out of here for some other reason."

"Nobody could know; I don't make mistakes. With perhaps one exception."

"What's that?"

"You, Sam. Telling you what I am. Fortunately for you, that was after the fact."

"Telling me was not a mistake," he said.

"I don't know what to think. Somebody tried to kill me, and you can bet I'm going to find out who." There was fire in her eyes.

"Be careful, Karen." Sam cautioned.

"Sam, I need to know about you." She searched his face for an answer.

"Prison," he said. He made the decision while he was running, knowing he was moving back into a life of risk. He would explain prison and the circumstances, but nothing else. Karen said nothing, just listened. Didn't register shock or disappointment, letting him know by her reaction that she believed his explanation was reasonable.

Cedrick Hamilton sat in the parking lot at Harry Tom Cooper's Boat Dock watching Skeeter Crewes, who was hosing down the dock. He would be getting off work soon. He didn't know what approach he would use, but figured it would come to him as they talked. He was good off-the-cuff, one of his greatest career assets.

At seven-thirty Skeeter walked out the door of the ship's store and started his solitary walk home. He did not see Hamilton sitting in his car watching him as he left. The man waited until Crewes was well out of the parking lot and then headed up the ever-darkening road toward Route 37. *Goin' home*, Hamilton thought. *Just another poor nigger goin' home to nothin'*. Like someone speaking a foreign language, he often reverted to the language of his beginnings when he was thinking. *Won't be long before the anger at beatin' his head against a wall of debt takes over, then it'll be beatin' his wife and drinkin' and settin' with the wire-spool crowd*. He had seen it happen to some of the best of them. "That's your future, boy," he muttered to the silence of the car, "And I'm here to help you." He was trying hard to make himself believe that.

Skeeter was halfway to Route 37 when he heard a car approaching from behind. He didn't turn around, just held his thumb in the air as he continued to walk. He took only a few steps before the car sidled up next to him. He went up to the window to look in; he never got into a car without first checking to see who or what was inside. The window lowered in front of his face.

"Skeeter?" the driver asked.

"Seed?" Skeeter said, bringing up the old nickname by which everyone in high school knew Cedrick Hamilton.

"Hadn't heard that one in a long time," Hamilton said. "Get on in. I'll give you a ride home."

"Don' want to take you outta your way, but I sure would appreciate it," he said as he opened the door and got into the car.

"How've you been, Skeeter. How long's it been? A year? Two?"

" 'Leas' that. I been doin' all right, far as it goes."

"Ettie and the kids doing okay?"

"We managin'. How 'bout you?"

"I'm doin' fine. Just have to work everyday to keep the good ol' boys off my back. You still live in the same place?" Hamilton asked as he approached Route 37.

"Me an' my daddy, an' his daddy befo' him. Same ol' place. 'Bout to fall down though. What you doin' out here on a Sunday? I ain' seen you at the boat dock, an' ain' much else down that road."

"Just takin' a ride. Sometimes I get tired of all I have to put up with at the office, and I just need to get out. Go back home, so to speak."

"I can understand that, but I don' think you got no complaints comin'. Done better than most of us." Hamilton was a little taken aback that Skeeter's speech had deteriorated as much as it seemed. He didn't remember him sounding like a field hand.

"In some ways, yes, I have. In others not so good. Look at you. A wife and two kids, nobody important to answer to. Something to be said for that, Skeeter."

"I guess. Hard though."

"Money?"

"What else? Ain' no work except at the dock. Ain' got no transportation, an' cain't afford to get none, but I ain' complainin' an' Ettie don't complain. She's good with the kids and that's good."

"What would you do if you could afford some transportation? Any ideas?"

"Might get a job in town. I don't know." Skeeter Crewes was thinking. And dreaming. Cedrick Hamilton began to feel confident for the first time since Clay suggested Skeeter as a mark.

"Not that many jobs in town from what I hear. What would you really like to do? Forget about money; what would you really like to do?"

"Get your job," Skeeter said and laughed. Hamilton laughed with him. "House is right up yonder," he said, nodding straight ahead.

"You don't want my job, I'll guarantee," he said. "Mind if we stop up here in the drive and talk for a couple of minutes? I have something that might help you out."

"Okay by me, but you better turn out the lights, so's it don't scare Ettie."

Hamilton stopped the car and turned off the lights.

"Now back to what I asked you. What would you do if you had some money?"

"Never thought about it much, 'cause I don't ever expect to get any."

"But if you did?"

"I don't fill my mind with 'what if,' Seed. You know I ain' one of those brothers sits around a spool an' talks about every damn thing that was done to them yesterday and every damn thing they're gonna do tomorrow."

"I know that, Skeeter, but I'm tryin' to help you here. Suppose you had twenty-five thousand dollars. What would you do?"

Skeeter laughed again. "You outta your mind, Seed. I'd hafta win the lottery to have that kinda money, an' I cain't even afford to buy a ticket."

"Okay, Okay, I understand that, but I'm interested. I don't get a chance to talk with friends I grew up with much anymore. I miss that, sharing those dreams we used to talk about."

"As I recall, we spent more time talkin' about pussy than dreams," Skeeter said with a smile.

"I guess you're right about that," he laughed.

"Twenty-five thousand dollars. Whew! Never much thought about it." He paused for a minute. "There is one thing I thought about once. A yard bidness. You know, cut grass, trim, sweep the walks, maybe cut the dead fronds outta the palmettos, spread pine straw, stuff like that. You know."

"Sounds like you've thought about it a lot."

"Did a long time ago." There wasn't any talk in the car for a minute or so, Skeeter visualizing; Cedrick Hamilton waiting. When enough time had passed, he spoke.

"How bad do you want that, Skeeter? A truck and mowers and the other tools it would take to do that kind of work?"

Skeeter Crewes turned toward him and stared.

"How bad?" Hamilton repeated. "It would take the pressure off, wouldn't it? You could do a lot better for your family than walking to the boat dock and working for Harry Tom every day. What's he paying you? Three, four dollars an hour?"

"What're you up to, Seed? Why you so interested in me all of a sudden? We ain' talked in three or four years, and now you're talkin' to me about twenty-five thousand dollars and what I want to be doin'?"

"Just trying to help a friend. You are a friend aren't you?"

"I don't know. I thought so, but I b'lieve you tryin' to get me into somethin'. I think I better go in the house with Ettie and the kids."

"Give me just a couple of minutes. If I tell you what's on my mind—whether you agree with it or not—can you keep it to yourself? I mean absolutely to yourself, not tell Ettie or anybody else?"

"I know how to keep things to myself. Been doin' it all my life." Hamilton suddenly felt nervous. He reached behind his back, as if he were scratching an itch, and felt the gun he had stuck in his belt before leaving his office. He felt ridiculous. He couldn't kill Skeeter Crewes. He couldn't kill anyone, but he thought maybe it would be useful in convincing the man he was serious. He was putting his whole life and career in Skeeter Crewes's hands without knowing whether he would go along or not. It didn't make any sense at all except his desperate need to stay on Charles Clay's good side.

"I know I can trust you, but I had to ask."

"Just what are you askin' me to do, Seed?"

"Take a couple of days off. Take the family up to Myrtle Beach, go visit relatives somewhere. That is really all I'm asking you to do, be gone for a couple of days. I can't tell you anything beyond that."

"How'm I suppose to take the family somewhere? And why? What the hell's goin' on? I better go on in the house." He reached for the door handle.

"Wouldn't Ettie and the kids like a vacation? Don't you think they deserve it? Wouldn't you like to give it to them?" Skeeter looked at him, his hand resting on the door handle.

"What're you gettin' me into, Seed? You still ain' told me how."

"Leave the 'how' up to me, and I'm not getting you into anything. All you'll do is take a three- or four-day vacation, and when you get back, you'll have enough money to start that business of yours."

"Say what?" There was a frown on Crewes's face that Hamilton couldn't read.

"Twenty-five thousand dollars when you get back. Just for being out of town." No further explanation was needed. Skeeter Crewes knew exactly what he was being offered.

"Twenty-five thousand dollars? Just for usin' my dock?"

"I didn't say anyone was going to use your dock." Hamilton smiled.

"Twenty-five thousand dollars. Truck, trailer and mowers. Shee-it!" He paused and looked out the window at nothing. "That would be nice all right."

"It's up to you. The offer's there."

"When?"

"Not exactly sure, but you'd need to be ready to go on a moment's notice."

"What'd I tell Ettie? Have to explain it somehow."

"Tell her you found a partner for your business. Have to go to Myrtle Beach to talk to him. He's footing the bill. That ought to work, shouldn't it?"

"Guess it would. I 'preciate it, Seed, but I'm gone hafta think about it. Kinda scary. I'll think about it, but I got to get on in the house. Ettie'll think somethin' happened to me." He opened the door, got out, and then looked back in through the open window. "What if I say no, Seed."

Cedrick Hamilton put his hand behind his back and pulled out the gun, which he laid on the seat where Skeeter Crewes had been sitting.

"We're serious, Skeeter." Skeeter's face turned sad, but there was no fear.

"Come on, Seed, you'd shoot me? You think I b'lieve that?" Hamilton could not look at his friend. His eyes were on his own lap.

"No, I wouldn't, but it might not be up to me. You think about it. I'll be in touch." He switched on the headlights, backed out onto the road, and was gone.

"Lawdy, Lawdy, Lawdy," Skeeter said to himself as he began the walk to his house. "Twenty-five thousand dollars and a vacation or we might shoot you. That'll take some thinkin'. Boy, yesterday was sure friendly compared to today. Lawdy."

Sunday was a loss for Sam Larkin. What he had told Karen roiled in his mind. She had listened to what he had to say and left it at that. No comments, no questions and no prolonged discussion. Her head was still hurting, she said, and her body—by her description—felt like it had been run over by a road grader. The day was lost to the physical exhaustion of the accident, its aftermath, little sleep and the emotional maelstrom created by both of their revelations. Karen slept most of the day, and at six o'clock Sam drove her home.

Brad Coleman relaxed in a lounge chair by a large swimming pool comparing the emerald green of the water in the pool to the deep blue of the Caribbean Sea, which lay several hundred yards from the pool area. Although he was back in Jamaica, he had neither seen nor spoken with Peter Walker, didn't even notify him he was going to be on the island. This was not a business trip. He had come as soon as negotiations for the boat to be used in the Carolina venture were completed. It was a spur-of-the-moment decision to call in an "anytime" invitation to spend five days at the Hedonism resort in Negril. Coleman often received such open invitations, where he could just show up at the registration desk and be awarded luxurious accommodations.

It was time to step back and assess what he was doing. In another day it would be back to the mainstream of business. That idea did not elate him as it had done in the past. Success fades the thrill of risk. When it ceases to be a challenge is when it all comes tumbling down, he thought. He had more money than many young millionaires on the rise could conceive having in their best moments. If *Forbes* or Dun and Bradstreet included smugglers on their "richest" lists, Brad Coleman would be well up on the list, over nine hundred million circulating in various accounts and corporations throughout the world, not to mention forty-plus million in real estate and stocks, most of it so insulated the best paper chaser in the world couldn't find it.

A nude woman of about thirty walked by and looked at him admiringly. It was a wonderfully free resort. One could dress or undress as one chose. Most who were in reasonably attractive physical condition chose nudity. Brad Coleman wore nothing, and his lean, hard body collected more than its share of second looks. However, sex and romance were not what he had come to Jamaica for. It was to relax and decide what he would do after the South Carolina operation was completed.

There would be time after that for one more venture somewhere before the tropical storm season began, but if he chose to do that, arrangements would have to begin immediately. He wasn't sure he was up to it. It had been a big year, and the constant travel was beginning to wear on him.

He was looking forward to his return to South Carolina in two weeks. He hadn't told Charles Clay exactly when he was coming because he wanted some time to see the area and get a feel for the place before he contacted him. And there was Morgan Hannah, the lady with the fascinating name. In their one brief encounter, she had captured his imagination, something not many women were able to do. The problem, as always, was the life he led. He owned homes on Eleuthera Island and Antigua, apartments in Miami and New York, and a home in St. Tropez, but he was never in any one for more than a few days at a time, sometimes not visiting a property for more than a year. It was a nomadic life. It didn't give anyone a chance for a clear shot. He couldn't imagine the woman Morgan Hannah appeared to be ever being willing to become a part of that even for a short term, which was typical of his relationships.

He turned his thoughts to the magic around him. The heat of the sun was cleansing and energizing. He was surrounded by generally beautiful people; his life exciting. It was to be enjoyed by itself, and Brad Coleman had mastered, truly mastered, the art of fully experiencing the moment. The problem was that it was all passing by too quickly. There would be an end to it, sometime, someplace.

He understood early on that the ability to take pleasure when it presented itself was a necessity in his line of work because he knew all of those things would likely be taken from him, suddenly, for awhile at least. He expected to be caught sooner or later. It was fair payment for the rewards of the life he led, of every pirate's life, and it never caused him great concern. The key was to be ready, and he was as prepared for that likelihood as it was possible to be.

A smile of contentment crossed his lips. He closed his eyes to better feel the heat and moisture escaping through his pores. He liked to feel that and enjoy the fragrance of the cascades of bougainvillea and other tropicals that were in abundance around the pool area. And he liked to listen to the sea. His smile grew wider. Maybe he could quit before they got him. They hadn't even come close yet.

CHAPTER 19

Karen Chaney didn't call Neil Dougherty on Monday morning to tell him what she had learned about Sam Larkin. Her head still ached and her back and muscles were stiff, but that wasn't the reason. It didn't take much of a back or many muscles to lift the receiver of a telephone. Larkin had given her an empty box, and she didn't know what to do with it. The four missing years were accounted for—she didn't doubt that he had been truthful—but he hadn't mentioned the money and there was no apparent willingness, on his part, to cooperate or assist her should she need him. She felt no more secure than she had before their mutual disclosures.

Finally, unable to put it off any longer, she picked up the phone, then put it down again. She didn't know what to tell him. He would want to hear all the details and would then ask what revealing herself had accomplished. Again, she picked up the phone. This time she dialed his number.

"Dougherty."

"Neil?"

"Yeah?"

"Sorry. It didn't sound like you."

"I seldom sound like me. Part of my training as a covert operations specialist."

"What are you on?" she asked. "Or are you just drunk?"

"No, Belle, I am not drunk, but ' 'tis a consummation devoutly to be wished.' Unfortunately, I have to work, so that makes being drunk out of the question. What can I do for you? No information on Larkin yet, if that's what you want."

"Prison," she said.

"Prison? He told you?" The word captured his attention.

"Yes, but it's not what it seems."

"Never is, Belle. Tell me," he said.

210

Karen told him, in detail, everything she had learned. When she was finished, there was a pause before Dougherty spoke.

"Who was the judge? Did he say?"

"Hunnywell, Hunnycut? Something like that."

"Sounds like something Thornton Hunnycut would do."

"Who the hell is Thornton Hunnycut?"

"Used to be a federal judge in Louisiana. Had people calling him senator before he ever ran for office. Corrupt as they come. I'm surprised he ever admitted his error," Dougherty said, "but I guess when you are an ex-federal judge who becomes a United States senator, you can do most anything you want and get by with it."

"According to Sam, he didn't."

"What?"

"Admit his error. A federal prosecutor called on Sam's attorney. They worked out a deal, including the money I assume, though Sam didn't mention that, and their absolute silence, as well as a complete expunging of the trial."

"You mean his record."

"Not from what Sam says. The whole arrest and trial was removed from the records. State, local and federal. It never happened, and there's nothing to prove it did. Blue, how could a federal judge send him to a state prison?"

"Consider the state and consider the government. But it is strange. Hunnycut or the feds must've made one hell of an error. What's Larkin gonna do?"

"About what?" Karen asked.

"You."

"I was afraid you'd ask that," she said. "To tell you the truth, Blue, I don't know. Have no idea."

"Oh, that's great. You expose yourself, and you're not sure you can count on him?"

"I think I can, but . . ."

"You can't think you can depend on someone when you're in our business, Karen. It's hard enough to have faith in the people you work with every day of the week, not to mention someone with a questionable past who won't commit to you. I think you've gotten yourself in a mess of trouble, young lady."

Exasperation turned to anger. "You should have better sense. I can't believe this."

"Blue, listen to me. I'm not going to jeopardize myself and whatever operation I have going here, which I can't define at the moment because there doesn't seem to be anything going on. At least I haven't been able to spot it. I know this is a prospecting mission."

"I did get one thing on your Mr. Clay. His name was mentioned in conjunction with the Descarté investigation. Just a phone call in the records, but my eyes widened when I saw his name. I'm not saying he's involved in anything, but it seems logical, all things considered. Could be anything. There were a lot of numbers."

"I'll see what I can find out. I pray he is a player. I need a target. The can is here, I'm sure. I've just got to find the opener to let out the worms. People are pretty close-mouthed and protective in this place. What else is happening on Descarté?"

"Just observation and investigation at the moment, but we know he's networked. I don't think he's aware of what's going on. Something will happen. Keep me posted if you learn anything about Clay."

"I will."

"And, Belle, don't trust Larkin, not until he's willing to earn it."

"I promise. Good night, Blue."

"Take care of you, Karen." The phone went dead in her hand. She got up, walked to the window and looked out at the river. Sam Larkin's house was over there on the other side of Matthew's Island. So near and so far out of reach on so many levels.

"Damn you, Sam Larkin," she said out loud and slammed her hand against the sill.

"Shit! Shit! Shit!" She pulled the drapes together, turned out the lights and went up the circular stairway to bed.

When the yellow school bus creaked to a halt on the dirt road in front of Bitta Smalls's house, Marvon Jefferies was waiting. Marvon's bus came earlier because he was in middle school. It was all planned: Bitta would drop off his book bag, and they would head to Turner Lockett's trailer, just as they had done the day before. Bitta had leaned a piece of scrap lumber he found in the yard against the trailer door, so they wouldn't have to go inside to see if anyone had been there while they were in school. No one had come on Monday.

From their hiding place, someone would have to come through the woods and marsh to approach without their knowing well in advance. Sitting quietly and watching was exciting for the first hour, talking enthusiastically in low voices about what they would do with the money if no one showed up, less enthusiastically about what they would do if anyone did. After an hour and a half, they were tired, hungry and ready to pack it in and head home when they heard the sound of a boat coming up the creek. There was no reason for anyone to venture up this far unless they were coming to Turner Lockett's trailer. The creek petered out not more than twenty-five yards beyond it.

Bitta Smalls struggled to keep from shaking. Marvon sat, eyes wide as full moons, watching the creek for sight of the boat. Seeing it round the final bend caused their fear to grow even greater.

"It be de po-lice," Bitta whispered, seeing Ray Breslin's brown uniform and the gun on his hip.

"What de po-lice doin' up here?" Marvon asked.

"Come to see de trailer, I reckon. What else dey be up here fo'?"

"Why you spec' de po-lice won' see dat trailer?"

"Man dead, ain' he? Dey has to check an' see what goin' on," the younger boy said.

"What happen he go inside an' see what we done?"

"He ain' see us do it. Be quiet."

The boat eased into Turner Lockett's sad excuse for a dock. Breslin got out and tied up. He carried a fire ax with him.

"What you reckon he gone do wid dat ax?" Bitta asked.

"I don' know, but it don' look good. I think we ought to get outta here an' go home. I ain' got no truck wid dis. Come on." He started to get up, but Bitta put his hand on Marvon's shoulder and held him down.

"I won' see what he be doin'. Maybe he jus' walk aroun' an' look things over. Dat what dey do."

"How you know?" Marvon asked.

"I seen it on TV. Cops always walkin' aroun' quiet-like, an' dey say a curse under dey breath when dey do it. 'At's what dey do."

Ray Breslin did not walk around and look at anything. He went straight to the door of the trailer, pushed the board aside and looked at the broken lock.

"Fuck!" he said and went through the door. "Holy Christ!" his voice echoed from inside the trailer. Bitta and Marvon looked at each other and would have run, but they were locked in place by fear.

He looked around in amazement. The cabinet doors under the sink were open, and everything stored under there was scattered on the floor. The ceiling light fixture was smashed. And it looked as if someone had tried to pull the wiring out of the wall, for whatever reason. Had to be kids, he thought. They wouldn't know what they were looking for, but then he didn't really know what to look for either. Lockett was a crazy old fart. No telling where he might have hidden his money.

He began by emptying all the cabinets and drawers, throwing the hanging clothes on the floor and tapping on walls for hollow sounds, but the whole damned trailer was hollow-sounding. He emptied all of the open containers of rice, flour and cornmeal, thinking maybe Turner had stuffed it in one of those and just covered the top so it appeared full. None of them contained any money. Frustrated, he began pulling the paneling off the interior walls. Nothing. He didn't have to get up on a chair to pull the remaining water-stained acoustical tiles from the ceiling; he could reach them from where he stood. Nothing hidden there either.

"Motherfucker!" the boys heard after the hammering and ripping inside the trailer stopped.

"Le's go," Marvon said. "He lookin' fo' sumpin', an' he ain' gone find it. I don' wan' be 'round when he finished."

"We try to go, he gone see us."

Breslin came out of the trailer and looked in all directions. His shirt had turned dark with sweat, and his hair clung wetly to his forehead. He went to the edge of the trailer, got down on his hands and knees and crawled underneath. By turning onto his back, he managed to traverse the whole underside of the structure looking for any sign that the money might be hidden there. Satisfied there was nothing to be found, he worked his way out from under. Brushing off his clothes made little dent in the filth that had accumulated on his uniform. Breslin was not aware of the six eyes watching every move he made.

The trailer was a dead issue. He had examined every possible hiding place. If anyone else came to check it out, there would be no question in their mind that someone had ripped it apart looking for something. The only remaining possibilities were that Turner buried it somewhere on the property or, God forbid, that someone else had found it. The prospect of locating buried money was unlikely, but he had to give it a try. He still couldn't believe it wasn't somewhere in the trailer. "How stupid could Turner be?" he asked himself silently, then realized the question didn't make sense. "Not stupid enough," he muttered to himself. Charlie would not accept his not finding it.

He noted his position and began walking in a grid pattern, forward and backward and side to side, doing five-yard squares. The only giveaway would be freshly disturbed ground or soft earth. He paced from the trailer outward toward the woods and back. Just before he reached the area where Bitta and Marvon had secreted themselves, they began to creep away. They had no choice. He would come face to face with them if they waited. They might have made it, but halfway to the tall trees, Marvon straightened up, and Ray Breslin caught the movement out of the corner of his eye. Kids. He started to run after them, but when he reached the edge of the woods, something hit him from behind and he fell forward.

Breslin's next conscious thought was of the pulsating ache in his head. He pulled himself to his knees and looked around. There was no one to be seen. When he stood up, his knees went weak, not from the blow he had received, but from the realization that the holster on his belt was empty. He fell to the ground, trying to shield himself from whomever had taken his weapon. There was still no sound or evidence of anyone being in the area. After a cautionary wait, he began crawling toward the trailer.

By the time he got to the dock, he was shaking. The more he thought about the kids having found the money, the more panicked he became. He saw two of them, but maybe there were three. Somebody had to have hit him. New questions kept presenting themselves. If they found it, what would they do with it? Who would they tell? They would tell someone. Maybe not. Maybe they'd just hide it. Unlikely, they were kids. What if they went on a spending spree? They'd get caught. Of that he was certain. Then they'd tell where they found it. But they would also mention seeing him ripping the trailer apart.

He didn't know what to do. The obvious solution was to get rid of them, but it was difficult to imagine killing little boys. It would be easy enough to get away with because nobody would ever find them. He could lose anything in the creeks and marshes. That would be no problem at all. But what about the money? With the kids gone, how would he ever recover it unless he forced them to tell before he killed them. He had to call Charlie. When he started the motor on his boat, he took one look behind him at where he'd been. He didn't see the eyes looking back at him

"Nothin'," he said into the telephone.

"Hard to believe Turner was that clever," Charlie Clay said, wondering if Breslin found the money and planned to keep it all for himself. He wouldn't mind that. The money itself wasn't important. It was someone else finding it that worried him.

"Charlie? I'm sure someone else was there before me," Breslin said reluctantly.

"What makes you think that?" Breslin described the condition of the trailer: the open cabinets, the broken light fixture on the floor and the wire pulled out of the wall.

"Sounds like kids," Clay said.

"Yeah. That's what I figure. I saw a couple of little nigger boys playing in the woods near the trailer."

"Don't use that word, Ray. It demeans you." Breslin didn't respond. "I'll have to think about this. It could be a big problem. Whatever it is, it's going to have to be resolved one way or another. Think you can do that?"

"Whatever you say," he answered.

"Find those boys and watch 'em for a couple of days and get back to me."

"I'll do that."

Breslin left the phone booth, got in his car and headed back out to the road that ran behind Turner Lockett's trailer. It was time to take an inventory of mailbox names. His head was still hurting, and the loss of his gun was as humiliating as it was frightening. It was out there somewhere in someone's hands. He would never tell Charlie Clay or anyone else he had been suckered.

Bill Reichert sat in his office with nothing to do. He wondered how he had filled all his time in the past. The fact was there were things to be done, but he just couldn't bring himself to do them. He sat or drove. He went out to dinner rather than going home. Isabel had developed an unusual sense of detachment from him, virtually ignored anything he said. All of the normal things about him had ceased to function. He hated Mexico, Ortega, Las Brisas, Isabel, the bank, and sometimes he hated Morgan Hannah and what he perceived she had done to him.

Depression was smothering him. He was underwater and there was no surface. Morgan had killed him, or at least what he was. She was right when she said he didn't know how to handle it. If it was love, he had tasted it and it was bitter. It would never happen again. Honestly, he suspected it was pride and ego more than love that brought this humiliation upon him. No woman had ever discarded him before. It was maddening because there was nothing he could do about it. In optimistic moments, he told himself he was waiting her out. In reality, he knew there was nothing to wait for.

Reichert looked around his office and saw nothing of value. It was a nice office with absolutely no personality. There was not a personal touch in the whole room. He could as easily have been sitting in the showroom of an office furniture store as in the office of the president of the Covington National Bank. There was nothing to reveal its identity. Looking at it and thinking about himself, it was clear the office perfectly reflected where his life was at the moment.

He was also panicked about the millions of dollars he would be in charge of handling in a few weeks. Charlie had gone too far with all this foreign investment, bringing in more people, dealing with real criminals. It was a mistake.

He stood up, reached into his pocket for his car keys and left the office. He wouldn't be back, he told his secretary. Everything was running smoothly as he passed the teller line and went out the door. The bank would be fine. They didn't need him. No decisions to make except where in hell was he going.

CHAPTER 20

Skeeter Crewes didn't sleep the night after his ride with Cedrick Hamilton. Not the next, or the next. He was more than troubled; he was scared. But not so much by Hamilton's offer or threat, as by his own vulnerability. The money could change his life and the lives of Ettie and the children. It was a way out of a four-walled room of helplessness with no doors. A high school diploma only qualified you for pumping gas or flipping burgers, and, hell, where he lived you had to have transportation to do even that. Maybe it was the opportunity he had been waiting for, or maybe it was what the Covington County Schools had prepared him for.

On the other hand, he had never purposefully broken the law in his life, and, despite the fact that he "would only be taking a three-day vacation," as Cedrick characterized it, the implications went far deeper than that. He was astounded that Cedrick had allowed himself to get involved in drug smuggling. Because it was virtually impossible to effectively patrol all of the creeks, inlets and estuaries along the coastline, smuggling was rampant in the lowcountry, had been since Joe Kennedy brought Scotch in during Prohibition, but to think that Cedrick Hamilton, Covington County's black superstar, was part of it was hard to believe. He was one slick operator. Skeeter wondered who else might be involved.

And what if they got caught? He would get caught, too. Nobody was going to protect Skeeter Crewes if they could deal him for a few years' reduction in sentence. What would Ettie and the kids do if he went to jail? They couldn't survive. Welfare wasn't an option. They made a pact when they married that welfare would never be their solution for want or need. Neither he nor Ettie wanted to be a part of that stereotype. Before she accepted his proposal of marriage, she had looked him square in the eyes and asked, "Am I gonna ever see you sittin' on the porch or around a spool table eatin' pork rinds and drinkin' beer on government money?" He had answered, "No." She never had and he never would. That was another train of thought. Problem was the two trains weren't on the same track. They were going in opposite directions, and he was in the middle.

There are times, he thought, when a man can't go to his wife for help, no matter how much he loves her or respects her wisdom. There are decisions a man has to make to protect his loved ones from the pain of that decision-making process and its results. In those moments he is completely alone. For three days he had walked around with heavy lids, longing for sleep that wouldn't come, for an answer, a direction. He even said a few prayers, but he wasn't very faithful about going to church, so he wasn't sure God was listening.

All of this was taking his life away, and he wasn't even seriously considering what Cedrick and his group might do if he said no. The man had flashed a gun in response to that question. Cedrick wouldn't do it, but someone else might. From a man of respect and admiration, an icon for every young black man and child in the county or country to emulate, Cedrick Hamilton had, in Skeeter Crewes's mind, degenerated into just another worthless nigger who educated himself in order to take advantage of his brothers along with the whites he pandered to. The man had become everything Skeeter hated, if he hated anything. He was no salvation for anyone, black or white, maybe not even Cedrick Hamilton.

Skeeter was sitting on his front porch in a cane-bottomed rocking chair that Ettie had just redone. It wasn't quite comfortable yet; that would take some wearing in. Finishing the woven seat and back had taken her awhile. A lot of years had passed since she spent her days at her mama's side, weaving the sweet grass baskets they sold on the roadside on Route 37. She told him that even as a little girl, she would go to bed with her fingers aching and sometimes bleeding from grass cuts. She was a better-than-good woman, he thought, as he watched the sun burning out on the horizon. No way on earth could he hurt her.

There were no answers in the yard he was staring at, or in the trees, or up in the sky where God was supposed to live. That made him angry. He hadn't spent a lot of time in his life looking for answers because he didn't have many questions. He was what he was. He accepted that, but it seemed that when you did need an answer, there should be one there for the taking. He was also where he was: back in that four-walled room, wearing a pair of Chinese finger-cuffs that left him helpless. He smiled when he remembered the little woven tubes they had played with when they were children. Put a finger in each end, try to pull them out, and you were stuck. The harder you pulled, the more firmly caught they became. He wondered what brought that memory to the surface. A lot of strange thoughts occurred when one felt trapped, he guessed.

"Ettie," he called out from where he was sitting, "I'm gonna walk over to Sam's." He had made his decision.

"Okay," he heard from inside the house. "You be long?" She didn't question her husband. She knew he did the best he could. She never doubted that.

"I don't think so. I'll be back directly. I'll see if I can talk Sam into bringing me back."

"Be careful," she said. Ettie always said "be careful," no matter who was leaving or what anyone was going to do.

It was a twenty-minute walk to Sam Larkin's house, which would give him time to think and make sure he was doing the right thing. He trusted Sam, but it still amused him that a white coon-ass from Louisiana had come to be his best friend.

Sam was dozing in the sun room when he heard footsteps on the stairs leading up to his deck. He couldn't imagine anyone coming to call on him. He got up and went to the door as Skeeter Crewes was cocking his hand to knock.

"Got me," Skeeter said.

"Hi, Skeeter. Come on in. What brings you out tonight? Anything wrong?"

"No, nothin's wrong, Sam."

"Something happen?"

"Naw, nothin' like that. Well, somethin' happened all right, but not like at the house or nothin'."

"Come on in and sit down. I was about half asleep when I heard you. Want a beer?" Sam asked.

"A beer would be fine. Am kinda thirsty."

When Sam brought in the beers, Skeeter was looking out over the marsh. This was no social call. He put the beers down and sat down himself. Neither of them said anything for a moment. There was no sound, but Sam could hear trouble like an echo in the wind.

"What's the matter, Skeeter?"

"I'm tired, Sam. Tired of beatin' my head against a wall. Tired of livin' in a beat-up double-wide where there ain' decent room for four people. Cain't even have privacy with your own wife without bein' worried about the children hearin'. I was thinkin' the other night, used to be when me and Ettie was gettin' it on, she'd scream and yell, and I'd grunt and moan, and now we have to be as quiet as if we was in church doin' it behind the choir loft. Don't seem much fun. We hardly ever think about it any-more."

"Did you ever do that? In the church, I mean?" Sam asked with a grin.

"I ain' tellin', but you know what I mean." He looked at Sam, his best friend. "No, I don't guess you do."

"Tell me what's wrong, Skeeter. Nothing we can't take care of."

"What I'm gonna tell you has to be between us. Nobody else for right now. I ain' even told Ettie and I don't plan to."

"You know me, Skeeter. The only people I ever talk to are you and myself, and I can trust both of them with a secret."

Skeeter related the story of being picked up by Cedrick Hamilton, all of the innuendoes Hamilton threw at him before he got to the point, and, finally, the offer he made. Sam listened in silence. Nothing he heard was much of a surprise except who had offered it and the amount: twenty-five thousand dollars. That figure made Cedrick a serious player, more serious than he wanted Skeeter to know. That they would pick on Skeeter made him angry. They had done their homework and knew he was defenseless. When he was working in Louisiana, Sam had been offered deals from importers, their thinking being that if they could corrupt an environmental officer, they would be in a candy store of opportunity.

"Cedrick Hamilton. Hard to believe." Sam was astounded.

"That's who did it."

"Does Hamilton have anything to hold over your head, Skeeter?"

"No."

"I just can't imagine him offering you that kind of deal without being afraid you'd go to the police. Big chance for him to take."

"Who's gonna believe me, I tell 'em Cedrick Hamilton offered me twenty-five thousand dollars to take a vacation. Ain' nobody," Skeeter said. Sam knew he was right.

"I don't like the man even though technically I work for him. Never did feel like he was trustworthy. He's too slick. Still it's hard to believe."

"Sometimes you cain't make an empty bag stand up."

"Any idea who he might be in business with?" Sam felt strange when he heard the long-buried law enforcement officer in his thinking and his voice. He was already trying to put pieces together.

"Didn't mention nobody, but I don't reckon he would."

"Well, that answers the question about Turner," Sam said.

"What do you mean?"

"That had to be what he was doing out here," Sam said.

"What?"

"Scouting for an off-load site. He was probably checking me out as well."

"I don't think they'd ever come on to you, Sam," Skeeter said.

"They would if they had any leverage. They're hungry and they've got a fork. They've got to stick it in something and eat. What're you gonna do?"

"That's what I come to ask you about. One minute I think one way, and the next minute I think the other. I ain' a cryin' man, but I sure have felt like it a coupla times the last few days."

"What's your gut feeling, Skeeter?" It was all getting deeper, becoming a swirling vortex that was sucking him in. Now he knew why Karen Chaney was in Covington. He wondered if she knew about Cedrick Hamilton.

"I don' want to get in trouble. I cain't go to prison."

"No, you don't want that, believe me," Sam assured him. Skeeter looked at his friend curiously.

"I don't want to get killed either. That wouldn't do Ettie and the kids no good. I ain' got no life insu'ance."

"Killed? Did Cedrick Hamilton threaten you?"

"Showed me a gun when I asked what he'd do if I say no."

"You didn't tell me that," Sam said.

"I don't want to think about it. Makes it worse. That's what keeps changin' my mind. I cain't figure why this has to happen to me. I ain' done nothin' to nobody."

"That's not the way it works, Skeeter. You don't have to do anything. Things happen. It's just the luck of the draw. What else did he say?" It was decision time for Sam Larkin, and a decision was the last thing he wanted to make. He had put this kind of stuff behind him, walked away, and that's what his brain was telling him to do now, but his heart and his conscience wouldn't let him.

"He didn't say nothin' else. Just that he would be in touch with me."

"Skeeter, I don't want to get involved in anything. That's why I came to the lowcountry. But you're my best friend, maybe the only one I've got here. I'll help you in any way I can, and I might be able to do some things, but you've got to decide what side of the fence you're gonna live on before I can say yes or no."

"You know me, Sam. You think I could ever join up with them pieces of shit? Cedrick Hamilton ain't nothin' but a pimple on a mus'rat's ass, but I ain't so sure about who he's workin' with. I cain't put Ettie and the children in no trouble."

"I don't think you have to worry about them. I have to believe if Hamilton's involved, they're all locals, and locals have to live here. Getting rid of a guy is one thing. But taking out a family or hurting children is not a local's way of handling things."

"If you say so," Skeeter said, not feeling any relief, yet looking for hope. "So what am I s'pose to do?"

"Did he say when he'd get back to you?"

"Naw. Jus' he'd be in touch. Could be tomorrow."

"I doubt it. They'll want you to start spending that twenty-five thousand dollars in your head and convincing yourself you're doing no wrong. When he does get back to you, you're going to have to stall him. Whatever you do, don't say no."

"What you gonna do?"

"You're going to have to trust me, Skeeter, but I promise I won't let you get hurt. I sure as hell don't want in on this, but I don't seem to be able to stay out and that pisses me off."

"Sam, I didn't mean to . . ."

"You didn't do anything. What's the point of having a friend if you can't go to him. And you're not the only one who's asking for help. I had a feeling something was about to happen. Know one thing, Skeeter, this is not going to be easy. And we're going to have to deal with a lot more than Cedrick Hamilton. Like you said, he's just a pimple on a coon's ass."

"Mus'rat's ass," Skeeter said and smiled. "Thank you, my friend."

"You're welcome. Let me give you a ride home. It's dark out there."

"I'll let you do that. Was plannin' on it anyway."

Relief was wonderful, almost as good as an exceptional orgasm. She once heard a therapist on a talk show discussing something called a full body orgasm, wherein all the muscles and nerves of the entire body experience the same physical response and reaction that a small number of nerves and muscles do in what is accepted as a normal climax. Although she had never experienced one herself, she had a friend in New Jersey who claimed several such reactions, describing them as pleasure bordering on pain and requiring a full-day recovery period. Her friend added that it was worth the price.

Morgan was fascinated and did some research to see if such a thing really did exist. She found it was a medical reality. Releasing herself from Bill Reichert and all he brought with him felt almost as good as she imagined that level of orgasm to be. She didn't realize how uncomfortable and constricting the last few months had been until they were over.

The four days since her return from Mexico had been glorious. Reichert was never a smothering entity in her life—she wouldn't allow that—but he was a burden, a cloud in the distance that once in awhile passed over, dropping rain at its whim. The days of sunshine they experienced in the beginning had become few and far between, which made her wonder why she let it go on so long.

Morgan did not allow negatives much thought. Her husband had spent their whole married life and his own life before they were married living frugally to amass a fortune, so they could live well when he retired. There were many things he wanted to do. He told her his dreams, and she shared them with him. It would be a magnificent life. Then, out of the blue, old Master Death visited, pushed him in the chest and left laughing. She vowed that the sum total of her life would never be measured in unfulfilled dreams and presumptions on the future. Needs came first; prudence and frugality be damned.

It was not a good beach day. The sun came out for brief periods, then tucked itself behind light clouds. The day was restless, couldn't make up its mind what it was going to do and neither could she. Shopping was a consideration, but she didn't need anything. A movie was a possibility. However, when she looked in the newspaper, there was nothing showing that held any interest for her. Charleston or Savannah were thoughts. She could spend the night, have a nice dinner, and there were friends in both places she could call. It was a plan. While she was mulling over which city she would rather visit, the telephone rang. She made herself comfortable on the couch, looked out to the ocean and picked up the phone.

"Hello?" Her voice wasn't designed, though a few friends good-naturedly accused her of that. The natural softness of her speech, rounded pronunciation with no hard edges and a pitch that was resonant and earthy, made it gloriously sensuous. It was the way she spoke all the time unless she was angry.

"Is this the lady with the fascinating name?" The question caught her momentarily off guard. It was a man's voice, gentle and unfamiliar.

"Some people have said that," she said, her lips forming a smile. "Who is this?"

"You haven't told me who you are. How do I know I'm speaking to the right person?"

"You called."

"So I did. All right, let's start again. I am trying to reach Morgan Hannah. If you're not she, you might know her or have seen her: lovely, blond, wouldn't dare guess her age, tall, statuesque and elegant. From a purely physical standpoint. Of course I've never had a conversation with her, so she might have the intelligence of a fig. I really couldn't say. Know her? Seen her around?" Morgan was amused.

"Are you insane?"

"Some people have said that."

"Touché. Yes, I am Morgan Hannah and I'm quite smart. Though I'm not a member of Mensa, I do read books that require above average intelligence. I also read some that don't require much beyond the ability to read. Now that you have my resumé would you please tell me who you are before I hang up?"

"If I tell you my name, you won't know me. Few people if any do." He heard the line disconnect.

Morgan Hannah did not put the telephone down. She sat back, watched the ocean and waited. Within a minute the telephone rang again.

"Is this the madman?" she asked.

"Some people have said that. My name is Brad Coleman. I'm sure you don't remember me."

"Walking on the beach with Charles Clay." Morgan felt an acceleration in her chest, not only because she had probably blasted him out of his chair with her memory, but also that he called. Twice. It was hard to forget the tanned, lean body, its height, the sandy-colored hair and the warm smile. Nor had she forgotten the gentlemanly, if somewhat reserved, attitude he had displayed in their brief meeting. There was little about what she had seen of Brad Coleman that was forgotten.

"You are amazing," he said.

"I don't think you believe that. I'm sure you fully expected me to remember you, or you wouldn't have called and tried to overwhelm me with glibness." She was smiling. She didn't know him, as he said, but, given the opportunity, she intended to correct that.

"Hope and surety are far apart."

"May I ask what brings this call? And, by the way, how did you remember me? Are you amazing, too? And don't say, 'Some people have said that.' "

"You are a memorable woman. Whether my remembering you qualifies as amazing, I don't know, but I'm certain you know all that. The reason for my call is that I'm going to be staying at Charles's beach house for a few days next week and wanted to ask if you might show me around if you're free."

"I'm flattered. I think that would be lovely. When are you arriving?"

"Probably Thursday."

"I shall look forward to it," Morgan said.

"I'm not a madman."

"That will have to be determined," she said. "Call me when you get here."

"I will do that," he said, "and thank you."

Morgan Hannah got the feeling that she was about to embark on an adventure new to her experience. She had thought about Brad Coleman a few times, wondered who he was and why he was with Charles Clay. He was handsome with an élan that was not distinguishable in any of the men she knew in Covington. It would be interesting. His call made her decision about the day. Charleston. Shopping. Now there were things she needed. She was humming as she began to dress.

Charlie Clay sat at the desk in his office, looking over a report he had received from an aide to the Covington congressional district's representative. It had taken some fancy finagling, money and pressure to get the information on the school district audit, and he wasn't pleased with what he saw. What he now realized, what Cedrick Hamilton neglected to tell him, was that the audit was just a small part of a massive effort to clean house. He wondered if Cedrick knew he was about to be skewered. It would take time, of course, months, maybe a year or two, but whoever was behind the investigation was serious. It had gone into places no one ever looked.

According to the report, there were conflicts of interest in awarding virtually all new construction contracts to the district finance officer's brother, unfair hiring practices, fraud involving the money path between individual schools' budget requests and disbursements that allowed thousands of dollars to go unaccounted for, possibilities of sales tax fraud, secret board meetings that violated the Freedom of Information Act, kickbacks, falsification of certification records, civil liberties violations and more. It was a mess that was beyond Charlie Clay's ability and influence to handle. Cedrick Hamilton had put himself in an untenable position. He was becoming a liability, which was one thing The Company did not need. Nothing would happen before the next venture, but that was not a great relief. The man might survive the locals and the state, but not the federal government. Someone with a knowledge of what he was doing had blown the whistle.

CHAPTER 21

The opening chords identified the song. It was familiar, and Sam knew where it was going. Waylon's harsh voice with all the miles of three lifetimes lived between thin and thin. He sat against a side wall watching the patrons of the bar. It was the perfect setting for the song, made it easy for him to settle in and get taken away by the lyric.

> *Everybody's lookin' for some way in,*
> *I'm lookin' for some way out.*
> *I've been wastin' my time, standin' in line,*
> *If this is what it's all about.*
>
> *All I've got is a job that I don't like*
> *And a woman that don't understand*
> *So tonight at the bar, I'll get in my car*
> *And take off for the promise land.*
>
> *Drinkin' and dreamin', knowin' damn well I can't go,*
> *I'll never see Texas, L.A., or ol' Mexico,*
> *But here at this table, I'm able to leave it behind,*
> *Drink till I'm dreamin' a thousand miles out of my*
> *mind.*

"I hope that's not prophetic," the female voice behind him said.

"Not sure," Sam answered. "It's awful tempting."

"This one of your all-time favorite hangouts?" Karen asked.

"One of them. I like it. You can lose yourself in here without going anywhere."

"That's what the song said."

"Sometimes that's a good thing," he answered.

"I've never been here before."

"Then you've been missing out."

The Hermit Crab was one of many small, backwoods, shotgun bars scattered throughout the lowcountry. Larkin spotted it one day, early in his time in the area, while he was exploring the creeks and sloughs within a forty-mile radius of the home site he had chosen on Matthew's Island. It was the kind of bar he liked: dark, quiet—except for the music, which he found to his taste—no questions, no pretensions, and far enough away from where he lived to avoid people he normally came into contact with. It was sixteen miles out of Covington and a million miles from anything familiar.

A bar ran the length of the small, square, cinder block building. There was a pool table set in an out-of-the-way corner, a small bandstand with an equally small dance floor, an old, neon-lit jukebox and a few tables. Wednesday night was burger night, complete with huge bowls of potato salad, baked beans, garden salad, sliced tomatoes, corn on the cob, macaroni and cheese, all-day-cooked snap beans, and sheet cakes. All for six dollars and ninety-five cents, including sales tax that, Sam guessed, the governor would never see.

"Sam, are you going to ask me to sit down? You did, after all, call and invite me here, much to my surprise," she said.

"I'm sorry. Have a seat," he replied with a smile.

"How gracious of you. Now, do you want to tell me what this is all about? I wondered what happened to you."

"What would you like to drink?"

"What you're having. Corona's fine."

"Shot?"

"You?" she asked.

"Why not?"

"Good." Sam got up and went to the bar for the drinks.

Waylon was still living in the world of straight-eights and heavy bass and belting out life-lesson song-poems about it. Karen watched Sam walk across the floor, the perfect "don't bother me and I won't bother you" attitude showing in his body and his stride. Not cocky, threatening or hostile, just Sam Larkin at his damnable, independent best. He could have been created by Tennessee Williams or William Faulkner. She wished she knew how to achieve that. For all of her professionalism in the work she did, the instability and danger of it, she was still a woman, with a woman's mentality and a woman's needs. Sam didn't appear to need anyone, which made her wonder why he called after three days of silence and asked her to meet him at an off-the-beaten-path bar, miles out of Covington.

He put the drinks on the table, lifted his shot glass, said "Cheers," drank it down and followed it with a swallow of beer. Karen sipped from her shot glass and let the beer sit.

"It's a good stop," she said.

"I like it occasionally. Don't come here often."

"I wondered if I'd ever hear from you again," she said.

"Would you have called if I hadn't?"

"No, I don't think so."

"Then I guess it's a good thing I did."

"Would you like to tell me why? I'm sure it wasn't to dazzle me with romantic intentions. When you gave me directions, I thought maybe you were embarrassed to be seen with me."

"I'm not sure where to start. Something's happened that I think you should know about, and yet it goes against all of my personal resolve to tell you about it."

"You want to try to explain that?"

"I didn't want to get involved in all of this, Karen, but I don't seem to be able to avoid it," he said. "I would have liked to have said no to you when you explained why you were here and what you wanted. Spent a lot of time thinking about it. However, now something has come up that makes 'no' impossible." Sam took a drink of his beer. "The problem is you're going to have to let me have input on how you proceed with the information I have and promise to let me know what you're doing."

"I can't do that, Sam. You must understand. This is a covert operation."

"Then I will have to handle this on my own," he said. "Just wanted to give you the opportunity to cooperate." She couldn't tell whether he was serious or being glib. She smiled and shook her head. He didn't say anything. He was dead serious, she decided.

"Are you telling me you're going from not being involved to being a 'loose cannon' out there on your own?"

"Something like that. I don't have a choice, Karen. A friend of mine has been threatened by the people you're looking for."

"You're sure it's the same thing I'm working on?"

"Yes, and I have a way in, but I've got to protect some people and I need some guarantees. Believe me, I know what can happen when the government decides it's got enough information to proceed without restraint and anyone who gets in the way be damned. I paid four years to get that knowledge. I can handle this with you or without you, but with you would make a lot more sense and both of our jobs easier."

"It's a job now?" She smiled.

"Looks like it." He wasn't smiling. She realized she had never seen such resolve and genuine concern in Sam Larkin before and wondered if it were the first time she was really seeing him at all.

"Sam, I'm missing something here. I don't know what's going on, so it's pretty hard for me to agree to anything. If you tell me something that has a bearing on what I'm working on, I can't ignore it under any conditions. On the other hand, you can trust me not to share any information you give me with any federal cowboys. I don't like them either, and beyond that, I don't trust them any more than you do. You're going to have to believe in me, Sam. It's the best I can offer."

Sam looked at her. It was hard for him to have faith in any organization that did what government agents and a federal judge had done to him. He felt himself sweating. He always did when there were no options.

"In for a dime, in for a dollar, I guess."

"I'm not going to let you or anyone you're involved with get hurt, not if they're innocent."

"Do you want to tell me what you're working on, or do you want me to tell you?"

"You first," she said.

"Have it your way. I could have guessed—living here—that it's a drug bust. It's a primary industry in the lowcountry. People here barely look askance at smuggling. From what I've heard, it's always been a subculture that's accepted as long as you don't get caught, but I didn't know how big." He saw a surprised reaction in her face. "You don't know either?"

"No, as a matter of fact, I don't. I really don't know much of anything. You're right about the target. As I told you, I'm on a prospecting mission, but I wouldn't be here for someone selling nickel bags of grass. What's happened?"

"Skeeter's been threatened."

"Skeeter?"

He told her the story of Cedrick Hamilton's offer, Skeeter Crewes's reluctance to get involved, and his coming to Sam for help.

"Hamilton. Wow." She paused to let that sink in. "You said the operation was big. How do you know that?"

"He offered Skeeter twenty-five thousand dollars and expenses to take his family on a three-day vacation. Has to be tons to make that worthwhile," he said.

"Not if coke is involved."

"I don't believe that's hit here yet, and I don't think the locals would get involved in it, especially people at Hamilton's level. Coke people are dangerous. I'm guessing these people are playing at it, as much as one can 'play' at it. At this point, I think the coke trade is still heading north and getting most of the DEA's attention, which until now has given the local grass importers an open field."

"No coke? I don't know."

"I believe I do," he said.

"Think Cedrick's the head of the operation?"

"No, but I would imagine whoever is, like Cedrick, is a man or men of influence and respect. Otherwise, Cedrick wouldn't be involved. I know the man, somewhat, and I don't believe he's got the balls to do it on his own. Whoever they are, they're not amateurs—the volume attests to that—but they're not pros either."

"You said Skeeter was threatened. Verbally or what?"

"A little more than that. Hamilton flashed a gun," Sam said.

"That's surprising, considering what you think about who might be involved and the fact that they're not pros."

"It was just a threat, probably something Cedrick did on the spur of the moment to make his point."

"Could I have another one of these?" She lifted her shot glass.

"Driving?"

"I can handle two," she assured him. Sam came back with one drink.

"Not having one?"

"One of us needs to be capable," he said.

"You're too perfect, Sam. Ever made a mistake?"

"Obviously one."

"That wasn't your mistake," she said.

"For a long time after, I thought it was, that it was a mistake to ever try to be straight. Prison taught me straight was better."

"I'd like to hear about that someday."

"Maybe someday."

"Where do we go from here?" she asked.

"Your call for the moment."

Karen Chaney was quiet. She needed to discuss it with Dougherty. Her dilemma was how to tell Sam. It was a calculated risk.

"I need to consult with someone." She held up her hand. "Don't say anything. I'm not going to give away any vital information. It's something I have to do, not because of rules and regulations, but because of me. He's an old friend who I would trust with my life." Sam didn't say anything. "Let me ask you something. What do you know about Charles Clay?"

"The lawyer?" There was disappointment in his face, and she wondered if she had lost him with her ultimatum. "Not much. I've never met him, but I've never heard anything bad about him. Old Covington family. If you're in trouble and can afford it, he's the one to get, or so I've been told, not because of his skill necessarily, but because of his connections. He on your list?"

"I don't have a list. I've been here two months, and Cedrick Hamilton is the first real lead I've gotten. And that came from you. Could make a girl feel inadequate. Actually, Clay's name did come up in another investigation. Only a phone call. It could be nothing, but it's the same kind of case, and, with Hamilton involved, he might be a better prospect than I thought."

"That would be interesting. I guess we also ought to check out the mayor, the police chief, various ministers, doctors and other lawyers." He said with a smile.

"Don't be too sure. You may not be far off the track. Are you hungry? I'm getting a little tired of working. I need time for all of this to simmer."

"I could eat," he said.

"Such enthusiasm. I'm tired of thinking. I need some fun. I believe tonight's the first time I've seen Sam Larkin start to come down off his pedestal of isolation and join the rest of us mere mortals."

Sam smiled. "I think that's a compliment, but I'm not sure. Okay, we'll quit thinking. And working. Why don't I take you to dinner, and . . ."

"Go to my place," she said with a grin. "I want to see if you're any different now that you're human. Could be interesting."

"I wasn't human before?"

"Human, maybe. Not involved."

While they were eating, there was no conversation regarding the case or any other subject that bordered on serious. The weather had changed during dinner. When they left the bar, Karen followed Sam's red tail lights through the rain, which was not heavy, but stimulated a chilling memory of her disastrous trip to Sam's house the week before. Sam kept her headlights in his rearview mirror as he led the way.

Not a lot of personal revelations had come to the surface at The Hermit Crab, yet there was a heightened sense of ease in each other's presence that was different. It was a welcome break in the emotional armor Sam had put on the day he entered prison.

At her townhouse Karen made coffee while Sam poured them a brandy in snifters he found in her sparsely furnished china cabinet. They sat on the couch, looking out at the rain on the river, touching each other and enjoying their new freedom. It was as if a veil of caution had been lifted. There would be time later for Cedrick Hamilton, Charlie Clay, Skeeter Crewes, and Neil Dougherty.

After more than an hour, which passed without notice, Karen curled into him even deeper.

"You're a different man tonight, Sam."

"Not really. A little more confused maybe, kind of like a buoy that's broken away from its anchor. The tide's taking me somewhere. I just wish I was more comfortable with the ride."

"Will you ever tell me about you?"

"I wouldn't know where to begin."

"We'll find a place."

She took his hand and led him upstairs. In the shower, she soaped his back and enjoyed the sensuous, slick feel of her soapy hands sliding across his skin. He turned and pulled her to him. The hot water, the soap, her breasts pressing into his chest, as he bathed her with his body, caused him to rise against her. She lifted up on tip-toe to position him between her legs. He didn't enter her, just allowed her to hold him there as their tongues explored each other's mouth. Without words, they rinsed the soap off their bodies and went to her bed.

Sam kissed her eyelids, her neck and the softness of her lips. He was aware of every reaction her body gave him. Karen wrapped her legs around him and undulated slowly beneath him. She could feel the wave coming and tried to grip it and let it unfurl against her efforts. The anguish of release rose from the very center of her body, in her stomach, beneath her lungs, and freed itself through every part of her. She watched Sam's mouth open in a soundless gasp and felt him flood her with himself.

Afterwards, after breath returned and nerve-endings were silenced, Sam lay with his head between her breasts, his arms circling under her. It was an exquisite time, a peace derived from the shattering of cares, of pain and of thought. They were left blank, the world gone like a shadow, dissolved, leaving nothing behind. And then they slept.

Chapter 22

Monday did not start out well for Isabel Reichert. She was ten minutes later than usual, and the buses were already arriving at the John C. Calhoun Middle School. It was her own personal charge to be in the building before the students came on the campus. It gave her a proprietary feeling to be there when the first bus pulled in; it was her school, at least for the present. With what she had in mind, being a principal in the public schools of Covington County might no longer be a necessity.

A sheriff's deputy was waiting in the main office when she came in. There had been a fight on one of the buses, and the parents were on their way to the school. It wasn't an unusual occurrence. However, it wasn't something she wanted to deal with this morning. Fortunately, she got there before the parents, which allowed her to turn over the disciplinary conference to her assistant principal. He wouldn't handle it well, but he would handle it. There were a number of financial reports concerning the closing of school to be completed for the audit, and, at eleven o'clock, she had an appointment with Julia Prescott in Charleston.

Known in legal circles as "The Predator," Julia Prescott was recognized as the leading South Carolina divorce lawyer. And it wasn't just in South Carolina. Though she was only licensed in two neighboring states, she was frequently called on to consult in high-profile cases throughout the country. Isabel didn't need a piranha, not with the grounds she had against Bill Reichert. But she gleefully anticipated the fear that Julia Prescott's name would strike in Mr. Self-Assured once he heard it.

At eight-thirty Isabel's phone rang. As she picked it up, she resolved not let to anything disturb the remainder of her day's calendar.

"Mrs. Reichert? Superintendent Hamilton is here to see you," her secretary said.

"He's in the office?"

"Yes, he is."

"Thank you, Martha. I'll be right out."

In front of the receptionist's desk, Cedrick Hamilton was doing what he did best, schmoozing with the office staff, the custodians, and anyone else who happened to be present, making them equals, a part of the team. He's amazing, she thought, as she approached him.

"Good morning, Cedrick," she said with a broad smile. "Did we have a meeting or something?"

"Good morning, Isabel. No, no meeting. Just paying a visit." Cedrick Hamilton didn't just "pay visits." Behind his smile and friendly greeting, she could discern an anxiety level in the man that was unusual. He didn't look well.

"Well then, come on back to my office, and we'll visit," she said. Hamilton excused himself from the small group that was gathered around him and followed her. After entering the office, he shut the door and sat in the chair that faced her desk. He said nothing.

"You look like hell, Cedrick. What's wrong?"

"Thanks for the compliment, but I know you're right. I feel like hell. The Harold Taylor situation hit the fan this morning. I'm trying to deal with it, but I think a female's input might be helpful, thus my visit."

"What happened?"

"Evidently, our Mr. Taylor, as has been rumored, is getting a bit more aggressive in his behavior with a couple of female teachers. One, in particular, is going to file charges against him and possibly the board, if we don't do something about it."

"What's he done?"

"The teacher who contacted me this morning says he threatened her several times with the loss of her job, said he'd see to it that she never teaches anywhere again, calls her at all hours, and then, on Friday night he called her a brainless cunt and said if she went to me I wouldn't do anything. He made a mistake on that count. I'm just not sure how to proceed without creating a public uproar. We did hire him after all."

"And with the bond issue, you don't need that. It's a shame she never read Dorothy Parker."

"What do you mean?" he asked.

"Dorothy said she was called a cunt for ten years before she realized it was a compliment." Hamilton smiled. "Are you going to talk to him before you take any action?"

"I already have. This morning," Hamilton said.

"And?"

"According to him, she's lying like all the others, is a terrible teacher, has no control, and has done everything but verbally offer herself to him, which frustrated her because he didn't take her up on it. And that under no circumstances will he resign."

"Probably looking for a buy-out. He knows the position you're in."

"He might just get it. I'd hate to see that, but you know the board philosophy: 'Keep the water flat at all costs.' I thought you might have a suggestion. Think talking to this teacher would do any good? Hold her off awhile? Let it be forgotten?"

Isabel looked at him and then away. The man had fallen a long way from the idealist who took over the district. There were many who questioned his genuine concern for the district and its students. Now it appeared he was giving credence to their doubts.

"Cedrick, that demeans you. You're talking about one of your teachers who is being threatened by a man who is obviously very sick. Getting rid of him should be a feather in your cap, not something that would submarine a bond issue. Suppose she goes to the opposition? What then?"

"I'm not sure the people of Covington County care much about something like this."

"If they don't, it won't hurt you either way, but I believe, and I think you believe, they do. They're not going to crucify you for doing your job. You're a superstar, remember?" Isabel smiled, hoping to relieve some of his stress.

"Yeah," he said. "Of course, they usually lynch my kind of superstar." He gave a weak smile.

"Cedrick, is there something else? Not just Harold Taylor?"

"Not at the moment. I'm just concerned. You're one of the few people I know who doesn't have an agenda involving me. I thought you might have a suggestion."

If you only knew about my agendas, she thought. "I'm sorry I can't be of more help, Cedrick."

After seeing the superintendent to the door, she noticed Ray Breslin, the wildlife officer, in the attendance office. She couldn't imagine what he was doing at the school. He didn't have any children, as far as she knew, and if he did, they didn't attend Calhoun. She hurried back to her office and closed the door. The last thing she needed on top of everything else was to have to talk with a wildlife officer regarding some environmental prank one of her students might have instigated.

Because of Cedrick Hamilton's unexpected appearance and several other school items that demanded her immediate attention, Isabel knew she would be late for her appointment with Julia Prescott. She called and advised the secretary of her delay and was relieved to find out that Prescott had scheduled an office day and would be available.

Isabel chose Julia Prescott because of the legends she had heard. Prescott was enigmatic: she wouldn't take just any case, no matter how much money was offered, nor would she do charity work. She wasn't an idealist, yet she was pragmatic in her choice of clients. Her practice was limited to those who could afford her and who fit her personal moral profile for divorce, a hangover from her own. She wouldn't work a case for a wealthy man who wanted to dump the wife, marry a bimbo and get off cheap, nor would she represent a man who had used his wife to establish a career and then wanted to discard her. The same exclusion applied to women who married for money and wanted out for romance and sex. When she did take a case, she had a reputation for legally removing the gold from the defendant's teeth.

She listened to Isabel's story about the background of the marriage: her husband's blatant infidelities, the fact that he no longer shared their bed on a regular basis, that he spent more money than he made as an officer of the bank, yet never explained where it came from. Isabel described periods of mental and emotional abuse he had put her through, his flaunting of his affairs, which were humiliating to her, and his arrogant attitude about their whole relationship, as if he were doing her a favor by remaining married to her. During the time she was speaking, Julia Prescott said nothing. After a moment of thought, she started asking questions.

"How long have you been thinking about filing for divorce, Mrs. Reichert?" the lawyer asked.

"This time?" There was no response. Julia Prescott obviously had no time for humor.

"Sorry. I didn't mean to be glib. The idea has been around for a long time. Years, in fact. But that's all it was, an idea. About a year ago I finally made up my mind that something had to be done. However, as much as I hate to admit it, I guess I held out some hope. Don't ask me why. I don't know. Lost causes don't normally interest me."

"So why now?"

"Because it's about damn time. That's the only reason I can give you. That it's time for me."

"Good enough. Any physical abuse?"

"No."

"Drinking, substance abuse problems?" Prescott asked matter-of-factly.

"No."

"What about you? Alcohol, prescription drugs, any of the other things women are prone toward?"

"No."

"Affairs?"

"I've already told you, he—" Isabel started.

"No, not him. You."

"I wish." Again, a moment of stony silence.

"Does he have anything morally he can throw at you?"

"Again, I wish."

"Mrs. Reichert, we're talking seriously here. This is not a game I play. Now. Important question: How much is your salary in the school district?"

"Fifty-seven thousand and all benefits."

"So you don't need his money," Prescott said. The statement caught Isabel by surprise. It wasn't an attitude that she expected Julia Prescott to have.

"Not to survive," she answered.

"I ask you that because as long as you don't need his money, we can probably get most of it. That is, if I decide to go forward with this. Does your husband have any idea what you are doing?"

"No, not yet."

"Good. There are a couple of ways we can go with this, Isabel, but I do have to make sure that you understand a few things. I don't know you yet, nor do I know your husband or his attorney, so I can say nothing definite about how we should proceed or how long it might take. Those things are all interdependent. Only if we do go forward will I be able to answer those questions. You know my fee."

"Yes. I knew that before I called. Money is not an issue; results are."

"Good. Who is your husband's attorney?"

"I'm sure he will use Charles Clay in Covington. He does all the work for the bank, and he's been our family attorney for years."

"I've heard of him, but I don't know him. How will your husband react to this? Any idea?"

"Outrage first, accusation second, and, hopefully, compromise third."

"What kind of compromise do you want?"

"I want him to compromise, not me. It should cost him money, of course, that's one of his most jealous mistresses. And I should get the house, which he loves. By losing that, he will also lose a good part of his own personal security and identity. It's where he runs when he's in trouble."

"So, personal revenge, ruining his reputation is not important to you?" Prescott asked.

"I don't think anyone would be surprised."

"That's the right answer. I don't get involved in suits that have revenge as a payoff. It's not spendable, doesn't hurt as badly as financial loss and doesn't last as long, so, ultimately, it's not the sweetest revenge. Does he have a passport, Isabel?"

"Yes. I saw him with it before he went to Mexico."

"Why did he go to Mexico?" There was a look of concern on the attorney's face.

"He said he was going to Salt Lake City, but I found some travel brochures and knew he was lying. His mistress du jour went with him, but I think she may have dumped him on the trip."

"And how would you know all of this?"

"I followed them."

"To Mexico?" she asked astonished.

"Yes. I even sat behind them in the Dallas airport on the way back. Their conversation led me to believe that she was finished with him. No shrinking violet that one. Bill got what he deserves."

"I guess I don't have to worry about your losing your nerve during this litigation then." Prescott smiled and shook her head in wonder. "So the Mexico trip was just a romantic getaway?"

"I don't think so. He went by himself to see a man named Ortega, a banker of some kind. I found that out from the clerk at the resort where Ortega was staying."

"That's interesting." Again she smiled. "You ever thought about being a private investigator?" Isabel laughed. It was the only vague attempt at humor Julia Prescott had made in their entire meeting. "Does he have any accounts in Mexican banks that you know of?"

"I've never heard him mention any, but nothing would surprise me."

"I hope not. Do you have any ready cash? Some that's yours personally, that's not in his bank?"

"I have a private account that he doesn't know about. I opened it a couple of years ago when I began considering this. It's at a bank in Charleston."

"Is the account in your name?"

"My maiden name. I was pretty paranoid at that point."

"Good. Here's how I will proceed, Isabel, and the conditions I give you must be agreed to, or I will not represent you. I will need to get a complete file constructed before I build a complaint. I will try—and I'm usually successful—to get a judge to grant an early hearing. I'd like to go *ex parte*, meaning only we will be there. I will ask that Mr. Reichert's assets be frozen until we can get an accurate inventory. Do you want him out of the house?"

"Yes." Isabel was surprised at her own immediate decision. She hadn't really thought about that part before because she usually saw so little of him.

"I believe we can manage that, but it might be tricky. Are you afraid of him?"

"Not really."

"I believe you are and aren't being honest with yourself." Isabel could see the attorney's point. "In any case, the less he knows about what you're doing, the better, so I will ask you to agree to say nothing, to threaten nothing or even mention that you've talked to an attorney until we have everything in order and are ready to move. Surprise may get you what you want. All of this we will discuss in detail at our next meeting. Some time within the next two weeks." Prescott, once again, didn't leave the decision up to Isabel Reichert.

"That's fine," Isabel said. At that point, a great weight lifted from her, and she felt the shackles fall.

CHAPTER 23

Karen Chaney was in a fog, not knowing if she had slept at all, if she had just awakened frequently, or if her sleep was so restless that her metabolism continued to work at full-speed all night long. She was exhausted. It was something she would have liked to attribute to several sessions of intense love-making with Sam Larkin during the weekend. However, despite her lack of conditioning in that area over the last couple of years, she knew it wasn't that.

On Saturday and Sunday Sam called Skeeter Crewes to ask if there had been any further contact from Cedrick Hamilton, but there was none. They were giving him time to think. It was what Sam expected. Giving the man time to think about all that money, Karen knew, was Sam's biggest fear for Skeeter. Money and the need for it can overcome a lot of honesty and apprehension.

Sam had left the townhouse late in the afternoon on Sunday, and by eight in the evening, she was in bed asleep. It had been a glorious weekend. As tired as she was when she awoke, her body was stimulated. There was little energy to get out of bed, yet all of the nerve endings under her skin were standing at attention, as if two days of Sam Larkin in her bed had revitalized a part of her that was in hibernation.

After a shower, a cup of coffee and refocusing her thinking toward the work at hand, she dialed Dougherty's office. Putting her mind on a different track, she was anxious to tell him of the new developments Sam had brought to her and what she had learned about the man himself.

"Dougherty."

"That official TV-cop dialogue?" Karen asked with an amused smile on her face.

"Hey, Belle. Kind of unusual for you, isn't it? Regular business hours? The sun shining? I'm not in bed sound asleep?"

"I have some new developments up here that might finally be opening things up."

"Well, well. Tell me, darlin'."

"First, Sam Larkin is onboard somewhat."

"On board? In what sense?" he asked sarcastically. There was silence. "I get your point."

"No, Blue, I don't think you do."

"Tell me about 'somewhat.' What does 'somewhat' mean? 'Somewhat' is not a real good thing in our business."

"Okay, maybe I used the wrong word." She paused, then reconsidered. "Or maybe I didn't."

"You're making me nervous, Belle."

Dougherty was silent as she told him about her meeting with Larkin at The Hermit Crab, his revelation about Cedrick Hamilton's threat to Skeeter Crewes, and his take on Hamilton, the man. She also told him of Sam's reluctance to work, in any way, with the government without some guarantees of confidentiality, that he was willing to do so only under his conditions in order to protect his friend. She mentioned that he would go it alone if she didn't agree to his terms and keep the "cowboys" out and added that she knew he was perfectly capable of that.

"That's quite a package, Karen." She was aware of the name change and knew he would be talking from his prescribed position.

"Don't go straight on me, Neil. I don't want this to go down the tubes because of 'official procedure.' You and I both know the only thing that ever happens when official procedure is followed are 'official fuck-ups,' followed by 'official mistakes' made by 'official incompetents,' followed by an 'official bureaucratic mess.'"

"Don't lecture me, Karen. I don't want you putting yourself in jeopardy. You have no backup in your situation."

"I prefer it that way, Blue, and I do have Larkin."

"Old Somewhat and Maybe? An ex-con, who doesn't trust the government or probably you, if the truth were known, whose story is so implausible that it's highly questionable?"

"I'm not lecturing you, Blue. Don't try to pull that. I just don't want this thing to get blown away by some overzealous 'hot dogs.' That's why the powers-that-be agreed to let me operate without local police cooperation or knowledge of what I'm doing and who I am. If what we believed when I was sent here is true, this has been going on a long time, and, even though they may not be pros, they're smart and sophisticated. And, judging by the size of the bribe, much bigger than we dreamed. Top that off with the fact that they've been one hundred percent successful, as far as we know, and we've got a major operation. I need some help here; I thought you'd congratulate me."

"I do, but I also worry about you," he said.

"Give me your thoughts."

"Well, what you just told me casts a new light on our investigation down here."

"Descarté?" she asked.

"Yes. Descarté. I'm beginning to think that what you're doing and what I'm doing are connected."

"Fill me in."

"Descarté is more an engineer than anything else. Occasionally, he will broker a deal and arrange and provide product, but always on a small scale. His biggest function is putting people together: financing, purchasing, transportation, delivery and, ultimately, hiding and laundering the money for larger operations. I'd hate to play bridge with the man. He's a brilliant strategist and knows how to keep his cards covered. That's why we've had no success in bringing him down, although I do think we're close this time."

"How long have you known about him?" Karen asked.

"When did his name first come to our attention? Eight years ago. We've been concerned that he'd retire and we'd never get him."

"You said you thought our operations might be connected. How?"

"Over the last month, Descarté has been putting together something large. Calls to Mexico, several islands, hell, even one to Denmark, which we finally figured out was to investigate purchasing a sailboat, but, as far as we can determine, neither he nor any of his contacts bought. Of course, I'm sure we don't know all of his contacts. Anyway, in amongst all of those calls was the one I mentioned to that lawyer, Clay, in Covington, South Carolina. Now that you're telling me about a big operation going down and the class of people involved, I'm beginning to believe it's all one package."

"Possible. What can I do to help you?" she asked.

"If what I'm thinking is correct, Clay might be the key. There's also a big time broker-smuggler who we've known about for years, but haven't been able to get close to, whose name has come up several times in relation to Descarté. He's been such a magician at evading us that I'm not even making my staff aware of his presence in the investigation, so don't ask. My suggestion is to watch Clay, see what you can learn. And the school guy. If they're both involved, you'll find out. Might also come up with a few others if you keep a close watch on them."

"Blue, I'm here by myself as you pointed out. How can I watch two people, and, no, again, I don't want anyone sent in or the local police involved."

"What about a customs agent?"

"No one yet. When the time comes that I have to have somebody, what about you? Can you come to my rescue?"

"If they're connected, there's no problem. I can bring in a unit, but we'd have to have proof that they are tied together."

"And if they're not?" she asked.

"Then I might have to renegade and come by myself. Off the record."

"Thanks. I think things could happen rather quickly once the ball starts rolling."

"Me, too. Will Larkin back you up? Help you with the leg-work?"

"I don't know. As I said, he left his role undefined except to protect his friend. I'll talk to him today and try to pin him down."

"I would do a couple of other things, Karen. Check out Clay and the school guy through your resources. Not anything local like SLED, but the Southern States Criminal ID Base and AFIS, the national computer base. See what you come up with. I'll see what I can get from the IRS without making any waves."

"Thanks, Blue."

"Be careful, Karen."

"As I can," she said.

All of the energy was gone from the room. The tables had been cleaned, no forgotten textbooks or backpacks left behind by distracted students, charts and posters were gone from the walls, and supplies were stored in cabinets. The elementary and middle schools were still in session, but for all intents and purposes, the high school was closed.

Exams were over, grades were averaged and put on report cards, budgets for the coming year were completed and submitted, along with each teacher's Personal Improvement Plan, called PIPs by the administration, much to the amusement of the faculty. They were not done with any degree of seriousness by the teachers and looked at with even less concern by the administrators. It was just another stone on the trail of endless paperwork given to the faculty, so the central administration and the board could point to them and say: "This is what we are implementing to improve the quality of education in Covington County." And the tax-paying public bought it.

Sam sat at one of the tables in the back of the room taking in the scene in front of him. Once again he was faced with another new direction in his life. When he made the decision to open up his past to Karen Chaney and ask for her cooperation in helping Skeeter Crewes, his whole identity and position in Covington had changed. The life he'd designed when he was released from prison served its purpose, but he had known from the beginning it wasn't a long-term solution. It was a recuperative period, and it had come to an end. Life was a contact sport. He had avoided that ever since coming to Covington.

He would not return to Covington County High School when the doors reopened in mid-August. Where his life would be then was a matter for conjecture. His involvement with Skeeter and Karen Chaney contributed to his decision, but it was inevitable even without them. He had just refused to see it. Teaching, and all that went with it, was not what he thought it would be. He realized that his purpose in pursuing it was idealistic, but even after the first year and a number of illusions destroyed, he hoped it might still work out. It didn't and each year became more frustrating.

Unconsciously and through naïveté, he had gone into the classroom to regain his honor and self-respect. Prison had stripped him of those qualities after a time. It had nothing to do with shame or guilt, just what he came to believe about himself. A man in a dishonorable position often considers himself dishonorable, he realized from a distance. He wasn't aware of the positive parts of him leaving, didn't know where they had gone, but his innocence ceased to be a consolation, a place where he could protect himself from everything that was going on around him. In prison he had fallen into a daily life of depression and acceptance. Ambivalence. He saw the same probabilities in education.

Tired of analyzing and rehashing what had been going through his mind on a daily basis, he got up from the table and began putting his personal items—things of his life that he brought in to share with his students—into boxes. There was a degree of sadness at the idea of never returning. Some of the kids were really good, bright, anxious and creative, but not enough of them to live on.

Maybe with Hamilton going, which appeared inevitable, things would change, though he doubted it. Down with the old incompetent, up with the new. It was the way it worked. The one positive note was that with school closing for the summer, Cedrick Hamilton might have his hands too full to put pressure on Skeeter Crewes for awhile. It was possible the school calendar might buy Karen Chaney some time.

Sam left as soon as his boxes were loaded into the back of the Rover. Teachers were scheduled for two days of end-of-the-year meetings, but his work was complete. There were no backward glances as he pulled out of the parking lot. To have made his career decision was a relief, but what he would do for the rest of his life and how he would survive remained a quandary. Financially he could make it, but it would require conscientious frugality. The positive side of that was that he wouldn't be able to afford to do anything except read and paint, what he had come to the lowcountry to do.

It was a shock when Sam walked up the steps to his deck and found Ray Breslin sitting at the table smoking a cigarette.

"Larkin. How you doin'?" the man asked. Sam stared at him.

"Officer Breslin, can I ask what you're doing here? Last I heard this was private property." Sam's mind was running wild with questions. Had Breslin been inside his house? Did he know about Skeeter's problem? Had Karen broken her promise about confidentiality? Did Breslin know about Cedrick Hamilton? Did he think Sam Larkin was involved?

"That bother you?" There was hostility and challenge in his voice.

"What?"

"That I'm here."

"You're damned right it bothers me." Sam tried to control his anger. "Now, do you want to tell me why you're here on my deck when I'm not at home?"

"What was that you said about private property? Ain't no private property where the law's concerned. I know you're just a schoolmarm and 'artist,' " he said with a visible sneer, "but even you oughta know that. I pretty much go where I want and nobody questions me. And, even if they do, I don't hafta answer." The man was dumber than Sam had suspected. "But I'm gonna tell you this time. I'm tryin' to find out who trashed Turner Lockett's trailer. Whoever did tore it up somethin' awful. Looks like they went at it with an ax or somethin'. You know anything about that?"

"No, I don't."

"Well, seein' as how you live out here and all, I thought you mighta been out in your boat and seen somebody around there. Maybe some little nigger boys playin' around? You seen anybody like that? They's plenty around there. Maybe they jus' got carried away—didn't mean no harm—and tore it up. Or maybe they did it outta pure meaness."

"I don't have to answer either, but I can tell you that my boat hasn't been away from the dock for awhile. Needs some work. Besides that, I don't often go up in Turner's creek unless I'm shrimpin', and you know that's not in season now, so why would I be in there?"

"Just thought I'd ask. Looks to me like someone was lookin' for somethin'. Cain't imagine what ol' Turner woulda had that anybody'd want." He paused. "Can you?"

Breslin tried to stare him down.

"Not a thing in the world that I can think of. Of course, I've never been to his trailer, so how would I know?"

"Guess you wouldn't, but you think on it, and if you come up with anything, let me know," Breslin said and got out of his chair.

"Guess I'd better get on about my bidness." He turned to Sam. "You mighty friendly with that Karen Chaney, ain't you?" Sam tensed.

"I know her. You introduced us, remember?" he said.

"Oh, yeah. I remember. Thought I might get a little piece of that. Then I heard she was a muff diver. Maybe you could enlighten me on that, wipe out that dirty rumor."

"I don't go around trying to disprove rumors. I'm a school-marm and an artist, remember?" Sam said with a smile.

"Don't get smart with me, Larkin. That's not a real good idea. You want, I can give you a list of people that did."

"I'm not getting smart, Ray. Just don't know about Miss Chaney's sexual preference and don't really care. Let people believe what they will, I always say. Maybe she is."

"That's what you always say, huh? Well, she coulda had a real good friend in ol' Ray Breslin, but she didn't want to. You know ol' Ray: bait a trap with pussy, and you'll catch him every time." He laughed and started for the steps.

"Ray?" Sam said.

"Yeah? You think of somethin'?"

"The next time you need to talk to me? Call." There was a coldness in Larkin's eyes that shook Breslin visibly. "You would make a grave mistake not to."

"You threatenin' me, Larkin? You gonna shoot me?" he asked, regaining his momentary loss of composure.

"You never know, Ray. Might mistake you for someone try-ing to do me harm. All alone out here, I can't be too careful. You just never can tell."

"I'll keep it in mind," he said and headed down to the dock and his boat.

Sam was furious. The idea of someone like Breslin having access to his house, with little he could do about it, was akin to rape. It would not be forgotten. His other line of thinking told him Ray Breslin had just made a significant blunder. He was con-cerned with something more than finding some kids who tore up an abandoned trailer. He indicated the possibility that someone was looking for something, and then threw in that he couldn't imagine Turner having anything that anyone would want. It was no puzzle to Sam. If Turner was a bird dog for off-load sites, as he suspected, who knew what his other responsibilities might have been? Who could know how much money he might have salted away over the years?

Sam went in the house, pulled a shoe box from behind the books on the top shelf of the bookcase in his study. He put it on his desk, opened it and removed the soft cloth that was wrapped around a stainless steel, k-frame, .357 magnum Smith & Wesson. It was not a subtle weapon, which was his reason for choosing that particular model. He thought the sight of the weapon might prevent him from ever having to use it. It was purchased as soon as his record was cleared in Louisiana, as a protection against prison paranoia that told him the good Judge Hunnycut would never let him leave the state alive. Other than a few practice rounds, the gun had never been fired. He checked to make sure it was loaded, wiped it off and put it in the pocket of a rain slicker that hung by the door. He then placed the rag and the box back behind the books.

He opened a beer and dialed Karen Chaney's home office telephone. He knew she wouldn't be there, but while he was at her place, she had given him the code that would allow him to leave a secure message. He heard a soft click, a short hum and another dial tone. He punched in the code numbers, heard another click and began to speak.

"It's Sam. I think Ray Breslin is another piece of the puzzle. He was waiting for me when I got home. Asked questions about someone ripping Turner Lockett's trailer apart. I think whoever did it—and it might have been Breslin himself—was looking for money. My guess would be there's quite a bit of it. I'm headed over to the boat dock to check on Skeeter right now. Call me tonight. And watch your back."

Late Monday afternoon Charlie Clay sat in his office awaiting a telephone call from Brad Coleman. When he had arrived at his office earlier in the day, he'd found a message on his private answering machine arranging for a four o'clock call. Clay was beginning to feel the excitement of the venture coming together. It was one thing to talk about doing such a thing, quite another to actually accomplish it. If this were to be the last operation, he wondered how much he would miss the excitement.

It appeared, barring any complications from Coleman, that everything was pretty well in place. Jerry Salyer had set up the off-load crew, Reichert had the money path covered, and all of the equipment and storage areas had been arranged. The one remaining element to be decided was the exact off-load site. Cedrick assured him there would be no problem with Skeeter Crewes, but Clay never took anything for granted.

His only worry was that Ray Breslin had not come up with a line on Turner Lockett's money. If it were found and made public, no one would have any doubts about what kind of enterprise generated it. Clay looked at his watch. Four o'clock. The telephone began to ring.

"Right on time," he said.

"It's necessary to be punctual," Brad Coleman said. "I'll be coming to Covington on Thursday, Charles. I want to take in some of the area while I'm there, so I'll just rent a car at the airport."

"You sure I can't have you picked up? It's no trouble."

"I'm sure. But I will take you up on your offer of the beach house if it's still available."

"Of course. I'll leave a pass for you. What name would you like me to use?"

"Charles Woodson."

"Charles Woodson," Clay repeated. "Think you can find it? You've only been there once."

"I'll find it."

"Any idea what time you'll be getting in?" Clay asked.

"Not definite. I'm still working on some arrangements. In any case, I should be at the beach house in the early afternoon on Thursday."

"Do you want to meet then or on Friday morning? I'm at your disposal."

"I think Friday would be better. I'm sure I'm going to be tired, and I'd like to get some rest. I'll call you to arrange a time."

"Would you like to come to the restaurant for dinner?"

"Low profile, Charles. The less I'm seen around Covington, the better."

"Nothing to worry about here, Brad. Nobody's lookin'."

"No way to tell that. You never know, and it's not worth the chance. I'll see you Friday. Maybe lunch at the restaurant would be all right. I'll call. And thanks." The phone went dead.

CHAPTER 24

When she was seventeen, Isabel Reichert—Isabel Jordan, then—had a date with Walker Shelton for the senior prom. She decided that she would lose her virginity on that night. It was her decision. She liked Walk, as she called him, and enjoyed it when he fondled and kissed her breasts. She even permitted him to put his hand between her legs a few times. Very briefly. There was some "dry humping," as it was called in those days, but they never came close to sexual intercourse, and she had never experienced an orgasm with a boy. From what she read, she was smart enough to know that wasn't likely to happen the first time. However, there had to be a first time, and she selected prom night as the night to get it over with.

When she saw him in the halls at school, the situation and her decision gave her a tremendous sense of power. Walker Shelton had no idea what was in store for him. The anticipation during the day of the prom was excruciating; she couldn't imagine an orgasm could feel much better. Her whole body was electric.

Isabel was feeling much that same kind of excitement as she drove home from Charleston. She had called Bill earlier in the day to ask his plans for the evening, and, as usual, he was not planning to come home until late. She pretended regret, while rejoicing at the prospects ahead. She had fucked him, and he didn't even know it. She was in control, and that was sexual in nature to her. All things considered, things were going quite well.

"What's this about Breslin?" Karen Chaney asked when she finally reached Sam.

"I don't know that it's anything. He was waiting for me when I got home from school and that bugs the hell out of me. I have no idea how long he was here, but he appeared ready to wait as long as it took. Made himself comfortable at the table on the deck."

"Did he go into your house?"

"Not that I can tell, and I'm sure I would know if he did. I don't think he's that clever."

"I doubt it. You said in your message he was asking about Lockett's trailer."

"Yes, someone evidently trashed it. Breslin said it looked like they used an ax. He also said it looked like they were trying to find something. The only thing I can imagine Turner might have had would be money, which would confirm my suspicions.

"What suspicions?" she asked.

"That he was part of the operation. That he was out here looking for an off-load site when he drowned. Checking out the traffic. Especially if they're considering Skeeter's."

"What about your place? You've got a dock and road access."

"Maybe. Whatever money Turner might have made, he obviously didn't spend. Look at how he lived," Sam said.

"Whoever was looking for it would have to know Turner was involved."

"That's why I think it was Breslin who tossed the place. Why else wouldn't he just turn it over to the sheriff's office and forget about it? I think it was him, and he didn't find what he was looking for, so he's out fishing."

"And that's your reason to suspect him?"

"It's a guess," Sam said. "The money would be a major problem if it's found. I imagine whoever else is part of it is doing a little sweating right now."

"Did he say anything else?"

"Dropped a thought that it might have been a couple of black children playing around, knew the trailer was deserted and tore it up out of meanness."

"I hope if that's true, they didn't find the money."

"The alleged money," Sam said.

"Right. Do you believe that could have happened?" she asked.

"That the kids might have found it? Not really, though I can't imagine why he brought that scenario up, unless there was a reason."

"Maybe he saw somebody like that over there," she said.

"Or somebody saw him. That would be more dangerous than finding the money."

"I think you're right. Anything else?"

"I had the uncomfortable feeling he thought I might have it."

"The money?"

"The money. Oh, he did ask me if I could satisfy his curiosity about your being a dyke."

"And?" she asked.

"Told him you might be for all I knew." Sam heard her snicker.

"Why would he want to know that?"

"Give me a break, Karen. He's trying to convince himself that's the reason you haven't invited him to your bed. Of course, it could be that he's not attracted to you at all and just wants to pick my brain to learn more about you. The other possibility is that he was letting me know our relationship is not a secret. I think we're going to have to be a little more discreet about being seen together."

"I love sneaking around, makes everything seem so much more illicit," she said.

"Most women do."

"And I suppose men don't."

"Of course we do," he answered.

"Want to sneak over here tonight?"

"Not tonight. I want to be available should Skeeter need me, and besides, you wore me out over the weekend. I need to recoup."

"Your loss," she said.

"I know."

"Sam, do we have a relationship?"

"I'm not sure what that word means, but I wouldn't bet on our having one," he said. She hoped he was smiling.

"Bastard," she said.

"Call me about the same time tomorrow or anytime if you get anything."

"I will."

When she hung up the phone, she realized she hadn't told him about her conversation with Neil Dougherty. More significant, she thought, he didn't ask. What a piece of work.

Summer heat was in the air, and it was only six-thirty in the morning. The rising sun painted a scarlet cast on the marsh, lightened by the veil of heat-generated mist that rose from the smaller creeks and rivulets that stemmed from the main branch of Jones Run Creek. It was beautiful and frightening at the same time, a conjunction that greeted the transition days between spring and summer. The physical beauty was obvious; the fear more psychological, spawned by the gothic drear of early morning haze that held the true nature of the coming day in hiding.

It had taken Ray Breslin no more than a day to identify the two young boys he had seen at Turner Lockett's trailer. A search of mailbox names, a couple of questions at the school, and he had them nailed. Marvon Jefferies and Bitta Smalls. They were easy. What kept him awake at night was the one he didn't know, the one who had hit him from behind and stolen his gun. He was afraid, and that unnerved him.

Breslin was parked in a stand of trees that gave him protection from the view of anyone getting on the school bus that passed and stopped in front of Bitta Smalls's double-wide, mobile home. He wanted to catch one of the boys alone, but it appeared they were inseparable. He wasn't sure what his plan of attack would be if he did manage to get one of them alone, but he had to do something. Charlie Clay was getting impatient. The last call from him was angry, not typical of the man.

Every possible scenario he came up with resulted in the same conclusion: the boys had the money. That knowledge stimulated the same frustration he had experienced as a child when his mother, worried about his pudginess, put all the sweets in the house on the top shelf of the pantry. He knew where they were, could see them, but there was never enough time to pull up a chair and get to them without being caught and punished. Instead, he would just stare at the shelf, sitting right up there, just out of reach. He could live without sweets. The money was a different matter.

When the long, yellow school bus pulled to a stop—caution lights first, then red lights, then the little stop sign extending itself out from the body of the bus—Bitta Smalls and Marvon Jefferies walked from Bitta's house together and got on board. Breslin remained hidden in the trees. Today he would go a step further, a risky one, but necessary. When Bitta's parents left for work, he was going into the trailer to see what he could find. If the money was there and he took it, the problem was solved. They couldn't tell anyone, and if they did, who would believe them?

It was seven-thirty when the Smalls left for work. The way the trailer was situated on the property, there was an easy approach through the trees that allowed him access without ever coming in sight of the neighbors or anyone passing down the road. He got out of his truck and made his way to the back door. Getting in was no problem. He used the "trailer twist," a technique in which the door handle is twisted, jerked, and pulled simultaneously. He had learned it from a B&E specialist he had met early in his career. The lock flipped on his first attempt to open it.

Breslin was surprised when he entered the home. It was immaculate. The furniture was not typical of any trailer he'd ever been in. It wasn't luxurious or the most expensive, but it was of a quality that anyone would consider nice. Solid, not laminated, and the decor—lamps, wall hangings, throw rugs on top of a decent quality carpet—appeared designed. Everything worked. The standard, mobile home cabinetry in the kitchen had been replaced with custom-made built-ins, and the appliances were better-than-manufacturer's quality. It was a home, substantial and enduring.

He went straight for the boy's room, which was also neat and well kept. The bed was made, and there were no child's toys or collectibles scattered on the floor, as in most children's rooms. Discipline, Breslin thought. If the boys had the money, their parents didn't know. From what he could see, he knew these people would have gone straight to the sheriff. That was a minor relief. His search had to be done with care; anything out of place would be noticed.

He put on a pair of latex gloves and began opening drawers and cabinets. There was a small desk, drawers built-in under the bed, a night table and two small closets. Even they were orderly. He found nothing. Several shoe boxes stored on the top shelf of one of the closets yielded only the typical young boy's treasured memorabilia: rocks, baseball cards, sea shells, a flashlight key chain, a small looking glass—the kind that usually held a picture of a naked woman—which Breslin was surprised to find showed the faces on Mount Rushmore, and a number of other things that only a child could value enough to save. There was no money. He wiped the door handle after relocking the latch and moved out toward the shed.

Everything the double-wide was, the shed was not. Breslin stood inside the door looking at the maze of rusted farm machinery, gunny sacks full of who knew what, old tools, wooden boxes, an old tractor, long retired, broken appliances and most anything else one could imagine that was totally useless and decomposing with time. The thought of trying to do any kind of meaningful search was ridiculous. The money might be within feet of where he stood, but without a total demolition project, only the person who put it there would ever be able to find it. The kids would have to tell him. He closed the door and went back to his truck.

When he returned to Miami from his sojourn to Jamaica, Brad Coleman had a few things to tie up before he left for South Carolina. He was looking forward to seeing Morgan Hannah even more than he had anticipated when he called her. There were a number of messages waiting for him, along with a sizable number of correspondences. Sizable for a man whose location was, at best, guessed at. Much of the correspondence was from banks, investment services, real estate brokers, and attorneys, who handled the business of his international interests. Most of it was originally sent to private mail boxes, collected by the personal assistant he employed at each of his residences, packaged and sent to whatever location he left with them as a forwarding address. Like his money, his mail passed through a lot of stops before it reached him. It was a simple method of determining if anyone was tracking him. Somewhere along the path, they would make a mistake and be exposed.

There was nothing unusual in any of the mail and only one telephone call of any consequence. It was from a man Brad Coleman was more than familiar with. The man had been after him for several years to include cocaine in the inventory he smuggled and found it difficult to take "no" for an answer. Trafficking in grass and hashish was one thing, in Coleman's mind and philosophy, dealing in cocaine and any other hard drug was quite another.

The business had started as a lark back in his college days, done on a very small scale with a few friends, a typical scenario. Nobody thought about getting enormously rich or going big time. It was not an unusual story. He and his friends philosophically justified what they were doing with the old clichés: herbs were not a deadly drug; the fact that, until the government took away the profit motive, they weren't really serious about stopping its importation; and, the bottom line, morality can't be legislated. Something that should have been learned during prohibition. At times the ideas, even in their own minds, seemed sophomoric justifications. However, as time passed, the old homily that clichés are only clichés because they are true seemed accurate.

The vacation in Jamaica had been an epiphany. The excitement of the business was diminishing according to the law that governed such things. It had been a long career, but its time had come, and fortunately, he thought, he was smart enough to realize it. Now it was just a matter of cleaning things up, divesting and disappearing. There was no guilt to take with him. The old beliefs were still his guide, and he stuck to them. In addition to not dealing in hard drugs, and, in spite of the activities in which he was involved, he had never committed nor ordered any kind of violent act. It was one of the few virtues with which he credited himself.

He looked around the condo to assess its personal worth to him. It was luxurious and spacious, over three thousand square feet with an ocean view, yet there was nothing in it that was meaningful to him. It was one of his stopovers, never a place he lived. Of all the properties he owned, only one did he consider home: the large villa in St. Tropez in the south of France. It was there that he set up his life-to-be. The rest were business locations, and business never touched his beloved French villa. There he was at peace with the world and all of the cares it held. The rest were nothing.

By the time he boarded the plane for South Carolina, the condo in which he stood would be up for sale, and within a week it would be gone with no connection to Brad Coleman ever established. Removing himself from his physical holdings was no more than the act of removing the accouterments of battle, something to be left behind and forgotten, not a matter for sadness.

Morgan Hannah. He didn't even know the woman, had said little more than "hello" to her, yet he thought he recognized some brand of spiritual synergy between them. Not the "love-at-first-sight" variety. He wasn't sure what love was, but he knew there was something that bordered on "interesting-at-first-sight." He saw it in her eyes when they met on the beach, was sure she recognized it in his eyes as well. It was the lady he was anticipating more than the enterprise he would be there to orchestrate.

The round, brass and walnut paperweight on his desk was receiving all of Cedrick Hamilton's attention. School was, for all intents and purposes, over for the year. Normally he would be busy making the rounds of the district schools, shaking hands and wishing everyone a happy, well-deserved summer vacation. This year he wasn't able to bring himself to do it. With all that was circulating around him privately and professionally, he felt like a hypocrite. The idea of being a leader was laughable.

He was startled out of his thoughts by the telephone.

"Cedrick Hamilton," he said in a commanding voice that was more habit than any show of strength or confidence. He even recognized the sham in that.

"Good mornin', Cedrick. How's your day goin'?"

"Fine, Charles. Fine." That it was Charles Clay was a cautionary relief. However, there was no assurance that talking with him would be a cause for celebration.

"Cedrick, I got some disturbin' news this mornin'. I wonder if you even know about it. If you don't, I'm sure it will be less than welcome news."

"You might as well tell me, Charles. Nothing could surprise me at this point."

"Well, unless you've been leadin' me down the primrose path, this, I believe, will be a surprise."

"I've never led you anywhere, Charles. Will you tell me what it is, so I can add it to what I'm already drowning in?"

"We've got a problem with the auditors," Clay said.

"I told you that. What's different?" There was a sense of foreboding as he waited for the attorney to answer.

"No, this is a different kind of problem. It doesn't look like my contacts are going to be able to exert any pressure to direct the audit toward those with a friendly attitude." Hamilton's stomach began to churn. His lids got heavy. He wished he could just go to sleep and never wake up.

"What happened? I thought you said—"

"I did say, Cedrick, but I didn't know then what I know now."

"Would you please tell me what's going on?" He wasn't able to hide the impatience and dread in his voice.

"The audit is going to be done by a South Carolina firm, all right, but nobody we can work with. They are, according to my source, to be assisted by the South Carolina Department of Internal Revenue and the IRS." There was silence on the line. Hamilton didn't know what to say, how to respond. There was a scream inside him that threatened to burst all of the blood vessels in his brain, but he couldn't let it out. Cedrick Hamilton and everything Cedrick Hamilton was perceived to be was imploding. Think, he told himself. Right now. This moment. Think. He was always able to think logically under pressure, but this time his mind was blank. He had to get Clay off the phone. His mind, for once, couldn't function on two tracks at the same time, and his panic was accelerating.

"Jesus! How did you find this out?"

"One of my contacts in Columbia. He had no information as to how or why the federal government got involved. Said he just heard about it yesterday and thought he ought to let me know. I don't think it will happen for some time, so you might have a chance to get your wagons circled. What I can't understand is why they're interested."

"I have no idea, but I'm not sure circling the wagons will have any effect. I was beginning to think we were in pretty good shape, along with your help, but this. I don't know. Any suggestions?" Cedrick asked.

"No, my contact said he'd let me know if he heard anything. Try to keep a low profile for awhile. We might be able to get you out of this yet. What about our friend? Is he going to the reception?"

"Haven't heard anything yet. I think he's sufficiently interested, but I wanted to give him until the weekend to decide how he's going to spend it."

"We need his cooperation, Cedrick. Be hard pressed to come up with another site. And we have to count on you for that," Clay said. Cedrick sensed worry in the man's voice, something he didn't need added to his own.

"I'll take care of it, Charles. Keep me posted on the other situation. Do what you can for me." There was hopelessness and resignation in his voice.

"I will, Cedrick. I will. Are you all right?"

"I'll make it."

"Don't worry. We'll come up with an answer."

Hamilton hung up the telephone and went back to rolling his paperweight. There was nothing else he could do.

CHAPTER 25

It was the first full day of summer vacation. Marvon Jefferies and Bitta Smalls had put their books away, stored their lunch pails in the closet and were ready for summer. Normally, they would have been ecstatic, thinking of the fish they would catch, the exploring they would do, sitting on a blanket in the shade of an old live oak on days too hot to play and just generally being lackadaisical, doing what they wanted when they wanted to do it. But things weren't normal. They had a man in a green truck watching them. They had seen him. There was no ease to be found.

The boys were sitting in the back of the shed. They had put a barrier up against the door on the outside chance that someone might try to get in, but they weren't really worried about that. If they were asked why they barricaded the door, they could always admit to looking at the old *Playboy* magazine they had found in the trash last winter. What they were really doing would get them in a lot more trouble than looking at naked women.

It was almost time for Bitta's parents to be home, and Marvon was getting nervous. They both stared down at the small piles of money spread out on an old oilcloth they had pulled off a pile of musty and mildewed magazines gathered in the corner of the shed. The foil wrappers in which the money had been wrapped lay next to the oilcloth. The small stacks of bills were neatly arranged, so they would all fit on the cloth.

"Cain' be," Marvon said. "Jus' cain' be. I don' b'lieve it."

"Well, it is. We done coun' it three times," Bitta Smalls said, looking at the older boy.

"You done made a mistake."

"I ain' made no mistake. You coun' it dis time. One mo' time, an' then we bes' put it away and decide what we gone do."

"Las' time," Marvon said and began counting the money. Bitta watched him as he pointed to each pile and said the number out loud. The younger boy was silently counting with him, his lips moving in concert with Marvon's sounds. It seemed they had been counting for hours.

"Forty-four, forty-five, forty-six, forty-seven, forty-eight, forty-nine. Forty-nine piles. Fifty hunderd dollar bills in each pile. Dat's five thousand in a pile, right?"

"Right." Bitta shook his head emphatically in agreement.

"Den dat's two hunderd and forty-five thousand dollars."

"Cain' be," Bitta said, shaking his head.

"Damn it, Bitta, it two hunderd and forty-five thousand dollars, an' we got it, an' we in trouble. Now wha' we gon' do wid it?"

"Put it away, dumb ass. We cain' leave it layin' out here."

"Help me," Marvon said and began rewrapping the money in foil.

"Where you s'pose dat ol' man git all dis money?"

"Stole it, I reckon," Marvon said.

"Well, if he stole it, he ain' got no right to it, right?"

"I guess."

"Well den, we didn't steal it. Cain' steal somepin' already been stole," Bitta said.

"I ain' sho' 'bout dat. We in trouble any way you look at it. 'At po-liceman ain' care who stole it from who. He ain' gone go away."

"He gots to catch us, an' we ain' got to go to school no mo' 'til nex' year."

Marvon wrapped the last bundle, placed all of them back in the shopping bag, and Bitta put it back in the box seat on the old tractor.

"Bitta, we gots to decide wha' we gone do. I done say dat a thousand times. I ain' foolin' no mo'. We gots to decide."

"We gots to trus' somebody," Bitta said.

"Who?"

"My uncle. I b'lieve we gots to trus' him. Ain' nobody else, an' he smart. Axe him what to do."

"When?" Marvon asked.

"He off on Mondays. Le's go Monday. Maybe dat po-liceman give up on us by den."

"He ain' gone give up, Bitta. He don' fin' dat money, he gone do somepin' bad to us."

"You scarin' me again, Marvon." Bitta's eyes teared up. It seemed to be happening all the time. He hadn't even told Marvon about waking up in the night with bad dreams about the policeman and crying himself back to sleep.

"We bes' stay scared 'til we go talk to yo' uncle. Afta' dat I ain' got nothin' to do wid it. Help me get des' boxes away from de do'. I gots to go home."

"Me, too," Bitta said, wiping his eyes as if they were burning and helping Marvon take the barrier down.

It was seven o'clock when Sam pulled out of the driveway to his house and headed toward Route 37. Karen had called the night before and asked him to meet her at The Hermit Crab at nine o'clock. He told her he would arrive early to make sure no one was there who would put them together as a team. In all of his significant life-experiences—the Merchant Marine, law enforcement and prison—his caution never caused him embarrassment. It had, however, saved his life on occasion. Now that he was in, there was no room for mistakes. He, Sam Larkin, was an unknown element to the bad guys, and he wanted to keep it that way.

He had spoken with Skeeter several times since Hamilton made his overtures, but he made it casual. His contact with Chaney was kept to a minimum and only by telephone. Until tonight. There was no reason to suspect that anyone was monitoring either of them, but, to his way of thinking, vigilance was preferable to surprise.

Shortly after turning onto Route 37, he was blinded by the headlights from the vehicle behind him, reflecting off his rearview mirror. Even when he adjusted it to cut the glare, they still bore into his eyes. There was no open highway where he could put any distance between the vehicles without breaking the speed limit. He didn't think the other driver had his high-beams on. It was the level of the lights that was causing the problem. He guessed it was some kind of jacked-up truck. The driver probably wasn't even aware he was creating a problem. He thought about pulling off the road and letting whoever it was go ahead, but the shoulder was narrow, so he pushed the mirror aside instead.

When he turned off the main highway and headed toward The Hermit Crab, the other vehicle continued down the road. That was a relief, but the idea of the same driver being behind him all the way from Matthew's Island put his senses on alert. All of his perceptions and intuitions were armed and on guard, something he hadn't experienced since prison where it was a way of life. They would stay that way until the present situation was resolved.

The Crab had a good early-evening crowd, which was not unusual on a weeknight. It was home away from home for local shrimpers, fishermen, sportsmen of all varieties, assorted outlaws, ladies shopping for someone to go home with and other classic lowcountry types. It smelled of spilled beer, cigarette smoke, loud perfume and sweat, with a few other unidentifiable elements thrown in the mix. The odor was familiar and comfortable for most of the people there, who listened and tried to override Moe Bandy blaring from the jukebox what Larkin thought was probably their common biography.

> You wrote "Your Cheatin' Heart" about
> a gal like my first ex-wife;
> And you moaned the blues for me and for you;
> Hank Williams, you wrote my life.

The whole scene fit. Scripted for a Hollywood movie, Larkin thought, as he stood in the doorway, scanning the room. He was the stranger come to town. He got a beer and went to a table in the back of the room, adjacent to the darkened dance floor. He sat in the shadows, trying to think himself invisible as he analyzed everyone in the place and watched for Karen Chaney. There was no one there he knew or had any recollection of ever seeing. Observing the patrons doing their personal dances was more entertaining than television. They were masters of their craft, no matter what their purpose in being there was, and they were probably there more nights than not, practicing their same steps.

Sipping his beer, Sam caught a familiar face coming through the door. The man stopped, looked around briefly and went to the bar. Ray Breslin was not in uniform. He wore jeans, broken-down cowboy boots and a tee shirt with a skull and *Kill 'em all. Let God sort 'em out!* emblazoned across the back. It made Larkin smile. The man was soft, but that was of no consequence; the fact that he was in The Crab was.

It was no coincidence. He was looking for someone, and that someone, Sam suspected, was right under his nose, sitting at a table in the shadows. Breslin had followed him, continued up the highway when he turned off and then doubled back. Sam watched him. Breslin didn't appear to know anyone else either. It would be only a couple of minutes before he was served and turned to take a closer look at the surroundings. It was decision time. The one thing he couldn't allow was for Breslin to see Karen Chaney come through the door.

Breslin's back was still to the room when Sam came up behind him.

"You following me, Ray?" he asked. Breslin started at the sound of his voice and quickly turned. He looked at Larkin, but said nothing. "I asked if you were following me?"

Breslin smiled. "Why the fuck would I be following you, Larkin? I know where you live."

"I have no idea, but I'd be willing to bet that if I went out to the parking lot, I could find the jacked-up vehicle that was behind me all the way from Matthew's Island still making cool-down sounds."

"Go fuck yourself, Larkin. I imagine that's what you long-haired artists do all the time anyway. Just sit around smokin' dope and spankin' the monkey." Breslin laughed and looked around for approval. No one was paying any attention.

"I guess you're right, Ray. Now let me explain something. You pissed me off two days ago when I came home and found you sitting on my deck. I invite people to do that. People I like. I didn't invite you. You had no right to be there, and you better not ever be there again when I'm not at home unless you've got legal authority. Now, Ray, now you're following me, and don't tell me this is one of your favorite watering holes because I'll ask the bartender and everyone sitting at the bar if they've ever seen you before. We both know what the answer to that would be. No one would know who the fuck you are. Don't follow me, Ray. Ever again. It would be a mistake." By this time a few patrons, who were sitting close, were listening to the exchange, but only because the jukebox had gone dry.

"You threatenin' me again, Larkin?" The man tried to smile, but it didn't play.

"Read it any way you like. You've been forewarned." Sam turned and walked toward the door. He heard a muttered "Fuck you" as he left.

Outside, he found a spot next to a hi-jacked Ford mud-runner from which he could see the door of the building, the Rover and what he thought was probably Ray Breslin's pickup truck. He didn't have to wait long. Breslin burst out of the bar and headed for his truck. On the way he noticed that Sam Larkin's Rover was still parked where it was when he got there. He looked around, walked over to it and looked in. He knew he had been had. He turned just as Larkin stepped out from behind the mud-runner.

"I asked you not to follow me," Sam said as he approached. This wasn't something he wanted to do; it was necessity. Karen was getting close.

Breslin stood at full height, threw his shoulders back and stuck his chin out.

"As I said before, Larkin, fuck you."

"You threatening me?" Sam asked.

"No, Larkin, I'm not threatenin' you. I'm gonna whip your ass and love doin' it," he said and gave him a shove in the chest that forced him back a couple of steps.

"You don't want this, Ray. You're not in uniform, can't hide behind your badge, and it's not going to do either of us any good," he said, but, inside, the animal part of him wanted Breslin to push it. "Worst part of it is, you're going to get hurt."

Breslin laughed and came at him with a right hook that Sam managed to avoid by moving his head to the side. All Breslin caught was air. His second shot was more effective, catching Sam squarely on the side of the head. He ducked and moved in, focused on Breslin's belly. It was soft and moved independently of the rest of him. He got off three hard punches to the gut before Breslin saw them coming. Sam heard the air go out of the man as Breslin staggered backward. Sam stood his ground, knowing Breslin would come in with his head lowered. When he did, Sam caught him with an uppercut that snapped his head back. He threw another punch into the gut, which doubled

Breslin over, and caught him with another uppercut as he was coming down. Breslin tried to weave, but he was clumsy, and Sam landed three lightning-fast blows to his ribs.

"Bastard. Motherfucker," Breslin screamed and threw a punch that glanced off the man's shoulder. While he was off-balance, Sam hit him head on and heard gristle and bone crunch as Breslin's nose exploded, covering his face with blood and spraying Sam.

"I'm gonna kill you, you son of a bitch," Breslin said and rushed toward him again.

It was a bad move. Sam stepped aside and hit him in the kidney, turned him around and hit him square in the throat, pulling his punch to avoid killing the man. It was a prison skill, part of his rehabilitation-learning that would make him a useful member of society.

Breslin grabbed his throat with both hands and was squawking like a chicken. His eyes bulged as he saw Larkin coming toward him with the same cold look in his eyes that he had seen when he was going down the steps of the man's house. Sam hit him in the left ear with a right and brought a left cross into his chest, just under the heart. The big man's knees buckled, and he went down.

"I'm tired of warning you, Ray. Try again and you'll lose every time." Sam went to the Rover, got in and pulled out of the parking lot. In his rearwiew mirror, he saw Breslin pitch forward and lay flat on the ground. He had made an enemy for life. The man would never let it go.

He headed toward the highway, planning to stop at the turn-off and warn Karen away, but before he made the intersection, he saw her car coming toward him. He was going too fast to stop, so he blinked his lights furiously, hoping she would recognize him. In his mirror, he saw her taillights come on and her car slow. She turned around and came back to where he had managed to stop. As she pulled up beside him, she lowered her window.

"Where the hell are you going in such a hurry? Posse after you?" she asked.

"Maybe. Breslin's at The Crab. I'll meet you at your place, but I'll come on foot. Leave the door open. Now get the hell out of here."

"Okay, but—"

"No 'buts.' Go! He might be right behind me. I'll run inter-ference." He didn't have to say any more. Karen Chaney floored the accelerator and was on her way.

A clock powered by anxiety moves slowly; Karen Chaney's clock was moving so slowly, she was afraid it had stopped. She was anxious, to say the least. It had been more than two hours since the meeting on the road to The Hermit Crab, and there was no sign of Sam. She had never seen him as animated as he was when he gave her orders to go home. He was a different person, a stranger. She couldn't guess whether it was panic or energy or something within him that the situation awakened. The fact that Ray Breslin was at The Hermit Crab was unnerv-ing. Waiting, not knowing the details, was worse. She looked at the clock. It was taking too long for him to get there. There was a temptation to call Dougherty, more to pass the time than any-thing else, but there was nothing to tell him. She went out to the parking lot twice and stood for ten or fifteen minutes, hoping Sam would come walking down the street. He didn't. Back inside, she lay on the couch, building endless scenarios, some without happy endings.

At twelve-thirty, she was beginning to nod off when the door opened and closed quietly. By reflex action, even in the dregs of near-sleep, without moving her body or giving any indication that she was anything but asleep, she slowly slid her hand between the cushions of the couch and closed her fingers around the grip of the .357 she had put there when she laid down.

Sam was already far enough inside the room to see her hand movement, even though she was giving a performance that would convince any random intruder that she was sound asleep. It would have been funny, if it were not dangerous.

"Don't shoot," he said quietly, trying not to cause panic. A smile broke across her lips. She got up and crossed to where he was, put her arms around him, and pulled him in tight to her body.

"I was worried," she said.

"Really worried?"

"Really worried." She pulled back and looked at him, ran a finger across the evolving bruise on his face, took him by the hand and led him to the couch. "Where have you been? I would've gone out to look for you, but I didn't know where to start. What happened to your face? Where were you?"

"Outside."

"Outside? Outside my door? In the parking lot? That outside?" She looked at him in astonishment. "Why?"

"I wanted to make sure Breslin didn't follow me. I parked downtown and walked over, but I didn't use Main Street, kind of wound myself around. I was pretty sure I was clear, but better safe than sorry. We've got a lot riding on keeping this little partnership hidden."

"So what did you see outside?" She had to test him one more time, knew the testing would never stop until she was totally secure with Sam Larkin, which she wasn't sure was possible.

"What did I see? Well, I saw you come out the door twice, stand in the shadows for ten or fifteen minutes and then go back inside."

"Where were you?" she asked.

"Within ten feet of you."

"That's frightening. I told you I was wor—"

"And I saw the woman two doors down being brought home by her boyfriend. I guess it was her boyfriend. He didn't go inside or walk her to the door, but they disappeared from sight inside the car for twenty-five minutes, and it looked like she was buttoning her blouse when she got out."

"You're a pervert. You timed them?"

"I was bored."

"I'll accept that. Tell me what happened. How did you get bruised?"

"I wondered if you were going to get around to that; you were so worried and all." He was smiling.

"I was, but you're here now, so I'm not worried about you anymore. And you distracted me. Are you going to tell me, or do I have to get a goose-neck lamp to shine in your eyes. One way or the other, Larkin, you're going to spill your guts," she said, hands on her hips.

"You better get the lamp," he said.

"Come on, Sam."

He replayed the whole evening for her, detailing each event: the vehicle with the bright headlights following him, seeing Breslin come in The Crab, knowing he had to get out and warn her, the confrontation, and making his way to where he sat. She listened, absorbed in every circumstance he described. Again, she realized it was a different Sam Larkin. His essential self hadn't changed, but he was stimulated and invigorated.

"You left him lying in the dirt in the parking lot?" she asked. This was a Sam Larkin she found unfamiliar.

"He was on his knees when I left him. He fell forward after I got in the Rover." Karen didn't say anything for a moment.

"You're not through with him you know."

"I know and I'll handle it when it happens, but I also think his following me is a pretty strong indication that he's involved with whomever Hamilton's working with. I figure it was Breslin that drove you off the road."

"I'll have to find a way to check out his truck," she said.

"Anything positive there would pin it down. He probably was taken on board because of his job, or they might have thought they could use him as muscle if it was ever necessary."

"Guess they were wrong about that," she said. "Did you enjoy it?"

"Why would you ask that?"

"From your attitude, I get the feeling you might have."

"No." The answer came quickly, without qualification. "I've had enough of that kind of enjoyment to last a lifetime."

"You must be good at it."

"It wasn't an even match. Breslin's never been in prison." He appeared to be getting uneasy. "Could we talk about something else? You never told me about your conversation with the friend you called."

"You never asked."

"I figured if and when you were ready to tell me, you would, but after tonight, it seems pertinent for me to know what's going on."

"Would you like something to drink?" she asked, rising from the couch. "I'm going to have one."

"Jack on the rocks would be good. I could use it."

"I guess you could and I can do that."

She came back with the drinks, curled her feet under her on the couch and faced him.

"Confidential?" she said.

"Confidential," he replied.

"His name is Neil Dougherty. He's a federal officer, DEA, and my supervisor. Right now he's working with the Florida Law Enforcement Unit investigating what they believe is a major international drug smuggling operation. The guy they are zoning in on is named Descarté. He's a broker, financier, basically an engineer, putting everything together for large consortiums. He's been in the business for years. That's where Charlie Clay's name came up. He called Descarté at one point. Only one call, but I'm sure it connects. It's just too coincidental to be . . ." She paused, looking for a word.

"Coincidence," he said.

"Right," she said with embarrassment.

"What did he say when you told him about Hamilton?"

"He was surprised at the size of Hamilton's offer and agreed with our assessment. Told me to keep an eye out for Clay, see if there's any connection between him and Hamilton and to keep him advised."

"That's all?"

"And to watch my back. I'm hearing that a lot lately."

"I would surely do that," Sam said. He sipped his drink. "How do you plan to keep an eye on Clay?"

"With your help," she said with a smile.

"You ask a lot. Is there a plan, or do we just follow people like Inspector Clouseau?"

"Don't be sarcastic. I'm not sure we can develop a plan until someone makes a move."

"I have a feeling Breslin just did," Sam said. "Something's got him going, and when that happens, people usually screw up. What occurred tonight may have rattled him, as well. At this point he'll either get more aggressive or run and hide, and I don't believe whoever is behind this is going to let him do that. If I'm right about Turner Lockett's money being lost, they've got to find it or risk exposure."

"Other than the restaurant and the law office, do you have any idea what Clay does with his time?" Karen asked.

"None. He has a house on the beach out on Sangaree, but I have no idea if he spends much time out there. I could check it out."

"Can you get on the island?"

"I know a couple of the security guys that work the gate, or I can just pick one of the resident's names, call security, pretend I'm that person and leave a pass for myself."

"You're larcenous, Larkin. Is the security that lax?"

"Sometimes. I like that. Larcenous Larkin. I'll see what I can find out. A walk on the beach would do me good. So, how did you hook up with Dougherty?"

"Knew you'd ask that eventually. I met him when I was in college. I was a freshman, he was a graduate student. Both in Law Enforcement. He's been my friend, my mentor and my help-mate my whole career. And I know the next question. Was he my lover?"

"I would never ask that."

"But you want to know, so I'll tell you. Yes, we were lovers and then we were married for a short time, little more than a year. Job and jealousy interfered. His, before you ask. End of marriage; we're still friends."

"I would never have asked you," Sam said.

"I know you wouldn't. You're too much a gentleman. A rare commodity in this day and age, but I wanted you to know. Get it out of the way."

"Good." Sam stood up.

"You're not leaving are you?" There was a look of shock and disappointment on her face. "Because of what I just told you? I can't believe . . ." Sam's fingers found her lips.

"That's the most ridiculous thing I ever heard," he said. "I want to protect my house. Who knows what state of mind Ray is in. I don't want to find it burned to the ground."

"I'm disappointed."

"So am I. It would be easy to stay. I'll call you when I get up. Maybe you can sneak out tomorrow night." He looked at his watch. "Uh, I guess that's tonight."

"I love sneaking."

"So you told me." He took her in his arms, kissed her and then he left.

CHAPTER 26

Mornings on the beach at Sangaree were more than a wake-up call for Morgan Hannah. They were the essence of everything living: the bounty of sunshine, warm breezes, the ocean, its salt smell, the hush of sound it emitted, sandpipers chasing the receding surf and scurrying away on twig-legs as it returned. Dune grasses bending to the wind, and—if one knew where to look and recognized them for what they were—loggerhead turtle tracks, tire-tread evidence of the propagating journey out of the sea to the nest and back again.

Even in the height of the season, Sangaree was not crowded by the standards of most island resort communities. The usual plethora of high-rise condominiums, pushed tightly together and arranged to allow the maximum number of window-sized views of the ocean, was nonexistent, not allowed. By Morgan Hannah's description, it was a small piece of the paradise writers tried to capture and never could, as much a deserted island as civilization, security and real estate developers would allow.

This day was anticipated from the moment Brad Coleman called and said he was coming to South Carolina and wanted to see her. The man knew how to create an aura about himself. His remembering her was a compliment, which she was able to reciprocate. That alone was enough to create interest. Morgan Hannah met many men and women whose names and appearances were gone as soon as they were. She was not a woman in need. Consequently, other people were not always assessed as an opportunity to be remembered when useful. This was not a result of financial independence. She was grounded within herself and knew it would be the same if she were dirt-poor.

There was no way to know what time she might hear from Brad Coleman, and she was not one to sit anxiously waiting. She got up early, as she did four days a week, took her morning walk to the end of the island and back, had a breakfast of fresh fruit, an English muffin and coffee, then dressed for the beach.

At eleven-thirty her allotted time for the sun was over. She was gathering her beach paraphernalia to go back inside, when she saw a lone figure walking toward her from the direction of Charles Clay's house. She left her beach chair and beach bag and walked down to the water's edge. It was pleasant to stand ankle-deep in the ocean. It cooled the whole body.

The figure was still too far away to recognize, but Morgan felt her heart-rate increasing. It was silly, difficult to understand. She wasn't one to respond in such a way toward a man she didn't know, but, for some reason, Brad Coleman, at first sight, stimulated that reaction.

"Good morning," he said when he was within speaking distance. His tan was deeper than the first time she saw him. He was wearing white shorts, a yellow golf shirt and sandals, a contrast from the slacks and blue Oxford cloth dress shirt she held in her memory.

"Good morning to you," she said and walked out of the water toward him.

"You're as stunning as I remembered." His smile was infectious. Late thirties, early forties, she guessed, maybe a little more. It was hard to tell. The sun had lightened his hair a bit, highlighting it and adding to his youthful appearance. He wasn't movie-star handsome, but damned close to it. And he had presence, even standing on the beach.

"Do you always say the right thing?" she asked.

"Only when it's truthful."

"Your flattery is duly noted and more than welcome. When did you get in?"

"Early this morning. Took a walk on the beach, but your house showed no signs of life or I would have knocked on the door and tried to beg breakfast. Charles doesn't keep a lot of food at the house. Of course, I guess when you own a restaurant . . . Why am I talking so fast?" He smiled.

"I have no idea; I was just listening. Are you trying to beg lunch?"

"Probably. Yes. I think so."

"Then you're invited. Give me thirty minutes to wash the sand off, and I'll see what I can come up with." Coleman looked at his watch.

"Twelve-thirty okay?" he asked.

"That would be fine."

"Can I help you carry this?" He gestured toward the chair and the beach bag.

"That would be nice. Thank you."

At twelve-thirty, Morgan watched Brad Coleman as he approached the steps to her house. The table on the deck was set with white linen place mats and napkins, silverware and tall, Waterford crystal iced tea glasses. A pitcher of tea sat, sweating, to one side of the small flower arrangement that graced the center of the table. As he came up the steps, she walked through the French doors to meet him.

"How many people do you have working for you?" he asked, looking at the table.

"Just little ol' me, actually. I thought you might be available for lunch, so I had everything ready. You're very prompt. Do your social graces and charm have no end?"

"I don't believe being late is ever fashionable. And if my graces ever fail to come up to standard, let me know. Looking at your lunch table, I think I may already be in trouble."

"I hope so," she said. "Would you open the umbrella for me while I get the food?"

"Yes ma'am," he said.

Lunch consisted of a crab salad on mixed greens with avocado and alternating slices of papaya and yellow tomato. There were fresh rolls and small side plates for the herbed olive oil that she brought out on the food tray.

"It looks wonderful," he said. "I'll have to beg lunch more often."

"I won't apologize. The only thing I did was slice the fruit. The rolls come from the bakery—what they call half-baked, so you just put them in the oven to finish them—and the crab salad came from the deli in Covington."

"No need to apologize. May I be honest with you?"

"That depends on what about, or if listening to you being honest requires me to be honest in return."

"No requirements. I just have to tell you that I have come across very few people in my life whom I found impressive enough to feel the need to see again."

"I'm not sure how much of this I can take or believe."

"I know so little about you. Are you retired?"

"Oh, no." She chuckled.

"What do you do?" She looked at him with an amused and coy smile on her lips that said more than her words.

"Anything I want." Brad Coleman lifted his hands in a helpless gesture.

"I guess I can't probe into your life," he said.

"Not yet."

When they finished eating amidst small talk and politeness, there was nothing left to do, yet having something to do didn't seem important. Brad helped her clear the table and enjoyed watching her as she moved about her kitchen. The luncheon food might have come from the deli, but he could tell she was no stranger to the maintenance of a home. There was confidence in the way she did things. He realized, with wonderment, that he was perceiving her as an equal, and, with astonishment, that he had never placed any woman and very few men in that position before. It was illogical and out-of-character for him to do so with anyone, not to mention someone he hardly knew.

He watched as she put the dishes in the dishwasher and wiped the counter clean.

"Are you up for another short walk on the beach?" she asked.

"Yes," he answered and bent to take off his sandals. He looked up. "Don't want to ruin them."

"They're from Mexico, aren't they?"

"Probably, but I got them in Miami. How did you know?"

"I was there recently for a short vacation. The country was lovely. The vacation wasn't," she said.

"I'm sorry to hear that. There's much about Mexico I love."

He led her down to the water's edge. As they walked, the water would occasionally break over their feet. Even though the high sun had brought the day's heat to its peak, the slight chill of the water was still refreshing.

"Question time," she said. "I can't believe you're retired at your age, unless you have had major work done and look younger than you really are." He laughed.

"No work done, and, no, I'm not retired."

"So what do you do that brought you to South Carolina? Or is it just a vacation?"

He didn't say anything for a few minutes. He was perplexed, wondered if Morgan Hannah had cast some kind of supernatural, occult spell on him. He had an urge to come right out and tell her, honestly, what his business was. It could put him in jail or end the relationship before it began, which would be best, if he were pragmatic about it.

"Well? I told you what I did."

"Anything you want. I remember. Actually I do pretty much the same thing, I guess. However, if you want to put a name to what I do, I guess you'd have to say I'm a pirate."

He felt dizzy as the words came out of his mouth. Morgan laughed.

"I can believe that. You have an Errol Flynn quality about you. More depth, of course. Where do you practice this piracy? Do you have a ship with a Jolly Roger flying from the highest mast?"

"No ship," he said with a smile.

"You almost had me believing you."

"Would it bother you if it were the truth?" he asked.

"That would depend on what kind of pirate you are."

"A good, happy, successful, less-than-heroic pirate."

"I can accept that. We're all guilty of some degree of larceny, I think."

"Good," he said. "Now that we have that settled, can we change the line of conversation for the moment?"

"Of course. Where are we going for dinner?"

"Did I ask?"

"Weren't you going to?"

"Yes. You know the restaurants here, I don't. Somewhere out of the way where your friends won't be bothering you while we eat."

"Do you mind a drive?" she asked.

"Not at all."

"In that case, I know a wonderful little French restaurant on Palmetto Island. It'll be about an hour and a half each way."

He realized that at some point they had turned around and were back at her house.

"What time?" he asked.

"Six? I'll make a reservation for eight to be safe."

"Good. That'll give me some time to make a few phone calls and do some business."

"Piracy?" she asked.

"Sort of." He paused and looked at her. "I like you, Morgan. I'm looking forward to this evening."

"Me, too," she said and started up the boardwalk through the dunes to her house.

"See you at six," he said. Brad Coleman didn't know what he had expected, certainly not what he got. Morgan Hannah was mesmerizing. He had often wondered if he would ever meet a woman who could capture him. He conjectured that he might have.

Ray Breslin was still sore. His jaw hurt, and he could hardly speak from the punch to the throat that Larkin had given him. When he did try to speak, his broken nose gave a nasal quality to the squawk he was able to produce. His gut and his kidneys hurt, as well. Initially he tried to tell himself that Larkin had surprised him, caught him off guard, but he knew that wasn't true. Sam Larkin had whipped his ass, and he would never forget it. What surprised him was how tough the man was and the way he fought. He wasn't a barroom brawler, nor did he show any signs of having been trained to fight professionally. He was practiced and skilled and knew how to take another man apart. Their next encounter would not be a parking lot brawl. It would be planned, and Sam Larkin would never see it coming.

The truck was getting hot. He was stiff and uncomfortable from sitting. Unfortunately, there was no help for it. He couldn't risk getting out and being seen. The kids had to come out sooner or later. It was ten o'clock in the morning, and they didn't have school. It was summer vacation, for Christ's sake. Breslin shook his head. He had been talking to himself mentally for three hours. When he was a kid, he always went out to play when he didn't have school: fishing in the river, swimming, playing base-ball. "These fuckin' kids just stay in the house all day. Prob'ly watchin' TV," he thought.

He wasn't made for stakeouts. This was his first, and, if he had anything to say about it, his last. They didn't look so bad on TV, but there they only lasted three or four minutes. He had been watching Bitta Smalls's house since seven o'clock. They wouldn't have gotten out before then. The windows in the truck were down, but the heat was already imposing. If they didn't move by noon, he'd give up and come back another day. The problem with that was, every day they had the money gave them another day to do something with it. The longer they had it, the farther away it got. That's how he saw it, and he was sure he was right.

If he didn't get them today, he didn't know when he could get back. Clay had told him to keep Friday open, that there might be a meeting and he wanted everybody available if needed. Clay had also said he expected him to have the question of Turner's money solved by then. Well, if he could, he could. If he couldn't, he couldn't. He had already begun developing scenarios for get-ting rid of the kids. Even if he got the money back, how could he let them go? Drowning was the best idea. Everybody knew niggers couldn't swim worth a damn, and if a gator got them, so much the better. Everybody would just assume they drowned. Happened every summer. The key was to make it look like drowning, not murder. He was confident he could do that. It was after eleven o'clock.

Bitta Smalls and Marvon Jefferies were watching the truck from their hiding place in the trees. Their parents thought they had gotten up early to go fishing. They had been in position since a quarter after six, which they had decided the night before was early enough. They knew where he'd park. The dumb-ass parked in the same spot every time he came to watch for them.

"How long you think he gone be here?" Bitta asked.

"How'm I s'pose to know? Dumb-ass oughta know we ain' come out by now, we ain' comin'."

"Maybe he gone be here all day. Wha' we gone do den? We gotta go home fo' dark."

"Le's wait and see. What I'm hopin' fo' is Monday. We gots to get to yo' uncle. I don' wont no mo' truck wid dat money. I b'lieve it got a curse on it," Marvon said, "an' I ain' foolin' wid no curse. I done been scairt long enough."

"Me, too. I ain' got no truck wid it either. Wha' dat mean, Marvon?"

"Wha'?" He turned and looked at the younger boy.

"Truck. Like I ain' got no truck wid dat money." Marvon thought for a minute.

"I don' know fo' sho'. My granddaddy say it when he don' wont sompin' aroun'. Like my Aunt Tonya. He don' never wont her aroun'. He always say he ain' got no truck wid her. She done always tellin' him he drink too much and smoke up de house wid cigarettes. An' it his house. Dat why he say he ain' got no truck wid her 'cause he don' wont her aroun'. I ain' got no truck wid dat money, cause I don' wont it aroun'."

"Me neither," Bitta said, and they resumed their concentration on the truck.

Karen Chaney was keeping watch on Charlie Clay's movements in town, while Sam Larkin lay on the beach at Sangaree Island noting any comings and goings that might occur at the attorney's beach house. At five o'clock in the afternoon, after their watches were over, Karen called Larkin's house, as agreed.

"Hello?" He sounded like he was asleep.

"Sam? Did I wake you?" she asked.

"I was dozing. All that fresh air and sun. I feel fried."

"Better than being in town and playing hide and seek. Anything going on out there?"

"You first," he said. "I'm alert enough to listen, not sure about speaking coherently."

"Not much here. Appeared to be business as usual. He spent most of the morning in the office. I wish we had a phone tap, but that's out of the question at the moment."

"What about your friend? Couldn't he help with that?"

"Not unless we can connect this with what he's working on. Otherwise, we're left with probable cause, which we couldn't use without exposing Skeeter even if we had probable cause, which we don't."

"I'll figure that one out in a minute," he said. "Anything else?"

"Let's see," she said, checking her notes. "He met the vice-president of the bank, Bill Reichert, and they went to lunch at The Covington House. Neither of them looked very happy when they left, but that might have been indigestion."

"They don't serve indigestion at The Covington House."

"Don't know. I've never eaten there."

"It's pink," he said.

"Pink." She didn't know how to respond to that statement, so she didn't.

"Anyway, there was nothing else. He was still in his office when I unleashed him. Bad day for law. He didn't have a single client that I saw."

"Not sure he needs them," Sam said.

"What about you? See anything or were you too distracted by the bikinis out for an early tan?"

"Didn't see many of those. Sangaree's pretty dull except for the holiday weekends in the summer. I'm not sure whether I saw anything or not. There is someone staying at Clay's beach house, a guy. I've never seen him before, so I don't have a name."

"Single male?"

"I don't know whether he's single or not, but I can call and ask, if you're interested."

"Damn it, Sam. Be serious. You know what I mean. Is he by himself?"

"I don't know that either, for sure, but I'd guess he was. I didn't see anyone else at the house. He walked the beach early and then again later. Hooked up with a lady who lives a short distance down the beach. They walked. Seemed to know each other, ate lunch on the deck at her place, took another short walk, and then he went back to Clay's. I stayed another half hour and left."

"God, you sound like a cop. Do you know the lady's name?"

"I checked the mailbox on my way out. Morgan Hannah. I've seen her around town on a few occasions, and I've heard stories."

"But you don't put much stock in stories."

"No, I don't."

"What kind of stories?"

"That she's widowed and wealthy, which is obviously true judging by where she lives. And, rumor has it, that she does or did have a thing with your bank president. That seemed to be pretty common knowledge for awhile."

"My bank president?"

"Bill Reichert. You tapped his wife's conversation in the beauty parlor, remember?"

"Interesting. Anything on the wife?"

"Nothing that I would consider significant at the moment. There have been rumors. . . ."

"Covington seems to be a breeding ground for those."

"Small southern town. Southerners have always considered insanity, suicide, murder, alcoholism, and infidelity romantic and normal behavior. You can attribute all the rumors to that."

"So what were the rumors?"

"Varied. Some have said Isabel's a lesbian, some bisexual and some miscegenist."

"Miscegenist?" Karen looked at him puzzled.

"Crosses the color line."

"Any idea who?" Her mind was already working.

"Cedrick Hamilton."

"Wow! Do you think it's true?" she asked.

"Personally, I would doubt all of them. I guess she could go both ways, but that's only a personality judgment. It really doesn't make any difference anyway."

"But if she's involved with Cedrick . . ."

"I doubt that. She and Cedrick are both too career-oriented and smart to play with someone at work."

"It's interesting though. Seems like all of these people are connected somehow."

"It's a small town. Everybody's connected."

"Tell me about this guy at Clay's beach house," she said.

"Six-three or four. Well-built. Tan. Good-looking from what I could tell. I didn't get too close. Sandy hair, looks sun-bleached. I'd guess he's in his late thirties or early forties, and I'd say he has money."

"Why?"

"Just the look and physical attitude wealthy people have. Confident. Classy. Assertive without being aggressive. Tell you anything?"

"Do you have his phone number?" She laughed. "No, it really doesn't tell me anything. I'll check with Nell on the description, but it's pretty vague."

"I'll try to do better," he said.

"I didn't mean it that way, Sam. It just fits a lot of beach people. We'll see. When?"

"When what?" he asked.

"When am I going to see you?"

"We need to talk about how to pull that off. I don't perform well looking over my shoulder."

"I haven't complained."

"Don't," he said. "You'll scare me off."

"I believe that. So when am I going to see you?"

"What about tomorrow night. Depending, of course, on what happens tomorrow day."

"You're going to come here?" She sounded surprised.

"I will creep in after midnight on little cat's feet."

"I don't like cats."

"I'll be stealthy."

"Good. I like stealthy," she said.

CHAPTER 27

Charlie Clay and Bill Reichert were sitting in Clay's office. It was after five o'clock. The attorney was angry, at least as angry as he ever was of late. He suspected that all of his emotions had withered. Things had become too complicated and he was tired. At times, he believed it was all because of the size of the venture. Perhaps his ego had gotten in the way, and he was misguided into thinking they were capable of a major operation. He wasn't sure why he decided to do it, other than the smaller ones were becoming a simple matter of processing. He was no more experienced in the business than the others. The difference was, he wasn't afraid of the consequences. Other times, he lay the fault at the feet of the people involved. This was the first time any of them had ever considered consequences and become skittish.

"I'm sorry, Charlie," Bill Reichert said, his head hanging.

Clay said nothing. There were a couple of directions they could go. The whole venture could be scrapped, the result being a few angry buyers and fulfilling The Company's financial commitments. The other would be to reorganize The Company, but time and risk were against that. The best avenue, as far as Clay was concerned, was to convince, by any means necessary, those who were shaky to simply do their jobs as they always had.

"Sorry doesn't mean anything, Bill. Sorry is a character evaluation, not a reason or an excuse. I don't believe you have a choice here. You can't just fold up and withdraw. You're the only one of us who knows exactly how the money is to be handled, and you're the only one Ortega knows. I don't believe he would be amenable to involving a stranger at this juncture. I think you're in, Bill, like it or not. At least until this one is complete. Then you can do whatever the hell you want." Reichert looked lost and defeated.

"I don't know, Charlie."

Clay slammed his fist on his desk. "Damn it! I do know. You're in. You're the money man. We've already committed to more than a million dollars. We could cancel, but are you willing to cover that?"

"Well, I—"

"And that's not all. You'll have a lot of expenses to cover. All the moneys that have been put out for storage space, equipment, not to mention some of our silent backers will be very unhappy with you. Your time in Covington would be over. Have you thought about those things?" Charlie Clay was staring him straight in the eyes.

"I guess you're right. It's just that I'm getting nervous, and my heart's not really in it anymore."

"Hell, I know what's going on in your head and your heart. You're still mourning Morgan. I know what it's like to lose someone, but there are thousands of Morgan Hannah's out there, Bill. You have to let it go."

"It's not just that." Reichert paused for a moment. "Can I be honest? You won't think I'm crazy or anything?"

"Of course not."

"Sometimes, Charlie, I feel like I'm mourning my own passing. I spent two days last week—forty-eight hours with no responsibility—trying to figure out what I'd like to do for fun. What I would enjoy and be happy doing even for a day. And do you know what? I couldn't come up with anything. Not one thing or one person that I'd walk a block to do or see. I've got more money than I can ever reasonably spend and I'm worthless. There's plenty in the bank and nothing inside. For all intents and purposes, I'm dead."

"Bit dramatic aren't you, Bill?"

"I don't know. I don't know if I am or not."

"If you're asking me to feel sorry for you, I can't and won't," Clay said.

"I guess I don't have much of a choice."

"Not really. Listen, everything's gonna work out. Relax. Don't worry." The banker looked up at him with skepticism. "Look, I'm expecting a call very shortly, and depending on what I hear, I may need you for a meeting in the morning or say lunch tomorrow. You be available?"

"I'll be in the office. Call me."

"I will."

Clay saw Reichert to the door and wondered why he hadn't heard from Brad Coleman. Even though they weren't meeting until Friday, he expected a call to set up the meeting. He was on the island. Security told him that Mr. Woodson had arrived before seven A.M.

As these thoughts went through his mind, the telephone rang.

"Charles Clay."

"Good afternoon, Charles. Sorry I'm late in calling, but I got captured and held hostage by the beach. It's been a wonderful day out here, and I want to thank you for the privacy."

"I did check with security to make sure you got in all right. I figured you'd need some rest-up time from all the travelin'. You said you'd call, so I just left it up to you when."

"I appreciate that. About tomorrow. When and where would you like to meet?"

"How about lunch at my restaurant about twelve-thirty? We'll make it low profile. If that's okay, I can give you directions or pick you up."

"That's fine. I think I can remember where it is. I saw the turn-off and the sign as I was driving out here this morning."

"Good. I'd like to have my banker join us, if you don't mind, and anyone else you'd like to meet."

"The banker's okay. You can tell me about the rest. If I think I need to see them, I will before I leave. The fewer who know I'm here, the better. And, Charles, use Mr. Woodson at the meeting if you would."

"I understand."

"Everything progressing smoothly?" Coleman asked.

"Just fine." It was a lie. But one way or another, it would be running smoothly when the time came.

"Well, then I guess I'll see you tomorrow. I'm going to drive over to Palmetto Island for dinner tonight. I've never been there, and a friend said I should see it while I was in the area." It was a good way to avoid refusing the dinner offer he was certain Clay would extend.

"I think you'll enjoy it. It's a nice island. Let me know if you need anything in the meantime."

"I will, Charles. Thanks."

Four additional calls and the business of the day was concluded. Coleman went to the bar, poured some Scotch over ice and walked out on the deck. He could probably live on this island, he thought, if it were not in the states. That would be tempting fate. Besides, the villa at St. Tropez was home. He smiled when he thought about it. There was a great deal of relaxation in considering retirement.

Les Pyrenees was the most expensive restaurant on Palmetto Island. It wasn't unusual for a dinner for two, with a good wine, to cost over two hundred dollars. In terms of grace, continental atmosphere and the accouterments of fine dining, it could not be equaled anywhere in the state.

It was quiet, and, despite the presence of other diners, seemed private. Everything was done in the traditions of the finest restaurants of Europe; however, unless one were directed to it, there would be no way to know of its existence. There were no signs to identify it, no valet parking attendants grouped hungrily at the door, not even a doorman to be seen. From the outside it was nondescript. Once inside, the atmosphere of refinement and dignity was boundless.

If her choice of a restaurant was any indication, Coleman thought, Morgan Hannah's perceptions of his character and tastes were very much on target. For a man who spent his life trying to be invisible, he must have been awfully transparent to her, and, considering the short time they had spent together earlier in the day, it was amazing, if not frightening.

Morgan suggested the grouper nicoise. They shared a baked brie. As they finished their drinks, Brad chose the wine to go with dinner. The food was magnificent, the conversation light. The way they related was different than it had been at the beach. They saw a more formal side of each other, as opposed to the casualness of their afternoon.

Coleman enjoyed looking at her through the candlelight. She was beautiful. Not perfection, but as close in the combination of physical beauty, style and class as anyone he could imagine. After dinner, they went back to Morgan's house for brandy. Sangaree

Island was softer than the city-like streets of Palmetto, more fitting for what had been a soft evening. Neither of them wanted that to change.

Sitting on the deck, listening to the ocean and watching the moon in its rising made the evening more romantic than real.

"I'm not sure when, if ever, I've been as much at peace as I have this evening. That's a compliment to you, Brad, and I thank you for it," Morgan said, without taking her eyes from the moon.

"I'm glad. It's been wonderful for me, too."

"Then thank you. I wasn't sure I could compete with the life a pirate must lead. Sailing the Seven Seas, looting, carrying off women in the night. I guess I should consider that a compliment as well."

"By all means." He took a sip of his brandy. "Actually though, pirates—myself excluded, of course—are by and large an unsavory and unsanitary lot. Living at sea for months at a time, always on the run, sneaking into port at night and out before dawn, and taking the town fathers' daughters with them for sport. It's not something to be done for a lifetime."

"I always thought pirates had very short lives and usually wound up on the gallows."

"Only the ones who aren't smart. According to history, many, over the years, quit the sea and led very respectable lives."

"Sir Francis Drake."

"And even some of his modern day counterparts," Coleman said.

"Are you considering becoming respectable?" she asked with a smile.

"I've never considered myself anything less," he answered.

"Nor have I, though I've only known you for twelve hours."

"I wish I could understand why it seems I've known you longer than that."

"Maybe it's because you're comfortable with me, or that we're comfortable with each other," she said.

"I hope that's the case. It's very strange. I have a compulsion to open up to you. Let you know and see things about me that no one has ever known. That goes against the very grain of everything I have always been, and I find it impossible to rationalize."

"Make you feel vulnerable?" she asked.

"Exceptionally," he said. "Maybe you're my one mistake."

"Maybe. Come over and sit with me," she said. He got up from the chair in which he was sitting, brought the bottle of brandy with him and joined her. After freshening both of their drinks, he put his arm around her, so she could lean against him.

"You don't seem to have a lot of curiosity about me," he said. "That's either impressive confidence on your part or shows a distinct lack of interest."

"It's not a lack of interest. I think a man is entitled to his secrets just as a woman is. In the beginning anyway. If things should continue and you don't confess your sins willingly, then I may start asking a few questions."

"You are remarkable," he said, looking at her.

"For right now, I hope so."

"You are." He pulled her to him. When he kissed her, he felt their bodies meld, felt the softness of her breasts, was aware of them flattening against his chest, could feel the heat under her arms when she put them around his neck. Her lips were warm and parted slowly, allowing his tongue to enter her mouth a little at a time. In all his experience, a kiss had never been such a singular and complete act. Not just a step in a process or part of a necessary ritual, but an end in itself. She buried her face in his chest and they held each other. They remained in that position for a long while and were fading into sleep when he realized what was happening.

"It's time for me to go," he whispered. Morgan looked at him without saying anything. "I want to stay," he said, "but I need to go. I need to think about you, tonight and all that we didn't say. You've done something to me, Morgan Hannah, and I need to find out just what that something is." Coleman stood and looked down at her. He leaned over and kissed her lightly on the forehead. "I will call you in the morning," he said.

"I'll be walking the beach at seven."

"I'll join you." He paused. "Thank you is too insignificant to say."

"I know." As he walked off the deck and started up the beach toward Charlie Clay's house, she wondered where Brad Coleman would take her. It was a thought filled with trepidation and excitement. Much like the first time she fell in love.

Rain swept across the land in wind-blown sheets, obscuring any view beyond the surf. The parking lot of Harry Tom Cooper's Boat Dock was awash with puddles in the deep ruts created by years of car and truck traffic. The thunderstorm popped up without warning, wiping out the moon and stars that had shown so brilliantly the night before. It wouldn't last long. It was that kind of storm. Hit and run. It did, however, postpone the daylight and prevent any work being done on the dock.

Skeeter Crewes stood inside the store sipping a cup of coffee and looking out at the rain. Fortunately, it hadn't begun until he was within several hundred yards of the dock. He was damp, but not soaked. His mind was heavy and his body tired from lack of sleep. Ettie had noticed his condition and asked what was bothering him. She wouldn't accept his evasions, and there were several arguments over his reluctance to share his troubles. He hated arguing with Ettie; life was hard enough without taking on the guilt of being angry and short with your family.

Several times he came close to giving in and conceding to join Cedrick Hamilton in his enterprise, but the fear of being just another black man, taken away in handcuffs and sent off to jail, leaving his family to fend for themselves, held him back. That and the things he had been taught and still believed in. Those lessons were his grasp on dignity. His grandmother, who raised him, always said, "Be proud. It don't take nothin' to be a nigger, and I don't raise no niggers. Be a man and act like one. Don't nobody owe you nothin'." She also said, "Don't go to trouble. Let it come to you. Then handle it." The wizened old woman started branding those things into him before he was six years old. Living up to them was at times difficult. Excuses came easy.

Standing at the window, he saw the rain began to slacken and the sky lighten. A car came down the road, pulled into the lot and parked close to the side of the building where it could not be observed by anyone inside. Harry Tom was in the storeroom doing an inventory. It was what he did on stormy days when there was no traffic. Skeeter went out the door, ran to Cedrick Hamilton's car and got in.

"Little wet for you to be all the way out here ain't it, Seed?"

"I needed to see you, Skeeter. I have to have an answer. We can't wait until the last minute to know whether or not you're going to cooperate," Hamilton said.

"Well, I got a problem, Seed. You tol' me not to let Ettie know what was really goin' on, but she ain't gonna buy the idea that I'm goin' to Myrtle Beach about a job, and the man is gonna pay for it. Ettie ain't dumb. You got any other ideas? I mean, I want to do it, but, you know, my family an' all. I cain't risk gettin' that messed up."

"You sure you really want to do it, Skeeter?" Cedrick Hamilton looked at him hard, trying to see what was behind his eyes, looking for honesty or betrayal.

"Who wouldn't want twenty-five thousand dollars? What I still cain't understand is you, Cedrick. I mean, I didn't have much choice about what I do. I mighta done better, but I wasn't smart enough to know it at the time, and then Ettie got pregnant, but you, you got it all. I imagine twenty-five thousand dollars is pocket change for you now, and even before you got into this, twenty-five thousand dollars wasn't a life for you. It is to me, and that's the only reason I'm listenin' to you. I'll come up with somethin'. Why don't you come by the house in a few days, and I'll see if I can have it worked out."

"I'll try to get you a few days, but, Skeeter, you figure out what you have to do. Remember, it's not up to me. I think they plan to use your dock with or without your cooperation. Hell, take the money and give yourself a start. It's not too late to get where you could've gone. Otherwise, you're going to be right where you are ten, twenty years from now."

"If I am at all?" Skeeter looked at Cedrick, who lowered his head.

"If you are at all."

When Skeeter went back into the store, Cedrick remained parked next to the building. He couldn't move. Regardless of what happened, he was over. There was nowhere to go, nowhere to run. He had, without thinking, destroyed himself. That thought kept coming back to him, over and over. He had never imagined what hell it was to find yourself in an untenable position with no way to escape it and no one to blame for it except yourself.

When the rain stopped, steam rose from the black-top road in front of Bitta Smalls's house like vapor from a boiling kettle. Blades of grass, wet and green, picked up the sun's rays and glistened like a field of carved crystals. The earth was fresh and clean. Stepping outside his back door, Bitta watched a banana spider continuing the construction of a massive web that ran from the porch railing to the rain gutter above his head. The web was wet with droplets of moisture that made it easy to see in the bright morning light.

Standing there, Bitta couldn't imagine anything better than going to Marvon's house, smelling the fresh biscuits his mother baked every morning before work, spreading one with butter and jelly before he and his best friend spent the day doing whatever caught their attention for the moment. Complete freedom. But they couldn't do that, not until after Monday when the money was gone. He and Marvon would be together, but there would be no freedom, only fear.

He ran at full speed to Marvon's house, staying as far from the road as he could. He jumped over a yellow and black-shelled terrapin that in any normal time he would have picked up and adopted for a day or at least until he and Marvon got tired of playing with it. His eyes checked the road for the green truck as he ran, but there was no sign of it yet.

After collecting Marvon, Bitta felt more secure. They'd been best friends since they were old enough to have a friend. Now they were as close as brothers. Fear and a common enemy can beget those bonds. The hunter was still out there, his presence as strong as if he were standing directly in front of them. They feared the moment when they would turn and find him standing next to them or feel a shadow descending over them while they were looking in another direction.

The boys headed for the woods. There was safety there. They made a pact not to go to the shed or to pull out the shopping bag of money again until they went to Bitta's uncle's house, maybe not even then. Whether to take the bag with them or just tell Bitta's uncle about it had become a contentious argument.

There was an old tree house, not far from the road yet well-hidden by the new spring growth on the trees, put up by some other young adventurers years before. It afforded them a view of the road and the marsh that led out to the creek. They would be able to see anyone approaching from any direction. They could even see part of the creek that ran in front of Turner Lockett's trailer.

It was Marvon's day to bring the food. He had gotten up early, before anyone else in his house was awake, made bologna sandwiches with mustard, threw in some cookies and filled a jug with ice and Hawaiian Punch. No matter how much food either of them brought, it was always gone by ten-thirty, and they went hungry for the rest of the day. Even school was better than spending the day watching the road and the marsh.

At ten-thirty, they heard a boat. It was pretty far away, but, as they listened, it sounded like it was coming in their direction.

"You think he comin' by boat dis time?" Marvon asked.

"Might. Think so?"

"How'm I s'pose to know? You think I call him on de telephone an axe 'You comin' by boat or road today?' Dumb-ass question."

"You axed me. You mus' not thought it was too dumb-ass to axe."

"S'pose he come an' pull dat boat in de marsh and git out an' come ova' here? Wha' we gone do den?" Marvon asked.

"I reckon we climb down an' run in differ'nt directions, like we said befo'." The boat was getting louder. Bitta and Marvon edged up to the marsh side of the tree house and looked out, keeping their heads down, only their eyes above the weathered planks that slatted its sides.

"I see 'im," Bitta said. "An' dat sho' be him."

"He comin' out here?"

"I don't think so. He gots sumpin' on he face, like a white stripe 'cross his nose."

"A disguise? He comin' disguised now?"

"If dat wha' it s'pose to be, it ain' workin'. I know dat sumbitch, an dat's him."

"Wha he doin' now?"

"He lookin' through some binoculars, but he lookin' mo' toward de house." Suddenly Bitta ducked his head and whispered. "We gone know soon if we hid. He turnin' dis direction."

"I wish somebody shoot dat sumbitch. I'm tired a bein' scairt. He gone ketch us some how, some way. I know it," Marvon said.

"Naw, he ain'. Jes keep you head down. I'll watch." Bitta eased his head up until he could see the boat. Ray Breslin was still there, but he was sitting down, not looking at anything, letting the boat drift at idle.

"Wha' he doin' now?"

"He ain' doin' nuffin. Jest sittin'. Lettin' de boat drif'," Bitta said.

"I be glad when Sunday come."

"Why you wont Sunday?"

"Cause we be in church," Marvon said. "He ain' gone come in de church. Plus, de nex' day be Monday, an' we gone see you uncle." They heard the boat's motor accelerate. "Wha' he doin' now?"

"Headin' back down de creek. I b'lieve he done give up."

"I don' " Marvon said.

"Me neither. You hungry?"

"Yeah, le's eat. We ain' stayin' here all day. Aunt Tonya comin' dis aftanoon 'bout one o'clock. We gon' go to my house an' watch TV. Dat man try to git us wif Aunt Tonya 'roun', he get his neck wrung and he balls kicked fo' sho'. She a straight-razor totin' woman, my granddaddy say, an' he know."

"Wha dat mean?" Bitta asked.

"Totes a straight-razor, I reckon. I don' know wha' dat is, but it mus' be bad de way granddaddy talk 'bout it. He scairt of Aunt Tonya, says she can yell the feathers off a chicken."

Bitta laughed. "I like to see dat."

"Yeah. Be fun to watch."

Jared Barnes watched the boat head back down the creek. He couldn't see it clearly because everything he looked at had a halo around it that blurred clarity. It had been that way ever since he pulled himself from the creek. The man in the boat seemed familiar, but he couldn't remember much. Just Turner Lockett. "Turner think Jared dead," he said to himself. "Jared ain't dead; Turner dead." He turned his attention to the tree house, wishing he could climb up and sit with the boys.

CHAPTER 28

It took Brad Coleman several hours to fall asleep and then he awakened frequently, unsettled and restless. He had set the clock for six A.M. When the alarm went off, he was awake, listening to a hard rain beating against the house in the pitch black darkness. The morning walk would not happen. It was then he fell into a deep sleep and didn't awaken until after ten o'clock. The sun was shining. He called Morgan, but she wasn't at home. Her answering machine picked up. He explained what happened, said he would call her mid-afternoon, and for her to make dinner plans.

The lunch hour was in full swing when Coleman arrived at The Oyster Creek Inn. Typically, the bar was filled with watermen and construction workers, the dining room with women out for a day of shopping, and an assortment of professional types. It was a bigger crowd than Charles Clay had indicated. Wearing a blue blazer, tan slacks, a powder blue, open-collared shirt and tan loafers with no socks, there was nothing to distinguish him from any of the dining room crowd except his looks. Several women gave him a second look while he waited to be seated. Clay got to him before the host.

"Mr. Woodson, good to see you," Charlie said. "Could I invite you to join me for lunch?" He found it difficult not to get angry at the show Clay was enjoying putting on.

"That would be very nice, Charles. Thank you," he said, not getting caught up in the charade. "You have a nice place here. Was it like this when you bought it?" Clay was guiding him to a table in the corner of the dining room closest to the boat dock. It provided an unobstructed view of the entire dock, the marsh, the creek that gave the restaurant its name and the Chester River in the distance. The table was somewhat removed from the rest and up one step on a small platform, so the attorney could not only

301

enjoy privacy while he dined or conferred, but also oversee the whole room.

"No, I put quite a bit of money in it. Redid the whole place from kitchen to rest rooms. Everything except the bar. And I'm proud of it," he said as they sat at the table. "Don't think I'll put The Covington House out of business, but some of their regulars have started comin' out here occasionally. I took the liberty of puttin' our order in earlier; I hope you don't mind."

"Not at all."

"It's cold, so it won't take long to prepare. What would you like to drink?"

"Iced tea would be fine," Coleman said. Clay raised his eyebrows.

"Henry?" Clay called out and a waiter appeared immediately. "Would you bring Mr. Woodson an iced tea, and I'll have a little bourbon over ice."

"Yes, sir," the waiter said and was gone.

"So, you enjoyin' the beach?" Clay asked. Coleman could tell he was probing. Lawyers were never very subtle.

"Very much. Your house is beautiful, and Sangaree has so few people, it's like having a private island. I thought your banker friend was going to be here."

"He will be. I told him one o'clock, so we'd have a few minutes to chat first. No need for everybody to know everything. I think we have everything in place as far as you're concerned. Couple of little local things to finalize, but that'll be done in a day or so. They have no relation to your part of the operation. You said you would give me instructions regardin' coordinates for the meeting at sea. Identification codes and so forth?"

"Yes." Coleman pulled a thick envelope from his inside blazer pocket and gave it to Clay. "They're all in there, as well as instructions for communications during the last twenty-four hours before the meet. I don't like a lot of communication. We use a variety of frequencies, sometimes changing every few words, so that no one can pick up a coherent conversation. By the time they find where we are, the words are gone. No contact should be more than twenty seconds. Ten is preferred. I know changing frequencies is awkward, but it's safer. And only one

person is to be in contact and know the communication procedures."

"I don't see that as a problem," Clay said.

"It can't be. What kind of boat do you have meeting us?"

"It's a sixty-eight-foot shrimper. Won't take any notice going
out or coming in. Plenty of space and she moves pretty good,"
Clay said.

"Be sure it meets with all Coast Guard regs; you don't want
to fall because of some simple oversight."

"Don't worry. I know you probably think of us as amateurs,
and I guess in the great scheme of things we are, but we've been
doing this for awhile and successfully, I might add."

"No offense intended," Coleman said.

"None taken. How soon can you deliver?"

"Once you give the word, we can have the boat moving
within a day. From Jamaica, with the southeast trade winds at
this time of year, four days on the water, five at the outside. You
tell me."

"When can you sail?" Clay asked.

"Soonest? Sunday night, Monday."

"That would put you here next Thursday or Friday. We can
be ready."

"Do you have buyers lined up?"

"The word is out, and they're anxious. Within a week of
delivery, this business should be out of our hands."

"That's the way to do it."

"When are you planning to leave South Carolina?" Clay
asked.

"Sunday afternoon. I'll need the bearer bonds Sunday morning. I don't want them before then and would prefer you deliver
them, Charles."

"That's no problem. I have them available."

While they were talking, Reichert passed through the bar. He
didn't see Ray Breslin, having a beer and observing Charlie
Clay's table. Breslin's eyes were blackened and purple as if he'd
had a nose job, which, in essence, he had. There were several
strips of tape across his nose, an amateur and futile effort to hold
it straight.

Charlie Clay saw Reichert working his way through the tables.

"Here's my banker now," Clay said, rising from his chair. "Glad you could make it, Bill. Meet Mr. Woodson, our southern representative." He reached across the table to shake Coleman's hand.

"Mr. Woodson." The food Charlie ordered for the three of them arrived as they were seating themselves.

"Looks wonderful, Charles," Coleman said.

"It's our seafood salad sampler. Shrimp, fresh tuna, and crab," Clay said, pointing out each one. "I think you'll find it enjoyable. It's kind of a kick owning this place. I hope I own it forever, whatever forever is."

"Then I hope that for you, too," Coleman said.

"Bill, to catch you up, we've discussed all the logistics and arrangements and decided that our meeting should take place next Thursday or Friday."

"That soon?" Reichert said. Clay didn't acknowledge the question, Coleman noticed.

"I'll need to get Mr. Woodson's package from you on Sunday morning. Perhaps we could meet for an early breakfast at The Covington House."

"I see no problem with that. Everything's ready." Reichert turned to Coleman. "What about the balance of the . . ."

"One of my attorneys will be contacting you with instructions on how to proceed with clearing that out," Coleman said. "As I told Charles, he will be contacted with all of the last minute details. If you have your end taken care of, there should be no problems."

"Will you be making the trip?" Reichert asked.

"I have a lot of interests to manage, Mr. Reichert, and they require my presence. My crews are very efficient, capable and trustworthy."

"I hope so," Reichert said.

"Be assured," Coleman said with an edge in his voice.

"Enough business," Clay said. "Let's enjoy lunch. You said you were going to Palmetto last night. What did you think?"

"I had no idea how big it is. It's a city. I did have a great meal, place called Les Pyrenees. Are you familiar with it?"

"Can't say as I am," Clay said.

"I am," Reichert said. "How did you find out about it? It's a pretty well-kept secret over there. The residents like to keep it for themselves."

"A friend introduced me to it." Coleman saw Bill Reichert tense, but didn't know why he would.

"You are in your friend's debt. I think it's the best in the South."

Coleman watched Bill Reichert throughout the meal. He trusted Charles Clay, but the banker seemed unstable.

After graciously refusing Charles Clay's offer of an evening together, Coleman left the restaurant and drove toward Sangaree Island and Morgan Hannah. He had just engineered an operation that would net millions of dollars, yet he was more excited about the dinner plans for the evening than he was about the risk of his venture and all of the money involved. That was a glorious feeling.

Karen Chaney sat in the parking lot of the Oyster Creek Inn for more than two hours after following Charlie Clay from his office in downtown Covington. She saw Ray Breslin park and go into the bar and was amazed at the damage Sam Larkin had done to his face. The man looked like he had tried to take on an eighteen-wheeler head-on. Her respect, as well as her wariness, for Sam Larkin grew. There was a dark corner in the man that he kept well-hidden. She wanted to check Breslin's truck for front-end damage, but there was no way to do it without being seen. There would be time.

She also watched Bill Reichert pull in the parking lot and go inside. Other people came and went, and she was ready to call it an afternoon when she saw Charlie Clay usher Bill Reichert and another man out on the porch to say their farewells. The man, whom she hadn't seen enter because she wasn't looking for him, grabbed her attention. His presence was commanding. He was handsome, a word that didn't do him justice. She guessed he was Charlie Clay's house guest. It was obvious what Larkin meant when he described him as having confidence and money. It showed without effort.

As soon as the man and Bill Reichert left the parking lot, Karen drove home. There were no messages on her answering machine. She picked up the phone to call Dougherty, but there was no dial tone. She pressed the disconnect button twice, and there was still nothing.

"Hello?" she said.

"Hello?"

"Sam?"

"It never rang," he said.

"I know. I just picked up to call Neil."

"I didn't expect you to be at home. I was going to leave a message."

"What's happening? I thought you'd still be at the beach."

"I was, but no one was moving. About noon I went for a walk off the beach, and both Clay's guest's car and Morgan Hannah's were gone. So, with nobody left to watch, I came home."

"Well, I'm pretty sure the house guest was with Clay at his restaurant. And you're right. He does look rich and he is handsome. I hope he's not involved, 'cause I think I'm in love."

"That sounds like him."

"Bill Reichert was there, too. I guess they all had lunch. Oh, and so was Ray Breslin, but I don't think he was invited to be part of the others' lunch date. He didn't come or go with them. Sam, Ray looked like he was hit by a truck. His eyes were black, nose taped. You sure did a job on him."

"I didn't have a choice."

"I know," she said, sensing that was the end of that line of conversation.

"I went by Harry Tom's on the way back to the house. Cedrick stopped by to see Skeeter again."

"And?"

"Came early. During the storm. Skeeter talked to him and got another threat. Cedrick said they couldn't wait much longer, that they'd use his dock with his cooperation or without it. Didn't leave him much choice."

"What did Skeeter say?"

"Told him to give him a couple of more days to set it up at home. I think Hamilton will get out there over the weekend."

"Probably. I'm beginning to think things are getting close, and we're essentially nowhere," Karen said.

"I know."

"Listen, since I'm home early and you're home early, why don't you go to the grocery store, pick up what we need for a good dinner and a nice breakfast and come over early. I believe with all your vast experience, you can tell if someone's watching you and get in without being seen."

"I can do that. Leave the patio doors open. I'll probably come in through the back."

"With stealth?"

"With stealth."

As soon as she was off the phone with Sam, Karen dialed Neil Dougherty's office number. She got the machine and left a message for him to call. She then dialed his pager, which she didn't often do. Pagers always sounded like an emergency, which this wasn't.

She dialed in her number at the command and hung up. He would call when it was convenient. If it were an emergency, she would have dialed the pager again immediately, which would alert him to drop everything and call. She had only done that once, while working undercover in Panama City, Florida. She'd been badly beaten and left for dead by a street dealer who'd caught her in her apartment alone and, thinking she was a snitch, tried to teach her a final lesson. She couldn't identify herself to him without jeopardizing the whole operation, so she'd tried to fight it out. She lost. It was the closest she had ever come to dying. At times the violence of her job caused her to rethink her career path, but two bad situations in all the years she had worked was better than average.

At five o'clock Sam had not arrived, and there was no word from Neil. She was ready to give him another try or call Sam to see what was keeping him. Two days of watching Clay and only two brief telephone conversations left her feeling isolated and alone. It made it easy to understand why women, or men for that matter, left at home all day alone, made the decision to drink for a living. The telephone rang before she could call anyone.

"I don't care who you are," she said. "Stay on the line. I want to talk to you." There was silence.

"Belle?"

"Hey, Blue." Back to normal.

"What in hell was that all about? Are you okay?"

"I'm fine. I just haven't had anyone to talk to and I'm lonely. I've been staking out Charlie Clay for two days and Sam's watching his beach house. We've only talked twice. Briefly. On the telephone. I think things are heating up and I've got nothing."

"And you're horny," he said.

"And I'm horny. Satisfied?" Her brusque comment cut him short.

"Why don't you give me a run-down on what's happened since we talked."

Karen went through every detail of the past few days: Sam's confrontation with Breslin, Cedrick Hamilton's second visit to Skeeter, and Charlie Clay's meetings with Bill Reichert.

"And that's all I have. One threat. Nothing else. Oh, and Clay has a guest at his beach house. I forgot that. He met for lunch with Clay and Reichert today while Clay was on my leash."

"Can you describe this house guest?"

"Six three or four, well-built, sandy hair, looks rich and is handsome beyond reason."

"Very Tan? Like George Hamilton tan?"

"He's better looking than George Hamilton and much more masculine, but, yes, very tan. What's on your mind, Blue?" Karen was suddenly getting a lump of excitement in her stomach."

"Can you get a picture of him and fax it to me?"

"I don't know. I don't even know if he's still here."

"Try tomorrow."

"Blue, what's going on? Who is this guy or who do you think he is?"

"Obviously, I can't tell who he is from down here, but it sounds a lot like a guy named Brad Coleman. If it is, you're going to see me real soon."

"Who's Brad Coleman?"

"Probably the most sophisticated and successful importer of marijuana and hashish alive today. Estimated to be worth hundreds of millions of dollars from smuggling alone. Heaven only knows how much from investments, properties and companies he owns. I met him once in person during an investigation we were conducting on someone else. We questioned him, but he wasn't involved. And you know what? I liked the guy."

"Why haven't you been after him? Because you liked him?" Karen chuckled.

"Oh, we've been after him. He's on everyone's list, including Interpol. The problem is, he's out in the open. He moves around, but he manages to hide all his dealings, and his money is so well-covered that we've never been able to prove he's anything other than a legitimate businessman. He's uncanny."

"No paper trails?"

"The guy's a financial magician. Majored in International Finance at Cornell. We know he's running a Continuing Criminal Enterprise, which could put him away forever, but nobody can prove it. Bust him and they'll make you director of something," Dougherty said. "I am an idiot. Duh! Why don't I fax you a picture. We've got a couple of old ones. Give me about ten minutes. Karen, if I'm right, you were on the mark about the size of this operation. Coleman doesn't deal in small stuff."

"Get it to me, Blue."

"You want to marry me again?"

"Blue," she said with exasperation.

"I would, you know."

"I know you would," she said and hung up the phone.

The ten minutes took forever. There was still no word from Sam. Finally, she heard the fax machine ring, the click and the drone of the roller as it pushed the picture out. She didn't go over to the machine until she heard the signal that the transmission was complete, didn't want to see half a picture and get confused. When she ripped it off and looked at it, a smile came across her face.

"Bingo!"

She picked up the phone and dialed Neil Dougherty's pager, hung up and dialed again.

There was a small envelope stuck in the front door of Charlie Clay's beach house when Coleman returned from lunch. The flap was embossed with Morgan Hannah's address. Her handwriting was exquisite, not calligraphy, but close to it.

Dear Sir,

Knowing that you are a pirate and all, and know-
ing that I am not only putting my person, but also my
dignity in extreme jeopardy—though your gentleman-
ly behavior last evening would indicate otherwise—
why don't you join me for dinner at my home at six
o'clock? I will expect you unless I hear differently.
Affectionately,
Morgan

He folded the note and put it back in the envelope. What he said the night before—that he needed to think about her—was true. There was little in life he hadn't done and almost nothing he couldn't do, if he so chose. He could build a skyscraper, put up his own satellite, buy twin Lear jets, all things that only a handful of people in the world could even imagine doing, yet none of these things created any personal worth to his way of thinking. He liked the money, what it could do, but never considered it a monument to anything. Maybe because of the shallowness of what he did to earn it.

Now there was Morgan Hannah. The problems she presented were numerous and complicated. Time was a factor. In two days he would be gone. It was more dangerous to come to the states than stay away. After the Clay venture, he would never come back to South Carolina again. It was a rule. He couldn't imagine Morgan Hannah ever throwing her life to the wind to gamble on him. He was a poor risk. The authorities would never stop trying to indict him. His only choice was to give it all up and distance himself from every part of the life he was living and had lived. That would also include the majority of the money he possessed.

He didn't want to run, though he could do it in style. Being a fugitive wasn't a life. The other possibility was a long shot, but not out of the question. He could become respectable. As far as he knew, the authorities had nothing they could prove to this point; if they did, he would be in jail. If they didn't get him on this operation, which was unlikely since there was nothing to prove his involvement, and he retired to France, he could be home free. There would always be questions, but his moneys were so insulated and so few people in his business knew who their employer was, the likelihood of jeopardy was slim. It was something to think about.

At six o'clock he knocked on Morgan's door. He was dressed casually: white linen slacks, Mediterranean sandals, a pale blue, open-collared shirt with long sleeves and epaulets. It was the moment he had looked forward to since the night before. When she opened the door, she was even more impressive than he remembered. She, too, wore white slacks, but with a silk, taupe-colored blouse and a wide belt with a two-piece gold buckle in the shape of a crab.

"You look wonderful," he said. "I've missed you today."

"Thank you." She led him into the living room. "Do you mind eating in? Anywhere I suggest after last night would be an anticlimax."

"It's a luxury for me. I eat in restaurants most of the time." He took her by the elbows and kissed her lightly on the lips. "Are we deli-ing tonight or cooking?"

"We are cooking and you can help. But before that, why don't you mix us a drink? Unless you're starved, of course."

"Martinis?"

"Vodka martinis on the rocks, down and dirty"

"I'll do my best."

For dinner Morgan prepared black sea bass she had purchased fresh in the afternoon. It was rolled in almonds, baked, and drizzled with a light cream sauce. She served it with Florentine potatoes and fresh asparagus spears. It was a delightful dinner, and they enjoyed the playfulness and camaraderie of the kitchen.

He helped Morgan clear the dishes and put them in the dishwasher. He couldn't remember the last time he'd done that. Years. It felt good. When everything was put away, he poured a brandy for each of them, and they went to the deck to watch the sky transfer itself into full night. The moon and stars appeared more three-dimensional here than in any other place in the world that he had been.

"Did we accomplish any piracy today?" Morgan asked, smiling.

"I think so. I have many ships sailing the seas. Surely one of them must have come up with some booty or a wench or two."

"What do you do with the wenches? When you're through with them, I mean."

"Throw them away or sell them."

"Ahh. What did you really do today, if I may be so personal."

"Slept late after waking at six and seeing a deluge outside my window. Didn't think it would be comfortable walking the beach. Then I had lunch with Charles at his restaurant and came back here to wait for six o'clock."

"Still throwing the charm around, aren't you?"

"I hope it's working." There was silence for a moment. "What are you thinking, Morgan?"

"Seriously?"

"Seriously." She didn't say anything, just held her brandy snifter in both hands, warming it and looking out at the stars.

"I'm not sure what I think," she said. "I'm not avoiding the issue. It's just that all the things going through my mind are confusing, and I'm not used to being confused."

"Tell me," he said and closed his arm around her shoulder.

"I was married once. It wasn't a fantastic marriage, but a good one. Solid. Since my husband died, I have never considered any kind of permanent relationship, have no need for one, yet for the past two days, every now and then, a stray thought regarding that has run through my mind. I don't even know you." She chuckled. "We've never been to bed together. Maybe we wouldn't be physically compatible, though I find that hard to believe. Those thoughts are presumptuous, and they scare me, Brad. You scare me."

"I scare you?" He turned to look at her.

"That you could make me think that way. I have no idea what you do, who you are. You say you're a pirate and that's romantic and cute, but I don't know where romantic and cute end and reality begins." Brad shook his head and smiled.

"That's pretty scary all right," he said.

"It is. What about you? What are you thinking?"

"How much can I trust you?" He faced her. "Seriously."

"Implicitly." There was no quarter in her answer.

"I have to take you at your word because I think there is something going on here that I'm not very experienced with. Those thoughts you just mentioned, I've had some of those, too.

The difference is, Morgan, I've never been married, never been part of a permanent relationship in my life. My work wouldn't allow it. Rarely have I ever spent more than a week in one other person's company or in one place. I have no family, so there have never been any ties. You're right. To think of that now is scary. For me, too." He took a deep breath, felt a little dizzy and began a confession he never thought he would make.

"I think before we go any further, I must tell you something I have never told anyone who is not involved in my industry, and this may solve both of our problems. I am truly a pirate of sorts." He paused.

"Please?"

"I arrange for, and sometimes participate in, the smuggling of marijuana and hashish. I've never been involved in hard drugs: cocaine or heroin or anything like that, and I've never been arrested nor served any time. Of course, that has been and always is a possibility. I've been able to accept that with a settled mind until now. Now the idea of spending years in prison is uncomfortable. That is my story." He finished and realized he had been rehearsing that speech all afternoon. "I'll leave if you prefer." Again, there was silence. She was considering her answer.

"You're not putting me in any jeopardy. I'm not sure what I think about all of this. It will take some thought. I don't like what you tell me you do, but I appreciate that you did. It certainly indicates a great deal of trust. And, no, I don't want you to leave."

Morgan looked up at him. He pulled her forward and kissed her. There was no tentativeness, no exploring as there had been the night before. She opened her mouth and let his tongue come inside. It was a strong kiss, one followed by another, his tongue circling the outside of her lips, feeling the smooth slickness of them.

"I want you to make love to me, Brad Coleman. That first and then I'll think."

He kissed her as they walked to her bedroom. His fingers were difficult to control when he unbuttoned her blouse. It was a new experience for him, something he couldn't describe even to himself. When her blouse was off, she loosened her bra and let it fall to the floor. Her breasts were magnificent. He kissed each one, as his hands undid the buckle of her slacks.

Morgan went to the bed while Brad undressed. His body was lean and muscular, as she had imagined. There were no tan-lines. The skin was smooth and unblemished. She watched the muscles in his back move when he bent over to remove his slacks and underwear. He was beautiful, and she needed to tell him that, she thought, in those words. She had never thought of a man that way.

"You're beautiful," she said as he approached the bed. He lay down beside her with no words, kissed her deeply, felt her move against him. The heat of her body enveloped him. A rose tint colored her face. His hands went down to her hips, a blind man sensing through his fingers the sculpture of her. He could feel her breath in his ear and knew her eyes were closed as were his. They shut out the rest of the world and existed in a universe of each other.

CHAPTER 29

After leaving The Oyster Creek Inn on Friday afternoon, Bill Reichert got drunk. It was becoming a more frequent occurrence. So far it had caused no problems. He always managed to function if he were called on to do so, which wasn't often. Usually, by one o'clock, he was gone from the bank for the day, and when he got home, Isabel was in bed asleep. It was never a struggle getting up in the morning; his body managed to repair itself quickly. At least until now.

He was in the guest room bed. It was Saturday and the sun was up. That was all he could be sure of. His head ached, and his face and all the muscles in his body hurt. If he had been in a fight or an accident he didn't remember. A box. A cardboard box. He remembered something about that, but there was no definition to the memory. His brain was sore and empty. When he managed to sit up, he realized he was still fully dressed, still had his tie and jacket on, though the tie was loosened.

His clothes weren't dirty, so he assumed he hadn't been in a fight. He didn't get another thought in before he threw up. He pulled his knees together to keep the spume from getting on the carpet, but was only partially successful. Removing his pants while trying to not to make a bigger mess was impossible. He gave up and pulled them off, vowing to clean the carpet as soon as he got himself together. The acrid, whiskey smell of his vomit made his stomach lurch, but there was nothing left to come up. The dry heaves lasted for five or ten minutes. Tears were streaming down his face and drool was coming from his lips. He didn't want to close them for fear of swallowing the taste in his mouth.

Wearing his shirt, tie, jockey shorts and socks, he went to the bathroom, turned on the shower and stepped in, not knowing or caring whether the water would scald him or send him into uncontrollable shivering. He needed wet, didn't care what kind. The water was cold, but quickly warmed to the point that he had to adjust it to avoid being burned. He removed the clothes he was still wearing and let them lay in the floor of the shower, moving them with his foot when necessary to free the drain.

When the water began to chill, he turned it off and leaned against the stall. His head remained foggy and the rest of him was no better. His stomach was cramping. He couldn't control his fingers and his hands were shaking. He stepped out of the shower and lay down on the oriental rug that covered most of the tiled area between the shower stall and the bathtub and went to sleep.

Awaking a second time in the same day, shivering, again not knowing how he got where he was, frightened him. Looking at himself in the mirror, he surmised that he looked ten years older than he had two months ago. There were dark, grape-colored circles under his eyes. His cheeks were sunken from the fifteen pounds he had lost, and his lips were an unnatural crimson.

Going back into the bedroom, being hit by the sour smell of stomach acid and stale whiskey, seeing his trousers bunched next to the bed amidst the mess that came out of him, brought back the memory of waking and getting into the shower, but nothing else. He went back to the shower to wash, didn't think he had done that the first time. He couldn't stand his own stink. Bill Reichert, Compulsive Bill, best dresser in Covington, South Carolina, was a disaster.

While he was shaving and dressing, he attempted to reconstruct the night before. There'd been a meeting with Charlie Clay and Woodson or whatever his name was in the afternoon. He recalled leaving The Oyster Creek Inn and starting back to Covington. Then he had turned left instead of right onto Route 37. He'd headed toward Sangaree, lost his nerve halfway there, and gone into The Sea Horse, a quasi-biker bar, not so rough that it was not frequented by other classes of people. That was where he had loosened his tie. He clearly remembered doing that before he'd gone inside. Funny.

And he was meeting Charlie for breakfast in the morning to deliver the bearer bonds. That much was certain. There was also something about the bank, but it was vague. A brown cardboard box. Nothing else. There was no recollection of the night or going home or anything specific after he'd gone into the tavern. His thoughts were like fireflies. They presented themselves and were gone. It was the third blackout in the last few weeks.

He went to the bedroom window to see if Isabel's car was in the driveway. It wasn't. It was Saturday. Hair and nails would take her until at least two o'clock. By then he would be gone. He wondered if she had looked in on him before she left. The thought made him sweat. The telephone startled him. He debated whether or not to answer. Who knew what news might be out there awaiting him?

"Bill Reichert," he said, trying to sound normal.

"Mr. Reichert?" Why would his secretary be calling him at home on Saturday?

"Yes?"

"I just wanted to see if you were okay."

"Why shouldn't I be?" His mind was racing, begging for memory. The moisture on his skin began to chill.

"Well," she hesitated, "you seemed ill when you came back to the bank yesterday just before closing. I didn't want to leave you there, but you insisted." He felt like he was going to be sick again.

"I'm glad you called, Doris. I was just trying to explain to Isabel why I was late for dinner. It's good to know I have a perfect alibi." He tried to laugh, but it didn't play. "What time was it exactly, when I got to the bank? About five o'clock?"

"Actually twenty after. I was just leaving and had to unlock the door to let you in."

"Oh, yes, I remember. I'd left my keys on my desk."

"Yes," she lied, recalling his struggle to get his key into the lock.

"And what time did you leave?"

"I went to the storage room to get you the box you asked for and then I left. That was about six."

"Well, I had some work that needed doing whether I was ill or not, so I worked my way through it," he said. The box.

"You were there until six-thirty. I waited in the parking lot to make sure you locked up. Since you were ill and all," she added.

"I appreciate that, Doris. So, six-thirty."

"Yes. You came out, put the box in your car and went back and locked the door. After you left, I checked to make sure."

"Thank you. Can we keep this private, Doris?"

"Of course."

"I think I need you to take care of me all the time. Thank you again. I guess I'll see you bright and early Monday morning." Monday morning. Monday morning, he thought. The boat would sail on Monday morning.

"Take care of yourself, Mr. Reichert, and if you need me for anything, don't worry about calling."

"Thank you, Doris."

After he hung up the phone, he felt like collapsing or going to bed or dying or something. Instead, he went down to the bar, pulled the top from a bottle of vodka and turned it up. It threatened to come back on him, but he closed his throat. He gagged, reached for the empty ice bucket, just in case, but managed to hold it down. His eyes were watering. They felt tight, stretched.

"My God," he whispered to the room. "What in Heaven's name did I do? Where did I go after the bank? What the hell was the box for?" His memory had deserted him. He lifted the bottle again and took two big gulps, struggling to keep it down. It was beginning to burn away the fear, but it wasn't clearing the mind.

Doris said he had put the box in his car after the bank closed. He hurried outside to the driveway. The car was there, which was some relief. It wasn't locked, which was strange if he had left something in it. He wasn't that trusting. There was no box in the front or back seat. He popped the trunk and went around and looked in. There was nothing there. It was maddening. A box. A brown corrugated box. He could see it, remembered it, but had no idea why he asked for it, what he put in it or where he took it. His stomach was queasy. He went back to the bar, turned up the bottle again and waited for the pain to stop.

With credit for service time Ray Breslin had six more years until retirement. He would be forty-five years old, young enough to build a whole new life. This was not a time to screw up. With what he had and at least half of what Turner stashed, he could live the kind of life his dreams were made of. The bonus thought was that he could take all of Turner's money if he wanted, just tell Charlie there was nothing to be found.

It was getting toward seven A.M. Neither of the kids had made a move. Friday was a loss because he'd chosen to come by water and then he had gone to Charlie's restaurant for lunch. The fact that Charlie hadn't included him in the meeting didn't sit well. Maybe he'd just keep Turner's money if he found it. No loyalty to him? No loyalty to them. After thirty minutes of waiting, he got out of the truck and walked to the door of Marvon Jeffries's home.

Marvon and Bitta felt safe in the house. It was Saturday. Marvon's mama and daddy were at home. Bitta slept over and by seven o'clock, the two boys were curled up on the couch with blankets wrapped around them to keep off the morning chill. The TV was on and two bowls of Frosted Flakes were on the metal tray-table in front of them. They were hypnotized by the cartoon characters and never took more than one spoonful of cereal at a time before sitting back and readjusting their blankets. They talked during the commercials.

"You won' go fishin' dis aftanoon?" Marvon asked, taking a spoonful of soggy flakes.

"Be good, I reckon, but ain' too smart."

"You mean 'at ole po-liceman? He din't even come back yestiday. We sat out dere all mawnin' fo' nuffin. He might not eva' come back."

"You funnin' yosef, you don' think he comin'. He be back. You watch," Bitta said.

"Wha' time we gone go to yo' uncle's Monday?"

"I don' know. He pro'bly get up early."

"But s'pose de po-liceman catch us while we on our way?" Marvon asked.

"I don' know."

The commercial was over and Deputy Dawg was back on. When it was Mattel time, they talked again.

"Well, s'pose he do?" Marvon asked.

"Hafta be careful, I reckon. Make sure he don't. If we stay off de road, he won't see us. He don't like to leave dat truck."

"I wonder what happen to he face. Look like he got beat up or run into a tree or sumpin'. How long it gone take us to git over to yo' uncle's?"

"Don' know. Ain' never walked. Only been in de car."

"We ain' gone be walkin'. Dat's fo' sho'," Marvon said. "We bes' be runnin'." Marvon stopped speaking. It had nothing to do with the TV show. The shadow of a man appeared in the sheer curtain stretched from the top to the bottom of the front door window. Bitta turned to Marvon and then to the door. His jaw dropped and his mouth fell open. Neither of them moved or said a word. They hunkered further under the blankets.

The man knocked. When no one answered, he knocked again. The boys tried to hold their breath.

"Anybody home?" the man shouted. "Law Enforcement."

Marvon's daddy came out of the bedroom. He looked at the boys on the couch.

"Why didn't y'all answer the door?" He shook his head and opened it. "Yeah?" Ray Breslin flashed his badge. Marvon's daddy didn't look at it. "Wha' you wont? Wakin' us up this early."

"I'm sorry 'bout that. You got a young boy name of Marvin Jefferies livin' here?"

"Why you won' know?"

"I need to ask him some questions. Now does he live here?"

"Firs' of all, his name ain' Marvin; it's Marvon. And second of all, he ain' a boy, he's a child or a young man. Third of all, wha' eva' you got to axe him about, you axe me."

"I believe him and his friend, Bitta Smalls, know somethin' 'bout who tore up that trailer down on the creek yonder. Belonged to a Mr. Lockett. Drowned awhile back. Now maybe they know somethin' and maybe they don't, but you can bet, one way or another, I'm gonna find out. Are they here and can I talk to 'em, or do I have to go get a warrant for their arrest?"

Marvon's daddy began to laugh.

"A warrant fo' dey arres'? You crazy? Dey little boys, an' you don' even know dey done nothin'. Now I could tell you to go get dat warrant, but I won't. I'll axe 'em and dat will be dat," he said.

"I'm 'fraid not. I got a bunch of questions to ask, and I think I'd get better answers if I talked to 'em myself." It wasn't going the way Breslin had hoped. He knew he was on testy ground.

"You might, but you ain'. Marvon, Bitta, come on ova here."

The two boys clutched their blankets around them, the bottoms dragging the floor like bridal trains. They shuffled toward the door, their eyes as big as saucers, their mouths open.

"Dis man say he wont to axe you 'bout a trailer down on de creek. Y'all ever been down there?" They couldn't lie; the man had seen them there.

"Seen it," Marvon said. "Everbody know where it is."

"You know anything 'bout who trashed it?" Breslin asked before Mr. Jefferies could say anything. Both boys looked at him; neither said anything.

"Do you?" Marvon's daddy asked. "Now don' you be foolin' with me."

"Nawsuh," Bitta said. "Don't know nuffin' 'bout trash."

"Tearin' it up. You boys tear it up?" Breslin asked.

"Nawsuh," Marvon said. "We ain' tore nuffin' up."

"Pull wires out of the walls? Knock out the ceilin'?"

"Why anybody won' do dat?" Bitta asked. "I gots to go to de bafroom." He started toward the back of the house.

"Me, too." Marvon said and followed him.

"Wait a min—" Breslin started.

"I think they done told you, Officer. Dey don' know anythin' about it."

"I believe they do, and I am gonna find out."

"I been nice so far, but you ain' gone come roun' here and scare dem childrens. I don' wont to see you roun' here again less you got some proof dey done it. Dey good boys. Ain' neva been in no trouble. Dey do somethin' wrong, dey get a whippin' and dey know it. Now you get on and leave us alone."

"I guess I'll just hafta get the police to come out an' get 'em," Breslin said.

"I guess you will, but you won't. Police ain' got no cause to come out here, an' you know it. You go get 'em." With that, he shut the door and left Breslin standing on the porch.

Mr. Jeffries went to the back of the house.

"Marvon? Bitta? Come on out here." The two boys came out of the bathroom, not knowing who they should be most afraid of. "You know anythin' 'bout all dis? Now don't you lie to me."

"We don' know nuffin 'bout it," Bitta said. It was easier for him to lie to Marvon's daddy. A technique the two friends had used since they were little. Marvon did the lying to Bitta's parents and Bitta to Marvon's.

"If you lyin' 'bout it, you know what you got comin'. I'll do dat firs', and den let the police take you to jail." He turned and went back into the bedroom.

"Holy shit," Marvon whispered when they were back in the living room. "He done come to de door."

"An' you say he ain' comin' back."

"I say he might not come back."

"Same thing," Bitta said.

"Ain' de same thing, dumb-ass. Ain' and might differ'nt."

"I'm gone get under de cova an' go to sleep. I'm tired," Bitta said.

They pulled the covers over their heads and closed their eyes. They enjoyed the warmth, the closeness and the safety of being curled up together on the couch. They were both too afraid to talk about what happened.

"We ought to stay here 'til Monday," Bitta heard Marvon say.

Breslin slammed his fist against the hood of his truck, got in and drove a mile and a half up the road and parked it on an old, farm road, overgrown by lack of use. He walked back through the woods and stationed himself where he could watch the Jefferies' house. Perhaps his visit would cause some activity. If not, Daddy wasn't aware of the money, and the boys were too scared to tell. At least that question would be answered. For brief moments, he wondered if he were chasing a pale horse, a scenario that existed in his mind only. Maybe the boys didn't have it. They had to. His thoughts flip-flopped back and forth, but he was convinced they were his best bet. It was his money, and they stole it.

The pain in Jared Barnes head was getting worse. Sometimes he could sleep after the lights in the boys' trailers had gone out, and when he awoke, it would subside for a few hours. On this morning it was excruciating, like steel beams being forced through his brain. His blurred vision was made worse by the pain-tears that filled his eyes as he watched the wildlife man go into the house and come out angry. He couldn't leave the boys to themselves; the man wanted to hurt them and all because of

Turner Lockett. He couldn't let him do that, though he possessed no reasoning to tell him why.

Sam Larkin felt soft kisses on his back. He didn't open his eyes. Karen was lying against him, her right leg across his, her skin warm against the fading night chill. For him, it had been a restless night, his thoughts vacillating between his feelings about the woman lying next to him and her news about Brad Coleman, which definitely added Bill Reichert to the growing list of those involved. The lady possessed so many qualities he admired. The difficulty lay in their goals and plans; they were polar opposites, and he couldn't see either of them changing. For the present, her life was her job. She was in charge in most everything she did. Sam knew, from his own experience, that she would not give it up at this juncture for his life of peace and solitary work. It would be wise to keep a governor on his emotions.

He turned over and looked up at her.

"Good morning," he said.

"You were sleeping so soundly, I thought about feeling guilty for waking you, but decided not to." She leaned over him, allowing her right breast to fall just within touching distance of his chest, coming in and out of contact as she breathed. Sam felt the heat rise in his loins and desire building within him.

"Are you looking for something?" he asked. Her hand slid down his stomach and grasped him.

"Found it," she said, pushed back the light comforter and straddled him. She moved slowly, rising and falling. He watched the muscles in her stomach clutching and relaxing, the motion of her breasts. She began to bite her lower lip, leaned forward, her hair covering the sides of her face, and increased the momentum of her movements. He could hold off no longer and felt all his energy exit him as she let out a soft cry and collapsed.

She stayed on top of him, her head tucked between his neck and his chin. They floated in a sea of comfort, no thoughts, no desire for anything, no wishes, no hopes. He felt himself slip from within her and she sighed.

"It's gone," she said. "I feel empty."

"Resting from the rigors of battle, but not defeated," Sam said.

"I'm glad to hear that." She lay quietly, then said, "Where do we go from here, Sam?" He was staring at the ceiling, feeling their chests conflict as they breathed in opposing rhythms.

"You been readin' my mind?" he asked.

"You, too?"

"Yes."

"I'm afraid to say 'I love you,' " she said. "It's what I'd like to say. What I think I feel, but I'd screw it up and the two of us along with it."

"How?"

"It's me. Supergirl. The job. I can't imagine what I'd do if I didn't do what I'm doing. But three on a horse doesn't work for long. Everything inside me says go for it, but I know me, and I couldn't do that to me or to you. What am I talking about?" She laughed. "I don't even know if you're interested," she said.

"You're not traveling alone. I know where you are with the job. I felt the same way until I was sidetracked, so to speak. If that hadn't happened, I don't know how things might have turned out. The strain was already beginning to show in little ways."

"Think you'd ever like to get back into law enforcement?"

"Haven't given it much thought. I never even considered the possibility. Living here and doing what I do is what I've dreamed of ever since I went to prison. That experience pretty well soured me on public service, law enforcement, the bureaucracy, the government and most other people."

"A loner, huh?"

"But not a recluse." He smiled. "Not yet."

"I felt that."

"What?"

"It moved. Back to the question. Where do we go?"

"For the moment right here is safer for both of us."

"Can I say, 'I might love you'?"

"Yes." They squeezed each other, holding on to the relative peace.

They dressed for the beach and Karen packed a lunch. It was Saturday. No way to know when or where Charlie Clay would make a move. Karen believed Brad Coleman was the centerpiece as long as he was around. If anything significant were going to happen immediately, he would be the motivating force. Once he

left, it would be in Clay's hands. A day working at the beach with
Sam would be nice. She wondered if the very conflict they had
talked about in bed was already raising its head.

Daylight came and turned into mid-morning before Morgan
Hannah opened her eyes for good. She was tired, and when she
moved, she realized she was also sore. She couldn't recount the
number of times she and Brad Coleman had made love. He was
the consummate lover. Nor could she remember all the things
they'd done. But she knew that they had tried to reach into each
other's beings, to solidify what they had for the moment. They
both considered it fragile and ephemeral, something that could be
lost as quickly as it had begun.

She looked at him, sleeping beside her. She was in pain emotionally and frustrated. This was their last day together, and what
was she supposed to do? Put it all behind and chalk it up as an
interesting time and good sex? Her head was spinning. There
were a few unorthodox moments in her life to look back on, but
this was different. All her life, by her own standards, she had
maintained a relatively moral life; now she was being faced with
a major moral decision unlike any other.

The man had turned her world upside down. She was not of
an age to throw caution to the wind like an empty-headed teenager
and gamble everything, including herself and everything she
was, on passion and excitement. He was a criminal, a breaker of
laws. No matter what she felt or what he might promise, that was
a huge obstacle, and she didn't believe she could overcome it or
accept it. She wished he had never called, then was glad he had.

When he was up and dressed, they sat on the deck having
breakfast and discussed what they might do for the day and the
evening. The mood was different. Nothing was said of the conversation the night before, but it hung between them.

After breakfast, they walked the beach, feeling time chasing
them. As a matter of habit, Brad scanned the people they saw, but
took no notice of the couple who followed some distance behind
them. There were other things on his mind. The world was different, and he didn't know how to deal with it. This new life was
unfamiliar. He didn't want to be who he was any longer. He

wanted to be like Morgan or any of the other people he was seeing on the beach. He wondered what he would have to do to turn
things around. Could it be done? How would he do it? Could he
manage it? The evening stood before him like a gauntlet, as he
imagined it also did for Morgan.

CHAPTER 30

It was late afternoon, and Skeeter Crewes was washing down the tables and sinks where customers cleaned their day's catch. It was an ongoing task that couldn't be put off for more than an hour at a time. Half-drunk from drinking all day in the sun, the fishermen were less than considerate about cleaning up after themselves. Their leavings brought the green flies and gulls, scavenging for pieces of fish-gut dropped on the deck and left on the tables. The birds left their own mess as evidence of their presence.

He was almost finished when he saw Ettie and the children walking across the parking lot. The sight panicked him. It was a long walk in the afternoon heat, and Ettie wasn't one to leave the house without a purpose. The house was her place, her position in life. It was where she fit. He was relieved both children were with her. He put the mop down, turned off the water and went to meet her.

His wife had a worried look on her face as he approached. The children ran to him, the excitement of their adventurous trip causing an adrenaline rush they couldn't control.

"Ettie? What's the matter?" he asked when he reached her.

"I don' know, but somethin' must be. You want to tell me?"

"I don' know what you mean. What's happened?" Ettie's expression changed from worried to stern.

"Skeeter, I seen you get a ride home in a big car a week or so ago. I couldn't tell who it was, but you come in lookin' like you seen a ghos'. Somethin's been eatin' at you ever since. I didn't ask you about it, cause I b'lieve you'll tell me when you're ready. Now one of them fish and game men come by an' asked me a whole lot of questions about Turner Lockett's trailer, an' then Seed Hamilton called wantin' to know what time you be home from work an' actin' all friendly-like, like we jus' been together for a social occasion last Saturday night. Somethin's goin' on, an'

327

I want to know what it is. You ain't told me anything." Stern had turned to angry.

"You say an officer came by?" he asked.

"Uniform, gun an' all."

"Tell me what he said."

"Wanted to know if you ever shrimped or fished over near Turner Lockett's trailer. If you mentioned seein' anybody over there. Specially some little boys. Asked me if I knew Sam and did he ever go shrimpin' or fishin' over there. An' ever time I answer a question, he asked me another one, like he didn't want to leave." She paused, almost out of breath, the venting of her anxiety exhausting the flow of adrenaline. "He scared me." Skeeter could see her chin begin to quiver.

"I don't know. I don't know nothin' 'bout Lockett's trailer. Never been over there but a few times. No time recent. An' why don't he ask Sam if he ever been over there 'stead a askin' you?" he asked.

"He said Sam wadn't at home. Asked me did I know where he was."

"What'd you tell him?"

"I told him I don't know. I don't keep no track of the neighbors. He said don't get smart.'" She saw anger in Skeeter's eyes. "Now don't get all riled. Won't do no good."

"Seed just asked what time I'd be home?"

"He said he needed to talk to you. Didn't make no sense. Somethin' about a job in Myrtle Beach. He asked if you told me about it."

"Seed give me the ride home. He told me about a guy up there could give me a job better than what I got here and asked if we all wanted to go up an' talk to him, said the man would pay for it. Like a vacation." He didn't like lying to Ettie; their honesty with each other and sharing their feelings and discontents held them together. Hard money and hard times had nothing to do with that.

"You b'lieve that? Who gonna pay for all of us to go to Myrtle Beach just for you to talk about a job? What kind of job?"

"Somethin' to do with a boat dock. He didn't tell me any details 'cause I told him I wadn't interested. Dat's why I didn't say anything 'bout it. But you know Seed. He cain't let nothin' drop. Thinks he's helpin' me out, doin' his good deed." He attempted to sound casual, at the same time trying to figure out how to contact Sam if he wasn't at home. "You walk all the way over here to tell me this?"

"That officer scared me, Skeeter. He looked beat-up and his eyes was takin' in everything. Like he was lookin' for somethin'."

"Did he say anything else?"

"Just that he was investigatin' who tore up Turner Lockett's trailer. Thought maybe you or Sam seen somethin' over there."

"Somebody tore up the trailer?"

"That's what he said. An' then Seed callin' an' talkin' about somethin' I don't know nothin' about, made me nervous," she said. "I was thinkin' you was in trouble."

"No, honey, I ain' in no trouble. I don't know 'bout that trailer, an' I told you what Seed wanted. Everything's fine."

"You sure?"

"I'm sure. Lemme go ask Harry Tom to borrow the truck, an' I'll run you all home. Ain' no need for y'all to be walkin' in dis heat." He turned to go into the store. The children were throwing pieces of broken oyster shells that paved the lot. "Y'all hang on, kids. Gonna ride in the back of a truck," he yelled and gave them a big smile.

It was after four o'clock when Sam and Karen left the beach. The day was frustrating, with nothing accomplished. Coleman and Morgan Hannah had walked the beach, sat on her deck for awhile, and then Coleman went back to Charlie Clay's house. There was nothing else to see. Sam was tired. Nights with Karen didn't promote sleep, and the sun and heat had robbed him of what energy was left. He didn't argue when Karen said she had to get back to Covington.

He walked through the door of his house, dropped his bag on the floor, took off his clothes and stepped into the shower. After washing his hair and cleaning the oil and sand from his body, he began to feel human again. He put on a pair of olive bush shorts and a bleached-out denim shirt, poured some sour mash over ice, and was headed for the deck when he noticed the light on his answering machine flashing. He pressed the PLAY button and listened.

"Sam, this is Skeeter. I need to talk to you, man. This shit is gettin' outta hand. Gimme a call at the dock. I'll be here till six. Or you could come over and give me a ride home. I got a feelin' tonight's the night. Let me hear from you."

It was quarter to five. Sam called the dock and left Skeeter a message saying he would be there by six to pick him up. He went out on the deck, lit a cigarette and told himself again he'd quit tomorrow. Or maybe not. The whiskey was good and the cigarette better. He thought about what Skeeter had said in his message. At half past five, he called Karen and got her machine. He told her what he was doing and said he would call back when he knew more.

When he hung up, he got in the Rover and drove to Harry Tom Cooper's Boat Dock. He didn't go inside. Cedrick Hamilton had picked Skeeter up at work both times they talked. If he was coming tonight, Sam didn't want to be caught in the position of being left in the store while they drove off. He waited only a few minutes before Skeeter came down the ramp.

" 'Preciate this, Bro," he said as he got in the car.

"You sounded stacked. What's happenin'?"

"Let's move. I don' want to be around if Seed come out here." Sam started the Rover and drove toward Route 37.

"Okay. We're movin'. What's happened?" he asked.

"I'm not sure. Ettie and the kids walked all the way over here in the heat this afternoon. She was scared. Said a wildlife officer come to the house and asked her a bunch of questions about Turner Lockett's trailer. Was I over there? Seen anybody? Some little boys? He even asked her had you been over there? Had to be Ray Breslin. She said he looked all beat-up. You have anything to do with that?"

"Why would you ask that?"

"You tol' me you ran into him at that bar. Thought maybe y'all got into it." Skeeter was grinning.

"Anything else?"

"She said Cedrick called, too, and wanted to talk to me about a trip to Myrtle Beach this week. I had to lie to her and go along with the story."

"This week?" The time caught Sam by surprise. Neither he nor Karen thought it would come down so soon. It put a different color on things.

"I'm gonna hafta give him some kind of answer. Wonder what he'd do if we were both there when he came?"

"Probably nothin'. You'd be better off to talk to him. Just tell him Ettie wouldn't go along with it. See what happens," Sam said. "You think Ettie and the kids would go up to my house for the night?"

"Sleep up at de massa's house? Where de white folks do? I reckon she would." He laughed. "Why?"

"I don't think there's much chance he'll do anything, but if he does, it's best if they're not around." He saw the worried look on his friend's face. "I'll stay with you. You'll be okay."

"But what about the gun? I don't think he'd . . ."

"Don't worry. I'll cover it." Skeeter saw an unfamiliar look in Sam Larkin's eyes and didn't ask how.

Ettie wouldn't budge until Sam and Skeeter explained in detail what was going on. She found it hard to believe that Cedrick Hamilton could be involved in anything like they described, but reluctantly agreed to go when Sam said if there were an argument, it would be better if the children didn't hear it. Sam drove them to his house, left the Rover and walked back to Skeeter's to wait it out with him. He carried the K-frame S&W in his belt against his back. Skeeter saw it, but said nothing.

Shortly after nine o'clock, they heard the sound of a car pulling up to the house. Sam went into the bedroom and looked through the window. He felt a chill, knowing this was not going to go down easy. Cedrick Hamilton got out of the car and walked up the steps. Sam didn't see a second vehicle parked out on the road.

Skeeter opened the door to an agitated Cedrick Hamilton. He gave him a broad smile.

"Hey, Seed. Come on in. Ettie said you called."

"What the fuck are you doing, Skeeter?" Hamilton asked as he entered the room.

"Whoa, man. Settle down. What do you mean?"

"Did you tell Ettie what I offered you?" He looked around the living room. "Where is she, by the way? Perhaps she ought to be in on this."

"She's at her brother's with the kids. Why she need to be in on it?" Hamilton sat down on the edge of the couch.

"Did you tell her about our deal, Skeeter?"

"I ain' told nobody, an' you best leave her out of it. You don't want to get in that fight, Seed."

"You never told her about Myrtle Beach, did you? She told me she didn't know a thing about it." Skeeter shook his head and smiled, hoping Hamilton couldn't see the fear and anger that was roiling inside him. It was a good act.

"Seed, Seed. You think you can come in here, throw a bunch of money in my face an' lead me around like a puppy dog for the rest of my life? I ain' no drug dealer, an' I ain' gonna be one. You gonna take care of my wife and kids while I'm servin' my time?"

"You're not listening, Skeeter. I told you it's not up to me. You don't have any choice, and I don't want to think of what might happen if you try to go to anybody for help. Be sensible, man. Take the damned money, go away, come back and forget about it. Then all of our problems will be solved."

"What about the nex' time they want to use it or me?"

"There won't be a next time. They never use the same place twice." Skeeter turned away from him. He wondered if Sam were catching all of this from behind the door.

"You got that gun with you, Seed?"

"Yes, I do. Why?"

"I want to see it." Hamilton hesitated. "Come on. Get it out. Lemme see." Skeeter said.

Hamilton pulled the revolver from his coat pocket and held it in his hand. Skeeter, in a lightning fast move, grabbed Cedrick's hand in a firm grip and pulled the hand and gun to his own face. His anger exploded. "Pull the trigger, Seed. You been threatenin' me. Do it. All your problems be solved. Ettie cain't stand up to you without me. Come on. Pull it!" he yelled. "Then you'll be safe from your friends. I know that's what's drivin' you."

Hamilton jerked his hand away and swung the gun at Skeeter, making contact with the side of his head, knocking him to the floor. He then pointed the gun at him as Sam Larkin came through the door.

"Drop it, Cedrick," Sam said, pointing the K-frame directly at the superintendent's face. Hamilton turned, a look on his face as if his legs had been cut off at the knees and he had just looked down to find them gone. The gun fell from his hand. Before Skeeter recovered enough to reach for it, Sam felt a blow on the back of his head that brought pinnacles of light exploding in his brain. He tried to make his body turn to keep from collapsing, but it was no use. He was going down and couldn't stop the fall. His vision was foggy and blurred, but he recognized Ray Breslin standing over him with a hand-fashioned billy club in his hand.

"Looks like you dropped it, Larkin," the man said, smiling. Sam was trying to get up on spaghetti legs when Breslin leaned back and aimed a foot at his ribs. It hit its mark and drove the breath from him. He could feel bone crack as Breslin followed through with his weight. Breslin kicked him again, turning him over on his back. He was ready to cap Sam's knees with his club when Hamilton grabbed him.

"Stop it!" Hamilton screamed. Breslin turned to look at him.

"You ain't got the stomach for it, go outside. I'm gonna take care of this son of a bitch once and for all. He won't never walk straight again."

Hamilton lifted the revolver and pointed it at the big man.

"You're not going to do anything, Ray. You just fucked up big-time. I didn't call for you."

"I was comin' in whether you called or not. You don't ask these bastards for cooperation. You tell 'em. You ain't got the guts for that Cee-drick? Well, I do. Now get outta my way. I got a job to finish."

"I'll shoot you, Ray," Hamilton said, raising the gun. "Get back in your truck and get out of here, or I'll see that you're cut out of it. All of it. I'll take care of this." Breslin gave him a hard look.

"It's not over, Larkin, and if that nigger opens his mouth, I'll feed his kids to the alligators." He pointed his finger at Skeeter. "You just better pray no one finds out about this, boy, 'cause I'll come lookin'." Skeeter got up and started to go after him, but

Hamilton's gun stopped him. Breslin left through the back door, slamming it behind him.

Sam's head felt like it had been dropped from a five-story building and cracked open like a cantaloupe. He tried to get up, but his legs were mush. He couldn't think; everything was spinning.

"Sit down, Skeeter," Hamilton said, motioning him toward the couch. "Stay where you are, Mr. Larkin." Sam was still trying to focus on Cedrick Hamilton. It would be no challenge to take him if he could trust his body, but he knew he couldn't. His mind wandered to Ettie and the kids, his house, Ray Breslin, Karen Chaney; it all ran together.

Breslin would come after him. He didn't have any choice. For all his threats, the man knew he couldn't trust Larkin to do nothing. Sam cursed himself for looking forward to it.

"Can we work this out, Skeeter?" Hamilton asked. "Keep you and your family or Larkin there from getting even more hurt? It's out of my control now. I can't do anything about it. You weren't smart."

Skeeter Crewes looked at him, a tired, sad expression on his face. "You let us down, Seed. That's what hurts the most," he said. "Even more than you gettin' me or my family involved. I can protect them and I can keep me out of it, believe me. One way or another I can do that, but the sad thing is I can't protect you. You sold your soul, Seed. I don't know why, but you did. It's done and gone, and you'll never be able to get it back. I can't help you."

"You're making a mistake. Breslin meant what he said." The force was gone from Hamilton's voice.

"Might be, but I'll jus' have to play that as it lays. I ain' gonna say nothin', but I cain't help you." It was a standoff. Cedrick Hamilton was out of his league and didn't know what to do.

"You could get out of this," Hamilton heard Larkin say.

"What?" he asked, turning to the man on the floor.

"You could get out of this. I can arrange it."

"How?"

"Drop the dime. Give me names, times, anything. I can bargain for you," Sam said.

"Who are you?"

"Who or what I am doesn't make any difference. I'm your only hope."

"Listen to the man," Skeeter said.

Hamilton shook his head, looked to the ceiling and took a deep breath of resignation. "I have to make a call," Hamilton said. He looked around for the phone, spotted it and walked to it, keeping the revolver pointed in the direction of the two men. Sam looked at the S&W lying on the floor, but judged a move might make the man lose control and shoot. He watched as Hamilton dialed a number. He tried to move his legs. It was a struggle. Hamilton moved the gun more in his direction, and he ceased any movement.

"The off-load will have to be somewhere else," Hamilton said into the phone. "Skeeter Crewes couldn't work it out with his wife. He tried. He really tried. I don't know what else to tell you." His voice was tired and resolute. Charlie Clay wouldn't get the message until he went to the office on Monday. Hamilton turned to Skeeter. "I did the best I could for you. Maybe it'll work." He turned and walked out the door.

Sam managed to pull himself to his feet. He was dizzy and his head throbbed. He made the couch, but that was as far as he could go.

"He won't make it," Sam said.

"What do you mean?"

"Us or them. He'll go down. Whoever's behind him didn't mean for it to go this way, but it has and he can't stop it. I'm his only chance, and he won't take it."

"What about Breslin? He better not come near my family."

"He won't. I'll see to it." Skeeter was looking down at him with a quizzical look.

"Don't judge me on tonight, Skeeter. You can bet your life this won't happen again. Guaranteed. Call the house and tell Ettie and the kids we're comin'. I want them to stay there tonight."

"What about tomorrow? I got to work."

"We'll take care of tomorrow tomorrow. Give me a hand. My brain is still squeezing, and I think I might have a couple of broken ribs."

"Oh, you gonna be a big help. I can see that now," Skeeter said and laughed. The laughter sounded good in Sam's ears. "You think you can walk that far?"

"I'll make it," Sam said. He faltered. "I think."

Brad Coleman and Morgan Hannah spent the day walking on broken glass. They had a difficult set of circumstances, and neither of them knew how to avoid cutting their emotional feet. During the afternoon Morgan played every scenario she could imagine and still had no idea of what she would do if faced with a decision. Brad was quiet in the morning and no more open in the afternoon. She felt very alone.

Again, Morgan prepared dinner at home. Avoiding other people was one decision they had made without problem or pain. In the afternoon while Brad was at Charlie Clay's house making telephone calls, she prepared a shrimp lasagna and examined the pieces of her life that were dear to her and those that had no value. She also thought about risk and morality, all of the things that come to mind when one is trying to talk oneself in and out of some atypical behavior.

During dinner Brad remained quiet, preoccupied, knowing their situation had to be addressed, but not wanting to take on the guise of salesman. Morgan could see the ideas working behind the charm and smile on his face. He had been honest with her, put the decision, without pressure for which she was grateful, in her lap.

How to begin, she wondered. How to begin a conversation they were both avoiding, a life-changing conversation no matter how it was resolved, leaving both parties with a bounty of "what if's," "maybe's" and "if only's." It had to begin. She looked up at him and smiled. *Play it light; you can always stay as you are*, she thought to herself. And what's that? As you are. It's not so bad, that's what. Play it light.

"So, what have you got to offer, Mister Pirate Man?" she asked.

"That's a helluva an introduction to what's been on both our minds for the last forty-eight hours." He couldn't help laughing.

"We have to start somewhere."

"Well, to answer your question, I'm not certain what I have to offer. I'll tell you what I'd like to be able to offer and what I might be able to do to achieve that, but right now, this moment, that's all I can do. Morgan, everything I say tonight is speculation and would require an inordinate amount of luck and cooperation from some generally uncooperative sources to pull off."

"That's a mouthful, but I'm not sure what it says."

He reached for the bottle of brandy on the coffee table, gestured to her, and she shook her head. He poured an inch in his own glass and set the bottle down.

"What I said last night didn't tell you who I am, and I think you need to know that. I don't feel dishonored. I might and probably should have done some things differently, but I feel no real guilt. Maybe I'm naïve. I look at all the legal corruption going on and find it difficult to see myself as bad as some people might. Rationalization? Maybe, but my feelings about that are not going to change. I am responsible for everything I've done in my life, good or bad, and I'm willing to pay reasonable dues for it. What I believe is reasonable. Sounds pretty pompous, doesn't it?"

"Not really, though I'm not sure I can agree with it entirely."

"All of that's beside the point. I don't think I can offer you anything until I change my position. I wouldn't want you living my life, even if you would, which I doubt. Believe it or not, I was thinking of doing this before I ever saw you. I'm tired, and what was fun or thrilling or whatever you want to call it is no longer any of those things."

"Is there anything you can do?" she asked.

"It's complicated. I've been on the telephone all afternoon with my attorneys. They believe it can be worked out. They are very powerful people with significant connections. However, dealing with the government is like working out a corporate sale. What can you give me? What can I offer you?" Brad got up and moved to the glass doors that fronted the ocean. Except for the stars, it was black; there was no moon. "There are a couple of ways I can approach the problem. I could work a deal, go to court and hope for lifetime probation, which I couldn't accept, or I could be given immunity from all prosecution."

"How could they give you that?"

"Because they want me out of business, and they want what I have."

"Money?" she asked.

"Money and information, but information is not a bargaining point. I've worked with a lot of people who trusted me, and—right or wrong—I won't betray that trust. The money I will sacrifice. Most of it anyway. Their problem is they really have nothing on me they can prove, nor can they prove that any of my assets came from a criminal enterprise, so they can't do a seizure. It's out of reach. Whatever I give them will be a gift. They'll probably label it as back taxes or something, if they acknowledge receiving it at all."

"Is there that much?'

"Nine hundred million dollars is what I am offering. That and ceasing any operations now and in the future. They will probably also want my citizenship." Morgan felt her breath catch. The amount was inconceivable.

"You have that much?"

"Yes."

"And then what would you do?"

"Find out what we have," he said looking at her. Morgan was silent. "If anything."

"Oh, we have something. I just don't know what to do with it. You've come into my life and made my world topsy-turvy. I didn't expect you. This. For all my bravado, I feel like a young girl who knows little about the real world and how it operates. You scare me, Brad. I have few limits, but this? It goes against everything I have ever believed. I'm confused."

"So am I," he said.

"What time do you leave tomorrow?"

"Eleven."

"We don't have much time," she said.

"Not enough."

"Can I make you an offer?"

"I'm listening."

"Let's put this away for now. There's nothing we can do about any of it. Put it in our pockets, give ourselves time and see what happens. I've found a lot of feelings with you that have suffered from being ignored. I need to bring those feelings into focus, but with you sitting here next to me that is impossible. I want you, but I have to be sure it's all right with me and for you."

"I think that's wise, which is not surprising. If you weren't wise, I never would have considered falling in love with you."

"Somehow I don't think love is negotiable. Right or wrong, it happens."

"My first time," he said.

"And maybe your last." She looked at him and smiled. "I want to make love to you."

"I want you to," he said and kissed her.

At two-thirty in the morning, if anyone had been passing the marsh observation area, deep in the center of Henry Bell State Park, they might have seen a silent flash of lightning inside a car parked next to the water.

CHAPTER 31

Karen Chaney was sleeping soundly when the telephone rang. She glanced at the clock on the night table and reached for the phone. It was half past twelve.

"Hello?"

"It's Sam." His voice was strained and tired. The pain in his ribs and kidney was growing, making it difficult to speak. He had passed some blood earlier and wondered if Ray Breslin had done him serious harm.

"What's happened? You sound awful," she said.

"Thanks."

"Sam." His humor irritated her.

"We were right. Cedrick Hamilton showed up at Skeeter's. Problem was, he brought Ray Breslin with him. I think Cedrick's getting desperate."

"You're kidding."

"No, I'm not kidding. I got blind-sided."

"Are you all right? What about Skeeter? Is he okay? Tell me what happened."

"I caught a billy club on the back of my head and took a couple of kicks in the ribs. My stupidity; I got careless. I'll live. And Skeeter's okay. His wife and kids are at my house. I'm gonna be here with Skeeter for a few days. It's going down this week. That's when Cedrick told Skeeter to leave." His breathing was getting difficult.

"That's too soon. We need more time," she said.

"You don't have it. You'll have to take what you can get and hope somebody turns."

"What about Breslin? He can't just let you and Skeeter walk."

"I'll take care of Breslin."

"What are you going to do?"

"You don't want to walk in that neighborhood, Karen."

"Sam, I'm not hearing this."

"You're right. You're not. I'd suggest you give your friend a call and tell him what's happened. I think we need some help," he said.

"I'm coming out there."

"No. We're okay. You need to watch Charlie Clay tomorrow. Hamilton called someone and said they couldn't use Skeeter's place. I imagine that's gonna stir things up. When Skeeter goes to work, I'll call you. I think he'll be all right there."

"I think I should come out. Breslin might not wait that long."

"He's not ready yet. He knows he'll have to choose his moment, and he thinks he's got Skeeter panicked."

"Anything, I mean anything goes on, I'd better hear from you, Sam."

"Promise. Call Dougherty."

"I will. If you don't call by eight in the morning, I'm on my way."

"Gotcha." He hung up the phone and leaned back on the couch to ease the pressure on his ribs. Ettie had cross-taped them and wrapped him in an Ace bandage while he was at the house. The wrapping was too tight to be comfortable, but he insisted it be that way. If he needed to move quickly, he didn't want internal parts of him moving in the wrong direction. His head was still pounding, but he was no longer dizzy and his legs had feeling.

"You really don't think he'll come back tonight?" Skeeter asked.

"No. He knows we'll be on alert. Go on to bed. I'm gonna sleep right here. I'm sure it'll be more rest than sleep, but I'll be okay." The S&W lay on the table in front of him.

"Think you could use that, Sam?"

"I hope he doesn't try me."

"That's not an answer."

"It would be his mistake." Skeeter Crewes did not question the look in Sam Larkin's eyes. He got up and went into the bedroom.

At one time during the sleepless night, Sam thought he heard someone outside the house, human footsteps. He got up, took the gun and went outside to look around. The halogen lamp out next to the road cast some light as far as the house, but not enough to see anything human or inhuman that didn't want to be seen. It was probably imagination; all his nerves were on the surface. He went back inside and lay down, but his ears wouldn't rest. He held the gun on his chest instead of putting it back on the table.

Neil Dougherty looked at the clock and picked up the phone. It read 1:15, and outside was still dark.

"Good morning, Belle. I went to sleep, so you'd call and tell me what's going on up there." He waited for laughter, but there was none.

"It's serious time, Blue."

"What's up? Our boy Coleman done anything of note?"

"Walked on the beach with the lady next door. Appears he spent the night."

"I hope you didn't call just to tell me that."

"No, the off-load is happening this week. I just got word from Larkin." She explained all that had happened with Cedrick Hamilton, Skeeter, Larkin and Ray Breslin. "It looks like things could get real nasty up here. It doesn't fit the nonviolent profile I was given when I was sent in."

"Somebody's gotten greedy or scared," Dougherty said.

"Looks like. Neil, I think there are a lot more people involved than those I'm aware of. The load is too big for five or six people, but I'm not sure how I can put all that together in four days. And I'm sure it's not just here in Covington. If this guy Coleman is what you say he is, it's got to go way beyond this town. I think Clay may just be a branch office. Whoever in Washington planned this operation for me didn't do their homework."

"It was the only way to play it. If they had sent in a cadre of agents, everyone in town would have known they were there. It's a small town. A single person was the only way not to alert them. Hey, it worked."

"It's too big, Blue. I'm gonna need some help."

"And you still don't want the DEA 'cowboys' in on it?"

"They're not all cowboys, but you know what happens. I don't know which ones are and which ones aren't, and I don't have the time to separate them. I have to trust your judgment."

"If it's arriving this week, it's either already at sea or leaving immediately. We'll find it. I'll notify the powers that be and tell them I think Coleman's involved. That will allow my team to coordinate with you. I'm also going to get a couple of IRS people I can trust to come in on it. They are masters at turning suspects, which I believe is our only hope of a clean sweep. You're becoming quite a gunslinger, lady, uncovering all this corruption and crime."

"You know what bothers me the most?"

"What's that?"

"The only way we ever catch them is by accident."

"Most of the time," he said. "You'll hear from me tomorrow."

"Are you coming?"

"I don't know. Let's see what happens over the next forty-eight hours. And, Karen, if you page me, use the emergency signal. Don't try to cover too much territory. Cover the people you've got: Clay and Reichert. The others will come to them pretty quickly if things are getting close. Good luck."

"Don't leave me out here."

"I won't."

Two other people had a sleepless night, but it wasn't because of physical pain or Sam Larkin's kind of worry. After they made love, Morgan Hannah and Brad Coleman were back where they started, wanting immediate answers where there were none, fearing the insecurity of postponement and indecision. She wanted to go with him when he left in the morning, but he hadn't asked. If he did, she would say no. That was where they were. They were quiet, holding each other, feeling naked skin, warmth, pretending to sleep, each listening to the other breathe. Afraid of words.

Through lidded eyes, Morgan felt the sunrise. She looked at Brad, but couldn't tell whether he was asleep or not. She kissed his chest, his stomach. There was a soft moan from him, and she knew he had been awake. When he started to move his hips, she pulled him on top of her. The love-making was slow and the culmination a coda to all the thoughts and emotions that had grown within them during the long night that had passed too quickly. Afterwards, they lay looking at each other in silence, an occasional light kiss to a forehead, an eyelid, a neck. Whisper-kisses. The sun continued to rise. Unstoppable.

"I've never said 'I love you' to a woman," Brad said after he got up and dressed.

"There's time," she said. "If you said it right now, after only three days, after making love for hours, I would have to doubt you, as I doubt myself. I'm feeling the same thing, but, having been there before, I'm familiar with my own caution and trust it. We have time if it's supposed to happen."

"Thank you."

"It's realistic," she said.

"Think you could live in France?" he asked.

"I believe I could live anywhere under the right circumstances."

"You want to tell me what those might be?"

"I would have to be in love or at least very much in 'like,' which is what most people are when they think they're in love. I'd need to think it was relatively stable. I have no desire to live a 'jet-set' life or be a gypsy."

"I guess that lets out being a fugitive," Brad said. Morgan paused and looked at him. He read the answer in her eyes.

"I couldn't live like that, wondering every morning if my whole life was going to change by nightfall. I can't imagine how you've done it all these years." She smiled. "That doesn't mean an ex-fugitive, who made his peace with the world and whom no one is looking for, couldn't entice me to live abroad. I have no ties here," she said.

"I'm working on that first part," he said. "The second part's up to you."

"I gathered that from what you told me last night, but it has to be for you as well. This has to be because you want it. The freedom of it. Not because you want me. You've already had me."

"Not by a long shot, Morgan. I know that. It's not ending here, but I do have things to take care of before I leave. That time I've been sweating all night is here. I tried to practice a speech, but it didn't make sense because I was talking to myself, and I felt foolish." He looked at her face-on. "I want you with me. Somehow, some way, I'm going to make this work, but you're going to have to have a lot of faith. You won't know when you're going to hear from me, but you will hear, one way or another. If

I can accomplish what I'm trying to do, I will send for you. Then it's up to you. Don't change your life. I won't ask that of you, but know I'm there."

"I'll try. Don't make it too long, Brad. I have to be realistic. I may change my mind."

"As soon as I can." He took her in his arms and kissed her. "That's worth everything I have." No more was said.

When he was ready to leave, he handed her an envelope.

"If you ever need to reach me in an emergency, but only in an emergency, call this number. I will get back to you. I love you as much as I can right now, Morgan," he said and held her.

"I'll worry," she answered.

"Don't. I think it's meant to be."

He turned, walked out on the deck and onto the beach. He didn't look back as he walked to Charles Clay's house. Morgan got out of bed and watched him all the way.

"You look like hell," Skeeter Crewes said, looking down at Sam Larkin lying on the couch.

"That's strange. I feel perfect."

"You gonna protect me?" He said it with skepticism. "I'll be surprised if you can get off that couch."

"I can make it," Sam replied, struggling to get upright, which he finally managed. He wasn't sure he'd be good for much, but he didn't have a choice. What burned in his mind the most was Ray Breslin. In prison he had learned one primal concept and, though not proud that he did, lived by it out of necessity: "Allow no trespass on your personal space and freedom of choice to go unpunished." Several prisoners gained painful recognition of how strictly Sam Larkin adhered to that principle. Fortunately, no one had tested that resolve since he was released. Ray Breslin had trespassed, and Sam Larkin cringed at the thoughts that moved, like an unbridled storm, through his mind.

"Here. Take these." Skeeter held out two aspirin and a glass of water. Sam took them without argument.

"Did you call Ettie?"

"Yeah. They fine. Say the massa's house right comfortable and the TV reception's better 'n here. 'Course I knew that."

Skeeter laughed. "Other than take me to work, what else are you gonna do today?"

"Find Ray Breslin."

"I was afraid you would say that. You a crazy man? What are you gonna do with him when you find him? Point out the spots he missed and let him kick your ass again? You ain' in no shape to take him on. You gonna get hurt bad this time."

"You go after an animal like an animal. That's not always the righteous way to do it, but Ray Breslin is gonna wish he never heard of Sam Larkin."

"Don't sound like the Sam Larkin I know. What is it you always say? 'Don't go in that neighborhood.' You better take your own advice, and let it come down when it comes down. Let the law handle it."

"I wish I could, but he's not finished yet, and he is the law. He can't leave us standin' around, Skeeter. Not me, not you or your family. He's in too deep. It's the way he thinks. He's got a little power runnin' through his blood after last night, and he's gonna try to use it. I've got to stop that." Sam stood up awkwardly, bracing himself on the arm of the couch to gain his feet. "Come on. Let's check on Ettie and the children. See if they need anything and then get you to work."

"You reckon they gonna be . . ."

"Breslin won't come to my house. He's not smart, but he's already been warned. He knows better than to try to take a man on his own territory."

There was no one Bill Reichert could ask, nowhere he could look that he hadn't searched, no explanation hiding in his brain. He pictured himself on an ice floe, drifting into a warm sea with no way to save himself. The box was the key. Intuitively he knew that much. The key to what, he didn't know, but he was certain finding it would solve all his problems.

After searching the house the previous morning, he had gone to his office, but couldn't unearth a clue to what he might have needed a box for. He spent the rest of the day drinking, but neither drunken solace nor his lost memory kicked in. He even asked Isabel if she had seen a brown cardboard box anywhere. She smiled and said no, didn't ask what was in it, and dismissed him.

It was six o'clock in the morning. He lay awake, looking at the ceiling. In three hours he would meet Charlie Clay and hand over a million dollars in bearer bonds. They were in his briefcase; he had checked them ten times. The briefcase was under his bed, and God only knew how many times during the night he leaned over the side of the bed and felt for it. A million dollars to get caught, which he had convinced himself would be the ultimate outcome.

After showering and dressing and checking to see that Isabel was still asleep, he went to the bar and took several large swallows of vodka. The heat of the alcohol coursed through his body. A couple more and his brain would be back to normal, the fears numbed, solutions—rational or irrational—available. He took two more swallows. If he could get through this one day, he would be okay. He had made a decision during the night, and the alcohol was giving him the courage to believe he could follow through with it.

He was going to run; there was no other choice. Money was no problem, and he already knew how he was going to get it out of the country. In half a day, he could take care of the instrumentation and transactions that were necessary. Bernardo Hieronymous Ortega had taught him more than he realized. He wasn't even going to take any clothes. Bill Reichert was going to make himself disappear before the shit hit the fan. He took a couple of more hits from the bottle and began to feel good about his prospects. Fuck the box; fuck whatever might happen to the rest of them, and fuck Isabel. He wished no harm to any of them, but whatever came to them, they brought upon themselves. All except Isabel. He was beginning to feel better than good, confident again and superior. Leaving to meet Charlie Clay, he paused in the driveway and looked at the house he loved. One more night in you, and fuck you, too.

Breakfast was uneventful. Looking at Charlie, who lived within his own pose of wisdom, shrewdness and good judgment, made Reichert feel like giggling. If the man only knew what he planned to do. He was angry that he couldn't gloat over his new freedom. Most of his anger was directed toward Morgan Hannah. She was the only person in his life who had ever made herself more important to Bill Reichert than himself, and he knew she was lost.

When Charlie Clay left The Covington House with the brown manila envelope containing one million dollars in bearer bonds, Reichert felt a great weight lift from his shoulders. It was over; he had performed his last act for The Company. Let them carry on without him. Only then would they realize what he did for them.

From the dining room, he watched Clay pull away from where he was parked and another car leave behind him. There was a time he would have taken notice; now he didn't give it a thought. The alcohol was beginning to wear thin; it was time for another drink. There was a full bottle in the car; he was good for the day.

Most of the cars Karen Chaney saw on Route 37 on Sunday morning were filled with Matthew's Island residents on their way to the numerous churches along the road. The sun was bright, its light creating gold doilies out of the Spanish Moss that hung from the limbs of ancient live oaks. She was concerned that Clay might spot her following him. Once they passed the turn-off to his restaurant, she allowed more distance between them, confident he was on his way to Sangaree. She looked down Osprey Landing Road when they passed the intersection, hoping Sam was okay.

Karen's badge got her through the gate without question. She parked below Morgan Hannah's house, which gave her safety and allowed clear observation of Clay's front door. He was going up the steps carrying a bag of groceries when she arrived. She didn't see the envelope he had with him when he left The Covington House.

Clay was in the house for less than thirty minutes, then came out and got back into his car. As she pulled out of her parking spot to follow him, she saw Brad Coleman come through the front door with a suitcase and a briefcase. Her heart dropped, not knowing whom to watch. Coleman was leaving, and there was nothing she could do to track him. Clay was her object, and experience told her never to leave the object to chase a wild goose.

With luck, Clay would go home or somewhere else that would give her a chance to call Dougherty.

Despite the beautiful day, Henry Bell State Park was not crowded. By mid-June, it would be difficult to find a parking space at any of the marsh waysides. Wilbur Crowder and his family arrived in the park a little before eleven o'clock. There was only one other car parked in the area. The plan was to spend the day bird-watching—their ten-year-old daughter's latest fascination—picnicking and walking the park's nature trail. While Mr. Crowder was getting his camera bag and binoculars out of the trunk, his wife and daughter walked toward the boardwalk that led to an observation gazebo fifty yards into the marsh.

He was closing the trunk lid, when his blood turned cold at the sound of a scream so shrill and terror-stricken that his first thought was that a member of his family had been lost. He dropped the bag and the binoculars, turned and saw his wife shielding their daughter against the sight of the car parked facing the marsh. The screaming continued as he made his way toward them on legs weakened by fear. When he reached them, they were sitting on the ground, holding onto each other and sobbing. He reached out to his wife who gave him a head gesture toward the car.

Looking inside, Wilbur Crowder felt his stomach turn and bile come up into his throat. He wanted to turn away, but his eyes were locked on the grotesque scene inside the car. It was a man, what was left of a man. The top of his head was gone, its detritus splashed on the windshield, the dash and the back of the seat. Pieces of the headliner, ripped and heavy with blood and human tissue, hung from the roof of the car. When he managed to turn away from the carnage, he fell to his knees and cried. He didn't know why, didn't know the man; it was the overwhelming sadness of it that overcame him.

After getting his wife and daughter back in their car, Wilbur Crowder set out to find a park ranger. The binoculars and camera case remained on the ground.

CHAPTER 32

Pain was not unfamiliar to Sam Larkin; for four years it had been as predictable as bad food, something he had learned to live and function with. Breslin had done more damage than Sam had first thought. The ribs hurt with every movement, and he was still passing blood from what he judged to be a bruised kidney. His head had settled into a soft ache, punctuated by dizziness if he bent over or stood up too fast. He was taking four aspirin every three hours, but they were having little effect.

When he began his search for Ray Breslin, there were no thoughts of what he would do when he found him or how effective he could be in the condition he was in, but the man would suffer. He also knew in his mind and in his heart that if killing him were the only way to survive or protect his friend, he wouldn't hesitate, regardless of the can of personal worms it would open.

There was too much ground to cover. He checked Breslin's house, the city marina—his boat was there—drove through town, passed the Environmental Service office, even went as far as The Hermit Crab and out to Charlie Clay's restaurant. The man was nowhere to be found. He tried to think like Breslin, but came up with nothing, which made him chuckle. In the early afternoon, he stopped by Harry Tom's to check with Skeeter, but his friend had not seen or heard anything. It was like the previous night never happened. Hurting, he left the dock and went home to clean up and rest.

It was four o'clock when the telephone beside his bed rang. Ettie Crewes was out on the deck struggling with the crossword puzzle in the Covington paper, and the children were watching television. It was painful to reach over and pick up the phone.

"Hello?"

"Sam?" Karen asked.

"You got me."

"Did I wake you?"

"Yes, but it was time. What's up? You sound tense."

"Cedrick Hamilton's dead. I just got home, and there was a message from the office."

"How?"

"They found him in Henry Bell State Park. He blew the top of his head off. The coroner said he had been dead ten to twelve hours."

"Who found him?"

"A family out for a picnic. They found him and got the park ranger."

"Good Lord. What does this do to us?" Sam asked.

"I have no idea. I think there's got to be more to this than Skeeter's refusal to cooperate. There's surely enough potential off-load sites around here. That wouldn't be enough to kill your-self over. And who would he be afraid of anyway, unless there's a helluva a lot we don't know or even suspect," Sam was quiet for a moment.

"You know, now that I think about it, I believe maybe he had made up his mind to do it before he left Skeeter's."

"Why?" she asked.

"I don't know. There was something about his attitude, kind of a melancholy tone in his voice, the way he moved when he walked out the door. Lifeless."

"Well, he sure is now. It was pretty bad from what I was told."

"What about Clay?"

"Nothing. He went to The Covington House for breakfast; don't know if he met anyone there or not. Didn't see anybody. Then out to the beach house for thirty minutes, took in a bag of groceries and left. As I was leaving, I saw Coleman putting his bags in his car, but I couldn't follow both of them."

"Anything on Reichert?"

"Didn't see him. What about Breslin?"

"Couldn't find him, and he didn't show up at the dock, Skeeter's or here, so I came home to heal."

"Did you?" she asked.

"Not enough."

"I drove by Ray's house. His truck was gone and the boat's still at the marina. Be nice if he did us a favor like Hamilton did." There was silence on the line. "Sorry. That was a poor thing to say," she said. He heard the contrition in her voice.

"I'm not saying I wouldn't say it, but, yes, it was a poor thing to say."

"They sometimes bring it out in me, Sam."

"I know. I'm going to pick Skeeter up shortly. We'll be at his house."

"I may go over and watch Clay's house for awhile. If he gets the news, something might happen," she said.

"Don't do anything foolish and get caught. These guys are breaking their profile. Might be getting a little skittish. Call me if anything comes up."

"I will. Who knows, maybe I'll even spot Breslin over there."

"I doubt it. Call me," he said.

"You, too."

It was dark outside. Five o'clock in the morning. Time to make the desperate trek to Bitta's uncle's house. And it was raining. For all the beauty of the day before, Monday had come on with a rage of lightning and thunder and rain that blew sideways in the glow of the pole light in front of the Jefferies' house.

"How we gone get ova' there in dis mess?"

"Walk," the pragmatic Bitta said.

"Daddy say he never seen it rain so much. Mos' every day."

They were standing at the window in Marvon's living room. Their parents would be worried when they found them gone, but there was nothing they could do about it; they had lived with their secret too long. Marvon left a note on the kitchen table saying he was at Bitta's. Bitta had done the reverse at his own house. They hoped it would hold them off long enough. They put on their jackets and left the house. By the time they reached the shed, they were already soaked. Marvon climbed up on the tractor and brought down the shopping bag.

"We cain' carry it like dis," Marvon said. "De rain gone make de bag break, den wha' we gone do? You got any plastic or cloth out here?" They looked around, and Bitta found an old sheet. "Dat'll do. Wrap it up an' tie it." The boys put the shopping bag in the center of the sheet, pulled up the corners, twisted the cloth and tied it in a knot."Gone be heavy if we got far to go."

"You got de flashlight?"

"I got it, but I ain' gone turn it on till we get away from here."

"We got to see. Dat po-liceman ain' watchin' us in dis mess," Bitta said.

Ray Breslin was half-asleep. Since the rain began, it had become more and more difficult to keep his eyes open. From time to time, he would jerk himself awake, wondering if some movement or sound had stimulated his awareness. It was almost twenty-four hours since he began his watch, and it was a physical struggle to stay awake. Something brought him out of a shallow doze. He was disoriented. A sound. A movement. Something. It was difficult to see. He leaned forward, but it didn't help. He rolled down the window and put his head out. The cool rain brought his senses to attention.

There were no lights in either of the houses, no movement that he could see. He closed the window and leaned back in the seat, was ready to let his eyes close again, just for a minute, when he saw a zephyr of light. He leaned forward again. They were there; the boys were there. Coming out of the shed. They had a flashlight, and they were carrying something. Breslin felt his heart jump and his breath quicken. They were headed toward the woods. He got out of the truck, closed the door quietly, and started in their direction. Let them get far enough away from the house that no one could hear them if they yelled. The rain would help deaden the sound. This was going to be easy, he told himself.

After he got beyond the shed, it was difficult to keep track of them. He found the meandering path they were following, but it was not well-defined, and the scrub between the boys and him only allowed him to see the light intermittently. He picked up his pace. They weren't moving fast, and the distance between them was shrinking. Breslin didn't see the fallen log lying across the path; he was focused on the light. When he fell, he let out an involuntary grunt and cursed under his breath.

"You hear dat?" Bitta asked in a whisper.

"Yeah," Marvon said. "They's somebody back there."

"Turn out de light." Marvon fumbled to get it off.

"Holy shit! I bet it's dat po-liceman. I bet it is."

"Keep 'at light off. Le's wait a minute. We see him, we go in differ'nt directions."

Breslin lay quiet for several minutes. Listening. Maybe they didn't hear him. He got up slowly, couldn't see the light. He had no idea where they were, whether they had stopped or gone on. He began to move forward, focusing straight ahead, but taking careful steps to avoid falling again.

"I hear him," Bitta said. "He comin' afta' us. We gotta move. Follow me, an' keep 'at light off. I know where we gone; he don't."

"Where we gone? Sides yo' uncle's, I mean."

"We gone circle 'roun' and come out behind de Exxon station. Den we gone go down de road an' take dat road dat run down by de Texaco. Dat's de road where my uncle live," Bitta said.

"Dat po-liceman gone see us iff'n we go out on de road. You crazy."

"He gone still be lookin' in de woods. Come on."

They had disappeared. Ray Breslin stood in the path waiting to see a light, hear a sound, but the only thing he heard was the rain falling and dripping in a steady cadence. There were no voices, no footsteps. To try to follow them would be useless; it was their playground.

They came from the shed, and they were carrying something; it had to be the money. What worried him was he had no idea where they might be going with it. He tried to figure it out as he trudged back to his truck, but couldn't come up with an idea.

He stopped dead. The two boys had circled around and stood directly in front of him as if frozen. He dove for the white bundle, caught it and Marvon Jefferies arm. Bitta Smalls screamed as he saw a monster face appear from nowhere and a three foot piece of wood smash into the policeman's head, dropping him to the ground moaning. The bundle had torn open and several silver bundles had scattered on the ground. The boys couldn't move.

Jared Barnes said nothing. He knelt down, started picking up the foil packages and putting them back in the sheet. Bitta finally got the courage to move and began helping. Barnes retied the bundle and stood up. Bitta couldn't take his eyes off the scarred, misshapen face. One eye was lower than the other and milky white, half the man's forehead was dented in and part of his lower lip was missing. Barnes handed the bundle to Marvon.

"Ya'll get on out of here now," he said in a gurgling voice, like a rasp on iron. Bitta Smalls still held two foil-wrapped packages in his hands. Unshaken by what he saw, he looked at Jared Barnes and tentatively held the two packages out to him. The man's hands, callused and cracked by a life in the outdoors, reached forward and took them. He couldn't smile; his face wouldn't allow it, but he nodded his approval. "Ya'll get on out of here now. I'll be here; don't you worry."

The two boys turned for a last look and continued on their circuitous route toward the road.

Ray Breslin heard them running and saw a shadow disappear into the trees. He was addled, wondering how it had happened again with no idea who it might be. Sensing he was finally alone, he felt for his gun, pulled himself to his knees and looked around. There was no one there.

The boys weren't going home in the direction they'd left; he still had time. He needed coffee, something to clear the haze in his brain. It was his last chance. He stumbled toward his truck, got in, started the engine and headed toward the Exxon station out on Route 37. It would be bad coffee, but it was coffee.

Bitta and Marvon came around the side of the Exxon station and were crossing Route 37 when Ray Breslin, at the counter paying for his coffee, turned and saw them. The rain had lessened, and the light from the station caught them just as they reached the opposite side of the road. He left his cup on the counter and ran to his truck. He hit the ignition, the motor raced, and the tires squealed. The boys turned at the noise and saw him. Bitta yelled and they took off toward the fields and marsh behind the old, unoccupied buildings that lined the road. Breslin crossed the road, screeched to a stop where they had run between two buildings, got out and ran after them.

Bitta Smalls thought about crying, but knew it wouldn't help. Marvon Jefferies thought about being home on the couch watching TV. He felt like crying, too. The Texaco was no protection, not carrying all that money. Bitta ran toward an old live oak, dead from the encroachment of the marsh. Marvon, struggling with the growing weight of the bag, found it difficult to keep up, but managed to make it to the far side of the tree. They hit the water like infantrymen jumping for the trenches and hunkered behind the trunk.

"Y'all better come on out from there," Breslin shouted, having no idea where they were. The sky was beginning to gray around the edges, but there was still not enough light to see anything clearly. "You hear me? This is law enforcement. Y'all gone find yourself in jail, you don't watch out. They love little boys in jail." Neither boy moved; neither boy said anything. They waited. "Son of a bitch!" they heard him say. Minutes later they dared to look out, and he was nowhere in sight.

"I think he gone," Bitta said.

"We cain' go back out on de road; he see us fo' sho'," Marvon said.

"We gone walk de edge of de marsh. Dey's a bunch a churches and houses and stuff 'tween us an' de road. We don' need to cross de road till we get 'cross from Uncle Skeeter's house. Den we be all right."

"Skeeter? Dat be yo' uncle's name? Skeeter?"

"Yeah."

"Well, le's go; we ain' gettin' nowhere sittin' in dis here water."

The boys got up and took the curve of the marsh behind the Texaco station and followed it parallel to Osprey Landing Road. They were exhausted. The plough mud pulled at their sneakers like quicksand, testing the strength of their legs at every step.

Breslin figured there was only one direction they could go from where he last saw them. Sooner or later they would have to walk into deep water or come up to the road. Then he would grab them. The little bastards had finally boxed themselves in. Back in his truck, he began a slow drive down Osprey Landing Road, trying to move at the same speed he estimated they were traveling. Cars behind him honked, sped by when they got a chance and honked again. He scanned the side of the road with his spotlight, but the sky was lightening to the point that it wasn't a help.

Bitta and Marvon moved cautiously, fighting to keep their balance on the treacherous marsh bottom. Between the buildings set against the road, Ray Breslin's spotlight was visible. They both knew what it was. When they reached The Tabernacle of the South Baptist Church, Bitta left the marsh and led Marvon to the back of the building.

"Wha' we gone do now?" Marvon asked.

"Uncle Skeeter's is right across de road. We gone hafta get over there."

"How we gone do dat? Dat man out dere still lookin'."

"Gone hafta run. I'll watch de truck; when I say go, run yo' ass off. We get to de house, we okay," Bitta said. "Ain' much else we can do."

Bitta Smalls went to the side of the building where he could look out at the road. He saw the green truck move by slowly, but it didn't stop. As soon as the truck had gone far enough down the road, he signaled Marvon, and they began their race to safety. The heavy bag and fatigue exasperated their youthful strength and quickness. Breslin saw them in his rear view mirror, going into the dirt road that led to Skeeter Crewes's house. He cut a u-turn, going off one side of the road, just missing a drainage ditch, and then gunned the engine in pursuit of the boys.

Bitta and Marvon heard the truck noise and ran down the driveway, Bitta screaming Skeeter's name as loud as he could. Skeeter was making coffee, and Sam Larkin was sleeping on the couch. At the sound of the child's yelling, they both ran to the front door. The boys didn't hesitate; they ran up the steps and through the door Skeeter was holding open.

"Bitta?" Skeeter said in astonishment as he followed the boys inside. Sam didn't follow them; he saw Breslin's truck take a quick turn into the drive and watched as it came to a sliding halt in front of the steps. The man was out of the truck almost before it stopped.

"What the hell are you doin' here, Larkin?" Sam couldn't distinguish whether the look on Breslin's face was surprise or panic.

"Guess I could ask you the same question," Sam said.

"You got two kids just run in here that we been lookin' for. Now it's up to you how we do this, but one way or another I'm gonna get 'em. It's your choice." Breslin's voice was cracking, and there was blood on the side of his face. Regardless of the cause, it didn't seem to be slowing him down.

Sam tried to assess his body, wondering if it were up to whatever might happen. He wasn't sure, but knew it couldn't be avoided.

"If you can't give me a good reason, Ray, I guess it's gonna be the hard way."

"You ain't in no shape to be a smart ass. Them two kids destroyed Turner Lockett's trailer an' stole a bunch of stuff. This is somethin' different than you and me or Cedrick and Skeeter."

"Cedrick's dead."

"You're a lyin' sack-a-shit, Larkin." He was easing himself closer to the steps.

"He blew the top of his head off. It's all falling apart, Ray; you'd be wise to get yourself out of it." Just then Skeeter and the two boys came to the door. It was closed, but Breslin could see them through the screen wire. He lunged at Sam, knocking him backwards onto an old steel glider that didn't move.

"You're a dead man and so are they," Breslin screamed. He threw a punch that missed, and Sam took his feet from under him. Breslin fell backwards, cracking his head on the porch railing. Sam was on him, his rationale gone. He was back in Angola, in the yard, but there were no guards to pull him off. He grasped Breslin's Adam's apple between the thumb and clenched fingers of his left hand, as if he were going to pluck it from his throat. It was a paralyzing move, which also cut off the man's breath. He held him tightly while his right hand, in blows so rapid and furious that Breslin couldn't see them coming, hammered his face, making his already broken nose soft and putty-like, feeling the jaw give under the pummeling. He couldn't stop, wouldn't let himself stop. He didn't know how many times he hit the man, but when he saw his own hand covered with blood, he pulled back to see what he had done. Ray Breslin was unrecognizable. His eyes were closed, his nose caved-in between his cheek bones, his jaw slack and at an unnatural angle, which held his mouth open. There were no visible teeth. Skeeter stood beside Sam, staring at him in awe, looking at a man he had never seen before.

Skeeter put his hands under Sam's arms, lifted him off the helpless man, and helped him to the glider. Bitta Smalls and Marvon Jefferies stood behind the screen door, their mouths open, their eyes as big as silver dollars. Ray Breslin had not moved.

"Check and see if he's still alive," Sam said, trying to catch his breath. "It looks like his bladder released."

Skeeter got down on one knee and checked the carotid artery for a pulse.

"He's alive, but he ain't feelin' too good." He looked at his friend. "Sam?"

"I'm sorry you saw that, Skeeter. I thought it was behind me. He's all right?"

"Oh, he ain't all right. He ain't gone be all right for a long time if ever."

"Get his handcuffs and cuff him to the railing post. I need to call Karen and see how she wants to handle this. Who are the boys?" Sam asked.

"My nephew and the boy lives next door to him," Skeeter said, as he locked the cuffs. "Come on inside, and let's see how much damage you done to those hands."

When they walked through the door, Sam went to the couch. "I gotta sit down," he said. "Just for a minute. Then I'll clean up." He looked up at the two boys who were still staring at him, Marvon clutching the dirty white bundle in his hands. "That was a bad thing for you guys to see," Sam said. "I'm sorry."

"What you boys doin' comin' over here anyway, and why was that man chasing you? You steal somethin' like he said?" Marvon stepped forward and handed the bundle to Skeeter Crewes. "What's this?" he asked as he untied the sheet and the foil-wrapped packets of money fell out on his living room floor. He picked one up and unwrapped it. No one said anything. Skeeter Crewes's jaw dropped. Sam Larkin just stared. The two boys watched the two men.

"Good Lord, I ain't never seen nothin' like that," Skeeter said, surveying the number of packages. "I wonder how much that is? I ain't got no idea," he said in shock.

Bitta Smalls looked up at him, a frightened look on his face.

"Two hunderd and some thousand dollars," he said and gave Marvon a hard look. "We might not a counted it right, and I give two to the man helped us."

"What man?" Skeeter asked.

"I don' know. Some kinda monster man peered like. We seen him down at de trailer de firs' time. Den jus' now, he come up and hit dat man in yonder like he done de firs' time at de trailer."

"Who you think?" Sam asked Skeeter.

"I don't know. Jared Barnes lives out that way. He ain't pretty, but I don't know as I'd call him a monster man. Whoever it was ain't gone have trouble makin' ends meet. Not with two of these." He held up two of the packages and looked at Sam. "Unless you tell on him," he said with a smile.

"I don't know what you're talking about," Sam said and laid back on the couch.

CHAPTER 33

By the time Karen got to Skeeter Crewes's house, Sam and Skeeter had moved Ray Breslin inside and cuffed him to a bed in one of the back bedrooms. She stared down at the piece of human carnage that lay before her. Breslin's jaw appeared to be fractured, teeth were broken off at the gum line and his nose would require extensive surgery to look half-normal again. His eyes were swelling shut. None of his injuries appeared life-threatening on the surface, though the bleeding in his mouth, where he had bitten through his tongue, was a concern.

"Sam?" She was asking for an explanation and he had none.

"It couldn't be avoided. Come in here; there's something you should see," he said, leading her into the other bedroom where the foil packages were spread out on the bed. "From Turner Lockett's trailer; it was what Breslin was after at the expense of two little boys."

"Has Ray seen these?" she asked.

"No," Sam said, "and we filled up the sheet the kids brought it in with clothes In case anyone else came looking." Karen looked at him. "Like they're running away from home?" he explained.

"Do you think anyone else will come?"

"No. As far as we know, the boys, Skeeter, you and I are the only people who know it exists. Breslin was guessing; I'd stake my life on it." Karen didn't say anything.

"What are we gonna do about him?" Skeeter asked. "That man needs a doctor."

"Not in Covington," Karen said. "It's too risky. Maybe Charleston."

"Only if we can turn him," Sam said. "Hell, we might get charged with kidnapping if we take him to Charleston, and he doesn't want to go."

"What do you think? Can we do it?" she asked.

"Not without you coming out. You want to talk to Neil?"

"He's on his way here. Should be in this afternoon, but we can't hold Ray unless he cooperates. If I come out and he doesn't drop, we either feed him to the alligators or blow the whole operation." Skeeter looked at her with disbelief. "We're not going to do that, Skeeter."

"But what if he thought we were?" Sam asked.

"Threatening a witness? Confession by coercion? Harassment? How many charges can you handle, Sam?"

"We've either got to turn him, or you have to leave and let us take him to the hospital."

"He could pile up so many accusations against you, you'd never get out," she said. "And he would. I have to come out; I don't have any choice at this point."

"I'm sorry I put you in this position, Karen. I'll do whatever you want. Take him in and run if I have to. Until it's all out in the open."

"Put this stuff out of sight," she said, gesturing toward the money. "Let's go talk to him before I think about it."

On Sunday, the first person Covington Police Chief Harold Rhodes notified of the death of Cedrick Hamilton was the president of the Covington County School Board, who asked that a blanket be put on the announcement of the suspected suicide.

"I'd appreciate your giving us time to gather ourselves in the face of this tragedy," the man said, "and prepare a dignified announcement to the public. Just give us twenty-four hours." The chief agreed.

The board president then called Willie Bagwell, owner and editor of the *Covington County Times*, and told him Cedrick Hamilton was dead. He also told him to keep any mention of his death out of the newspaper until Wednesday. That it would be in the best interests of the community. The editor-owner agreed, as he always did when the 'best interests' of the community and Willie Bagwell were at stake.

It was Monday, and, as far as the board president was concerned, the blanket was in place. He had twenty-four hours to clean up whatever mess Cedrick Hamilton left. The superintendent

had done the board the greatest favor he could imagine. All the
worms could now go into one hole.

Ray Breslin opened his eyes, what little he could, and saw
Larkin and Karen Chaney standing over him. His face felt broken, each facet issuing its own pain; there was no way to
describe it. If he focused on the pain alone, he was sure he would
lose consciousness. What was Chaney doing here? Larkin would
pay. He was getting sleepy, but he couldn't allow that to happen.
He tried to move his right arm, realized he was cuffed to the bedpost, and experienced his first pang of fear.

"Ray, can you hear me?" Karen asked. He attempted to
answer, but the words were garbled; his jaw wasn't working, and
his tongue felt like it was in two pieces. Trying to move any part
of his face increased the pain. He had to consciously think about
forming words, but they came out in an angry hiss, barely under-
standable.

"Yeah," he said.

"Listen carefully. I'm going to identify myself, and I don't
want any confusion or misunderstanding."

"I know who you are," he mumbled.

"I don't think you do. My name is Karen Chaney. I am a federal officer attached to the DEA." Breslin's eyes registered shock
and then anger. "Before you say anything, I want you to confirm
that you understand what I just said." Breslin looked at her with
hate and betrayal in his glare.

"Him, too?" he asked.

"No," said Chaney.

"Then you're in trouble," Breslin hissed at Larkin.

"That shouldn't be your major concern right now, Ray," she
said and then Mirandized him. "Do you understand what I just
said?" Breslin looked confused. He was being arrested? They
didn't have anything on him. He wondered if anyone else was
being questioned, or if they planned to lay the whole thing on ol'
Ray Breslin. He should have killed the kids, taken the money and
run. If what Larkin said was true, Cedrick did it, turned on him
and then killed himself. They probably already had the whole
company, Cedrick's way of clearing his conscience. He moved
his head that he understood what she had just done.

"What the fuck's going on?" he asked. There was a problem with the *f* sounds. *Fuck* came out *plfuck*.

"We know about your operation. We've known for awhile; that's why I'm here. We know about Cedrick Hamilton, Charlie Clay, Bill Reichert, Turner Lockett, Brad Coleman and you." A questioning look came into Breslin's eyes. "What?" she asked.

"Pfrad Coleman?"

"Brad. He was here meeting with Clay the last few days. You saw him at Clay's restaurant." Surprise registered. "I was there, too, Ray. You can help yourself, but it has to be right now. You can wait and talk to a lawyer, of course, but I don't think that's going to help you. You know who I am now; that puts me in a dangerous position. We know your shipment's at sea; it's being tracked as we speak. It will never get here." Karen was making it up as she went along, but she had faith in Neil. "You will never make any more money smuggling, Ray, if you're thinking in that direction. Nobody's been killed yet, as far as we know, and that's a good thing, but it could happen. Somebody's going to turn; you're all going down. I'm giving you the opportunity to be first in line, before anything worse happens. Cooperate and I'm sure I can protect you. If you don't, you're on your own and God help you."

Breslin was silent; he didn't know what to do, was kidding himself, knew what he was going to do. Standup guys only existed in the movies. No matter what the situation, ultimately, he always thought of himself first; that wasn't going to change.

"Jail?" he asked.

"I don't know. I'll do my best. Not in South Carolina. Not state. Federal. And not where any of the others are going. That I can pretty well guarantee, but it's your call."

There was really no decision to make. He nodded affirmatively.

"Rest for a few minutes and then we'll talk. Don't change your mind, Ray. That would not be a good thing." She motioned Sam out of the room and followed him.

"What the hell are you doing?" he asked when they were back in the living room. "He was ready."

"I'm not screwing this up. I've got to get somebody in here to take his statement. You're not the best of all possible witnesses."

"There's an accountant out on 37 about two miles away. I've seen 'Notary' on her sign."

"Let's get her."

It took twenty minutes for Barbara Martin to get to the house on Osprey Landing Road. She was horrified at the sight of Ray Breslin and knew that if anyone asked, she would have to testify to his condition. She was relieved when Officer Chaney had her describe that in the peremptory to Ray Breslin's statement.

Though it was a slow and painful process, Ray Breslin was a wealth of information. It all started with another attorney, a college friend of Clay's who brought him in, then Charlie recruited Bill Reichert and Cedrick Hamilton and himself. He brought in Turner Lockett. Later, when more operating capital was needed, another Covington attorney, a doctor and some people from Charleston joined up. There were others, but Breslin didn't know their names. Word of the operation was spread through buyers, which eventually spread to a large portion of the East Coast. When asked if Morgan Hannah knew anything about it, Breslin looked surprised and shook his head "no."

"We need to get you to a hospital, Ray," Karen said when they were finished. Breslin signed the statement and watched Barbara Martin notarize it.

The Notary's eyes expressed shock at what she had heard. Karen repeated to her that everything she had witnessed was privileged information, and she could be prosecuted if she violated that trust. Barbara Martin wished she had not been at home to take the call.

"Where do you want us to take you?" Karen asked Breslin. "I'm not sure Covington County Hospital is the wise choice."

"Charleston," he whispered. He was getting weaker.

"Are you okay to ride that far?" He nodded. She looked at Sam and he shrugged his shoulders. "You and Skeeter take my car; it's more comfortable. I'll take the Rover. And, Sam, be careful; you can't afford to get stopped by the police. Doing it this way is about as illegal as it gets."

"I've never known the federal justice system to worry about that," he said. Karen ignored the barb.

"I'll have federal officers meet you at the hospital to take charge of Ray. Where is Skeeter?" she asked, noticing for the first time that he was gone.

"He walked the boys over to my place; I'll call him." Sam looked at Karen. "You handled that very well; I'm impressed."

"First time I've ever impressed you, Sam?"

"Not really," he said and left.

It was the first excitement Bill Reichert had felt about anything in months. Since Acapulco. By five o'clock on this day, he would cease to exist. Despite the drinking steadily over the past twenty-four hours, he felt exceptionally well, better than he could remember. He was ready to cast off all of his burdens; there was nothing in Covington County he would miss.

After showering and dressing, he poured the last cup of coffee he would ever have in that house. He smiled. He wouldn't miss it. It was eight-thirty, and there were a number of things to be done at the bank before he left. He had managed to avoid Isabel. That was important because he wasn't sure he could keep his secret and contain his glee.

Several of the tellers were already at the bank when he arrived. He issued his "good mornings," went to his office, closed the door and spent the early part of the morning preparing the documents he would be using. The box was no longer a concern. He called U. S. Airways and booked a flight from Jacksonville, Florida, to New Orleans. There he would get some new identities, which he had been told was easy, then book a subsequent flight under a different name and do the same thing in two more cities. Bill Reichert would be gone.

It was to be a two- or three-day trip to Myrtle Beach to attend an education seminar. That's what she'd told her husband. Isabel Reichert did not want to be around when the divorce papers were served on him. Julia Prescott said it would be Wednesday, and she wanted to be long gone; however, the trip was turning out to be quite different than planned. Instead of Myrtle Beach, she was going to Charleston. In the last hour, her whole life had turned upside down or downside up. Yes. Downside up.

She had awakened early and heard Bill showering and dressing, listened to him make coffee and go out on the gallery. She also heard him stop at the bar in the den several times before he left. She was beginning to perceive herself as an independent woman, and, for the moment, free of any responsibility. As soon as she heard him leave, she got up, bathed, dressed and began to pack the few things she was taking on her trip.

She was excited about her life for the first time in years. She was practically dancing as she readied herself. When the suitcase was packed, she went to the storage closet off the screened-in back porch to get the hanging bag she would put her three dress outfits in. Never knew what might come up in Myrtle Beach, and she wanted to be ready for whatever it was. She determined that libido was in direct relation to freedom, and hers was in high gear.

She tried to lift the hanging bag off the closet rod, but it was too heavy. It took both hands to get it down and onto the floor. She unzipped it to see what had been left in it from its last use and screamed at what she saw. It wasn't a scream of horror, but one of astonishment. She was looking down at more money than she had ever seen, except for the one time Bill had taken her on a tour of the bank's vault.

Her first inclination was to call him and ask what the hell was going on. She resisted that reaction. There were stacks and stacks of it. It couldn't be legal; he had to have stolen it. That being the case, she reasoned, he couldn't tell anyone if it were missing, and she could deny ever having found it. It was hers. She claimed it. "Finders keepers," she said to herself as she zipped up the bag and struggled carrying it to the trunk of her car. She went back in the house, got her make-up bag, suitcase, and threw the three outfits over her arm, even though she never expected to wear those two-year-old rags again.

Her body was shaking, her hands shivering on the steering wheel, and her stomach was turning 360s. Pulling out of the driveway, she began working on her plan. She would get two safety deposit boxes, and, as she said to herself into the rearview mirror, "Stash the cash."

Twenty miles out of Covington, She stopped at a gas station and dialed her husband's office. She was having a hard time stifling a giggle.

By ten o'clock, his phone calls completed, Reichert checked his desk, and rechecked the items in his briefcase. It was time for the next step. He pulled a nylon gym bag from his desk drawer, emptied the workout clothes that he used on his twice-weekly trips to the gym, and was ready to leave his office for the vault when his buzzer sounded. There was no hurry; his future was waiting for him. Two million tax-free dollars. He put down the gym bag and picked up the phone.

"Bill Reichert," he said, a bounce in his voice.

"Well, you sound happy."

"Isabel?"

"Just wanted to let you know I'm leaving for Myrtle Beach."

"Okay. You already told me you were going. Why are you calling? You don't have to check in with me; we agreed to that. Is this some new rule you're instituting?" he said sarcastically.

"No, I don't need rules after Las Brisas."

"What?"

"Just wanted you to know I'm getting off early. Didn't take long to pack. One suitcase and the hanging bag. See you, Bill." The phone went dead in his hand and his knees buckled. The hanging bag. The cardboard box. His money.

He dropped the phone and hurried to the vault, not caring whether anyone took notice. The hanging bag. Isabel's words had brought it all back to him. She'd even emphasized the two words. He knew what he would find when he reached his safety deposit boxes, but he had to go. Tears filled his eyes. He tried to tell himself that this couldn't be happening, that there was a mistake, his drunken memory had short-circuited, but he knew differently.

The boxes, the largest size, were located near the floor. He bent down, inserted the two necessary keys and pulled out the first container. He didn't have to look inside; it was empty. He felt a pain in his stomach and his breath became labored. He wanted to scream, but he couldn't. The second was also empty. His money was gone. All the exuberance, excitement, relief and safety, present for the past two days, evaporated. He couldn't go anywhere. Two million dollars, hidden in the hanging bag in a moment of paranoid, booze-induced panic, was gone, and there was nothing he could do about it.

In a daze, he took the containers back to their places, inserted them and locked the doors. Then went to his office and closed the door. He felt like he was having a stroke, a rushing of fluids in his head, hoped he was and that it would take him out, but it wasn't a stroke. He didn't know what to do, which had become a familiar situation. He sat at his desk, waiting for something to happen, not knowing or caring what.

Ettie Crewes and Karen Chaney spent an hour talking after Karen brought the boys and her home from Sam's place. It was a delicate situation, and Karen knew the whole procedure, thus far, was incredibly stupid as far as the law was concerned. She could wind up in jail. She felt vulnerable, which was neither a familiar nor comfortable position for her. If Breslin changed his mind or used the circumstances of his arrest against her, she was dead. The money was another problem. It would have to be held until it could be formally seized, which could leave the boys who discovered it and ultimately broke the case, unrewarded. She didn't want that to happen.

"It's all so crazy," Ettie was saying when Karen's mind came back to the present.

"It always is when something like this happens. Ettie, I need a favor."

"You don't have to ask, just tell me what it is."

"Legally this is a very delicate situation. I don't want any of these guys to get by with what they've done through some technicality. I think it's best if we can keep this whole thing quiet for the next twenty-four hours."

"I ain't gonna say nothin'," she said.

"I'm not worried about you. It's the boys."

"I'll call their momma an' tell her they here."

"Think you could get her to let them spend the night?"

"I believe so. Let me call."

Ettie called her sister and explained that the boys had gone on a 'planned' adventure, got caught in the rain, and wound up at her house. She said she had scolded them soundly, then asked if it was all right for them to spend the day playing with her children, who wanted them to sleep over. Bitta's mother was angry but laughed when Ettie described the two "wet rats" who came knocking at her door. She agreed they had probably learned their lesson and decided it wouldn't hurt them to sleep over. Karen Chaney let out a sigh of relief.

Karen went back to her townhouse to wait for Neil Dougherty. After making some notes, she sat back on her couch and sighed, knowing that if one of the balls she was juggling came close to falling, the whole operation could fail.

When the knock on the door came, she was greeted with a broad smile and the open arms of Neil Dougherty. He was tall, dark and not-so-handsome. Attractive and well-built, but not New York, male-model handsome. No Brad Coleman.

"Hey, Babe," he said as he hugged her

"Hey, yourself," she said. "Come on in."

"This is some place," he said, looking out toward the river. "A cop would be in front of Internal Affairs for living in a place like this." He sat down on the couch.

"They'd come up empty except for growing indebtedness. I refuse to be uncomfortable in my hideaway from the insanity. God, I'm happy you're here, Blue."

"Me, too. I brought a couple of IRS people with me and three additional feds in case we need them. They were more than anxious to see this part of the country. Florida's getting hot."

"Where are they?"

He described the motel, and she realized it was the same one she had stayed at when she came to Covington.

"I'm staying there, too," he said.

"Good luck." She laughed, which garnered a quizzical look.

"Okay, tell me what's going on and where we are."

Dougherty focused on Karen as she told her story. She knew he was taking in every word, filing it to be used at the proper time. He forgot nothing; it was his talent. It took more than forty minutes for her to fill him in. He did not interrupt. She also gave him Breslin's statement, which he read before he spoke.

"Now tell me anything new you've learned about Sam Larkin," he said. She wrinkled her brow. "Karen, I need to know who I'm working with."

She told him what she had seen and how he reacted to the events that had taken place.

"I've done a little further research on him myself since I found out where to look, and a lot of it substantiates what you just told me. He's an enigma. Had a perfect life until his arrest. It appears every right he has was violated in his trial. The most dangerous, which I am sure was its intent, was putting him in Angola instead of a federal facility. The good Judge Hunnycut assumed he wouldn't survive, and all his problems would be solved. As it turns out, Larkin was one tough prisoner. Minded his business, obeyed the rules and was quiet until aroused. Showed anyone who tested him they'd made a mistake."

"As I said, I've seen evidence of that. It's frightening."

"I can imagine. They gave him a tough time, and he gave them a tougher one back. When will he be here?"

"Most any time, depending on the weather and the traffic. I think you ought to get your crew, so we can make some decisions. I want Sam involved, Blue."

"He's not legal, not an officer." She gave him a determined look. "It's your show; I'll call the guys. Here okay?"

"Not goin' there," she said.

At eleven o'clock, Charlie Clay received a phone call from one of his courthouse informants telling him of Cedrick Hamilton's death. He had received Cedrick's message about the off-load site when he arrived at his office. Skeeter Crewes's dock was the best place, but it wasn't the only place. Not a problem, despite the threats and tough-talk, to take one's life over or any life for that matter. It was unnerving, knowing that when he'd heard Cedrick's voice delivering the message, the man was already dead. He was perplexed, caught up in his own game, and, maybe, in some way, he, Charlie Clay, was responsible. He wouldn't live with that. Cedrick wasn't afraid of him. It had to be the school problems, something out of Charlie Clay's reach. The IRS was untouchable. The fact that they were involved in Cedrick's case was, however, cause for concern. They wouldn't stop because he was dead, and if they dug deeply enough, what else would they find out about Cedrick and where would it lead?

Clay dialed Bill Reichert's number. His secretary answered.

"Good morning, Doris. It's Charlie Clay."

"I know your voice, Mr. Clay; it's hard to miss. I believe Mr. Reichert's in his office. Would you like me to put you through?"

"Yes. Thank you."

She buzzed her boss's phone. "Mr. Clay on line one, Mr. Reichert."

"Hello, Charlie." He said, his voice as empty and fragile as an abandoned spider web.

Clay did not acknowledge the pain he heard in the voice.

"Cedrick's dead, or have you heard?" There was silence.

"No, I didn't know."

"Bill, are you all right?"

"Why?" he asked without interest.

"I said Cedrick's dead. He committed suicide, and you sound like I told you a PTA meeting's been canceled. What's wrong with you?"

"I'm sorry, Charlie. I can't explain. What can I do? What does this do?" The lack of emotion in the man's voice startled Clay.

"I don't think there's anything any of us can do at the moment. Just don't react. I'm sure it has nothing to do with us. Probably something personal. I didn't want it to shake you when you heard it. We're almost there, and then it's over. I'm out."

"Yes. Me, too, Charlie. When?"

"Friday night is the present schedule. We should have the package ready for New York within a week."

"Sounds good. Oh, by the way, Charlie, I'll be out of town Tuesday and Wednesday on some bank business, but I'll call you when I get back."

"I'll wait for your call."

"Thanks. I'm sorry about Cedrick; he wasn't a bad man."

"No, he wasn't," Clay said.

Clay was disturbed when he hung up the phone. He was beginning to feel isolated, like all the guns were pointed at him. No word from Breslin, Cedrick's dead, and now Reichert's sounding spooked. He dialed Reichert's number again.

"Mr. Reichert's office," Doris Singleton said.

"Hi, Doris. It's me again."

"Oh, Mr. Reichert just left the office, but I can take a message."

"No, that's okay. Do you have a number where he can be reached for the next couple of days? He said he would be out of town on some bank business."

"He hasn't given me that, Mr. Clay. Let me check his schedule. I don't see anything here, but he may not have put it in yet."

"Thanks, Doris." He had learned nothing.

Chapter 34

The skies never cleared from the morning's storm. When Sam Larkin and Skeeter Crewes started back from Charleston, it was just after one, yet every car had its lights on. The wind was fresh, and wild Pampas and marsh grasses leaned at a forty-five degree angle toward the east. Creeks and rivers had whitecaps, and flashes of lightning and thunder were so sharp and loud that the two men driving toward Covington flinched at the Armageddon playing out above them. When the rain came, the oncoming cars' lights became ghost-like halos floating toward them and passing by.

"Looks like Judgment Day," Skeeter said, as they passed down the two-lane road.

"Was for Ray Breslin."

"That doc said a coupla more hours an' he mighta been dead. I'da hated to try to explain that."

"He took the first swing," Sam said stoically.

"You'd lose that defense, lookin' at him." Skeeter was silent for a moment. "You were right scary, Sam."

"Yeah."

"Why? I didn't know rightly what to do. I mean I know you was protectin' us and the boys an' all, but you'da killed him; I know you woulda."

"It's a long story, Skeeter; I'll tell you about it sometime. Somebody tried to do something to me once that I didn't want done. He didn't accomplish what he wanted to, but he left me in worse shape than Breslin is. I vowed that would never happen again."

"How'd you leave him?" Skeeter asked.

"He died. It was needless."

"Maybe not." They were quiet for a long stretch. When they made the turn onto Route 37 at Brownsboro; the rain began to let up, but the skies remained ominous.

"Wonder what Officer Chaney's been doin' since we left?"

"Getting ready, I guess."

"You think they'll move now or wait till the load comes in?"

"I'm not calling the shots, but I think, if they're smart, they won't wait. One of those people will drop, and then they can package it. Breslin, by himself, is not a lot of security."

"It ain' gonna stop, you know. The smugglin', I mean."

"No, it won't, but it might take a vacation."

"You think weed is wrong, Sam?"

"Doesn't matter what I think; it'll always be here. There's no way on God's green earth to stop that. Just seems there'd be a better way to handle it," he said as they came into Covington. "I'm going to go by Karen's and see what's happening. If she's there, I'll let you take the Rover home. You can call Ettie and tell her you're coming."

There were three cars Sam did not recognize in front of Karen's townhouse.

"Maybe I ought to wait out here," Skeeter said.

"Come in with me."

One question had not been addressed on the trip to and from Charleston. Skeeter was curious, and Sam was trying to figure out how to handle it. What would happen to the money that Bitta Smalls and Marvon Jeffries had shown up with that morning? It was the accident that appeared to have broken the whole thing open.

On Sangaree Island, Morgan Hannah walked in light rain. The beach was peaceful in the rain, hers alone, softer than when the sun baked the sand and people were about. The wet coolness was a balm to her bare feet and her spirit. The early morning hours had been spent watching the storm. There had been no sleep since Brad Coleman said goodbye. The hours since then were a confusion of thought and decision-making. He had given her nothing, yet she was left with something: hope, some promise and wishful thinking.

Passing Charles Clay's beach house, she looked at it wistfully, wishing Brad would step through the glass doors and wave. It wouldn't happen; she might never see him again. The prospect of that gave her pain. He had simply walked away from her without looking back, perhaps out of her life. It was hard to know whether to be angry at him for being what he was or at herself for even considering him a part of her future. Her feelings changed from moment to moment. In some of those moments, she was glad she didn't know where he was or how to reach him, fearing it might rush her into a bad decision.

A flight of pelicans glided overhead, carried along by invisible air currents. She watched them follow the shoreline out of sight. There was no effort in their flight; they sailed as smoothly as an ice cube on a piece of glass. No life was as calm and unruffled as the flight of those birds. Morgan struggled to put "if only" aside. She would wait, but not too long, and she would commit, but not impulsively. At best, she had found what she was looking for; at worst, she would be back where she had been a couple of weeks ago, a little more lonely, perhaps, a little harder and less vulnerable, maybe carrying a new emptiness, but Morgan Hannah had no doubts about surviving.

When Karen led Sam Larkin and Skeeter Crewes into the living room, Sam was uneasy. There were six men sitting in a room that he viewed as Karen's private domain. As far as he knew, he was the only one to have shared it with her, which stimulated a feeling of invasion. He picked out the man he assumed to be Neil Dougherty before Karen introduced any of them. There was an implied comfort and familiarity the man's body expressed without any words being spoken. He was correct in his assumption.

"I don't know which cliché is most appropriate, but it's good to meet you, Sam; I've heard a lot about you."

"I think that covers the field at both ends," Sam replied as they shook hands. After the introductions, Skeeter looked uncomfortable.

"Why don't you take the Rover and go on home, Skeeter," Sam said.

"I'll stay if you think you'll need me."

"No, go on. Ettie'll start to get worried if you don't show up soon. I don't think anybody'll come out there, but if they do, call here immediately and don't open any doors," Karen said. "I gave Ettie the number."

"Okay, but I hate to miss the party."

"Good to meet you," Dougherty said.

"You, too. See y'all," he said and left.

"He okay?" Dougherty asked.

"Don't worry about Skeeter," Sam said. "He's as cool as the other side of the pillow."

"Karen told me you had a little confrontation. I can see. You feeling all right?"

"I'm fine."

"What about him?"

"You'll have to ask him," Sam said. He didn't smile.

"Sam, I told Neil I wanted you in on this."

"I can't do that, Karen. I have no legal standing. Besides, I think you have plenty of help here."

"I want you in," she said. "Unless you don't want to be."

"I think that's up to Mr. Dougherty," Sam said. "You told me he was your supervisor." Dougherty made a motion of nonresistance with his hands. "Why don't you tell me where you are before I say yea or nay."

"You essentially know where we are," Karen said. "We've got a confession from Ray Breslin, who's in federal custody. Might get more from him tomorrow after he's questioned further. We've got one primary dead by his own hand, a banker, two lawyers and numerous others Breslin dropped, and we're tracking a large shipment at sea. Neil isolated that shortly after it left Jamaica."

"Sometime you'll have to tell me how you do that," Sam said to Dougherty.

"Did I miss anything, Neil?"

"Only Brad Coleman, who, thus far, we have nothing on that we can prove. Even if Clay or someone names him, what can we really prove he's done? We've tried to paper-trail him for six years and gotten nothing. I'd say unless we could catch him unloading, which Brad Coleman doesn't do, we might as well concentrate on what we have here. The question is who can we break? Who knows enough to corroborate Breslin's story? Then, if we can get an arrest announcement, the dominos may begin to fall," Dougherty said.

"A thought just occurred to me," Karen said. "Anyone seen a paper today?"

"I did," one of the IRS people said.

"Anything about the superintendent of schools committing suicide?"

"Not a word. I would have noticed."

"Somebody's holding it out," Karen said.

"Must be somebody with clout," Dougherty said. "However, I'm sure it's gotten out to the people who need to know. Any ideas on who's the most vulnerable, Sam?"

"We really haven't had enough investigative time to determine that," Karen said. "It's taken us this long just to find out who's involved, but, from what Breslin said, Bill Reichert, the banker, has been shaky about this deal from the beginning. Breslin doesn't like him or trust him. He also identified him as the money man, said he went to Mexico not too long ago, but nobody, including him, was supposed to know."

"Mexico was money, for sure, but looking for a connection there is like searching a honeycomb. He's probably our mark. Attorneys are particularly vulnerable to the IRS, but that will be slower. I think it's Reichert."

"I agree," Sam said.

"You know him?"

"Just by reputation. From what I've heard, he's not known to be strong or reliable."

"How do we do it?" Karen asked.

"He's a banker, and he's got Charles Clay behind him," Sam said. "I don't think legal threats alone are going to do much."

"The other kind are against the law," Dougherty said.

"I think we can make him come to us without doing anything illegal."

"You really think so?" Karen asked.

"Why don't we go see?" He looked at his watch. "The bank will close soon; I don't think you can wait. By tomorrow they'll know about Breslin and Hamilton from somewhere. You and I did pretty well this morning, why don't we go have a talk with Reichert? Worst that can happen is we go after somebody else tomorrow."

"Take a warrant with you, Karen," he said handing her an envelope. "It's open and signed."

Karen Chaney looked at Sam. "Any idea how to approach this?"

"Not a clue, but we'll know when we get there. I just hope he's in."

Bill Reichert had managed to pull himself together after Charlie Clay's call, but only with the help of a couple of long pulls from the pint bottle of vodka he had left the office to buy. To his way of thinking, he was reacting rationally to a set of irrational circumstances. Cedrick was dead. He knew the impact of that had not yet set in. All of the preparations were in place for a permanent disappearance. That disappearance, he believed, was unalterable.

It was possible; there was some money remaining for a start. In addition to what he kept at the bank, there was a hundred thousand dollars behind the trunk liner of his car, his psychological safety net. It was still there. There was also the four hundred thousand Ortega had arranged for him to place in Mexico City and Guadeloupe. The documentation had come in and it was available.

Everything was ready. He would leave as soon as the bank closed. He opened his briefcase, removed the bottle, held it to his lips and took a long swallow. He could make it through the next two hours.

Reichert was clearing the drawers in his desk when the knock came. Doris had been told not to disturb him. His anger flared, but he suppressed it. In two days, he would no longer exist; it wasn't worth getting upset over. He went to the door and opened it.

The secretary, some kind of officer—not a policeman or a deputy—and a scruffy-looking, long-haired man were standing there.

"Yes?" he said, trying to maintain his calm.

"These people would like to talk to you. They insisted, Mr. Reichert." Doris said, her tone as disapproving and frightened as the look on her face. Reichert continued to stand in the doorway, shoulders back, assuming the authority of his position.

"May I ask what this is about?"

"I believe it's a matter best discussed in private, Mr. Reichert," Chaney said. The banker looked into her eyes and saw no quarter would be given.

"Of course. I have a few minutes. Come in, please." He allowed them to pass, closed the door and went to sit behind his desk. His two visitors sat facing him, the desk in between. A game warden; that's what she was. He smiled at his concern and relaxed.

Everything would proceed as planned. These two would not take much of his time; he wouldn't allow it.

"Now. How can I help you?"

"First, Mr. Reichert, let me introduce and identify ourselves. My name is Karen Chaney. I am a federal law enforcement officer attached to the DEA. This is Sam Larkin. He is a local resident, teacher, and holds no official authority." Reichert stared at them without saying anything. The last two gulps of vodka had taken hold, but they weren't enough to overcome this.

"And?"

"Just so you know who we are officially."

"I think you've established that," he said. "Now what's this all about? You have me in the dark here."

"I thought you would know why we are here, Mr. Reichert," Karen said.

"I haven't the slightest idea."

"We're here to talk about your involvement with Charles Clay."

"He's my attorney," Reichert said with false irritation. He felt pain in his groin as the need to urinate exerted itself. He adjusted his sitting position and crossed his legs.

"Raymond Breslin, who is in federal custody; Cedrick Hamilton, who is dead; Jerry Salyer, Doctor Winthrop Bailey." Reichert's face fell with every name. "Turner Lockett, now dead; James Edwards, attorney-at-law; Brad Coleman, a fugitive; and others to be named."

There was silence. Bill Reichert stared at the green blotter, set so neatly in the leather corners of its pad on his desk. He squeezed his thighs together in an attempt to ward off the pain that threatened to overwhelm him. He couldn't let that happen. He couldn't ask to be excused because they would never allow that. They were here because he was a criminal in their eyes. They didn't understand. He wasn't that; he wasn't a bad guy. He looked at the clock. An hour and a half. He would be gone. It wouldn't happen. He knew it.

"Mr. Reichert?" Karen said.

"Yes?"

"We can help you if you cooperate."

"I don't think I could do that, Ms. Chaney," he answered.

"Have you ever been to prison, sir?" It was the first time the man with the long hair had spoken. He was nobody, no legal authority the woman had said. Despite his fear, he would not subject himself to the humiliation of being questioned by a long-haired school teacher. That's what she said he was. Why was he even here?

"Have you?" Reichert asked. He looked at Sam, trying to assert some degree of power. "I guess you might have." He looked away toward the window.

"Would you like me to tell you what it's like? I'm sure you're thinking of all the stories you've heard about country club prisons. You might get sent to one of those, and you might even see a golf course, but you won't have a club in your hand. Maybe a rake or a shovel or a pair of clippers. That's the easy part. Everybody serving time there will not be like you and Charles Clay. There will be some rough trade there who just lucked out and should be in a more secure facility."

Reichert felt the nausea in his stomach growing from the pain in the middle of him. His breath was becoming more labored. He had to work through it. For the first time in his life he would have to take care of himself, be responsible for Bill Reichert. Sitting there in his expensively furnished and sterile office, surrounded by all the symbols of respect where there was none, he realized he was being asked to do something he didn't know how to do.

"I don't think they'd put someone like me in with . . ."

"You ever hear of John Dean. Mr. Reichert?"

"Watergate."

"Know what his greatest fear was if he was convicted? Rape. And he was a presidential advisor. That worried him more than the time." Again Reichert said nothing. Karen thought she saw his chin pucker. "But that's not your biggest worry; maintaining your sanity is. You are losing your life. Solitude will become treasured and there is none. People outside are living by their own rules. Where you'll be, everything in your life will be according to someone else's rules. And you will live your life in the presence of others, no time alone to think or reason. You're going to have a hard time making it, Mr. Reichert; take my word for it. There will, of course, be ways to kill yourself if you're clever, but I don't think you have the courage for that." Bill Reichert closed his eyes as if to shut the whole scene out. "You could make it easier on yourself. I'm sure Officer Chaney can exercise some influence on your behalf."

Reichert was silent. Eyes closed. The pain was becoming unbearable. He couldn't speak, afraid he would lose control of his body if he opened his mouth. Bile, hovering in his throat, was threatening to explode all over his desk. He could feel tears forming in his eyes. Karen Chaney saw the transformation, the pain in the man's face. He grimaced to stave off the disintegration she saw occurring before her.

"Mr. Reichert, are you okay?" she asked.

"I need . . . I need to . . ." His eyes squeezed tightly shut. A look of helplessness overtook the pain on his face. He tried to stand and felt the warmth as his bladder began to empty itself. He sat back down. Pain and helplessness were replaced by humiliation. A flash of cognizance made him wish he were with Cedrick Hamilton. It was all over. Cliché of all clichés

"Mr. Reichert?" she said again. His face was that of a shamed child. Sam and Karen were both aware of what had happened and were embarrassed for him. He looked at each of them and they saw the plea in his eyes. His mouth was tight and his chin was breaking up.

"I had an accident," he mumbled as the first tears began their course down his cheeks.

"We know, Mr. Reichert. It's all right."

He took a tissue from the box on his desk and wiped his eyes. His chest heaved and a loud sob preceded his breaking down completely.

"We need to talk, Mr. Reichert. We can help you if you cooperate," Karen said.

Reichert put his head down, looking for the right answer, but there was nothing there. He had to stay in this office. As long as he was here, he would be safe. That was the goal, he decided, to stay behind his desk. These two people had destroyed him and he hadn't put up a fight, never even taken up for himself. He wiped his eyes again and sat up straight. He looked at Karen Chaney. She was his salvation.

"You would have to cooperate fully, Mr. Reichert, and it would have to be now. Everyone else is going to be arrested, too. The problem for you is that it's first come, first served. If we get what we need from someone else, your information won't be worth anything. And don't think for a minute that no one else is going to talk." Bill Reichert sat up straight in his chair, decision made. He wiped his eyes.

"I can give it all to you, Ms. Chaney, except Brad Coleman. Whatever I could say about him would be supposition and hearsay. I couldn't prove anything except maybe that he came to South Carolina. How much time?"

"That's not for me to decide," Karen said, "but I believe I can assure your safety, if not your comfort, in prison."

"What else is there to negotiate? I'm new at this."

"There is nothing, sir. I have a warrant and will advise you of your rights here; however, another federal officer will be driving you to Charleston, where you will be formally arraigned and have your statement taken. Be aware that whatever you say in the car on the way up there will be Miranda-protected. That applies to any conversation with any law officer from this point on. Do you understand that?"

"Yes. Yes, I do." He felt relieved. Knew it was coming and now it was here. "I guess I should get an attorney, but I don't know who to call."

"I would suggest someone in Charleston. I think things in Covington could get a little hot. Mr. Reichert, I have to advise you that any holding back of information or any attempt at further negotiation will render our agreement null and void. If you help us, we'll help you to the limits of our power. That's all I can guarantee. Once we have your information, a lawyer and a prosecutor might sweeten the deal, but I wouldn't count on it. Don't play games with us."

"I understand," he said.

"I hope you do." There was a warning in Karen Chaney's voice.

She advised him of his rights. When she was finished, the banker remained seated at his desk.

"We have to go now," she said.

"I can't." Reichert looked down at his pants and then to Karen for help. His tears began again and he wiped them away.

"Take off your blazer. Now, where is your briefcase?" He reached down beside his desk and lifted it up to her. She opened it, took out the almost empty vodka bottle, which Reichert looked at longingly, and after examining them, emptied the papers into a drawer, closed it. "Put your blazer over your left arm and hold your briefcase in your left hand in front of you. I won't cuff you, but we will hurt you if you try anything. We'll make it through the office as quickly as we can. I don't think anyone will notice. If they do, I'm sorry."

"Thank you," he said as he did as she suggested. "I'm not a bad guy am I? Like those real criminals you arrest?"

"You broke the law, Mr. Reichert. Put other people at risk. That makes you a criminal in the eyes of the law. One of the bad guys."

The three of them walked out of his office. Doris Singleton sat at her desk, looking at him for an explanation, wondering if the bank were being robbed. He stopped for a moment and turned toward her.

"Doris, if anyone calls, anyone," Reichert said with a smile to put her at ease, "tell them I am going to be out of town for a couple of days. I'll call you on Wednesday." He looked to Karen Chaney, and she nodded her head affirmatively. With Bill Reichert in the middle, they left the bank.

As soon as they were through the door, Doris Singleton picked up the telephone and dialed Charlie Clay's number. It was busy.

"Mrs. Breslin?"

"Yes," the woman said.

"This is Charlie Clay. Ray around?"

"No. No, he's not. Actually, I'm a little worried about him."

"And why is that, Miz Breslin?" Clay asked.

"Because he hasn't been home in two days. I s'pose he's on some kind of work for the service, but he usually calls in."

"Well, I wouldn't worry too much. I imagine in his line of work it's hard to tell when somethin's gonna come up that you have to handle."

"Yes."

"Listen, if you hear from him, would you have him call me; it's pretty important. He has my number."

"Yes, sir, I will."

"Just have him call."

"I will, Mr. Clay."

An uneasy feeling permeated Charlie Clay's thoughts. First Cedrick's death and now Ray disappearing, and, beyond these things, Bill Reichert's attitude. Too many unusual things were happening, and he wasn't sure how to view them. Wanted to toss it off to coincidence, but found it difficult to convince himself of that. The risk he had always found exciting and invigorating was becoming uncomfortable. He was lost in this train of thought when the telephone rang.

"Charles Clay."

"Mr. Clay, this is Doris Singleton. Over at the bank?" She sounded near tears.

"What's wrong, Doris?"

"I don't know, Mr. Clay. Two people came to the bank to talk to Mr. Reichert, and they just left with him in their car. He said he wouldn't be back for a couple of days. One of them was some kind of police officer, and the other one, the man, looked rough. He didn't look like a police officer. He had a pony tail and—"

"Hold on, Doris," he interrupted. "You're going so fast, I can't keep up. He left with them? Did he say anything?"

"Just that he wouldn't be in for a couple of days. Do you think it's some kind of bank robbery? I don't know what to do."

"No, I don't think it's a bank robbery, Doris. Did he look like he was being forced?"

"No, sir. He wasn't forced. What should I do? Call the police?"

"No, Doris. Please don't do that. Just take care of business as usual. I'm sure everything will be all right. And, Doris, I wouldn't say anything to anyone about those two people. Probably just taking him out to look at a property for a loan. Something like that. Don't you worry."

"If you say so, Mr. Clay. I'll try."

"You do that. If I hear anything, I'll let you know."

"Thank you, Mr. Clay."

Clay sat back in the large swivel chair behind his desk, his hands clasped, fingers interwoven across his middle as though he were glorying in the satisfaction of having won a big case.

"Well, I guess that's that," he said to the emptiness of his office. He didn't consider running, though there was plenty of money. He didn't have the energy or the desire. He reminisced about his wife—the one love of his life—their joy and excitement in building the house on Sangaree, his buying the restaurant, and her death, which he considered the end of both their lives. He felt drowsy and relaxed. There was nothing to do except close his eyes and wait for what he knew was coming. "No regrets," he whispered to himself.

Bill Reichert was on his way to Charleston; two of Neil Dougherty's team were on their way to Palmetto Island to pay a call on Jerry Salyer. Karen Chaney and Sam Larkin sat in her car, which was parked across from Charles Clay's office. Neil Dougherty and one of the IRS agents had just been admitted through the front door. Once it began to crumble, it fell fast. Often on a case, she found herself building a relationship with the people she was after. With this case, she hadn't had time, didn't really get to know them.

"Sam," she said as they waited for Neil to bring Clay out, "you know this case is as much yours as it is mine."

"You're wrong there, lady. All I was trying to do was stay away from it."

"You broke it, Sam. You got Breslin. You got Bill Reichert. I'm not sure what I did."

"Plenty," he said.

"You were pretty rough on Reichert. I don't think I could have stood up under the pressure you put on him."

"It was necessary for us and for him. He had to know what he was risking. I saved him. Maybe."

"How much did you know before we hooked up on this thing?"

"More than I wanted to. It just kept comin' at me and I couldn't dodge it," he said.

"I'm glad you couldn't." They were silent, feeling the same awkwardness they felt the first time they were alone together. "You know, I don't think they really thought they were bad guys," she said.

"Were they?" Sam looked at her.

"They broke the law."

"Lots of good guys break the law. Do you think they were bad guys?" he asked.

"I'm not sure. That's what bothers me. I don't know how I feel about it. If it were heroin or coke, it would be easy, but this? I don't know. I try to believe we stopped a lot of people from being hurt, but I think that's wishful thinking."

"You can't save people from themselves. Who the hell knows what we did? I don't."

"What I can't understand is why some of them got involved. I mean it couldn't have been just for the money; most of them had enough before this ever started."

"I'm sure greed had a lot to do with it; there's never enough. And yearning for excitement. I'd guess they saw themselves as harmless outlaws. I don't think these guys had a clue about what they were really doing, but that doesn't make them innocent."

"Accidental smuggling?" Karen laughed. "No, they're not innocent; I'm just not sure how guilty they are."

Neil Dougherty, another agent and Clay came out the door. The attorney was in handcuffs, which upset Karen Chaney; they weren't necessary, but Neil didn't know that. He went by the book. Sam watched every step Charles Clay took, felt the pavement under his feet. He had walked there.

"It's a painful thing to see a man destroyed," he said, "even when he brings it on himself."

The car with the three men in it rolled away toward Charleston. Karen Chaney and Sam Larkin were left with the same sense of emptiness people feel in airports when they watch a plane taxi away from the terminal or wave goodbye to visiting friends as they depart for home. There is nothing of them left and nothing to fill the void.

"Sam, can we go to your house?" Karen said when the car was out of sight.

"I wouldn't take you anywhere else," he answered and started the car.

EPILOGUE

It was the hottest summer Sam Larkin could remember. Sunrises and sunsets came on like back-drafts from raging forest fires, painting the clouds scarlet against the purple-smoke background of the lowcountry sky. They punctuated days filled with oppressive heat and humidity. He loved the heat. It was August and there was still no plan. Time and circumstances would tell him what to do. He took the days and nights like an alcoholic, one at a time, trying not to think about the "what ifs," the "maybes," or the "should haves." He was good at putting things behind him, but the past spring and early summer were hard to forget.

Bill Reichert told everything he knew without shame, justifying his actions by admitting he was too weak to stand up to what he might face if he didn't cooperate. It was self-preservation, he said, and what guarantees did he have that others would remain quiet and let the government see if they could prove their case? For his information, the court would go easier on him, but Sam wasn't confident Reichert would survive even the easiest of prisons. Intact.

The other twenty-seven persons, cited to date, all contributed to what Bill Reichert and Ray Breslin had told the authorities. When it came down to "save your own ass" time, it became a contest to see who could tell the most. It was a common phenomenon among part-time players.

The only holdout was Charles Clay. He decided, while he waited for the federal agents to pick him up, to remain silent. There was no doubt in his mind what the others would do. He figured on ten to fifteen years. He would be an old man by some people's standards when he got out, God willing, but he felt like an old man already. He wasn't concerned with the future. When he was asked if serving more time than the others wouldn't bother him, he said, "I have nothing better to do."

Turner Lockett's involvement surprised no one. He was a lowcountry outlaw, one of many who would do whatever was necessary to live without compromise. Times good or times bad. What did create conjecture was what he had done with his money. Scavengers and treasure hunters had torn his trailer apart piece by piece until one morning when the dross that was left was burned. Ray Breslin never said a word. Karen Chaney arranged for a reward of twenty-five thousand dollars to be put in trust for each of the boys until they were twenty-one and a twenty-five thousand dollar reward for Skeeter Crewes; the remainder was quietly seized. All except ten thousand dollars. Skeeter had seen a mutilated man he thought was Jared Barnes at the boat dock once or twice, but he couldn't be sure. It had to be the man Bitta and Marvon had described. No one else could look like that.

Bill Reichert found a pocket of redemption for himself by continually talking about the cardboard box he had lost in a drunken stupor. It was considered a product of his imagination or an hallucination until his secretary corroborated the story. Others believed he and his secretary had hidden it for future use. No one could prove anything. It never occurred to him that he had done the first loving thing for his wife in the course of their marriage. The "box" stories did, however, cause federal prosecutors to worry about his reliability on the witness stand when the time came.

Covington County, South Carolina, and the City of Covington remained in a state of shock over the events of early summer. Most people were divided, depending on who they were talking to, over whether they had known what was going on or had no idea. It became attractive for one to "know nothing" because that made everyone else suspect they did. The morality of the operation was debated from the day the arrests were announced and would be as long as there were people of differing opinions.

Nothing was said when word of Isabel Reichert's divorce became public before anyone knew she had even filed. Julia Prescott had worked her magic, and, with Bill Reichert's agreement, rushed the divorce through in thirty days. No one could blame Isabel; no one knew how long her husband would be gone.

And there was Morgan Hannah. Of all the characters in the scenario, she interested Sam the most. He admired what little he knew of her. In a way, she epitomized what he was looking for: an independence she didn't appear to compromise at any cost. That independence was exemplified, in his mind, when he heard that her beach house was for sale, and she had decided to live in France.

Sam was standing on the deck outside his bedroom as these remembrances rolled through his mind. The fire of the sun had transformed into the dead, gray dark of an approaching storm. Thunderheads had sprung from nowhere and created a fearsome sky. The moss on the oak trees waved with the grace of Sirens beckoning. He could hear the rumbling in the distance and knew it would rain before full-dark.

He thought about Karen Chaney and wondered what the sky was like wherever she was. It might be mid-day there for all he knew. She had remained in Covington for more than a week after the day of the first arrests, most of that time spent at Sam's house. The future was on hold, and they let it stay there. There were no doubts about what they felt, but they were smart enough to know that Sam had been right when he said she couldn't give up the job, and he couldn't give up his quest for peace. At least at this time in their lives. One morning he awoke and she was gone. There was a note on the counter.

> *Have to go. I will call in a few days. You take care of you, and I'll take care of me. Maybe we can put it all together when I come back. I think I "might" love you.*
> *Karen*

She called, as promised, and they talked. Nothing significant. She had been reassigned and said she would call regularly. She hadn't. There were a couple of messages left on his answering machine and a few mysterious hang ups, which he was sure was indecision. She would be back when the attorneys quit playing their games and the trials began, but there was no way to know when that would be.

He missed her, everything about her. In reflective times such as the one he was going through, Karen Chaney was larger than his quest for peace. At other times, he was happy just to be where he was. He would get through the night, and tomorrow would be another day. The rain began to fall as he stood there. Not the storm he anticipated, not yet. It began as a steady, warm, summer rain. Sam Larkin removed his clothes and stood naked, letting the water from the sky bathe him. It made him feel fresh and clean.

ACKNOWLEDGMENTS

This book could not have happened without friends and fellows to keep my head in the right place and my vision on target. First and foremost, Archer Lee Smith, without whom few words would have ever hit the page; David Stern and Holly Frederick, for editorial advice, support and showing me the way whether they realized it or not; Pat Conroy and Tom Robbins, and others whose opinions I respect and who were willing to read draft after draft and sharing their honest opinions; Joe and Nancy Dennis, Suzanne Barbarossa, Jody Richelle, David and Catherine Riddle, Cecelia Wiley, Ann Roberts, James "Buck" Hundley, and Mary Smith; and for those who contributed in countless ways, Chris Stanley, Will Balk, Margaret Holly-Evans, Tim Moore, John Cullinan for his photographs, and Paul Craft for his music.

I am also most indebted to my publishers, Carolyn and Dr. Al Newman, who believed in the project enough to give me the opportunity; ever grateful to my editor, Ashley Gordon, who saw more in the book and was more patient than I; Nancy Stevens, who designed this artful package; and Tangela Parker, who promoted *Lowcountry Boil* far and wide; and, most of all, Brewster Milton Robertson, who led me to the door of River City Publishing and made the introduction.

Thanks to all.

LOUISIANA BURN

an excerpt from the new novel by
CARL T. SMITH

coming in 2006 from River City Publishing

It was still dark. The South Carolina stars and the moon, full and bright, bathed the crisp morning in silver. Sam Larkin, lean and tan from the summer, carried a flashlight to the end of his driveway, turned it off, and judged that he could do his workout on nature's electricity. He put the light on the ground and began running his course down Osprey Landing Road. There was a slight chill, and the longer he ran, the more he enjoyed the cool air in his lungs.

His course was three miles long—in summer, even early, the heat would bear down on him during the last mile. Today, making the turn for home, he felt he could run the course again. Maybe it was the air; maybe it was something else. Energy that needed to expunge itself. In most cases that would be all right, but the forces stimulating his adrenaline were not positive. It was something he had been struggling with for a few weeks now.

After cooling down and stretching out the muscles in his back and his legs, he stripped off his running shorts and T-shirt, now soaked with perspiration, and stepped into the shower stall he had installed on the side of his house. The convenience had been a gift to himself. A small cabinet held towels and washcloths so he wouldn't drip when he went into the house.

He dried his body and shoulder-length hair, hung the towel on a hook, and then climbed the stairs to his deck. He was naked, but no one else lived within view of the

house. He put on a pot of coffee and went into the bedroom to dress. Today's uniform was the same as it had
been the day before and the day before that: shorts, a T-
shirt, and huaraches. There were no further responsibilities to this day other than pulling his sandy, graying hair
tightly against his scalp into a pony tail and securing it in
place with a hand-tooled, silver ring. And that's what
bothered him.

He sat on the deck of his house on Matthew's Island
in the lowcountry, sipped on the cup of chicory coffee he
had brought out with him, and took an occasional drag
on his morning cigarette. He always felt that if he could
avoid the morning smoke, he could eliminate the four or
five he lit up during the remainder of the day. But despite
frequent, conscious efforts to quit, it hadn't happened.
And the chicory coffee, a holdover from his Louisiana
beginnings, was a pleasure he would never deny himself.

It was his normal time of quietude, a clean and sylvan
way to begin the day; however, on this day he felt the
familiar rumblings of the storm that clouded his past. He
tried to focus his attention on a small snowy egret that
was creeping along the water's edge not fifteen feet from
his house. The bird lifted each leg separately in a choreo-
graphed strut, silent, creating no crack in the glass surface
of the mirror in which it walked. Hunting. Focused
entirely upon its purpose, something Sam had found difficult these past few weeks.

The memories falling on him now had never before
come to him on the deck while he was lost in the beauty
surrounding him. Sometimes they came in dreams that
awakened him in the cold wetness of his sheets. At other

times they came out of nowhere, while he was dining in a restaurant, or driving his car, arriving with no recognizable stimulus.

Sam had never thought himself capable of killing another human being. Even as an environmental law enforcement officer back in Louisiana, it had never seemed a possibility, and yet it had happened and never left him. He knew he had to let it go, let it expunge itself, get past it.

The man—Sam didn't know his real name; they called him Chooch—had watched him for days in the yard, his crew standing behind him, their flat expressions devoid of humanity or emotion, a survival mode most prisoners adopted. Gain anonymity and fit in. Sam Larkin had done the same thing on the day he entered the Louisiana State Prison at Angola. It was the way of prison life, a black-and-white film with all the color of reason, optimism, and hope removed. It became his life. The man stared at him, winked, smiled, and nodded his head. The gesture made a date, one Sam knew he could not refuse.

When Sam walked into the shower room some hours later, Chooch was waiting.

"Hey, baby," Chooch said. He was leaning against a sink, and two of his crew held Sam's only Angola friend braced on an adjacent wall—bait in case Sam hadn't come on his own. Another watched the door. There was a viperlike sneer on Chooch's face, the corners of his mouth turned downward in a smile that had lost its battle with hatred and anger. Black hair, long and greasy, hung below a red bandana do-rag. A scar like a white worm split his face from his nose through both of his lips. He was lean, and the skin of his sinewy muscled arms, chest, and neck were covered with crude jailhouse art, a billboard of rage.

Sam stood just inside the door, saying nothing while checking out the man's crew. Their eyes switched back and forth between Larkin and their leader. The Mex was short, nervous, and anxious, his eyes pinholes—a meth addict running on empty. A bunk-punk, young, solidly built, and pretty, had a look of wonder on his face. The third was a muscled black man who looked at no one, just watched the door, taking care of himself.

"You scared, honey?" Chooch's eyes glistened with the shine of pruno, julep, jump, or some other contraband. He moved closer and smiled. Sam could see his teeth, dark, stained brown and green with nicotine and mouth moss. "Ain't no need. You jus' gone get a little attitude adjustment, you." Sam had never heard the man speak before. He was Cajun or raised in Cajun country. "I'm gone keep you protected and happy forever, you," Chooch said. "At least however long I let you forever be. See, I love you. I'm gone bitch you up and be you daddy. Take care of you." His words were like a sentence handed down by a judge. His decision was final, the conse-quences to be paid.

The man stepped closer. Sam didn't step back. The Cajun raised his eyebrows, surprised. An odor, not unlike ether, emanated from his body. He reached out a hand to touch Sam's face, but before he could make contact Sam gripped the man's hand in his own, spreading the fingers and bending them backward, separating them. The third knuckled popped. Chooch screamed, his agony echoing off the shower tiles. Sam took in the crew as peripheral shadows. They didn't move.

Sam knew he could stop now and end it for this day, but it would never be over. This was the date the man had made, his dance. He grabbed the Cajun as if to pull the larynx from his throat. Chooch's eyes widened, and he grabbed at the hand stopping his breath. He could make no sound. Sam tightened his grip and felt the trachea fracture. His other hand grasped the man's long, black hair and pulled it down and back with a hard, swift jerk. There was a cracking sound as solid as that of an ax hitting concrete, and Sam watched life pass out of the man's eyes.

He let go, and in time too short to measure, the man lay in a heap at his feet, blood leaking in oxygenated foam from his mouth. One final effort for breath, and it was over. None of Chooch's crew moved to help. It had all happened too fast. Over before they could protect and defend, though Sam was sure they didn't have it in them. They released their prisoner and stared at Sam in awe, offering an allegiance he didn't want.

There would never be any guilt over killing the Cajun; that had been done out of necessity.

What the scene brought back time and again to Sam was the adrenaline flow he had felt when it was over—exhilaration despite what he had done. He had felt untouchable, and it had been easy. His instinctive reflexes had been frightening; fear of that potential kept the memory green no matter how hard he tried to assuage it from his soul.

The young snowy egret was gone, though Sam knew it was still working the shoreline. He was surrounded by the noise of nature waking to a new day. Jumping mullet splashing in the brackish water, animals leaving their nesting places to forage for food, and dried palm fronds clicking their wake-up call with every passing breeze.

The forecast called for cool and dry weather. It wouldn't be, though. The pink early-morning sky would become a refracted landscape of blood red as the sun moved toward full day. Intermittent gray and purple ropes of cloud—flat and thin—would move in during the late afternoon and increase in number toward the vanishing point of the horizon. And eventually, October rain.

Larkin scanned the salt marsh spread before him. His present life was good: he owned a wonderful, if unusual, house in one of the most naturally beautiful areas of the country; he had time to paint, which was one of the reasons he had come; and there were no social pressures to live up to. Nothing to complain about. Regret was a toxin he tried not to allow in his system, though there were the dreams and the memories, for which he had no defense.

The life he was living was one he had fantasized when times had not been so serene. Yet now he felt aimless and without direction and alone. It gave credence to the old cliché that realizing one's dream is not always what it's cracked up to be.

He sipped his coffee and concentrated on the marsh and the creek, closing his mind to introspection. His surroundings remained a wonderment to him, despite the lack of quietude in his soul.

Karen Chaney walked through the supermarket, not seeing the items on the shelves. She was having a difficult time even remembering what she had come for in the first place. She put a jar of peanut butter into her cart and was halfway up the aisle when she realized she hadn't looked to see if it was crunchy or creamy. It was crunchy.

She turned the cart around, almost hitting a fat little boy sitting on the floor and gazing, goggle-eyed, at the candies displayed on the bottom three shelves. Grocers are smart, she thought, putting the candy within reach of tiny hands. It was a logical, sensible business decision. To hell with health. Chaney wished that her decisions were as simple. Every decision in her business involved people's lives, sometimes their very existence, and, in the present case, people she cared about and a future she was considering for herself.

She exchanged the peanut butter, turned the cart around, reached over the little boy still sitting on the floor, and jerked a large bag of M&Ms from the shelf. He looked up at her and smiled. Karen Chaney did not grimace at him, as she felt like doing. In times of unmanageable stress, she found M&Ms a great tranquilizer. The bag would be empty before she got home.

Chaney, an agent in the special forces unit of the DEA, sat in her car in the parking lot, eating M&Ms, regretting having taken the assignment in Baton Rouge.

It had been a month, and she still wasn't able to connect with the place. It wasn't a bad city, and a short drive would take her into the breathtaking natural beauty of southeastern Louisiana. New Orleans, with its bounty of culture, unique architecture defined by lacy wrought-iron galleries, and underlying erotic and dangerous charm, was close. It should have been a good situation, but it wasn't.

Back in September when Neil Dougherty, her supervisor, best friend, and partner in a brief marriage, had called, she had been at her father's place on Pine Island, south of Fort Myers, Florida. She had been sitting on the deck, watching a flight of pelicans glide effortlessly down the shoreline. Her time there had been designated as a period of R and R after several months of undercover work on a drug assignment in Covington, South Carolina. Special assignment work was usually emotionally easy: in and out, no ties, get the job done and forget about it. That hadn't been the case in South Carolina. She had made connections, allowed it to get personal, and became emotionally involved with an enigmatic high school teacher, artist and—she later found out—former environmental law enforcement officer and ex-con named Sam Larkin. She had allowed that relationship to escalate to the point of unprofessionalism, an unwise and dangerous set of actions that left her at odds with herself.

Dougherty, whom she called Blue after the outlaw Belle Starr's husband, Blue Duck, had warned her about personal relationships in their line of work. They are appendages federal agents in any capacity cannot afford to have, he had said, like a millstone or an albatross around the neck that gets in the way of the work and can get you killed.

Dougherty was her mentor. She had always listened and abided by his advice without question—until she met Larkin. That man had caused a dip in her logic and made her doubt her sense of purpose. She had been trying to put all of these things in perspective when Dougherty had called.

Popping another few M&Ms into her mouth, she remembered the mixed feelings she had experienced when she answered the phone and recognized his voice. It had been awhile, and Dougherty's calls were usually a bright spot in any day. There was no reason for trepidation, but from the first word the tone of his voice—hesitant and cautious—had unnerved her. Now, a month later, she could still play the conversation in her mind. She had done it a thousand times, trying to determine why she hadn't refused the assignment.

"Belle?"

"Well, this is unexpected. What's up, Blue? Or is it that you realized you just couldn't go on any longer without hearing the sound of my voice?"

"Your voice obviously."

"Right." Nervous sarcasm, she thought.

"How are things in the Sunshine State? Your dad okay?" Matter-of-fact.

"He's healthy. Has a lot of friends on the island who keep tabs on him, though he does complain about widows coming to the door with mattresses on their backs."

"I'm glad I've got something to look forward to," he said. "What about you? Any gentleman callers?" Forced pleasantries.

"Five," she said, "but I'm only sleeping with three of them." It was said to hurt; his jealous curiosity was a constant irritation that had increased since her affair with Sam Larkin. "Okay, Blue, ready to quit making nice? You don't call unless there's a reason. What's going on? Where are you?"

"Baton Rouge."

"Are you going to tell me I have to go back to work, I hope? I'm moldering down here, having hallucinations. Even dreamt I was a housewife one night. No disrespect to housewives intended."

"You tried that once as I recall. Miserable failure," he said.

"Thanks. Enough. Tell me why you called." She was holding her breath and didn't know why.

"You are going back to work if you want to."

"I've been waiting for someone to call; I just didn't expect it to be you. I didn't think we'd caught all the bad guys but was beginning to wonder if I'd been forgotten. So what is it, and where and who am I working for?"

"Well, it's a bit unusual for our unit. Basically doing background on a political candidate."

"Doesn't sound too thrilling. Why would the DEA be doing that? He running drugs, or something?"

"Not that I know of, but I wouldn't put it beyond the reach of credibility. We're just doing a favor for one of the FBI director's political friends. The director doesn't want his own agents involved."

"So throw us to the wolves, huh?" she said. The assignment sounded bland, and the thought crossed her mind that it was fallout from Carolina. The mission there had been successful, but Dougherty never stopped criticizing her for her personal involvement. "Where?"

"Baton Rouge, New Orleans, Gulfport, and probably Washington, D.C."

"Louisiana, I like. Mississippi's okay. D.C. I don't like. For whom?"

"I'll be agent-in-charge."

"You don't sound too enthusiastic, or maybe after last time, you have doubts about me. Look, Blue, I—"

"It's not you or your work, Karen." Karen. Serious business, she thought. Not risky. Something else. His voice was dark and unsure. Not like Neil Dougherty.

"So why are you sounding like you're sounding, Neil?"

"Thornton Hunnycut," he said. The pause was more than pregnant.

"What?"

"Thornton Hunnycut."

"Oh, shit." The name opened a bag of worms. Judge Hunnycut had sent an innocent Sam Larkin to prison, had seen to it that all records of his trial and incarceration no longer existed. Even Neil Dougherty hadn't been able to discover the entire truth of Larkin's past; Sam had told them. Her mind was racing. There were reasonable objections and strong arguments for recusing herself that she knew would never be heard. "No," she said.

✪   ✪   ✪

Senator Thornton Willingham Hunnycut was counting his sins. Political sins. The other kind didn't count much; those sins held no cause for regret. He didn't really consider them sins but, rather, necessities. He was turning political misdeeds over in his mind. Early on he had learned that God and the public forgive; politicians do not. Most of the political transgressions were as fresh in his memory as the day they had been committed. Fresh, no matter how much time had elapsed, because he wore them as a badge of pride, a symbol of power and ruthlessness, qualities he admired in others and knew others respected if not admired in him. They allowed him to hold his shoulders back and his head high. He had never viewed them with any misgivings until now, as he wondered if they would come back to haunt him. He could not allow that at any cost.

The senator from Louisiana was on the gallery of his second home, in Gulfport and more elegant than the extraordinary plantation house outside Baton Rouge that was his personal residence. This house in Gulfport was a monument to the architecture of the Old South. Eight massive columns supported the gallery, and the formal grounds, where a blossom of clover was not tolerated, added austerity to the building.

He had sat on the gallery for most of the last half of the day. He watched the Gulf of Mexico swallow the red sun and the grass in the manicured lawn turn black. The stars begin to decorate the sky and a partial moon rose. During that whole metamorphosis, the same emotions passed through his mind over and over again—elation tempered with caution, joy marshaled by anxiety, and resolve supported by limitless determination.

Earlier in the morning, a good friend and senate colleague, Harrison James of New Jersey, had called to ask him an incredible question: If Senator James, who was the favorite for the Democratic nomination for the presidency, were chosen, would he, Thornton Willingham Hunnycut, consider being his running mate? It wasn't assured, of course, and James advised him that his wasn't the only prospecting call he was making. Despite that, it was a grand thing to consider. Vice-president of the United States. Thornton Willingham Hunnycut. And if anything should happen to Harrison James: president of the United States. His head was spinning. When he had said goodbye to the probable candidate, he almost slipped and said "Thank you, Mr. President."

He had come a long way for a boy whose father owned a rundown gas station in New Roads, Louisiana, a nondescript town north of Baton Rouge. Boylin Hunnycut was a good man, just never able to make any money. The Hunnycuts were not the dirt-poor, Bible-banging, drunken, incestuous, abusive, husband-took-off-seeking-answers-to-some-idealistic-riddle-he-could-not-define families that had made so many southern novelists famous and rich. The Hunnycuts were, at best, lower middle class, and the youngest child, Thornton, resented that, especially when he had to wear his cousin's hand-me-downs while said cousin attended the same school. Nothing was ever said, but he had been certain everyone knew. The one saving grace was that the clothes were better than any his father could afford to give him.

There had been a lot of scrapes along the way, and, try as he might, he could think of no one to give credit for his ascendancy into respectability other than himself. Hunnycut smiled as the moon and stars faded behind rain clouds moving in from the west. Seventh grade, he recalled, he had been suspended from school for the first time, for fighting. It was also the first time that any male from his school received a year-end report card with no grade less than A, a pattern that had continued through high school. He remembered Mr. Baxa, the soft-spoken principal, once telling him on the occasion of yet another suspension for some forgotten offense: "Thornton, you're making me look damned stupid." Thornton hadn't replied. "How can I keep on suspending the student with the highest average in the school? Hell, I might find my valedictorian unable to attend graduation because he's on suspension." It had seemed poor judgment to the boy also, and they both laughed. It was part of Hunnycut's charm.

At seventeen, academic scholarship to Louisiana State University in hand, Thornton Hunnycut left New Roads and headed to Baton Rouge. He had seldom returned. In Baton Rouge, he hadn't been sure what he wanted to do with his life other than not live the way he had been raised. He'd done a lot of thinking and conceded that his father, by all standards, was a decent man but a weak one, satisfied and afraid of confrontation. He had also known that he probably overcompensated for his daddy's weaknesses by fighting, taking unwise risks, and usually operating from the unpopular stance whether he believed in it or not.

As a college freshman, he had realized that he was shooting himself in the foot. It had come as a revelation. He saw that power and influence, used properly—legally or illegally—would not only bring money but would prove more valuable. They would be the graders on the bumpy road he was traveling, a road whose only promise was dissatisfaction, unhappiness, poverty, maybe jail, and a whole host of other things that intelligence had no way of protecting him from.

Planning and preparation were the tools; attitude and vision, empowered without any consideration of remorse, were the keys. This reasoning led to his decision to study the law. It offered all the possibilities and could be used at will in any way he wished.

Thornton had been a methodical, if impatient, young man and had begun his preparation for the future on his first day in college. Registration day. While filling out the various forms he had been given, he felt, once again, a little less than those around him; he didn't have a middle name and all of the forms asked for one. It was silly, he knew, but it bothered him. Thornton was okay, better than Jim or Bob or Joe Willy. It came from some distant relative. His mother liked the sound of it, but they had never bothered to come up with a middle name.

As he sat at the registration table filling out his forms, he decided to give himself one. He wanted something that would add a touch of sophistication to his name should its use ever become necessary, a name that would provide a screen to his past. He glanced at the book he had brought with him to read in case there were long waits in the registration process. *End as a Man*. The author's name provided two good possibilities: Calder and Willingham. Thornton Calder Hunnycut. Thornton Willingham Hunnycut. Willingham was better. Richer. It was as simple as that and filled in one of the blanks in his life.

He had often questioned the inscription above the portals of his high school that said, "Knowledge is power." It had taken him only a few weeks of classes to realize that it was indeed meaningless. Knowledge meant nothing if not used to advantage. Having knowledge did not confer power. It had been a simple conclusion; all he had to do was look at his teachers and college professors—many of the latter pseudo intellectuals who elevated themselves, by virtue of the acronyms after their names, to a state of educated grace. A position that was accepted and somewhat respected only in their own small circles. They had no power except over their students and not even all of those.

One professor, Doctor Woods, who taught poetry and was a former member, along with John Crowe Ransom, of the Fugitive group at Vanderbilt, had gained Thornton Hunnycut's respect. He did it with one statement: "Call me Doctor Woods and you will fail. Doctors cure people and make great scientific discoveries. I, and most other academics, Faulkner said, simply endure other miscreants like ourselves."

Now he was a United States senator. Though James's call had infused him with excitement and stimulated endless fantasies, it also uncovered fear, something he had never acknowledged. People had often tried to bring him down, but he had never been afraid of them, and they had never succeeded. This was different. He would be put under a national microscope, manned by experts, and not the naïve, wood-hook politicians and press he had used on his rise to power. In Louisiana politics, corruption was the accepted way of doing business. He had found it no different in Washington.

If he were smart, he would respectfully decline; it was the safe thing to do. He possessed more of anything than he could ever want or use, and there was virtually no possibility of losing any of it. In his present position, no one could threaten him for what he was or what he possessed or what he might have done to get it. If he stepped into the national spotlight, that blanket of security would be ripped off and examined for rents and stains.

Decline, he told himself, knowing all the while that he wouldn't. He had to identify his own vulnerabilities and eliminate them before anyone else exposed them. They were there in multitudes. It was time to start circling the wagons, and no one was better at that than Thornton Willingham Hunnycut. He would accept Senator James's offer and anyone who stood in his way be damned. "Lay on, MacDuff, whoever you might be," he thought.

To Be Continued . . .